The
Summons

MORE WILDSIDE CLASSICS

The Summons

A.E.W. Mason

WILDSIDE PRESS

THE SUMMONS

This edition published 2005 by Wildside Press, LLC.
www.wildsidepress.com

CHAPTER I

The Olympic Games

"Lutrell! Lutrell!"

Sir Charles Hardiman stood in the corridor of his steam yacht and bawled the name through a closed door. But no answer was returned from the other side of the door. He turned the handle and went in. The night was falling, but the cabin windows looked towards the north and the room was full of light and of a low and pleasant music. For the tide tinkled and chattered against the ship's planks and, in the gardens of the town across the harbour, bands were playing. The town was Stockholm in the year nineteen hundred and twelve, and on this afternoon, the Olympic games, that unfortunate effort to promote goodwill amongst the nations, which did little but increase rancours and disclose hatreds, had ended, never, it is to be hoped, to be resumed.

"Luttrell," cried Hardiman again, but this time with perplexity in his voice. For Luttrell was there in the cabin in front of him, but sunk in so deep a contemplation of memories and prospects that the cabin might just as well have been empty. Sir Charles Hardiman touched him on the shoulder.

"Wake up, old man!"

"That's what I am doing—waking up," said Luttrell, turning without any start. He was seated in front of the writing-desk, a young man, as the world went before the war, a few months short of twenty-eight.

"The launch is waiting and everybody's on deck," continued Hardiman. "We shall lose our table at Hasselbacken if we don't get off."

Then he caught sight of a telegram lying upon the writing-table.

"Oh!" and the impatience died out of his voice. "Is anything the matter?"

Luttrell pushed the telegram towards his host.

"Read it! I have got to make up my mind—and now—before we start."

Hardiman read the telegram. It was addressed to Captain Harry Luttrell, Yacht *The Dragonfly*, Stockholm, and it was sent from Cairo by the Adjutant-General of the Egyptian Army.

> *"I can make room for you, but you must apply immediately to be transferred."*

Hardiman sat down in a chair by the side of the table against the wall, with his eyes on Luttrell's face. He was a big, softish, overfed man of forty-five, and the moment he began to relax from the upright position, his body went with a run; he collapsed rather than sat. The little veins were beginning to show like tiny scarlet threads across his nose and on the full-ness of his cheeks; his face was the colour of wine; and the pupils of his pale eyes were ringed with so pronounced an *arcus senilis* that they com-manded the attention like a disfigurement. But the eyes were shrewd and kindly enough as they dwelt upon the troubled face of his guest.

"You have not answered this?" he asked.

"No. But I must send an answer tonight."

"You are in doubt?"

"Yes. I was quite sure when I cabled to Cairo on the second day of the games. I was quite sure, whilst I waited for the reply. Now that the reply has come—I don't know."

"Let me hear," said the older man. "The launch must wait, the table at the Hasselbacken restaurant must be assigned, if need be, to other cus-tomers." Hardiman had not swamped all his kindliness in good living. Luttrell was face to face with one of the few grave decisions which each man has in the course of his life to make; and Hardiman understood his need better than he understood it himself. His need was to formulate aloud the case for and against, to another person, not so much that he might receive advice as, that he might see for himself with truer eyes.

"The one side is clear enough," said Luttrell with a trace of bitterness. "There was a Major I once heard of at Dover. He trained his company in night-marches by daylight. The men held a rope to guide them and were ordered to shut their eyes. The Major, you see, hated stirring out at night. He liked his bridge and his bottle of port. Well, give me another year and that's the kind of soldier I shall become—the worst kind—the slovenly sol-dier. I mean slovenly in mind, in intention. Even now I come, already bored, to the barrack square and watch the time to see if I can't catch an earlier train from Gravesend to London."

"And when you do?" asked Hardiman.

Luttrell nodded.

"When I do," he agreed, "I get no thrill out of my escape, I assure you. I hate myself a little more—that's all."

"Yes," said Hardiman. He was too wise a man to ask questions. He just sat and waited, inviting Luttrell to spread out his troubles by his very qui-etude.

"Then there are these games," Luttrell cried in a swift exasperation, "—these damned games! From the first day when the Finns marched out with their national flag and the Russians threatened to withdraw if they did it again——" he broke off suddenly. "Of course you know soldiers have believed that trouble's coming. I used to doubt, but by God I am sure of it now. Just a froth of fine words at the opening and afterwards—honest rivalry and let the best man win? Not a bit of it! Team-running—a vile business—the nations parked together in different sections of the Stadium like enemies—and ill-will running here and there like an infection! Oh, there's trouble coming, and if I don't go I shan't be fit for it. There, that's the truth."

"The whole truth and nothing but the truth?" Hardiman asked with a smile. He leaned across the table and drew towards him a case of telegraph forms. But whilst he was drawing them towards him, Luttrell spoke again.

"Nothing but the truth—*yes*," he said. He was speaking shyly, uncomfortably, and he stopped abruptly.

"The whole truth—no." Hardiman added slowly, and gently. He wanted the complete story from preface to conclusion, but he was not to get it. He received no answer of any kind for a considerable number of moments and Luttrell only broke the silence in the end, to declare definitely,

"That, at all events, is all I have to say."

Sir Charles nodded and drew the case of forms close to him. There was something more then. There always is something more, which isn't told, he reflected, and the worst of it is, the something more which isn't told is always the real reason. Men go to the confessional with a reservation; the secret chamber where they keep their sacred vessels, their real truths and inspirations, as also their most scarlet sins—that shall be opened to no one after early youth is past unless it be—rarely—to one woman. There was another reason at work in Harry Luttrell, but Sir Charles Hardiman was never to know it. With a shrug of his shoulders he took a pencil from his pocket, filled up one of the forms and handed it to Luttrell.

"That's what I should reply."

He had written:

"I am travelling to London tomorrow to apply for transfer.—Luttrell."

Luttrell read the telegram with surprise. It was not the answer which he had expected from the victim of the fleshpots in front of him.

"You advise that?" he exclaimed.

"Yes. My dear Luttrell, as you know, you are a guest very welcome to me. But you don't belong. We—Maud Carstairs, Tony Marsh and the rest of us—even Mario Escobar—we are the Come-to-nothings. We are the people of the stage door, we grow fat in restaurants. From three to seven, you may find us in the card-rooms of our clubs—we are jolly fine fellows—and no good. You don't belong, and should get out while you can."

Luttrell moved uncomfortably in his chair.

"That's all very well. But there's another side to the question," he said, and from the deck above a woman's voice called clearly down the stairway.

"Aren't you two coming?"

Both men looked towards the door.

"That side," said Hardiman.

"Yes."

Hardiman nodded his head.

"Stella Croyle doesn't belong either," he said. "But she kicked over the traces. She flung out of the rank and file. Oh, I know Croyle was a selfish, dull beast and her footprints in her flight from him were littered with excuses. I am not considering the injustice of the world. I am looking at the cruel facts, right in the face of them, as you have got to do, my young friend. Here Stella Croyle is—with us—and she can't get away. You can."

Luttrell was not satisfied. His grey eyes and thin, clean features were troubled like those of a man in physical pain.

"You don't know the strange, queer tie between Stella Croyle and me," he said. "And I can't tell you it."

Hardiman grew anxious. Luttrell had the look of a man overtrained, and it was worry which had overtrained him. His face was a trifle too delicate, perhaps, to go with those remorseless sharp decisions which must be made by the men who win careers.

"I know that you can't go through the world without hurting people," cried Hardiman. "Neither you nor any one else, except the limpets. And you won't escape hurting Stella Croyle, by abandoning your chances. Your love affair will end—all of that kind do. And yours will end in a bitter, irretrievable quarrel after you have ruined yourself, and because you have ruined yourself. You are already on the rack—make no doubt about it. Oh, I have seen you twitch and jump with irritation—how many times on this yacht!—for trumpery, little, unimportant things she has said and done, which you would never have noticed six months ago; or only noticed to smile at with a pleased indulgence."

Luttrell's face coloured. "Why, that's true enough," he said. He was remembering the afternoon a week ago, when the yacht steamed between the green islands with their bathing stations and châlets, over a tranquil, sunlit sea of the deepest blue. Rounding a wooded corner towards sunset she came suddenly upon the bridges and the palace and the gardens of Stockholm. The women of the party were in the saloon. A rush was made towards it. They were summoned to this first wonderful view of the city of beauty. Would they come? No! Stella Croyle was in the middle of a game of Russian patience. She could play that game any day, every day, all day. This exquisite vision was vouchsafed to her but the once, and she had neglected it with the others. She had not troubled, even to move so far as the saloon door. For she had not finished her game.

Luttrell recalled his feeling of scorn; the scorn had grown into indignation; in the end he had made a grievance of her indifference to this first view of the city of Stockholm; a foolish, exasperating grievance, which would rankle, which would not be buried, which sprang to fresh life at each fresh sight of her. Yes, of a certainty, sooner or later Stella Croyle and he would quarrel, so bitterly that all the king's horses and all the king's men could never bring them again together; and over some utterly unimportant matter like the first view of Stockholm.

"Youth has many privileges over age," continued Hardiman, "but none greater than the vision, the half interpreted recurring vision of wider spaces and greater things, towards which you sail on the wind of a great emotion. Sooner or later, a man loses that vision and then only knows his loss. Stay here, and you'll lose it before your time."

Luttrell looked curiously at his companion, wondering what manner of man he had been in his twenties. Hardiman answered the look with a laugh. "Oh, I, too, had my ambitions once."

Luttrell folded the cablegram which Hardiman had written out and placed it in the breast pocket of his dinner jacket.

"I will talk to Stella tonight at dinner. Then, if I decide to send it, I can send it from the hotel over there at the landing-steps before we return to the yacht."

Sir Charles Hardiman rose cumbrously with a shrug of his shoulders. He had done his best, but since Luttrell would talk the question over with Stella Croyle, shoulder to shoulder with her amongst the lights and music, the perfume of her hair in his nostrils and the pleading of her eyes within his sight—he, Charles Hardiman, might as well have held his tongue.

So very likely it would have been. But when great matters are ripe for decisions one way or the other, the little accident as often as not decides. There was a hurrying of light feet in the corridor outside, a swift, peremptory knocking upon the door. The same woman's voice called in rather a shrill note through the panels! "Harry! Why don't you come? We are waiting for you."

And in the sound of the voice there was not merely impatience, but a note of ownership—very clear and definite; and hearing it Luttrell hardened. He stood up straight. He had the aspect of a man in revolt.

CHAPTER II

An Anthem Intervenes

Upon the entrance of Hardiman's party a wrinkle was smoothed away from the forehead of a *maître d'hôtel*.

"So! You have come!" he cried. "I began to despair."

"You have kept my table?" Sir Charles insisted.

"Yes, but with what an effort of diplomacy."; and the *maître d'hôtel* led his guests to the very edge of the great balcony. Here the table was set end-wise to the balustrade, commanding the crowded visitors, yet taking the coolness of the night. Hardiman was contented with his choice of its position. But when he saw his guests reading the cards which assigned them their places, he was not so contented with the order of their seating.

"If I had known an hour before!" he said to himself, and the astounding idea crept into his mind that perhaps it was, after all, a waste to spend so much time on the disposition of a dinner-table and the ordering of food.

However, the harm was done now. There was Luttrell already seated at the end against the balustrade. He had the noise of a Babel of tongues and the glitter of a thousand lights upon his left hand; upon his right, the stars burning bright in a cool gloom of deepest purple, and far below the riding-lamps of the yachts tossing on the water like yellow flowers in a garden; whilst next to him, midway between the fragrant darkness and the hard glitter, revealing, as she always did, a kinship with each of them, sat Stella Croyle.

"I should have separated them," Hardiman reflected uneasily as he raised and drank his cocktail. "But how the deuce could I without making everybody stare? This party wasn't got up to separate people. All the same——"

The hushed wonder of a summer night. The gaiety of a bright thronged restaurant! In either setting Stella Croyle was a formidable antagonist. But combine the settings and she took to herself, at once by nature, the seduction of both!

"Poor devil, he won't have a dog's chance!" the baronet concluded; and he watched approvingly what appeared to him to be Luttrell's endeavour to avoid joining battle on this unfavourable field. He could only trust feebly in that and in the strength of the "something else," the secret reason he was never to know.

It was about halfway through dinner when Stella Croyle, who had directed many a furtive, anxious glance to the averted face of her companion, attacked directly.

"What is the matter with you tonight?" she asked, interrupting him in the midst of a rattle of futilities. "Why should you recite to me from the guidebook about the University of Upsala?"

"It appears to be most interesting, and quaint," replied Luttrell hastily.

"Then we might hire a motorcar and run out there to luncheon. Tomorrow! Just you and I."

"No." Harry Luttrell exclaimed suddenly and Stella Croyle drew back. Her face clouded. She had won the first round, but victory brought her no ease. She knew now from the explosion of his "No" and the swift alarm upon his face that something threatened her.

"You must tell me what has happened," she cried. "You must! Oh, you turn away from me!"

From the dark steep garden at their feet rose a clamour of cheers—to Luttrell an intervention of Providence.

"Listen," he said.

Here and there a man or a woman rose at the dinner tables and looked down. Upwards along a glimmering riband of path, a group of students bore one of their number shoulder-high. Luttrell leaned over the balustrade. The group below halted; speeches were made; cheers broke out anew.

"It is the Swedish javelin-thrower. He won the championship of the world this afternoon."

"Did he?" asked Stella Croyle in a soft voice at his side. "Does he throw javelins as well as you? You wound me every time."

Luttrell raised his head. It was not fear of defeat which had kept his looks averted from Stella's dark and starry eyes. No thought of lists set and a contest to be fought out had even entered his head. But he did fear to see those eyes glisten with tears—for she so seldom shed them! And even more than the evidence of her pain he feared the dreadful submission with which women in the end receive the stroke of fortune. He had to meet her gaze now, however.

"I put off telling you," he began lamely.

"So that this evening of mine with you might not be spoilt," she returned. "But, my dear, my evening was already spoilt before the launch left the yacht gangway. I am not so blind."

Stella Croyle was at this date twenty-six years old; and it was difficult to picture her any older. Partly because of her vivid colouring and because she was abrim with life; partly because in her straightness of limb and the clear treble of her voice, she was boyish. "What a pretty boy she would make!" was the first thought until you noticed the slim delicacy of her hands and feet, the burnish of gold on the dark wealth of her hair, the fine chiselling of brow and nose and chin. Then it was seen that she was all woman. She was tall and yet never looked tall. It seemed that you could pick her up with a finger, but try and she warned you of the weakness of your arm. She was a baffling person. She ran and walked with the joyous insolence of eighteen, yet at any moment some veil might be rolled up in her eyes and face to show you for one tragic instant a Lady of Sorrows.

She leaned towards Luttrell, and as Hardiman had foreseen the perfume of her hair stormed his senses.

"Tell me!" she breathed, and Luttrell, with his arguments and reasons cut and dried and conned over pat for delivery, began nevertheless to babble. There were the Olympic Games. She herself must have seen how they were fatal to their own purpose. Troubles were coming—battles behind the troubles. All soldiers knew! They knew this too—the phrase of a young Lieutenant-Colonel lecturing at the Staff College.

"Battles are not won either by sheer force or pure right, but by the one or the other of those two Powers which has Discipline as its Chief of Staff."

He was implying neither very tactfully nor clearly that he was on the way to dwindling into an undisciplined soldier. But it did not matter in the least. For Stella Croyle was not listening. All this was totally unimportant. Men always went about and about when they had difficult things to say to women. Her eyes never left his face and she would know surely enough when those words were rising to his lips which it was necessary that she should mark and understand. Meanwhile her perplexities and fears grew.

"Of course it can't be *that*," she assured herself again and again, but with a dreadful catch at her heart. "Oh no, it can't be *that*."

"That," was the separation which some day or another—after a long and wondrous period—both were agreed, must come. But, consoling herself with the thought that she would be prepared, she had always set the day on so distant an horizon that it had no terrors for her. Now it suddenly dismayed her, a terror close at hand. Here on this crowded balcony joyous with lights and gay voices and invaded by all the subtle invitations of a summer night above the water! Oh no, it was not possible!

Luttrell put his hand to his breast pocket and Stella watched and listened now with all her soul. More than once during dinner she had seen him touch that pocket in an abstraction. He drew from it two papers, one the cablegram which he had received from Cairo, the other Hardiman's reply. He handed her the first of the two.

"This reached me this morning."

Stella Croyle studied the paper with her heart in her mouth. But the letters would not be still.

"Oh, what does it mean?" she cried.

"It offers me service abroad."

Stella's face flushed and turned white. She bent her head over the cablegram.

"At Cairo," she said, with a little gasp of relief. After all Cairo was not so far. A week, and one was at Cairo.

"Further south, in the Sudan—Heaven knows where!"

"Too far then?" she suggested. "Too far."

"For you? Yes! Too far," Luttrell replied.

Stella lifted a tragic face towards him; and though he winced he met her eyes.

"But you are not going! You can't go!"

Luttrell handed to her the second paper.

"You never wrote this," she said very quickly.

"Yet it is what I would have written."

Stella Croyle shot one swift glance at Sir Charles Hardiman. She had recognised his handwriting. Hardiman was in Luttrell's cabin while the rest of the party waited on the deck and the launch throbbed at the gangway. If a woman's glance had power, he would have been stricken that instant. But she wasted no more than a glance upon the worldly-wiseman at the head of their table. She turned again to the first telegram.

"This is an answer, this cablegram from Cairo?"

"Yes."

"To a cable of yours?"

"Sent three days ago."

The answers she received were clear, unhesitating. It was a voice from a rock speaking! So utterly mistaken was she; and so completely Luttrell bent every nerve to the service of shortening the hour of misery. The appalling moment was then actually upon her. She had foreseen it—so she thought. But it caught her nevertheless unprepared as death catches a sinner on his bed.

She stared at the telegrams—not reading them. His arguments and prefaces—the Olympic Games, Discipline and the rest of it—what she had caught of them, she blew away as so much froth. She dived to the personal reason.

"You are tired of me."

"No," Luttrell answered hotly. "That's not true—not even a half truth. If I were tired of you, it would all be so easy, so brutally easy."

"But you are!" Her voice rose shrill in its violence. "You know you are but you are too much of a coward to say so—oh, like all men!" and as Luttrell turned to her a face startled by her outcry and uttered a remonstrant "Hush!", she continued bitterly, "What do I care if they all hear? I am impossible! You know that, don't you? I am quite impossible! I have gone my own way. I am one of the people you hate—one of the Undisciplined."

Stella Croyle hardly knew in her passion what she was saying, and Luttrell could only wait in silence for the storm to pass. It passed with a quickness which caught him at loss; so quickly she swept from mood to mood.

He heard her voice at his ear, remorseful and most appealing. "Oh, Wub, what have I done that you should treat me so?"

Sir Charles Hardiman, watchful of the duel, guessed from the movement of her lips what she was saying.

"These nicknames are the very devil," he exclaimed, apparently about nothing, to his startled neighbour. "The first thing a woman does when she's fond of a man is to give him some ridiculous name, which doesn't belong to him. She worries her wits trying this one and that one, as a tailor tries on you a suit of clothes, and when she has got your fit, she uses it—publicly. So others use it too and so it no longer contents her. Then she invents a variation, a nickname within a nickname, and that she keeps to herself, for her own private use. That's the nickname I am referring to, my dear, when I say it's the very devil."

The lady to whom he spoke smiled vaguely and surmised that he might be very right. For herself, she said, she had invented no nicknames; which was to assert that she had never been in love. For the practice seems invariable, and probably Dido in times long since gone by had one for Æneas, and Virgil knew all about it. But since she was a woman, it would be a name at once so absurd and so intimate that it would never have gone with the dignified rhythm of the hexameter. "Wobbles" had been the first name which Stella Croyle had invented for Harry Luttrell, though by what devious process she had lighted upon it, psychology could not have discovered. "Wub" was the nickname within the nickname, the cherished sign that the two of them lived apart in a little close-hedged garden of their own. Luttrell's eyes were upon her as she spoke it. And she spoke it with a curious little wistful pursing of soft lips so that it came to him winged with the memory of all her kisses.

"Oh, Wub, must you leave me?" she pleaded in a breaking whisper. "What will be left to me if you do?"

Luttrell dropped his forehead in his hands. All the character which he had in those untried days bade him harden himself against the appeal. But his resolution was melting like metal in a furnace. He tried to realise the truth which Hardiman had uttered three or four hours before. There would be sooner or later a quarrel, a humiliating, hateful quarrel over some miserable trifle which neither Stella nor he would ever afterwards forgive. But her voice was breaking with a sob in a whisper at his ear and how could he look forward so far?

"Stella!"

He turned impulsively towards her.

"The game's up," reflected Sir Charles Hardiman at the end of the table. "Calypso wins—no, by God!"

For before Luttrell could speak another word, the music crashed and all that assemblage was on its feet. The orchestra was playing the Swedish National Anthem; and upon that, one after the other, followed the hymns of the peoples who had taken part in the Games. In turn the representatives of each people stood and resumed their seat, the music underlining their individuality and parking them in sections, even as rivalry had parked them in the Stadium. The majestic anthem of Russia, the pæan of the Marseillaise, the livelier march of Italy, the song of Germany, the Star-Spangled Banner; and long before the band struck into the solemn rhythm of "God save the King," Stella Croyle at all events knew that Calypso had lost. For she saw a flame illumine Luttrell's face and transfigure him. He had slipped out of her reach. The doubts and perplexities which had so troubled him during the last months were now resolved. As he listened to the Hymns, he saw as in a vision the nations advancing abreast over a vast plain like battalions in line with their intervals for manœuvring spaced out between them. In front of each nation rolled a grey vapour, which gradually took shape before Luttrell's eyes; and there was made visible to him a shadowy legion of men marching in the van, the men who had left ease and women and all the grace of life behind them and had gone out to die in the harness of service—one in this, one in that corner of the untravelled world, and now all reunited in a strong fellowship. The vision remained with him after the last strains of music had died away, and faded slowly. He waked to the lights and clamour of the restaurant and turned to Stella Croyle.

"Stella," he began, and——

"I know," she interrupted in a small voice. She was sitting with her head downcast and her hands clenched upon her lap so tightly that the skin was white about the points where the tips of her fingers pressed. "Perhaps I shan't suffer so very much."

She was careful not to lift her head, and when a few moments later their host gave the signal to move, she rose quickly and turned her back on Luttrell.

The party motored back through the Dyurgarden, past the glimmering tents where the Boy Scouts were encamped to the great hotel by the landing-stage. There a wait of a few minutes took place whilst Hardiman settled for the cars, and during that wait Luttrell disappeared. He rejoined his friends at the harbour steps and when the launch put off towards the *Dragonfly*, he found himself side by side with Stella Croyle. In the darkness she relaxed her guard. Luttrell saw the great tears glisten on her dark eyelashes and fall down her cheeks.

"I am sorry, Stella," he whispered, dropping his hand on hers, and she clutched it and let it go.

"Perhaps I shan't suffer so very much," she repeated and the next moment the gangway light shone down upon their faces. Stella dropped her head and furtively dried her cheeks.

"I want to go up last," she said, "and just behind you, so that no one shall see what a little fool I am making of myself."

But by some subtle understanding already it was felt amongst that group of people, quick to perceive troubles of the emotions, that something was amiss between the pair. They were left alone upon the deck. Stella by chance looking southwards to the starlit gloom, Luttrell to the north, where still the daylight played in blue and palest green and the delicate changing fires of the opal.

"What will you do, Stella?" Luttrell asked gently.

"I think I will go and live in the country," she replied.

"It will be lonely, child."

"There will be ghosts, my dear, to keep me company," she answered with a wan smile. "People like me always have to be a good deal alone, anyway. I shall be, of course, lonelier, now that I have no one to play with," and the smile vanished from her lips. She flung up her face towards the skies, letting her grief have its way upon that empty deck.

"So we shall never be together—just you and I—alone again," she said, forcing herself to realise that unintelligible thing. Her thoughts ran back over the year—the year of their alliance—and she saw all of its events flickering vividly before her, as they say drowning people do. "Oh, Wub, what a cruel mistake you made when you went out of your way to be kind," she cried, with the tears streaming down her face; and Luttrell winced.

"Yes, that's true," he admitted remorsefully. "I never dreamed what would come of it."

"You should have left me alone."

Amongst the flickering pictures of the year the first was the clearest. A great railway station in the West of England, a train drawn up at the departure platform, herself with a veil drawn close over her face, half running, half walking in a pitiful anguish towards the train; and then a man at her elbow. Harry Luttrell.

"I have reserved a compartment. I suspected that things were not going to turn out well. I thought the long journey to London alone would be terrible. If things had turned out right, you would not have seen me."

She had let him place her in a carriage, look after her wants as if she had been a child, hold her in his arms, tend her with the magnificent sympathy of his silence. That had been the real beginning. Stella had known him as the merest of friends before. She had met him here and there at a supper party, at a dancing club, at some Bohemian country house; and then suddenly he had guessed what others had not, and foolishly had gone out of his way to be kind.

"She would have died if I hadn't travelled with her," Luttrell argued silently. "She would have thrown herself out of the carriage, or when she reached home she would have——" and his argument stopped, and he glanced at her uneasily.

Undisciplined, was the epithet she had used of herself. You never knew what crazy thing she might do. There was daintiness but no order in her life; the only law she knew was given to her by a fastidious taste.

"Of course, Wub, I have always known that you never cared for me as I do for you. So it was bound to end some time." She caught his hand to her heart for a second, and then, dropping it, ran from his side.

CHAPTER III

Mario Escobar

Late in the autumn of the following year a new play, written by Martin Hillyard and named "The Dark Tower," was produced at the Rubicon Theatre in Panton Street, London. It was Hillyard's second play. His first, produced in April of the same year, had just managed to limp into July; and that small world which concerns itself with the individualities of playwrights was speculating with its usual divergencies upon Hillyard's future development.

"The Dark Tower" was a play of modern days, built upon the ancient passions. The first act was played to a hushed house, and while the applause which greeted the fall of the curtain was still rattling about the walls of the theatre, Sir Charles Hardiman hoisted himself heavily out of his stall and made his way to a box on the first tier, which he entered without knocking.

There was but one person in the box, a young man hidden behind a side curtain. Hardiman let himself collapse into a chair by the side of the young man.

"Seems all right," he said. "You have a story to tell. It's clear in every word, too, that you know where you are going. That makes people comfortable and inclined to go along with you."

Hillyard turned with a smile.

"We haven't come to the water jump yet," he said.

Hardiman remained in the box during the second act. He watched the stage for a while, took note of the laughter which welcomed this or that line, and of the silence which suddenly enclosed this or that scene from the rest of the play; and finally, with a certain surprise, and a certain amusement he fixed his attention upon the play's author. The act ended in laughter and Hillyard leaned back, and himself laughed, without pose or affectation, as heartily as any one in the theatre.

"You beat me altogether, my young friend," said Hardiman. "You ought to be walking up and down the pavement outside in the classical state of agitation. But you appear to be enjoying the play, as if you never had seen it before."

"And I haven't," Hillyard returned. "This isn't quite the play which we have been learning and rehearsing during the last month. Here's the audience at work, adding a point there, discovering an interpretation—yes, actually an interpretation—there, bringing into importance one scene, slipping over the next which we thought more important—altering it, in fact. Of course," and he returned to his earlier metaphor, "I know the big fences over which we may come a cropper. I can see them ahead before we come up to them and know the danger. We are over two of them, by the way. But on the whole I am more interested than nervous. It's the first time I have ever been to a first night, you see."

"Well, upon my word," cried Hardiman, "you are the coolest hand at it I ever saw." But he could have taken back his words the next moment.

In spite of Hillyard's aloof and disinterested air, the night had brought its excitement and in a strength of which he himself was unaware. It lifted now the veils behind which a man will hide his secret thoughts! He turned swiftly to Hardiman with a boyish light upon his face.

"Oh, I am not in doubt of what tonight means to me! Not for a moment. If it's failure, it means that I begin again tomorrow on something else; and again after that, and again after that, until success does come. Playwriting is my profession, and failures are a necessary part of it—just as much a part as the successes. But even if the great success were to come now, it wouldn't mean quite so much to me perhaps as it might to other people." He paused, and a smile broke upon his face. "I live expecting a messenger. There! That's my secret delivered over to you under the excitement of a first night."

And as he spoke the colour mounted into his face. He turned away in confusion. His play was nearer at his heart than he had thought; the enthusiasm which seemed to be greeting it had stirred him unwisely.

"Tell me," he said hurriedly, "who all these people in the stalls are."

He peeped down between the edge of the curtain and the side wall of the box whilst Hardiman stood up behind him.

"Yes, I will be your man from Cook's," said Hardiman genially.

His heart warmed to the young man both on account of his outburst and of the shame which had followed upon the heels of it. Few beliefs had survived in Hardiman after forty years of wandering up and down the flowery places of the earth; but one—he had lectured Harry Luttrell upon it on a night at Stockholm—continually gained strength in him. Youth must beget visions and man must preserve them if great work were to be done; and so easily the visions lost their splendour and their inspiration. Of all the ways of tarnishing the vision, perhaps talk was the most murderous. Hillyard possessed them. Hillyard was ashamed that he had spoken of them. Therefore he had some chance of retaining them.

"Yes, I will show you the celebrities." He pointed out the leading critics and the blue stockings of the day. His eyes roamed over the stalls. "Do you see the man with the broad face and the short whiskers in the fourth row? The man who looks just a little too like a country gentleman to be one? That is Sir Chichester Splay. He made a fortune in a murky town of Lancashire, and, thirsting for colour, came up to London determined to back a musical comedy. That is the way the craving for colour takes them in the North. His wish was gratified. He backed 'The Patchouli Girl,' and in that shining garden he got stung. He is now what they call an amateur. No first night is complete without him. He is the half-guinea Mecænas of our days."

Hillyard looked down at Sir Chichester Splay and smiled at his companion's description.

"You will meet him tonight at supper, and if your play is a success—not otherwise—you will stay with him in Sussex."

"No!" cried Hillyard; but Sir Charles was relentless in his insistence.

"You will. His wife will see to that. Who the pretty girl beside him is I do not know. But the more or less young man on the other side of her, talking to her with an air of intimacy a little excessive in a public place, is Mario Escobar. He is a Spaniard, and has the skin-deep politeness of his race. He is engaged in some sort of business, frequents some sort of society into which he is invited by the women, and he is not very popular amongst men. He belongs, however, to some sort of club. That is all I know about him. One would think he had guessed we were speaking of him," Hardiman added.

For at that moment Mario Escobar raised his dark, sleek head, and his big, soft eyes—the eyes of a beautiful woman—looked upwards to the box. It seemed to Hillyard for a moment that they actually exchanged a glance, though he himself was out of sight behind the curtain, so direct was Escobar's gaze. It was, however, merely the emptiness of the box which had drawn the Spaniard's attention. He was neatly groomed, of a slight figure, tall, and with his eyes, his thin olive face, his small black moustache and clean-cut jaw he made without doubt an effective and arresting figure.

"Now turn your head," said Hardiman, "the other way, and notice the big, fair man in the back row of the stalls. He is a rival manager, and he is explaining in a voice loud enough to be heard by the first rows of the pit, the precise age of your leading lady. Now look down! There is a young girl flitting about the stalls. She is an actress, not very successful. But tonight she is as busy as a bee. She is crabbing your play. Yesterday her opinion on the subject was of no value, and it will be again of no value tomorrow. But as one of the limited audience on a first night, she can do just a tiny bit of harm. But don't hold it against her, Hillyard! She has no feeling against you. This is her little moment of importance."

Sir Charles rattled on through the interval—all good nature with just a slice of lemon—and it had happened that he had pointed out one who was to be the instrument of great trouble for Hillyard and a few others, with whom this story is concerned.

Hillyard interrupted Hardiman.

"Who is the girl at the end of the sixth row, who seems to have stepped down from a china group on a mantelpiece?"

"That one?" said Hardiman, and all the raillery faded from his face. "That is Mrs. Croyle. You will meet her tonight at my supper party." He hesitated as to what further he should say. "You might do worse than be a friend to her. She is not, I am afraid, very happy."

Hillyard was surprised at the sudden gentleness of his companion's voice, and looked quickly towards him. Hardiman answered the look as he got heavily up from his chair.

"I sometimes fear that I have some responsibility for her unhappiness. But there are things one cannot help."

The light in the auditorium went down while Hardiman was leaving the box, and the curtain rose on the third act of "The Dark Tower." Of that play, however, you may read in the files of the various newspapers, if you will. This story is concerned with Martin Hillyard, not his work. It is sufficient to echo the words of Sir Chichester Splay when Hillyard was introduced to him an hour and a half later in the private supper-room at the Semiramis Hotel.

"A good play, Mr. Hillyard. Not a great play, of course, but quite a good play," said Sir Chichester with just the necessary patronage to tickle Hillyard to an appreciation of Hardiman's phrases—a ten and six-penny Mecænas.

"I am grateful that it has earned your good opinion," he replied.

"Oh, not at all!" cried Sir Chichester, and catching a lady who passed by the arm. "Stella, Mr. Hillyard should know you. This is Mrs. Croyle. I hope you will meet him some day at Rackham Park."

Sir Chichester trotted away to greet the manager of the *Daily Harpoon*, who was at that moment shaking hands with Hardiman.

"I congratulate you," said Stella Croyle, as she gave him her hand.

"Thank you. So you know Sir Chichester well?"

"His wife has been a friend of mine for a long time." Her eyes twinkled. "I wonder you have not been seen at his house."

"Oh, I am only just hatched out," said Hillyard. They both laughed. "I hardly know a soul here except my leading lady and our host."

They were summoned to the supper table. Hillyard found himself with the leading lady on one side of him and Stella Croyle opposite, and Mario Escobar a couple of seats away. Supper was half through when Escobar leaned suddenly forward.

"Mr. Hillyard, I have seen you before, somewhere and not in England."

"That is possible."

"In Spain?"

"Yes," answered Hillyard.

A certain curiosity in Escobar's voice, a certain reticence in Hillyard's, arrested the attention of those about.

"Let me see!" continued Escobar. "It was in the Opera House at Barcelona on the first performance of Manon Lescaut."

"No," replied Hillyard.

"Then—I know—it was under the palm trees in front of the sea at Alicante one night."

Hillyard nodded.

"That may well have been. I was up and down the south coast of Spain for three years. Eighteen months of it were spent at Alicante."

He turned to his neighbour, but Escobar persisted.

"It was for your health?"

Hillyard did not answer directly.

"My lungs have always been my trouble," he said.

Hardiman bent towards Stella Croyle.

"I think our new friend has had a curious life, Stella. He should interest you."

Stella Croyle replied with a shrewd look towards the Spaniard.

"At present he is interesting Escobar. One would say Escobar was suspicious lest Mr. Hillyard should know too much of him."

Sir Charles laughed.

"The Mario Escobars are always suspicious. Let us see!" he said in a low voice, and leaning across the table, he shot a question sharply at the Spaniard.

"And what were you doing under the palm trees, in front of the sea at Alicante, Señor Escobar?"

Mario Escobar sat back. The challenge had startled him. He reflected, and as the recollection came he turned slowly very white.

"I?" he asked.

"Yes," said Hardiman, leaning forward. But it was not at Hardiman that Escobar was looking. His eyes were fixed warily on Hillyard. He answered the question warily too, fragment by fragment, ready to stop, ready to take the words back, if a sign of recollection kindled in Hillyard's face.

"It is what we should call here the esplanade—the sea and harbour on one side, the houses on the other. The band plays under the palms in front of the Casino on summer nights. I—" and he took the last words at a rush—"I was sitting in a lounge chair in front of the club, when I saw Mr. Hillyard pass. An Englishman is noticeable in Alicante. There are so few of them."

"Yes," Hillyard agreed. No recollection was stirred in him by Escobar's description. Escobar turned away, but he could not quite conceal the relief he felt.

"Yes, my friend," said Hardiman to himself, "you have taken your water-jump too. And you're uncommonly glad that you haven't come a cropper."

After that noticeable moment of tension, the talk swept on into sprightlier channels.

CHAPTER IV

The Secret of Harry Luttrell

"Shall I take you home?"

"Oh, will you?" cried Stella Croyle, with a little burst of pleasure. After all, Hillyard was the great man of the evening, and that he should consider her out of all that company was pleasant. "I will get my cloak."

Throughout the supper-party Hillyard had been at a loss to discover in Stella Croyle the woman whom Hardiman had led him to expect. Her spirits were high, but unforced. She chattered away with more gaiety than wit, like the rest of Hardiman's guests, but the gaiety was apt to the occasion. She had the gift of a clear and musical laugh, and her small delicate face would wrinkle and pout into grimaces which gave to her a rather attractive air of *gaminerie*—Hillyard could find no word but the French one to express her on that evening. He drove her to a small house in the Bayswater Road, overlooking Kensington Gardens.

"Will you come in for a moment?" she asked.

Hillyard followed her up a paved pathway, through a tiny garden enclosed in a high wall, to her door. She led him into a room bright with flowers and pictures. Curtains of purple brocade were drawn across the window, a fire burned on the hearth, and thick soft cushions on broad couches gave the room a look of comfort.

"You live here alone?" Hillyard asked.

"Yes."

She turned suddenly towards him as he gazed about the room.

"I married a long while ago." She stood in front of him like a slim child. It seemed impossible. "Yes, before I knew anything—to get away from home. Our marriage did not go smoothly. After three years I ran away—oh, not with any one I cared for, he happened to be there, that was all. After a month he deserted me in Italy. I have fortunately some money of my own and a few friends who did not turn me down—Lady Splay, for instance. There!"

She moved to a table and poured out for Hillyard a whisky-and-soda.

"My question was thoughtless," he said. "I did not mean that you should answer it as you did."

"I preferred you to know."

"I am honoured," Hillyard replied.

Stella Croyle sat down upon a low stool in front of the fire. Hillyard sank into one of the deep-cushioned chairs. The day of tension was over, and there was no doubt about the success of "The Dark Tower." Stella Croyle sat very quietly, with the firelight playing upon her face and her delicate dress. Her vivacity had dropped from her like the pretty cloak she had thrown aside. Both became her well, but they were for use out-of-doors, and Hillyard was grateful that she had discarded them.

"You are tired, no doubt," he said, reluctantly. "I ought to go."

"No," she answered. "It is pleasant before the fire here."

"Thank you. I should like to stay for a little while. I did not know until I came into this room with how much anxiety I had been looking forward to this night."

He leaned forward with his hands clenched, and saw pass in the bright coals glimpses of the long tale of days when endeavour was fruitless and hopes were disappointed. "Success! Lord, how I wanted it!" he whispered.

Stella Croyle looked at him with a smile.

"It was sure to come to you, since you wanted it enough," she said.

"Yes, but in time?" exclaimed Hillyard.

"In time for what?"

Hillyard broke into a laugh.

"I don't know," he answered. He was silent for a little while, and the comfort of the room, the quiet of the night, the pleasant sympathy of Stella Croyle, all wrought upon him. "I don't know," he repeated slowly. "I am waiting. But out of my queer life something more has got to come—something more and something different. I have always been sure of it, but I used to be afraid that the opportunity would come while I was still chained to the handles of the barrow."

Hillyard's life, though within a short time its vicissitudes had been many and most divergent, had probably not been as strange as he imagined it to be. He looked back upon it with too intense an interest to be its impartial judge. Certainly its distinctive feature had escaped him altogether. At the age of twenty-nine he was a man absolutely without tradition.

His father, a partner in a small firm of shipping agents which had not the tradition of a solid, old-fashioned business, had moved in Martin's boyhood from a little semi-detached villa with its flight of front steps in one suburb, to a house in a garden of trees in another. The boy had been sent to a brand new day-school of excessive size, which gathered its pupils into its classrooms at nine o'clock in the morning and dispersed them to their homes at four. No boy was proud that he went to school at St. Eldred's, or was deterred from any meanness by the thought that it was a breach of the school's traditions. The school meant so many lessons in so many classrooms, and no more.

Hillyard was the only child. Between himself and his parents there was little sympathy and understanding. He saw them at meals, and fled from the table to his own room, where he read voraciously.

"You never heard of such a jumble of books," he said to Stella Croyle. "Matthew Arnold, Helps, Paradise Lost, Ten Thousand a Year, The Revolt of Islam, Tennyson. I knew the whole of In Memoriam by heart—absolutely every line of it, and pages of Browning. The little brown books! I would walk miles to pick one of them up. My people would find the books lying about the house, and couldn't make head or tail of why I wanted to read them. There were two red-letter days: one when I first bought the two volumes of Herrick, the second when I tumbled upon De Quincey. That's the author to bowl a boy over. The Stage-Coach, the Autobiography, the Confessions—I could never get tired of them. I remember buying an ounce of laudanum at a chemist's on London Bridge and taking it home, with the intention of following in the steps of my hero and qualifying to drink it out of a decanter."

Stella Croyle had swung round from the fireplace, and was listening now with parted lips.

"And did you?" she exclaimed, in a kind of eager suspense.

Hillyard shook his head.

"The taste was too unpleasant. I drank about half an ounce and threw the rest away. I was saved from that folly."

Stella Croyle turned again to the fire.

"Yes," she said rather listlessly.

Yet Hillyard might almost have become a consumer of drugs, such queer and wayward fancies took him in charge. It became a fine thing to him to stay up all night just for the sake of staying up, and many a night he passed at his open window, even in winter time, doing nothing, not even dreaming, simply waiting for the day to break. It seemed to him soft and wrong that a man should take his clothes off and lie comfortably between sheets. And then came another twist. When all the house was quiet, he would slip out of a ground-floor window and roam for hours about the lonely roads, a solitary boy revelling even then in the extraordinary conduct of his life. There was in the neighbourhood a footpath through a thick grove of trees which ran up a long, high hill, and, midway in the ascent, crossed a railway cutting by a rustic bridge.

"That was my favourite walk, though I always entered by the swing-gate in fear, and trembled at every movement of the branches, and continually expected an attack. I would hang over that railway bridge, especially on moonlit nights, and compose poems and thoughts—you know—great, short thoughts." Hillyard laughed. "I was going to be a poet, you understand—a clear, full voice such as had seldom been heard; my poems were all about the moon sailing in the Empyrean and Death. Death was my strong suit. I sent some of my poems to the local Press, signed 'Lethe,' but I could never hear that they were published."

Stella Croyle laughed, and Hillyard went on. "From the top of the hill I would strike off to the west, and see the morning break over London. In summer that was wonderful! The Houses of Parliament. St Paul's like a silver bubble rising out of the mist, then, as the mist cleared over the river, a London clean and all silver in the morning light! I was going to conquer all that, you know—I—

" 'Silent upon a peak of Peckham Rye.' "

"I wonder you didn't kill yourself," cried Stella.

"I very nearly did," answered Hillyard.

"Didn't your parents interfere?"

"No. They never knew of my wanderings. They did know, of course, that I used not to go to bed. But they left me alone. I was a bitter disappointment in every way. They wanted a reasonable son, who would go into the agency business, and they had instead—me. I should think that I was pretty odious, too, and we were all of passionate tempers. Besides, with all this reading, I didn't do particularly well at school. How could I when day after day I would march off from the house, leaving a smooth bed behind me in my room? We were thorny people. Quarrels were frequent. My mother had a phrase which set my teeth on edge—'Don't you talk, Martin, until you are earning your living'—the sort of remark that stings and stays in a boy's memory as something unfair. There was a great row in the end, one night at ten o'clock, when I was sixteen, and I left the house and tramped into London."

"What in the world did you do?" cried Stella.

"I shipped as a boy on a fruit-tramp for Valencia in Spain. And I believe that saved my life. For my lungs were beginning to be troublesome."

The fruit-tramp had not been out more than two days when the fo'c'sle hands selected the lad, since he had some education, to be their spokesman on a deputation to the captain. Martin Hillyard went aft with the men and put their case for better food and less violence. He was not therefore popular with the old man, and at Valencia he thought it prudent to desert.

Stella Croyle had turned towards him again. There was a vividness in his manner, an enjoyment, too, which laid hold upon her. It was curious to her to realise that this man talking to her here in the Bayswater Road, had been so lately a ragged youth scouting for his living on the quays of Southern Spain.

"You were at that place—Alicante!" she cried.

"Part of the time."

"And there Mario Escobar saw you. I wonder why he was frightened lest you too should have seen him," she added slowly.

"Was he?"

"Yes. He was sitting on the same side of the table as you, so you wouldn't have noticed. But he was opposite to me; and he was afraid."

Hillyard was puzzled.

"I can't think of a reason. I was a shipping clerk of no importance. I can't remember that I ever came across his name in all the eighteen months I spent in Alicante."

When Martin Hillyard was nineteen, Death intervened in the family feud. His parents died within a few weeks of each other.

"I was left with a thousand pounds."

"What did you do with them?"

"I went to Oxford."

"You? After those years of independence?"

"It had been my one passionate dream for years."

"The Scholar Gipsy," "Thyrsis," the Preface to the "Essays in Criticism," one or two glimpses of the actual city, its grey spires and towers, caught from the windows of a train, had long ago set the craving in his heart. Oxford had grown dim in unattainable mists, no longer a desire so much as a poignant regret, yet now he actually walked its sacred streets.

"And you enjoyed it?" asked Stella.

"I had the most wondrous time," Hillyard replied fervently. "There was one bad evening, when I realised that I couldn't write poetry. After that I cut my hair and joined the Wine Club. I stroked the Torpid and rowed three in my College Eight. I had friends for the first time. One above all"

He stopped over-abruptly. Stella Croyle had the impression of a careless sentinel suddenly waked, suddenly standing to attention at the door of a treasurehouse of memories. She was challenged. Very well. It was her humour to take the challenge up just to prove to herself that she could slip past a man's guard if the spirit moved her. She turned on Hillyard a pair of most friendly sympathetic eyes.

"Tell me of your friend."

"Oh, there's not much to tell. He rowed in the same boat with me. He had just what I had not—traditions. From his small old brown manor-house in a western county to his very choice of a career, he was wrapped about in tradition. He went into the army. He had to go."

"What is his name?"

Stella Croyle interrupted him. She was not looking at him any more. She was staring into the fire, and her body was very still. But there was excitement in her voice.

"Harry Luttrell," replied Hillyard, and Stella Croyle did not move. "I don't know what has become of him. You see, I had ninety pounds left out of the thousand when I left Oxford. So I just dived."

"But you have come up again now. You will resume your friends at the point where you dived."

"Not yet. I am going away in a week's time."

"For long?"

"Eight months."

"And far?"

"Very."

"I am sorry," said Stella.

It had been the intention of Hillyard to use his first months of real freedom in a great wandering amongst wide spaces. The journey had been long since planned, even details of camp outfit and equipment and the calibre of rifles considered.

"I have been at my preparations for years," he said. "I lived in a cubbyhole in Westminster, writing and writing and writing, but when I thought of this journey to be, certain to be, the walls would dissolve, and I would walk in magical places under the sun."

> *"Now the New Year reviving old desires,*
> *The thoughtful soul to solitude retires"*

Stella Croyle quoted the verses gaily, and Hillyard, lost in the anticipation of his journey, never noticed that the gaiety rang false.

"And where are you going?" she asked.

"To the Sudan."

It seemed that Stella expected just that answer and no other. She gazed into the fire without moving, seeking to piece together a picture in the coals of that unknown country which held all for which she yearned.

"I shall travel slowly up the White Nile to Renk," Hillyard continued, blissfully. He was delighted at the interest which Mrs. Croyle was taking in his itinerary. She was clearly a superior person. "From Renk, I shall cross to the Blue Nile at Rosaires, and travel eastward again to the River Dinder—"

"You are most fortunate," Stella interrupted wistfully.

"Yes, am I not?" cried Hillyard. It looked as if nothing would break through his obtuseness.

"I should love to be going in your place."

"You?"

Hillyard smiled. She was for a mantelshelf in a boudoir, not for a camp.

"Yes—I," and her voice suddenly broke.

Hillyard sprang up from his chair, but Stella held up her hand to check him, and turned her face still further away. Hillyard resumed his seat uncomfortably.

"You may meet your friend Harry Luttrell in the Sudan," she explained. "He is stationed somewhere in that country—where exactly I would give a great deal to know."

They sat without speaking for a little while, Stella once more turning to the fire. Hillyard watching her wistful face and the droop of her shoulders understood at last the truth of Hardiman's description. The mask was lain aside. Here indeed was a Lady of Sorrows.

Stella Croyle was silent until she was quite sure that she had once more the mastery of her voice. It was important to her that her next words should not be forgotten. But even so she did not dare to speak above a whisper.

"I want you to do me a favour. If you should meet Harry, I should like him to have news of me. I should like him also—oh, not so often—but just every now and then to write me a little line."

There were tears glistening on her dark eyelashes. Hillyard fell into a sort of panic as he reflected upon his own vaunting talk. Compared with this woman's poignant distress, all the vicissitudes of his life seemed now quite trivial and small. Here were tears falling and Hillyard was unused to tears. Nor had he ever heard so poignant a longing in any human voice as that on which Stella's prayer to him was breathed. He was ashamed. He was also a little envious of Harry Luttrell. He was also a little angry with Harry Luttrell.

"You won't forget?"

Stella clasped her hands together imploringly.

"No," Hillyard replied. "Be very sure of that, Mrs. Croyle! If I meet Luttrell he shall have your message."

"Thank you."

Stella Croyle dried the tears from her cheeks and stood up.

"I have been foolish. You won't find me like that again," she cried, and she helped Hillyard on with his coat. She went to the door to see him out, but stopped as she grasped the handle.

All Hillyard's talk about himself had passed in at one ear and out at the other. But every word which he had spoken about Harry Luttrell was written on her heart. And one phrase had kindled a tiny spark of hope. She had put it aside by itself, wanting more knowledge about it, and meaning to have that knowledge before Hillyard departed. She put her question now, with the door still closed and her back to it.

"You said that Harry *had* to join the army. What did you mean by that?"

Hillyard hesitated.

"Did he not tell you himself?"

"No."

Hillyard stood between loyalty to his friend and the recollection of Stella Croyle's tears. If Luttrell had not told her—why then—

"Then I don't well see how I can," he said uncomfortably.

"But I want to know," said Stella, bending her brows at him in astonishment that he should refuse her so small a thing. Then her manner changed. "Oh, I do want to know," she cried, and Hillyard's obstinacy broke down.

Men have the strangest fancies which compel them to do out of all reason, even the things which they hate to do, and to put aside what they hold most dear. Fancies unintelligible to practical people like women—thus Stella Croyle's thoughts ran—but to be taken note of very carefully. High-flown motives from a world of white angels, where no doubt they are very suitable. But men will use them as working motives here below, with the result that they wreck women's hearts and cause themselves a great deal of useless misery.

Stella's hopes and her self-esteem had for long played with the thought that it might possibly be one of those impracticable notions which had whipped Harry Luttrell up to the rupture of their alliance; that after all, it was not that he was tired of a chain. Yes, she wanted to know.

"Luttrell only told me once, only spoke about it once," said Hillyard shifting from one foot to the other. "The week after the eights. We rowed down to Kennington Island in a racing pair, had supper there—"

"Yes, yes," Stella Croyle interrupted. Oh, how dense men could be to be sure! What in the world did it matter, how or when the secret was told?

"I beg your pardon," said Hillyard. "But really it does matter a little. You see, it was on our way back, when it was quite dark, so dark that really you could see little but the line of sky above the trees, and the flash of the water at the end of the stroke. I doubt if Luttrell would have ever told me at all, if it hadn't been for just that one fact, that we were alone together in the darkness and out on the river."

"Yes, I was wrong," said Stella penitently. "I was impatient. I am sorry."

More and more, just because of this detail, she was ready to believe that Harry Luttrell had left her for some reason quite outside themselves, for some other reason than weariness and the swift end of passion.

"Luttrell's father, his grandfather and many others of his name had served in the Clayford Regiment. It was his home regiment and the tradition of the family binding from father to son, was that there should always be Luttrells amongst its officers."

"And for that reason Harry—" Stella interrupted impetuously.

"No, there is more compulsion than that in Harry's case," Hillyard took her up. "Much more! The Clayfords *ran* in the South African War, and ran badly. They returned to England a disgraced regiment. Now do you see the compulsion?"

Stella Croyle turned the problem over in her mind.

"Yes, I think I do," she said, but still was rather doubtful. Then she looked at the problem through Harry Luttrell's eyes.

"Yes, I understand. The regiment must recover its good name in the next war. It was an obligation of honour on Harry to take his commission in it, to bear his part in the recovery."

"Yes. I told you, didn't I? Harry Luttrell was cradled in tradition."

Hillyard saw Mrs. Croyle's face brighten. Now she had the key to Harry Luttrell. He had joined the Clayfords. And what was his fear at Stockholm? The slovenly soldier! Yes, he had given her the real reason after all during that dinner on the balcony at Hasselbacken. He feared to become the slovenly soldier if he idled longer in England. It was not because he was tired of her, that the separation had come. Thus she reasoned, and she reasoned just in one little respect wrong. She had the real secret without a doubt, that "something else," which Sir Charles

Hardiman divined but could not interpret. But she did not understand that Harry Luttrell saw in her, one of the factors, nay the chief of the factors which were converting him into that thing of contempt, the slovenly soldier.

"Thank you," she said to Hillyard with a smile. She stood aside now from the door. "It was kind of you to bring me home and talk with me for a little while."

But it seems that her recovery of spirits did not last out the night. Doubts assailed her—Harry Luttrell was beneath other skies with other preoccupations and no message from him had ever come to her. Even if his love was unchanged at Stockholm, it might not be so now. Hillyard rang her up on the telephone the next morning and warm in his sympathy asked her to lunch with him. But it was a pitiful little voice which replied to him. Stella Croyle answered from her bed. She was not well. She would stay in bed for a day and then go to a little cottage which she owned in the country. She would see Hillyard again next year when he returned from the East.

"Yes, that's her way," said Sir Charles Hardiman. He met Hillyard the day before he sailed for Port Said and questioned him about Stella Croyle discreetly. "She runs to earth when she's unhappy. We shall not see her for a couple of months. No one will."

CHAPTER V

Hillyard's Messenger

Hillyard turned his back upon the pools of the Khor Galagu at the end of April and wandered slowly down the River Dinder. From time to time his shikari would lead his camels and camp-servants out on to an open clearing on the high river bank and announce a name still marked upon the maps. Once there had been a village here, before the Kalifa sent his soldiers and herded the tribes into the towns for his better security. Now there was no sign anywhere of habitation. The red boles of the mimosa trees, purple-brown cracked earth, yellow stubble of burnt grass, the skimming of myriads of birds above the treetops and shy wild animals gliding noiselessly in the dark of the forest—there was nothing more now. It seemed that no human foot had ever trodden that region.

Hillyard's holiday was coming to an end, for in a month the rainy season would begin and this great park become a marsh. He went fluctuating between an excited eagerness for a renewal of rivalry and the interchange of ideas and the companionship of women; and a reluctance to leave a country which had so restored him to physical well-being. Never had he been so strong. He had recaptured, after his five years of London confinement, the swift spring of the muscles, the immediate response of the body to the demand made upon it, and the glorious cessation of fatigue when after arduous hours of heat and exertion he stretched himself upon his camp-chair in the shadow of his tent. On the whole he travelled northwards reluctantly; until he came to a little open space ten days away from the first village he would touch.

He camped there just before noon, and at three o'clock on the following morning, in the company of his shikari, his skinner and his donkey-boy he was riding along a narrow path high above the river. It was very dark, so that even with the vast blaze of stars overhead, Hillyard could hardly see the flutter of his shikari's white robe a few paces ahead of him. They passed a clump of bushes and immediately afterwards heard a great shuffling and lapping of water below them. The shikari stopped abruptly and seized the bridle of Hillyard's donkey. The night was so still that the noise at the water's edge below seemed to fill the world. Hillyard slipped off the back of his donkey and took his rifle from his boy.

"*Gamus!*" whispered the shikari.

Hillyard almost swore aloud. There was a creek, three hours' march away, where the reed buck came down to drink in the morning. For that creek Hillyard was now making with a little Mannlicher sporting rifle—and he had tumbled suddenly upon buffalo! He was on the very edge of the buffalo country, he would see no more between here and the houses of Senga.

It was his last chance and he had nothing but a popgun! He was still reproaching himself when a small but startling change took place. The snuffling and lapping suddenly ceased; and with the cessation of all sound, the night became sinister.

The shikari whispered again.

"Now they in their turn know that we are here." He enveloped the donkey's head in a shawl that he was carrying. "Do not move," he continued. "They are listening."

Shikari, skinner, donkey-boy, donkey and Hillyard stood together, motionless, silent. Hillyard had come out to hunt. Down below the herd in its dumb parliament was debating whether he should be the hunted. There was little chance for any one of them if the debate went against them. Hillyard might bring down one—perhaps two, if by some miraculous chance he shot a bullet through both forelegs. But it would make no difference to the herd. Hillyard pictured them below by the water's edge, their heads lifted, their tails stiffened, waiting in the darkness. Once the lone, earth-shaking roar of a lion spread from far away, booming over the dark country. But the herd below never stirred. It no more feared the lion than it feared the four men on the river bank above. An hour passed before at last the river water plashed under the trampling hoofs.

Hillyard threw his rifle forward, but the shikari touched him on the arm.

"They are going," he whispered, and again the four men waited, until the shikari raised his hand.

"It will be good for us to move! They are very near." He looked towards the east, but there was no sign yet of the dawn.

"We will go very cautiously into the forest. We shall not know where they are, but they will know everything we are doing."

In single file they moved from the bank amongst the mimosas, the donkey with his head covered, still led by the boy. Under the cavern of the branches it was black as pitch—so black that Hillyard did not see the hand which the shikari quietly laid upon his shoulder.

"Listen."

On his left a branch snapped, ahead of them a bush that had been bent aside swished back on its release.

"They are moving with us. They are all round us," the shikari whispered. "They know everything we do. Let us wait here. When the morning breaks they will charge or they will go."

So once again the little party came to a halt. Hillyard stood listening and wondering if the morning would ever come; and even in that time of tension the habit of his mind reasserted its sway. This long, silent waiting for the dawn in the depths of an African forest with death at his very elbow—here was another sharp event of life in vivid contrast with all the others which had gone before. The years in London, the letterbox opposite the Abbey where he had posted his manuscripts at three in the morning and bought a cup of coffee at the stall by the kerb—times so very close to him—the terms at Oxford, the strange hungry days on the quays of Spain, the moonlit wanderings on the footpath over the rustic ridge and up the hill, when he composed poems to the moon and pithy short, great thoughts—here was something fresh to add to them if he didn't go down at daybreak under the hoofs of the herd! Here was yet a further token, that out of the vicissitudes of his life something more, something new, something altogether different and unimagined was to come, as the crown and ultimate reason of all that had gone before. Once more the shikari's hand touched him and pointed eastwards. The tree-trunks were emerging from the darkness. Beyond them the black cup of the sky was thinning to translucency. Very quickly the grey light widened beyond this vast palisade of trees. Even in here below the high branches, it began to steal vaporous and dim. About them on every side now the buffalo were moving. The shikari's grip tightened on Hillyard's arm. The moment of danger had come. It would be the smash of his breastbone against the forehead of the beast, hoofs and knees kneading his broken body and the thrust and lunge of the short curled horns until long after he was dead, or—the new test and preparation to add to those which had gone before!

Suddenly the shikari cried aloud.

"They are off"; and while he spoke came a loud snapping of boughs, the sound of heavy bodies crashing against trees and for a moment against the grey light in that cathedral of a forest the huge carcases of the buffalo in mad flight were dimly visible. Then silence came again for a few moments, till the boughs above them shrilled with birds and the morning in a splendour of gold and scarlet, like a roar of trumpets stormed the stars.

Hillyard drew a breath.

"Let us go on," he said.

They advanced perhaps fifty yards before the second miracle of that morning smote upon his eyes. A solitary Arab, driving a tiny, overladen donkey, was advancing towards him, his white robes flickering in and out among the tree-boles.

Hillyard looked at his shikari. But the shikari neither spoke nor altered the regularity of his face. Hillyard put no question in consequence. The Arab was ten days' journey from the nearest village and, even so, his back was turned towards it. He was moving from solitude into solitude still more silent and remote. It was impossible. Hillyard's eyes were playing him false.

He shut them for an instant and opened them again, thinking that the vision would have gone. But there was the Arab still nearer to them and moving with a swift agility. A ray of sunlight struck through the branches of a tree and burned suddenly like a dancing flame on something the man carried—a carbine with a brass hammer. And the next moment a sound proved beyond all doubt to Hillyard that his eyes did not deceive him. For he heard the slapping of the Arab's loose slippers upon the hard-caked earth.

Oh yes, the man was real enough. For the shikari suddenly swerved from the head of the file towards the stranger and stopped. The two men talked together and meanwhile Hillyard and the rest of his party halted. Hillyard lit his pipe.

"Who is it, Hamet?" he cried, and the shikari turned with his companion and came back.

"It is the postman," he said as though the delivery of letters along the Dinder River were the most commonplace of events.

"The postman!" cried Hillyard. "What in the world do you mean?"

"Yes," Hamet explained. "He carries letters between Abyssinia and Senga on the Blue Nile. He is now on his way back to Abyssinia."

"But how long does it take him?" Hillyard asked in amazement.

"He goes and returns once a year. The journey takes him four months each way unless he meets with a party shooting. Then it takes longer for he goes with the party to get meat."

Hillyard stared at the Arab in amazement. He was a lean slip of a man, almost as black as a negro, with his hair running back above the temples, and legs like walking-sticks. He stood wreathed in smiles and nodding confirmation of Hamet's words. But to Hillyard, with the emotions of the dark hour just past still shivering about him, he seemed something out of nature. Hillyard leaned from his donkey and took the carbine from the postman's hand. It was an ancient thing of Spanish manufacture, heavy as a pig of lead.

"But this can't be of any use," he cried. "Is the man never attacked?"

Hamet talked with the Arab in a dialect Hillyard did not understand at all; and interpreted the conversation.

"No. He has only once fired his rifle. One night—oh, a long way farther to the south—he waked up to see an elephant fighting his little donkey in the moonlight and he fired his rifle and the elephant ran away. You must know that all these little Korans he carries on his arms and round his neck have been specially blessed by a most holy man."

The postman's shoulders, elbows, wrists and neck were circled about by chaplets on which little wooden Korans were strung. He fingered them and counted them, smiling like a woman displaying her jewels to her less fortunate friends.

"So he is safe," continued Hamet. "Yes, he will even have his picture taken. Yes, he can afford to suffer that. He will stand in front of the great eye and the machine shall go click, and it will not do him any harm at all. He has a letter for you." Hamet dropped from his enthusiasm over the wonderful immunity of the postman from the dangers of photography into a most matter-of-fact voice.

"A letter for me? That's impossible," cried Hillyard.

But the Arab was thrusting his hand here and there in the load on the donkey's back and finally drew out a goatskin bag. Hillyard, like other Englishmen, had been brought up in a creed which included the inefficiency of all Postmasters-general. A blight fell upon such persons, withering their qualities and shrivelling them into the meanest caricatures of bureaucrats. It could not be that the postal service was now to reveal resource and become the servant of romance. Yet the Arab drew forth a sealed envelope and handed it to Hillyard. And it bore the inscription of his name.

Oh, but it bore much more than that! It was written in a hand which Hillyard had not seen for seven years, and the mere sight of it swept him back in a glory of recollections to Oxford, its towers and tall roofs, which mean so much more to the man who has gone down than to the youth who is up. The forest, with its patterns of golden sunlight and its colonnades of trees crowding away into darkness, was less visible than those towers to Hillyard, as he stood with the envelope in his hand. Once more he swung down the High and across the Broad from a lecture with a ragged gown across his arm. Merton and the House, New College and Magdalen Tower—he saw the enchanted city across Christ Church meadows from the river, he looked down upon it from Headington, and again from those high fields where, at twilight, the scholar-gipsy used to roam. For the letter was in the hand of Harry Luttrell.

He tore it open and read:

> *"Some one in London is asking for you. Who it is I don't know. But the message came through in a secret cipher and it might be important. I think you should pack your affs. and hurry along to Senga, where I shall expect you."*

Martin Hillyard folded the letter and put it away in his pocket.

"He will find food in our camp," he said to Hamet, with a nod towards the postman. "We may as well go on."

Even if he returned to camp at once, it would be too late to start that day. The sun would be high long before the baggage could be packed upon the camels. The little party went on to the creek and built a tiny house of reeds and boughs, in which Hillyard sat down to wait for the deer to gather. He had one of the green volumes of "The Vicomte de Bragelonne" in his pocket, but this morning the splendid Four for once did not enchain him. Who was it in London who wanted him—wanted him so much that cipher telegrams must find him out on the banks of the Dinder River? Was this letter the summons to the something more and something different? Was the postman to Abyssinia the expected messenger? The miracle of that morning predisposed him to think so.

He sat thus for an hour, and then stepping daintily, with timid eyes alert, a tall reed-buck and his doe came through the glade towards the water. But they did not drink; they waited, cropping the grass. Gradually, through a long hour, others gathered, tawny and yellow, and dappled-brown, and stood and fed until—perhaps a signal was given, perhaps a known moment had come—all like soldiers at a command, moved down to the water's edge.

Six nights later Hillyard camped at Lueisa, near to that big tree under which it is not wise to spread your bed. He took his bath at ten o'clock at night under the moon, and the water from the river was hot. He stretched himself out in his bed and waked again that night after the moon had set, to fix indelibly in his memory the blazing dome of stars above his head, and the Southern Cross burning in a corner of the sky. The long, wonderful holiday was ended. Tomorrow night he would sleep in a house. Would he ever come this way again?

In the dark of the morning he struck westwards from the Dinder, across a most tedious neck of land, for Senga and the Blue Nile.

CHAPTER VI

The Honorary Member

At six o'clock in the evening Colin Rayne, a young civilian in the Sudan Service, heard, as he sat on the balcony of the mess at Senga, the rhythmical thud of camels swinging in to their rest in the freshness of the night air.

"There's our man," he exclaimed, and running downstairs, he reached the door just as Hillyard's twelve camels and his donkeys trooped into the light. Hillyard was riding bareheaded, with his helmet looped to his saddle, a young man, worn thin by sun and exercise, with fair burnt hair, and a brown clean shaven face. Colin Rayne went up to him as he dismounted.

"Captain Luttrell asked me to look after you. He has got some work on hand for the moment. We'll see after your affs."

"Thank you."

"You might show me, by the way, where your cartridges are."

Hillyard selected the camel on which they were packed and Rayne called a Sudanese sergeant to take them into the mess.

"Now we will go upstairs. I expect that you can do with a whisky-and-soda," he said.

Hillyard was presented to a Doctor Mayle, who was conducting a special research into the cause of an obscure fever; and to the other officers of this headquarters of a Province. They were all young, Hillyard himself was older than any of them.

"Oh, we have got some married ones, too," said Rayne, "but they live in houses of their own like gentlefolk."

"There are some Englishwomen here then?" said Hillyard, and for an appreciable moment there was silence. Then a shortish, square man, with a heavy moustache explained, if explanation it could be called.

"No. They were sent off to Senaar this morning—to be out of the way. Wiser."

Hillyard asked no questions but drank his whisky-and-soda.

"I haven't seen Luttrell since we were at Oxford together," he said.

"And it's by an accident that you see him now," said Rayne. "The Governor of Senga was thrown from his horse and killed on the spot down by the bridge there six weeks ago. The road gave way suddenly under his horse's hoofs. Some one was wanted here immediately."

"Yes, there's no doubt of that," said Mr. Blacker, the short square man, with emphasis.

"Captain Luttrell had done very well in Kordofan," Rayne resumed. "He was fetched up here in a hurry as Acting Governor. But no doubt the appointment will be confirmed."

Mr. Blacker added another croak.

"Oh, it'll be confirmed all right, if——" and he left his sentence in the air; but his gesture finished it.

"If there is any Luttrell left to confirm," Martin Hillyard interpreted, though he kept his interpretation to himself.

There certainly was in that room with the big balcony a grim expectation of trouble. It was apparent, not so much in words as in an attention to distant noises, and a kind of strained silence. The sound of a second caravan was heard. It was coming from the north. Rayne ran to the rail of the balcony and looked anxiously out. The street here was very broad and the huts upon the opposite side already dark except at one point, where an unshaded kerosene lamp cast through on open door a panel of glaring light upon the darkness. Rayne saw the caravan emerge spectrally into the light and disappear again.

"They are our beasts," he said in a voice of relief, and a minute later he called down to the soldier in charge. He spoke in the Dinka language and the soldier replied in the same tongue. Hillyard understood enough of it now to learn that the women had arrived safely at Senaar without any incident or annoyance.

"That's good," said Colin Rayne. He turned to Hillyard. "Luttrell's a long time. Shall we go and find him?"

Both Blacker and Dr. Mayle looked up with surprise, but Hillyard had risen quickly, and they raised no objection. Rayne walked down the stairs first and led the way towards the rear of the building across an open stretch of ground. The moon had not yet risen, and it was pitch dark so that Hillyard had not an idea whither he was being led. Colin Rayne stopped at a small, low door in a high big wall and knocked. A heavy key grated in a lock and the door was opened by a soldier. Hillyard found himself standing inside a big compound, in the midst of which stood some bulky, whitish erection, from which a light gleamed.

Colin Rayne led the way towards the light. It was shining through the doorway of a chamber of new wood planks with a flat roof and some strange, dimly-seen superstructure. Hillyard looked through the doorway and saw a curious scene. Two Sudanese soldiers were present, one of whom carried the lantern. The other, a gigantic creature with a skin like polished mahogany, was stripped to the waist and held poised in his hands a huge wooden mallet with a long handle. He stood measuring his distance from the stem of a young tree which was wedged tightly between a small square of stone on the ground and the flat roof above. Standing apart, and watching everything with quiet eyes was Harry Luttrell.

Even at this first glance in the wavering light of the lantern Hillyard realised that a change had come in the aspect of his friend. It was not a look of age, but authority clothed him as with a garment. Rayne and Hillyard passed into the chamber. Luttrell turned his head and welcomed Hillyard with a smile. But he did not move and immediately afterwards he raised his face to the roof.

"Are you ready up there?"

An English voice replied through the planks.

"Yes, sir," and immediately afterwards a dull and heavy weight like a full sack was dumped upon the platform above their heads.

"Good!"

Luttrell turned towards the giant.

"Are you ready? And you know the signal?"

The Sudanese soldier grinned in delighted anticipation, with a flash of big white teeth, and took a firmer grip of his mallet and swung it over his shoulder.

"Good. Now pay attention," said Luttrell, "so that all may be well and seemly done."

The Sudanese fixed his eyes upon Luttrell's foot and Luttrell began to talk, rapidly and rather to himself than to his audience. Hillyard could make neither head nor tail of the strange scene. It was evident that Luttrell was rehearsing a speech, but why? And what had the Sudanese with the mallet to do with it?

A sudden and rapid sequence of events brought the truth home to him with a shock. At a point of his speech Luttrell stamped twice, and the Sudanese soldier swung his mallet with all his force. The head of it struck the great support full and square. The beam jumped from its position, hopped once on its end, and fell with a crash. And from above there mingled with the crash a most horrid clang, for, with the removal of the beam, two trapdoors swung downwards. Hillyard looked up; he saw the stars, and something falling. Instinctively he stepped back and shut his eyes. When he looked again, within the chamber, midway between the floor and roof, two sacks dangling at the end of two ropes spun and jerked—as though they lived.

Rayne had stepped back and stood quivering from head to foot by

Hillyard's side; Hillyard himself felt sick. He knew very well now what he was witnessing—the rehearsal of an execution. The Sudanese soldiers were grinning from ear to ear with delight and pride. The one person quite unmoved was Harry Luttrell, whose ingenuity had invented the device.

"Let it be done just so," he said to the soldiers. "I shall not forgive a mistake."

They saluted, and he dismissed them and turned at last to Martin Hillyard.

"It's good to see you again," he said, as he shook hands; and then he looked sharply into Hillyard's face and laughed. "Shook you up a bit, that performance, eh? Well, they bungled things in Khartum a little while ago. I can't afford awkwardness here."

Senga was in the centre of that old Khalifa's tribe which not so many years ago ruled in Omdurman. It was always restless, always on the lookout for a Messiah.

"Messiahs are most unsettling," said Luttrell, "especially when they don't come. The tribe began sharpening its spearheads a few weeks ago. Then two of them got excited and killed. That's the consequence," and he jerked his head towards the compound, from which the two friends were walking away.

Hillyard was to hear more of the matter an hour later, as they all sat at dinner in the messroom. There were thousands of the tribe, all in a ferment, and just half a battalion of Sudanese soldiers under Luttrell's command to keep them in order.

"Blacker thinks we ought to have temporised, and that we shall get scuppered," said Luttrell. He was the one light-hearted man at that table, though he was staking his career, his life, and the life of the colony on the correctness of his judgment. Sir Charles Hardiman would never have recognised in the man who now sat at the head of the mess table the young man who had been so torn by this and that discrimination in the cabin of his yacht at Stockholm. There was something of the joyous savage about him now—a type which England was to discover shortly in some strength amongst the young men who were to officer its armies.

"I don't agree. I have invited the chiefs to see justice done. I am going to pitch them a speech myself from the scaffold—cautionary tales for children, don't you know—and then, if old Fee-Fo-Fum with the mallet don't get too excited and miss his stroke, everything will go like clockwork."

Hillyard wondered how in the world he was going to deliver Stella Croyle's message—a flimsy thing of delicate sentimentality—to this man concerned with life and death, and discharging his responsibilities according to the just rules of his race, without fear and without too much self-questioning. Indeed, the Luttrell, Acting Governor of Senga, was a more familiar figure to Hillyard than he would have been to Stella Croyle. For he had shaken off, under the pressure of immediate work and immediate decisions, the thin and subtle emotions which were having their way with him two years before. He had recaptured the high spirit of Oxford days, and was lit along his path by that clear flame.

But there were tact and discretion too, as Hillyard was to learn. For Mr. Blacker still croaked at the other end of the table.

"It's right and just and all that of course. But you are taking too high a risk, Luttrell."

The very silence at the table made it clear to Hillyard that Luttrell stood alone in his judgment. But Luttrell only smiled and said:

"Well, old man, since I disagree, the only course is to refer the whole problem to our honorary member."

And at once every countenance lightened, and merriment began to flick and dance from one to other of that company like the beads on the surface of champagne. Only Hillyard was mystified.

"Your honorary member!" he inquired.

Luttrell nodded solemnly, and raised his glass.

"Gentlemen, the Honorary Member of the Senga Mess—Sir Chichester Splay."

The toast was drunk with enthusiasm by all but Hillyard, who sat staring about him and wondering what in the world the Mecænas of the First Nights had in common with these youthful administrators far-flung to the Equator.

"You don't drink, Martin," cried Luttrell. A Socialist at a Public Dinner who refused to honour the Royal Toast could only have scandalised the chairman by a few degrees more than Hillyard's indifference did now.

"I beg your pardon," said Hillyard with humility. "I repair my error now. It was due to amazement."

"Amazement!" Colin Rayne repeated, as Hillyard drained his glass.

"Yes. For I know the man."

There was the silence that follows some stupendous happening; eyes were riveted upon Hillyard in admiration; and then the silence burst.

"He knows him!"

"It's incredible!"

"Actually knows him!"

And suddenly above the din Blacker's voice rose warningly.

"Don't let's lose our heads! That's the great thing! Let us keep as calm as we can and think out our questions very carefully lest the Heaven-sent Bearer of Great Tidings should depart without revealing all he knows."

Chairs were hitched a little closer about Hillyard. The care which had brooded in that room was quite dispelled.

"Have some more port, sir," said the youngest of that gathering, eagerly pushing across the bottle. Hillyard filled his glass. Port was his, and prestige too. He might write a successful play. That was all very well. He might go shooting for eight months along by the two Niles and the Dinder. That was all very well too. He was welcome at the Senga Mess. But he knew Sir Chichester Splay! He acquired in an instant the importance of a prodigy.

"But, since he is an honorary member of your mess, you must know him too," cried Hillyard. "He must have come this way."

"My dear Martin!" Luttrell expostulated, as one upbraiding a child. "Sir Chichester Splay out of London! The thing's inconceivable!"

"Inconceivable! Why, he lives in the country."

A moment of consternation stilled all voices. Then the Doctor spoke in a whisper.

"Is it possible that we are all wrong?"

"He lives at Rackham Park, in Sussex."

Mr. Blacker fell back in relief.

"I know the house. He is a new resident. It is near to Chichester. He went there on the Homœopathic principle."

The conjecture was actually true. Sir Chichester Splay, spurred by his ambition to be a country gentleman with a foot in town, had chosen the neighbourhood on account of his name, so that it might come to be believed that he had a territorial connection.

"Describe him to us," they all cried, and, when Hillyard had finished:

"Well, he might be like that," Luttrell conceded. "It was not our idea."

"No," said Colin Rayne. "You will remember I always differed from all of you, but it seems that I am wrong too. I pictured him as a tall, melancholy man, with a conical bald head and with a habit of plucking at a black straggling beard—something like the portraits of Tennyson."

"To me," said Luttrell, "he was always fat and fussy, with white spats."

"But why are you interested in him at all?" cried Hillyard.

"We will explain the affair to you on the balcony," answered Luttrell, as he rose.

They moved into the dark and coolness of this spacious place, and, stretching themselves in comfort on the long cane chairs, they explained to Hillyard this great mystery. Rayne began the tale.

"You see, we don't get a mail here so very often. Consequently we pay attention when it comes. We read the *Searchlight*, for instance, with care."

Mr. Blacker snatched the narrative away at this point.

"And Sir Chichester Splay occurs in most issues and in many columns. At first we merely noticed him. Some one would say, 'Oh, here's old Splay again,' as if—it seems incredible now—the matter was of no importance. It needed Luttrell to discover the real significance of Sir Chichester, the man's unique and astounding quality."

Harry Luttrell interrupted now.

"Yes, it was I," he said with pride. "Sir Chichester one day was seen at a Flower Show in Chelsea. On another he attended the first performance of a play. On a third day he honoured the Private View of an Exhibition of Pictures. On a fourth he sat amongst the Distinguished Strangers in the Gallery of the House of Commons. But that was all! This is what I alone perceived. Always that was all!"

Luttrell leaned back and relit his cigar.

"When other people come to be mentioned in the newspapers day after day, sooner or later some information about them slips out, some characteristic thing. If you don't get to know their appearance, you learn at all events their professions, their opinions. But of Sir Chichester Splay—never anything at all. Yet he is there always, nothing can happen without his presence, a man without a shadow, a being without a history. To me, a simple soldier, he is admirable beyond words. For he has achieved the inconceivable. He combines absolute privacy of life with a worldwide notoriety. He may be a stamp collector. Do I know that? No. All I know is that if there were an Exhibition of Stamp Collections, he would be the first to pass the door." Luttrell rose from his chair.

"Therefore," he added in conclusion, "Sir Chichester is of great value to us at Senga. We elected him to the mess with every formality, and some day, when we have leisure, we shall send a deputation up the Nile to shoot a Mrs. Grey's Antelope to decorate Rackham Park." He turned to Hillyard. "We have a few yards to walk, and it is time."

The two friends walked down the stairs and turned along the road, Hillyard still debating what was, after all, the value of Sir Chichester Splay to the Senga mess. It had seemed to him that Luttrell had not wished for further questions on the balcony, but, now that the two were alone, he asked:

"I don't see it," he said; and Luttrell stopped abruptly and turned to him.

"Don't you, Martin?" he asked gently. All the merriment had gone from his face and voice. "If you were with us for a week you would. It's just the value of a little familiar joke always on tap. Here are a handful of us. We eat together, morning, noon, and night; we work together; we play polo together—we can never get away from each other. And in consequence we get on each other's nerves, especially in the months of hot weather. Ill temper comes to the top. We quarrel. Irreparable things might be said. That's where Sir Chichester Splay comes in. When the quarrel's getting bitter, we refer it to his arbitration. And, since he has no opinions, we laugh and are saved." Luttrell resumed his walk to the Governor's house.

"Yes, I see now," said Hillyard.

"You had an instance tonight," Luttrell added, as they went in at the door. "It's a serious matter—the order of a Province and a great many lives, and the cost of troops from Khartum, and the careers of all of us are at stake. I think that I am right, and it is for me to say. They disagree. Yes, Sir Chichester Splay saved us tonight, and"—a smile suddenly broke upon his serious face—"I really should like to meet him."

"I will arrange it when we are both in London," Hillyard returned.

He did not forget that promise. But he was often afterwards to recall this moment when he made it—the silent hall, the door open upon the hot, still night, the moon just beginning to gild the dark sky, and the two men standing together, neither with a suspicion of the lifelong consequences which were to spring from the casual suggestion and the careless assent.

"You are over there," said Luttrell, pointing to the other side of the hall. He turned towards his own quarters, but a question from Hillyard arrested him.

"What about that message for me?"

"I know nothing about it," Luttrell answered, "beyond what I wrote. The telegram came from Khartum. No doubt they can tell you more at Government House. Good night!"

CHAPTER VII

In the Garden of Eden

Just outside Senga to the north, in open country, stands a great walled zareba, and the space enclosed is the nearest approach to the Garden of Eden which this wicked world can produce. The Zoological Gardens of Cairo and Khartum replenish their cages from Senga. But there are no cages at Senga, and only the honey-badger lives in a tub with a chain round his neck, like a bulldog. The buffalo and the elephant, the wart-hog and the reed-buck, roam and feed and sleep together. Nor do they trouble, after three days' residence in that pleasant sanctuary, about man—except that specimen of man who brings them food.

All day long you may see, towering above the wall close to the little wooden door, the long necks and slim heads of giraffes looking towards the city and wondering what in the world is the matter with the men today, and why they don't come along with the buns and sugar. Once within the zareba, once you have pushed your way between the giraffes and got their noses out of your jacket pockets, you have really only to be wary of the ostrich. He, mincing delicately around you with his little wicked red eye blinking like a camera shutter, may try with an ill-assumed air of indifference to slip up unnoticed close behind you. If he succeeds he will land you one. And one is enough.

Into this zareba Harry Luttrell led Martin Hillyard on the next morning. Luttrell had an hour free, and the zareba was the one spectacle in Senga. He kicked the honey-badger's tub in his little reed-house and brought out that angry animal to the length of his strong chain and to within an inch of his own calves.

"Charming little beast, isn't he? See the buffalo in the middle? The little elephant came in a week ago from just south of the Khor Galagu. You had something private to say to me? Now's your time. Mind the ostrich, that's all. He looks a little ruffled."

They were quite alone in the zareba. The giraffes had fallen in behind and were following them, and level with them, on Hillyard's side, the ostrich stepped like a delicate lady in a muddy street. Hillyard found it a little difficult to concentrate his thoughts on Stella Croyle's message. But he would have delivered it awkwardly in any case. He had seen enough of Harry Luttrell last night to understand that an ocean now rolled between those two.

"On the first night of my play, 'The Dark Tower,'" he began, and suddenly faced around as the ostrich fell back.

"Yes!" said Luttrell, and he eyed the ostrich indifferently. "That animal's a brute, isn't he?"

He took a threatening step towards it, and the ostrich sidled away as if it really didn't matter to him where he took his morning walk.

"Yes?" Luttrell repeated.

"I went to a supper-party given by Sir Charles Hardiman."

"Oh?"

Luttrell's voice was careless enough. But his eyes went watchfully to Hillyard's face, and he seemed to shut suddenly all expression out of his own.

"Hardiman introduced me to a friend of yours."

Luttrell nodded.

"Mrs. Croyle?"

"Yes."

"She was well?"

"In health, yes!"

"I am very glad." Unexpectedly some feeling of relief had made itself audible in Luttrell's voice. "It would have troubled me if you had brought me any other news of her. Yes, that would have troubled me very much. I should not have been able to forget it," he said slowly.

"But she is unhappy."

Luttrell walked on in silence. His forehead contracted, a look of trouble came into his face. Yet he had an eye all the while for the movements of the animals in the zareba. At last he halted, struck out at the ostrich with his stick, and turned to Hillyard with a gesture of helplessness.

"But what can one do—except the single thing one can't do?"

"She gave me a message, if I should chance to meet you," answered Hillyard.

Luttrell's face hardened perceptibly.

"Let me hear it, Martin."

"She said that she would like you to have news of her, and that from time to time she would like to have a little line from you."

"That was all?"

"Yes."

Harry Luttrell nodded, but he made no reply. He walked back with Hillyard to the door of the zareba, and the ostrich bore them company, now on this side, now on that. The elephant was rolling in the grass like a dog, the giraffes crowded about the little door like beggars outside a restaurant. The two friends walked back towards the town in an air shimmering with heat. The Blue Nile glittered amongst its sandbanks like so many ribands of molten steel. They were close upon the house before Luttrell answered Stella Croyle's message.

"All *that*," he cried, with a sharp gesture as of a man sweeping something behind him, "all that happened in another age when I was another man."

The gesture was violent, but the words were pitiful. He was not a man exasperated by a woman's unseasonable importunity, but angry with the grim, hard, cruel facts of life.

"It's no good, Martin," he added, with a smile. "Not all the king's horses nor all the king's men——"

Hillyard was sure now that no little line would ever go from Senga to the house in the Bayswater Road. The traditions of his house and of his regiment had Harry Luttrell in their keeping. Messages? Martin Hillyard might expect them, might indeed respond to and obey them, and with advantage, just because they came out of the blue. But the men of tradition, no! The messenger had knocked upon the doors of their fathers' houses before ever they were born.

At the door of the Governor's house Harry Luttrell stopped.

"I expect you'll want to do some marketing, and I shall be busy, and tonight we shall have the others with us So I'll say now," and his face brightened with a smile, as though here at all events were a matter where the bitter laws of change could work no cruelties, "it has been really good to see you again."

Certain excellent memories were busy with them both—Nuneham and Sanford Lasher and the Cherwell under its overhanging branches. Then Luttrell looked out across to the Blue Nile and those old wondrous days faded from his vision.

"I should like you to get away bukra, bukra, Martin," he said. "Half past one at the latest, tomorrow morning. Can you manage it?"

"Why, of course," answered Hillyard in surprise.

"You see, I postponed that execution, whilst you were here. I think it'll go off all right, but since it's no concern of yours, I would just as soon you were out of the way. I have fixed it for eight. If you start at half past one you will be a good many miles away by then."

He turned and went into the house and to his own work. Martin Hillyard walked down the road along the river bank to the town. Harry

Luttrell had said his last word concerning Stella Croyle. Of that he was sure and was glad, though Stella's tear-stained face would rise up between his eyes and the water of the Nile. Sooner or later Harry Luttrell would come home, bearing his sheaves, and then he would marry amongst his own people; and a new generation of Luttrells would hold their commissions in the Clayfords. He had said his last word concerning Stella Croyle.

But Hillyard was wrong. For in the dark of the morning, when he had bestridden his donkey and given the order for his caravan to march, he was hailed by Luttrell's voice. He stopped, and Luttrell came down in his pyjamas from the door of the house to him.

"Good luck," he said, and he patted the donkey's neck. "Good luck, old man. We'll meet in England some time."

"Yes," said Hillyard.

It was not to speak these words that Harry Luttrell had risen, after wishing him good-bye the night before. So he waited.

Luttrell was still, his hand on the little donkey's neck.

"You'll remember me to our honorary member, won't you?"

"Yes."

"Don't forget."

"I won't."

Nor was it for this reminder, either. So Hillyard still waited, and at last the words came, jerkily.

"One thing you said yesterday. . . . I was very glad to hear it. That Stella was well—quite well. You meant that, didn't you? It's the truth?"

"Yes, it's the truth."

"Thank you . . . I was a little afraid . . . thank you!"

He took his hand from the donkey's neck, and Hillyard rode forward on the long and dreary stage to the one camping ground between Senga and Senaar.

For a little while he wondered at this insistence of Harry Luttrell upon the physical health of Stella Croyle, and why he had been afraid. But when the dawn came his thoughts reverted to his own affairs. The message delivered to him in the forest of the River Dinder! It might mean nothing. It was the part of prudence to make light of his hopes and conjectures. But the hopes would not be stilled, now that he was alone. This was the Summons, the great Summons for which, without his knowledge, the experiences of his life, detail by detail, had builded him.

CHAPTER VIII

Hillyard Hears News of an Old Friend

At Khartum, however, disappointment awaited him. He was received without excitement by a young aide-de-camp at the Palace.

"I heard that you had come in last night. A good trip? Dine with me tonight and you shall show me your heads. The Governor-General's in England."

"There's a telegram."

"Oh yes. It came up to us from Cairo. Some one wanted to know where you were. They'll know about it at Cairo. We just pushed it along, you know," said the aide-de-camp. He dined with Hillyard, admired his heads, arranged for his sleeping compartment, and assured him that the execution had gone off "very nicely" at Senga.

"Luttrell made a palaver, and his patent drop worked as well as anything in Pentonville, and every one went home cheered up and comfortable. Luttrell's a good man."

Thus Hillyard took the train to Wadi Haifa in a chastened mood. Obviously the message was of very little, if indeed of any, importance. A man can hardly swing up to extravagant hopes without dropping to sarcastic self-reproaches on his flightiness and vanity. He was not aware that the young aide-de-camp pushed aside some pressing work to make sure that he did go on the train; or that when the last carriage disappeared towards the great bridge, the aide-de-camp cried, "Well, that's that," like a man who has discharged one task at all events of the many left to his supervision.

One consequence of Hillyard's new humility was that he now loitered on his journey. He stayed a few days at Assouan and yet another few in Luxor, in spite of the heat, and reached Cairo in the beginning of June when the streets were thick with dust-storms and the Government had moved to Alexandria. Hillyard was in two minds whether to go straight home, but in the end he wandered down to the summer seat of government.

If Khartum had been chilly to the enthusiast, Alexandria was chillier. It was civil and polite to Hillyard and made him a member of the Club. But it was concerned with the government of Egypt, and gently allowed Hillyard to perceive it. Khartum had at all events stated "There is a cablegram." At Alexandria the statement became a question: "Is there a cablegram?" In the end a weary and indifferent gentleman unearthed it. He did not show it to Hillyard, but held it in his hand and looked over the top of it and across a rolltop desk at the inquirer.

"Yes, yes. This seems to be what you are asking about. It is for us, you know"—this with a patient smile as Hillyard's impatient hand reached out for it. "Do you know a man called Bendish—Paul Bendish?"

"Bendish?" cried Hillyard. "He was my tutor at Oxford."

"Ah! Then it does clearly refer to you. Bendish has a friend who needs your help in London."

Hillyard stared.

"Do you mean to say that I was sent for from the borders of Abyssinia because Bendish has a friend in London who wants my help?"

The indifferent gentleman stroked his chin.

"It certainly looks like it, doesn't it? But I do hope that you didn't cut your expedition short on that account." He looked remorsefully into Hillyard's face. "In any case, the rainy season was coming on, wasn't it?"

"Yes, my expedition was really ended when the message reached me," Hillyard was forced to admit.

"That's good," said the indifferent gentleman, brightening. "You will see Bendish, of course, in England. By what ship do you sail? It's not very pleasant here, is it?"

"I shall sail on the *Himalaya* in a week's time."

"Right!" said the official, and he nodded farewell and dipped his nose once more into his papers.

Hillyard walked to the door, conscious that he looked the fool he felt himself to be. But at the door he turned in a sort of exasperation.

"Can't you tell me at all why Bendish's friend wants my help?" he asked.

It was at this moment that the indifferent gentleman had the inspiration of his life.

"I haven't an idea, Mr. Hillyard," he replied. "Perhaps he has got into difficulties in the writing of a revue."

The answer certainly drove Hillyard from the room without another word. He stood outside the door purple with heat and indignation. Hillyard neither overrated nor decried his work. But to be dragged away from the buffalo and the reed-buck of the Dinder River in order to be told that he was a writer of revues. No! That was carrying a bad joke too far.

Hillyard stalked haughtily along the corridor towards the outer door, but not so fast but that a youth passed him with a sheet of paper in his hand. The youth went into the room where Government cablegrams were coded. The sheet of paper which he held in his hand was inscribed with a message that Martin Hillyard would leave Alexandria in a week's time on the s.s. *Himalaya*. And the message strangely enough was not addressed to Paul Bendish at all. It was headed, "For Commodore Graham. Admiralty." The great Summons had in fact come, although Hillyard knew it not.

He travelled in consequence leisurely by sea. He started from Alexandria after half the month of June had gone, and he was thus in the Bay of Biscay on that historic morning of June the twenty-eighth, when the Archduke Franz Ferdinand and his wife, Sophia Duchess of Hohenberg, were murdered in the streets of Saravejo. London, when he reached it, was a choir of a million voices not yet tuned to the ringing note of one. It was incredible that the storm, foreseen so often over the port wine, should really be bursting at last. Mediation will find a way. Not this time; the moment has been chosen. And what will England do? Ride safe in the calm centre of the hurricane? No ship ever did, and England won't.

A few degenerate ones threw up their hands and cried that all was over—*they knew*.

Of these a gaunt-visaged man, stubborn and stupid and two generations back a German, held forth in the hall of Hillyard's club.

"German organisation, German thoroughness and German brains—we are no match for them. The country's thick with spies—wonderful men. Where shall *we* find their equals?"

A sailor slipped across the hall and dropped into a chair by Hillyard's side.

"You take no part in these discussions? The crackling of thorns—what?"

"I have been a long time away."

"Thought so," continued the sailor. "A man was inquiring for you yesterday—a man of the name of Graham."

Hillyard shook his head.

"I don't know him."

"No, but he is a friend of a friend of yours."

Hillyard sat up in his chair. He had been four days in London, and the engrossing menace of those days had quite thrust from his recollections the telegram which had, as he thought, befooled him.

"The friend of mine is possibly Paul Bendish," he said stiffly.

"Think that was the name. Graham's the man I am speaking of," and the sailor paused. "Commodore Graham," he added.

Hillyard's indignation ebbed away. What if he had not been fooled? The quenched hopes kindled again in him. There was all this talk of war—alarums and excursions as the stage-directions had it. Service! Suddenly he realised that ever since he had left Senga, a vague envy of Harry Luttrell had been springing up in his heart. The ordered life of service—authority on the one hand, the due execution of details on the other! Was it to that glorious end in this crisis that all his life's experience had slowly been gathering? He looked keenly at his companion. Was it just by chance that he had crossed the hall in the midst of all this thistle-down discussion and dropped in the chair by his side?

"But what could I do?"

He spoke aloud, but he was putting the question to himself. The sailor, however, answered it.

"Ask Graham."

He wrote an address upon a sheet of notepaper and handed it to Hillyard. Then he looked at the clock which marked ten minutes past three.

"You will find him there now."

The sailor went after his cap and left the club. Hillyard read the address. It was a number in a little street of the Adelphi, and as he read it, suspicion again seized upon Hillyard. After all, why should a Commodore want to see him in a little street of the Adelphi. Perhaps, after all, the indifferent official of Alexandria was right and the Commodore had ambitions in the line of revues!

"I had better go and have it out with him," he decided, and, taking his hat and stick, he walked eastwards to Charing Cross. He turned into a short street. At the bottom a stone arch showed where once the Thames had lapped. Now, beyond its grey-white curve, were glimpses of green lawns and the cries of children at their play. Hillyard stopped at a house by the side of the arch. A row of brass plates confronted him, but the name of Commodore Graham was engraved on none of them. Hillyard rang the housekeeper's bell and inquired.

"On the top floor on the left," he was told.

He climbed many little flights of stairs, and at the top of each his heart sank a little lower. When the stairs ended he confronted a mean, brown-varnished door; and he almost turned and fled. After all, the monstrous thing looked possible. He stood upon the threshold of a set of chambers. Was he really to be asked to collaborate in a revue? He rang the bell, and a young woman opened the door and barred the way.

"Whom do you wish to see?" she asked.

"Commodore Graham."

"Commodore Graham?" she repeated with an air of perplexity, as though this was the first time she had ever heard the name.

Across her shoulder Hillyard looked into a broad room, where three other girls sat at desks, and against one wall stood a great bureau with many tiny drawers like pigeonholes. Several of these drawers stood open and disclosed cards standing on their edges and packed against each other. Hillyard's hopes revived. Not for nothing had he sat from seven to ten in the office of a shipping agent at Alicante. Here was a card-index, and of an amazing volume. But his interlocutor still barred the way.

"Have you an appointment with Commodore Graham?" she asked, still with that suggestion that he had lunched too well and had lost his way.

"No. But he sent for me across half the world."

The girl raised a pair of steady grey eyes to his.

"Will you write your name here?"

She allowed him to pass and showed him some slips of paper on a table in the middle of the room. Hillyard obeyed, and waited, and in a few moments she returned, and opened a door, crossed a tiny anteroom and knocked again. Hillyard entered a room which surprised him, so greatly did its size and the wide outlook from its windows contrast with the dinginess of its approach. A thin man with the face of a French abbé sat indolently twiddling his thumbs by the side of a big bureau.

"You wanted to see me?"

"Mr. Hillyard?"

"Yes."

Commodore Graham nodded to the girl, and Hillyard heard the door close behind him.

"Won't you sit down? There are cigarettes beside you. A match? Here is one. I hope that I didn't bring you home before your time."

"The season had ended," replied Hillyard, who was in no mood to commit himself. "In what way can I help you?"

"Bendish tells me that you know something of Spain."

"Spain?" cried Hillyard in surprise. "Spain means Madrid, Bilbao, and a host of places, and a host of people, politicians, merchants, farmers. What should I know of them?"

"You were in Spain for some years."

"Three," replied Hillyard, "and for most of the three years picking up a living along the quays. Oh, it's not so difficult in Spain, especially in summer time. Looking after a felucca while the crew drank in a café, holding on to a dinghy from a yacht and helping the ladies to step out, a little fishing here, smuggling a box of cigars past the customs officer there—oh, it wasn't so difficult. You can sleep out in comfort. I used to enjoy it. There was a coil of rope on the quay at Tarragona; it made a fine bed. Lord, I can feel it now, all round me as I curled up in it, and the stars overhead, seen out of a barrel, so to speak!"

Hillyard's face changed. He had the spark of the true wanderer within him. Even recollections of days long gone could blow it into clear, red flame. All the long glowing days on the hot stones of the waterside, the glitter of the Mediterranean purple-blue under the sun, the coming of night and the sudden twinkling of lights in the cave-dwellings above Almeria and across the bay from Aguilas, the plunge into the warm sea at midnight, the glorious evenings at waterside cafés when he had half a dozen coppers in his pocket; the good nature of the people! All these recollections swept back on him in a rush. The actual hardships, the hunger, the biting winds of January under a steel-cold sky, these things were all forgotten. He remembered the freedom.

"There weren't any hours to the day," he cried, and spoke the creed of all the wanderers in the world. "I saw the finest bull-fights in the world, and made money out of them by selling dulces and membrilla and almond rock from Alicante. Oh, the life wasn't so bad. But it came to an end. A shipping agent at Alicante used me as a messenger, and finally, since I knew English and no one else in his office did, turned me into a shipping clerk."

Hillyard had quite forgotten Commodore Graham, who sat patiently twiddling his thumbs throughout the autobiography, and now came with something of a start to a recognition of where he sat. He sprang up and reached for his hat.

"So, you see, you might as well ask a Chinaman at Stepney what he knows of England as ask me what I know of Spain. I am just wasting your time. But I have to thank you," and he bowed with a winning pleasantness, "for reviving in me some very happy recollections which were growing dim."

The Commodore, however, did not stir.

"But it is possible," he said quietly, "that you do know the very places which interest me—the people too."

Hillyard looked at the Commodore. He put down his hat and resumed his seat.

"For instance?"

"The Columbretes."

Hillyard laughed.

"Islands sixty miles from Valencia."

"With a lighthouse," interrupted Graham.

"And a little tumbledown inn with a vine for an awning."

"Oh! I didn't know there was an inn," said Graham. "Already you have told me something."

"I fished round the Columbretes all one summer," said Hillyard, with a laugh.

Graham nodded two or three times quickly.

"And the Balearics?"

"I worked on one of Island Line ships between Barcelona and Palma through a winter."

"There's a big wireless," said Commodore Graham.

"At Soller. On the other side of Mallorca from Palma. You cross a wonderful pass by the old monastery where Georges Sand and Chopin stayed and quarrelled."

The literary reminiscence left Commodore Graham unmoved.

"Did you ever go to Iviza?"

"For a month with a tourist who dug for ancient pottery."

Graham swung round to his bureau and drummed with the tips of his fingers upon the leather pad. He made no sign which could indicate whether he was satisfied or no. He lit a cigarette and handed the box to Hillyard.

"Did you ever come across a man called José Medina?"

Eleven years had passed since the strange days in Spain, and those eleven years not without their sharp contrasts and full hours. Hillyard's act of memory was the making of a picture. One by one he called up the chain of coast cities wherein he had wandered. Malaga, with its brown cathedral; Almeria and its ancient castle and bright blue-painted houses glowing against the brown and barren hills; Aguilas, with its islets; Cartagena, Gandia, Alicante of the palms; Valencia—and under the trees and on the quays, the boatmen and the captains and the resplendent officials whom he had known! They took shape before him and assumed their names. He dived amongst them for one José Medina.

"Yes," he replied at last, "there was a José Medina. He was a young peasant of Mallorca. He always said jo for yo."

Graham's eyes brightened and his lips twitched to a smile. He glanced aside to his bureau, whereon lay a letter written by Paul Bendish at Oxford.

"He probably has a larger acquaintance with the queer birds of the Mediterranean ports than any one else in England. But he does not seem to be aware of it. But if you persist in sitting quiet his knowledge will trickle out."

Commodore Graham persisted, and facts concerning José Medina began to trickle out. José's father had left him, the result of a Spanish peasant's thrift, a couple of thousand pesetas. With this José Medina had gone to Gibraltar, where he bought a felucca, with a native of Gibraltar as its nominal owner; so that José Medina might fly the flag of Britain and sleep more surely for its protection. At Gibraltar, with what was left of his two thousand pesetas and the credit which his manner gained him, he secured a cargo of tobacco.

"Gibraltar's a free port, you see," said Hillyard. "José ran the cargo along the coast to Benicassim, a little watering-place with a good beach about thirty kilometres east of Valencia. He ran the felucca ashore one dark night." Suddenly he stopped and smiled to himself. "I expect José Medina's in prison now."

"On the contrary," said Graham, "he's a millionaire."

Hillyard stared. Then he laughed.

"Well, those were the two alternatives for José Medina. But I am judging by one night's experience. I never saw him again."

Commodore Graham touched with his heel a bell by the leg of his bureau. The bell did not ring, but displaced a tiny shutter in front of the desk of his secretary in the anteroom; and Hillyard had hardly ended when the girl was in the room and announced:

"Admiral Carstairs."

Commodore Graham looked annoyed.

"What a nuisance! I am afraid that I must see him, Mr. Hillyard."

"Of course," said Hillyard. "Admirals are admirals."

"And they know it!" said Commodore Graham with a sigh.

Hillyard rose and took his hat.

"Well, I am very grateful to you, Mr. Hillyard," said Graham. "I can't say anything more to you now. Things, as you know, are altogether very doubtful. We may slip over into smooth water. On the other hand," and he twiddled his thumbs serenely, "we may be at war in a month. If that were to be the case, I might want to talk with you again. Will you leave your address with Miss Chayne?"

Hillyard was led out by another door, no doubt so that he might not meet the impatient admiral. He might have gone away disheartened from that interview with its vague promises. But there are other and often surer indications than words. When Miss Chayne took down his address, her manner had quite changed towards him. She had now a frank and pleasant comradeship. The official had gone. Her smile said as plainly as print could do: "You are with us now."

Meanwhile Commodore Graham read through once more the letter of Paul Bendish. He turned from that to a cabled report from Khartum of the opinion which various governors of districts had formed concerning the ways and the discretion of Martin Hillyard. Then once more he rang his bell.

"There was a list of suitable private yachts to be made out," he said.

"It is ready," replied Miss Chayne, and she brought it to him.

Over that list Commodore Graham spent a great deal of time. In the end his finger rested on the name of the steam-yacht *Dragonfly*, owned by Sir Charles Hardiman, Baronet.

CHAPTER IX

Enter the Heroine in anything but White Satin

Goodwood in the year nineteen hundred and fourteen! There were some, throwers of stones, searchers after a new thing on which to build a reputation, who have been preaching these many years past that the temper of England had changed, its solidity all dissolved into froth, and that a new race of neurotics was born on Mafeking night. Just ninety-nine years before this Goodwood meeting, when Napoleon and the veterans of the Imperial Guard were knocking at the gates of Brussels, a famous ball was given. Goodwood of the year nineteen-fourteen, *mutatis mutandis*, did but repeat that scene, the same phlegmatic enjoyment of the festival, the same light-heartedness and sure confidence under the great shadow, and the same ending.

The whispered word went round so that there should be no panic or alarm, and of a sudden every officer was gone. Goodwood of nineteen fourteen and a July so perfect with sunlight and summer that it seemed some bird at last must break the silence of the famed beech-grove! All the world went to it. The motorcars and the coaches streamed up over Duncton Hill and wound down the Midhurst Road to pleasant Charlton, with its cottages and gardens of flowers. Martin Hillyard went too.

As he walked away from Captain Graham's eyrie he met Sir Chichester Splay in Pall Mall.

"Where have you been these eight months?" inquired Sir Chichester. "'The Dark Tower' is still running, I see. A good play, Mr. Hillyard."

"But not a great play, of course," said Martin, his lips twitching to a smile.

"I have been looking for you everywhere," remarked Sir Chichester. "You must stay with us for Goodwood. My wife will never forgive me if I don't secure you."

Hillyard gladly consented. It would be his first visit to the high race-course on the downs—and—and he might find Stella Croyle among the company. It would be a little easier for him and for her too, if they met this second time in a house of many visitors. He had no comfortable news to give to her, and he had shrunk from seeking her out in the Bayswater Road. Wrap the truth in words however careful, he could not but wound her. Yet sooner or later she must hear of his return, and avoidance of her would but tell the story more cruelly than his lips.

"Yes, I will gladly come," he said, "if I may come down on the first day."

He was delayed in London until midday, and so motored after luncheon through Guildford and Chiddingfold and Petworth to Rackham Park. The park ran down to the Midhurst Road, and when Hillyard was shown into the drawing-room he walked across to the window and looked out over a valley of fields and hedges and low, dark ridges to the downs lying blue in the sunlight and the black forests on their slopes.

From an embrasure a girl rose with a book in her hand.

"Let me introduce myself, Mr. Hillyard. I am Joan Whitworth, and make my home here with my aunt. They are all at Goodwood, of course, but they should be back at any moment."

She rang the bell and ordered tea. Somewhere Hillyard realised he had seen the girl before. She was about eighteen years old, he guessed, very pretty, with a wealth of fair hair deepening into brown, dark blue eyes shaded with long dark lashes and a colour of health abloom in her cheeks.

"You have been in Egypt, uncle tells me."

"In the Sudan," Hillyard corrected. "I have been shooting for eight months."

"Shooting!"

Joan Whitworth's eyes were turned on him in frank disappointment. "The author of 'The Dark Tower'—shooting!"

There was more than disappointment in her voice. There was a hint of disdain.

Hillyard did not pursue the argument.

"I knew that I had seen you before. I remember where now. You were with Sir Chichester at the first performance of 'The Dark Tower.' I peeped out behind the curtain of my box and saw you."

Joan's face relaxed.

"Oh, yes, I was there."

"But——" Hillyard began, and caught himself up. He had been on the point of saying that she had a very different aspect in the stalls of the Rubicon Theatre. But he looked her up and down and held his peace. Yet what he did substitute left him in no better case.

"So you have not gone to the races," he said, and once more her lip curled in disdain. She drew herself up to her full height—she was not naturally small, but a good honest piece of English maidenhood.

"Do I look as if I were likely to go to the races?" she asked superbly.

She was dressed in a sort of shapeless flowing gown, saffron in colour, and of a material which, to Hillyard's inexperienced eye, seemed canvas. It spread about her on the ground, and it was high at the throat. A broad starched white collar, like an Eton boy's, surmounted it, and a little black tie was fastened in a bow, and scarves floated untidily around her.

"No, upon my word you do not," cried Hillyard, nettled at last by her haughtiness, and with such a fervour of agreement, that suddenly all her youth rose into Joan Whitworth's face and got the better of her pose. She laughed aloud, frankly, deliciously. And her laugh was still rippling about the room when motor-horns hooted upon the drive.

At once the laughter vanished.

"We shall be amongst horses in a minute," she observed with a sigh. "I can smell the stables already," and she retired to her book in the embrasure of the window.

A joyous and noisy company burst into the room. Sir Chichester, with larger mother-of-pearl buttons on his fawn-coloured overcoat than ever decorated even a welshing bookmaker on Brighton Downs, led Hillyard up to Lady Splay.

"My wife. Millie, Mr. Hillyard."

Hints of Lady Splay's passion for the last new person had prepared Hillyard for a lady at once gushing and talkative. He was surprised to find himself shaking hands with a pleasant, unassuming woman of distinct good looks. Hillyard was presented to Dennis and Miranda Brown, a young couple two years married, and to Mr. Harold Jupp, a man of Hillyard's age. Harold Jupp was a queer-looking person with a long, thin, brown face, and a straight, wide mouth too close to a small pointed chin. Harold Jupp carried about with him a very aura of horses. Horses were his only analogy; he thought in terms of horses; and perhaps, as a consequence, although he could give no reasons for his judgments upon people, those judgments as a rule were conspicuously sound. Jupp shook hands with Hillyard, and turned to the student at the window.

"Well, Joan, how have you lived without us? Aren't you bored with your large, beautiful self?"

Joan looked at him with an annihilating glance, and crossed the room to Millie Splay.

"Bored! How could I be? When I have so many priceless wasted hours to make up for!"

"Yes, yes, my dear," said Millie Splay soothingly. "Come and have some tea."

"That's it, Joan," cried Jupp, unrepressed by the girl's contempt. "Come and have tea with the barbarians."

Joan addressed herself to Dennis Brown, as one condescending from

Olympus.

"I hope you had a good day."

"Awful," Dennis Brown admitted. "We ought to have had five nice wins on form. But they weren't trying, Joan. The way Camomile was pulled. I expected to see his neck shut up like a concertina."

"Never mind, boys," said Sir Chichester. "You'll get it back before Friday."

Harold Jupp shook his head doubtfully.

"Never sure about flat-racing. Jumping's the only thing for the poor and honest backer."

Joan Wentworth looked about her regretfully.

"I understand now why you have all come back so early."

Miranda Brown ran impulsively to her. She was as pretty as a picture, and spoke as a rule in a series of charming explosions. At this moment she was deeply wronged.

"Yes, Joan," she cried. "They would go! And I know that I have backed the winner for the last race."

Dennis Brown contemplated his wife with amazement.

"Miranda, you are crazy," he cried. "He can't win."

Harold Jupp agreed regretfully.

"He's a Plater. That's the truth. A harmless, unnecessary Plater. I sit at the feet of Miranda Brown, Joan, but as regards horses, she doesn't know salt from sugar."

Miranda looked calmly at her watch.

"He has already won."

Tea was brought in and consumed. At the end of it Dennis Brown observed to Harold Jupp:

"We ought to arrange what we are going to do tomorrow."

Both men rose, and each drew from one pocket a programme of the next day's events, and from the other a little paper-covered volume called "Form at a Glance." Armed with their paraphernalia, they retired to a table in a window.

"Come and live the higher life with us, Joan," cried Harold Jupp. "What are you reading?"

"Prince Hohenstiel-Schwangau, Saviour of Society," Joan returned icily. But pride burned through the ice, and was audible.

"He sounds just like a Plater," replied Harold Jupp.

Meanwhile Dennis Brown was immersed in his programme.

"The first race is too easy," he announced.

"Yes," said Jupp. "It's sticking out a foot. Peppercorn."

Dennis Brown stared at his friend.

"Don't be silly! Simon Jackson will romp home."

Harold Jupp consulted his little brown book.

"Peppercorn ran second to Petronella at Newbury, giving her nine pounds. Petronella met Simon Jackson at even weights at Newcastle, and Simon Jackson was left in the country. Peppercorn must win."

"Let us hear the names of the others," interrupted Miranda, running up to the table.

Harold Jupp read out the names.

"Smoky Boy, Paper Crown, House on Fire, Jemima Puddleduck—" and Miranda clapped her hands.

"Jemima Puddleduck's going to win."

Both the young men stared at her, then both plunged their noses into their books.

"Jemima Puddleduck," Dennis Brown read, "out of Side Springs, by the Quack."

"Oh, what a pedigree!" cried Miranda. "She must win."

Jupp wrinkled his forehead.

"But she's done nothing. Why must she win?" asked Dennis.

Miranda shrugged her shoulders at the ineffable stupidity of the young man with whom she was linked.

"Listen to her name! Jemima Puddleduck! She can't lose!"

Both the young men dropped their books and gazed at one another hopelessly. Here was the whole scientific business of spotting winners, through research into pedigrees, weights, records, the favourite distances and race courses of this or that runner, so completely disregarded that racing might really be a matter of chance.

"I'll tell you, Miranda," said Harold Jupp. "Jemima Puddleduck's a Plater."

The awful condemnation had no sooner been pronounced than the butler, with his attendant footman, appeared to remove the tea.

"We have just heard over the telephone, sir," he said to Sir Chichester, "the winner of the last race."

"Oh!" cried Miranda breathlessly. "Which was it?"

"Chewing Gum."

Miranda swept round to her husband, radiant. "There, what did I tell you? Chewing Gum. What were the odds, Harper?" She turned again to the butler. "Oh, you do know, don't you?"

"Yes, madam, twelve to one. They say he rolled home."

Miranda Brown jumped in the air.

"Oh, I have won a hundred and twenty pounds."

Harold Jupp was sympathetic and consolatory.

"Of course it's a mistake, Miranda. I am awfully sorry! Chewing Gum ran nowhere to Earthly Paradise in the Newberry Stakes this year, and Earthly Paradise, all out to win, was beaten a month ago by seven lengths at Warwick, by Rollicking Lady. And Rollicking Lady was in this race too. So you see it's impossible. Chewing Gum's a Plater."

Miranda wrung her hands.

"But, Harold, he *did* win; didn't he, Harper?"

"There's no doubt about it, madam," replied the butler with dignity. "I 'av verified the hinformation from other sources."

He left the two experts blinking. Dennis was the first to recover from the blow.

"What on earth made you back him, Miranda?"

Miranda sailed to the side of Joan Whitworth.

"You are both of you so very unpleasant that I am seriously inclined not to tell you. But I always back horses with the names of things to eat."

The two scientists were dumb. They stared open-mouthed. Somewhere, it seemed, a religion tottered upon its foundations. Sacrilege itself could hardly have gone further than Miranda Brown had gone.

"But—but," Harold Jupp stammered feebly, "you don't *eat* chewing gum."

Miranda flattened him out with a question.

"What becomes of it, then?" and there was no answer. But Miranda was not content with her triumph. She must needs carry the war unwisely into the enemy's camp.

"After all, what in the world can have possessed you, Dennis, to back a silly old mare like Barmaid?"

Dennis Brown saw his opportunity.

"I always back horses with the names of things to kiss," he declared.

Jupp laughed aloud; Sir Chichester chuckled; Miranda looked as haughty as good-humour and a dainty personality enabled her to do.

"Vulgar, don't you think?" she asked of Joan. "But racing men *are* vulgar. Oh, Joan! have you thought out your book today? Can you now begin to write it? Will you write it in the window, with the South Downs in front of your eyes? Oh, it'll be wonderful!"

"What ho!" cried Mr. Jupp. "Miranda has joined the highbrows."

Dennis Brown was too seriously occupied to waste his time upon Miranda's enthusiasms.

"It's a pity we can't get the evening papers," he said gloomily. "I should dearly like to see the London forecasts for tomorrow."

"I brought some evening papers down with me," said Hillyard, and "Did you?" cried Sir Chichester, and his eyes flashed with interest. But Harold Jupp was already out of the room. He came back from the hall with a bundle of newspapers in his hands, pink and white and yellow and green. He carried them all relentlessly past Sir Chichester to the table in the window. Sir Chichester to a newspaper, was a needle to a magnet; and while Dennis Brown read out the selections for the morrow's races of "The Man of Iron" in the *Evening Patriot*, and "Hitchy Koo" in *The Lamppost*, Sir Chichester edged nearer and nearer.

Lady Splay invited Hillyard to play croquet with her in the garden; and halfway through the game Hillyard approached the question which troubled him.

"I was wondering whether I should meet Mrs. Croyle here."

Millicent Splay drove her ball before she answered, and missed her hoop.

"What a bore!" she cried. "Now I shall have to come back again. I didn't know that you had met Stella."

"I met her only once. I liked her."

Millie Splay nodded.

"I am glad. There's always a room here for Stella. I told her so immediately after I met her, and she took me at my word, as I meant her to do. But she avoids Goodwood week and festivals generally, and she is wise. For though I would take her anywhere myself, you know what long memories people have for other people's sins. There might be humiliations."

"I understand that," said Hillyard, and he added, "I gathered from Mrs. Croyle that you had remained a very staunch friend."

Millie Splay shrugged her shoulders.

"I am a middle-aged woman with a middle-aged woman's comprehension. There are heaps of things I loathe more and more each day, meanness, for instance, and an evil tongue. But, for the other sins, more and more I see the case for compassion. Stella was hungry of heart, and she let the hunger take her. She had her blind, wild hour or two; she was a fool; she was—well, everything the moralists choose to call her. But she has been paying for her hour ever since, and will go on paying. Now, if I can only hit your yellow ball from here, I shall have rather a good game on."

Lady Splay succeeded and, carrying the four croquet balls with her, went round the rest of the hoops and pegged out.

"I must go in and change," she said, and suddenly, in a voice of melancholy, she cried, "Oh, I do wish——" and stopped.

"What?"

"Oh, it doesn't matter," she answered. But her eyes were upon the window, where Joan Whitworth stood in full view in all her disfiguring panoply. Lady Splay wrung her hands helplessly. "Oh, dear, dear, if she weren't so thorough!" she moaned.

When they returned into the drawing-room, Sir Chichester was still standing near to Harold Jupp and Dennis Brown, shifting from one foot to another, and making little inarticulate sounds in his throat.

"Haven't you two finished yet?" asked Millicent Splay.

"Just," said Dennis Brown, rubbing his hands together with a laugh, "and we ought to have four nice wins tomorrow."

"Good!" said Sir Chichester. "Then might I have a newspaper?"

"But of course," said Dennis Brown, and he handed one over the table to him. "You haven't been waiting for it all this time, Sir Chichester?"

"Oh no, no, no," exclaimed Sir Chichester, quickly. He glanced with a swift and experienced eye down the columns, and tossed the paper aside.

"Might I have another?"

"But of course, sir."

The second paper was disposed of as rapidly as the first, and the others followed in their turn.

"Nothing in them," said Sir Chichester with a resigned air. "Nothing in them at all."

Millie Splay laughed.

"All that my husband means is that his name is not to be found in any one of them."

"The occurrence seems so rare that he has no great reason to complain," said Hillyard; and, in order to assuage any disappointment which might still be rankling in the baronet's bosom, Hillyard related at the dinner-table, with the necessary discretions, his election to the mess at Senga.

Sir Chichester was elated. "So far away my name is known! Really, that is very pleasant hearing!"

There was no offence to him in the reason of his honorary membership of the Senga mess, which, however carefully Hillyard sought to hide it, could not but peep out. Sir Chichester neither harboured illusions himself as to his importance nor sought to foster them in others. There was none of the "How do these things get into the papers?" about *him*.

"I am not a public character. So I have to take trouble to keep myself in print. And I do—a deuce of a lot of trouble."

"Now, why?" asked Harold Jupp, who possessed an inquiring mind and was never satisfied by anything but the most definite statements.

"Because I like it," replied Sir Chichester. "I am used to it, and I like it. Unless I see my name in real print every morning, I have all day the uncomfortable sensation that I am not properly dressed."

Millie Splay and the others round the table, with the exception of one person, laughed. To that one person, Sir Chichester here turned good-humouredly:

"All right, you can turn your nose up, Joan. It seems extraordinary to you that I should like to see my name in print. I can tell you something more extraordinary than that. The public likes it too. Just because I am not a public character, every reference to me must be of an exclusively personal kind. And that's just the sort of reference which the public eats. It is much more thrilled by the simple announcement that a Sir Chichester Splay, of whom it has never heard, has bought a new pair of purple socks with white stripes than it would be by a full account of a Cabinet crisis."

Once more the company laughed at Sir Chichester's apology for his foible.

Lady Splay turned to Hillyard.

"And who is the ingenious man who discovered this way of keeping the peace at Senga?"

Hillyard suddenly hesitated.

"A great friend of mine," he answered with his eyes on Millie Splay's face. "He was with me at Oxford. A Captain Luttrell."

But it was clear almost at once that the name had no associations in Lady Splay's mind. She preferred to entertain her friends in the country than to live in town. She knew little of what gossip might run the streets of London; and since Luttrell was, as yet, like Sir Chichester, in that he was not a public character, there had been no wide-run gossip about Stella Croyle or himself which Millicent Splay was likely to meet.

Hillyard thought at first, that with a woman's self-control she turned a blank face to him of a set purpose. But one little movement of hers reassured him. Her eyes turned towards Joan Whitworth, as though asking whether this Harry Luttrell was a match for her, and she said:

"You must bring your friend down to see us, when he comes back to England. We are almost acquainted as it is."

No! Millicent Splay did not connect Harry Luttrell with Stella Croyle.

It would have been better if Hillyard, that very night, had enlightened her. But he was neither a gossip nor a meddler. It was not possible that he should.

CHAPTER X

The Summons

It is curious to recollect how smoothly the surface water ran during that last week of peace. Debates there were, of course, and much argument across the table. It was recognised that great changes, social, economic, military, would come and great adaptations have to be made. But, meanwhile, to use the phrase which was soon to be familiar in half a million mouths, people carried on. The Brown couple, for instance. Each morning they set out gaily, certain of three or four nice wins; each evening they returned after a day which was "simply awful." Harold Jupp was at hand with his unfailing remedy.

"We'll go jumping in the winter and get it all back easily. Flat racing's no good for the poor. The Lords don't come jumping."

Joan Whitworth carried on too, in her sackcloth and sashes. She was moved by the enthusiastic explosions of Miranda Brown to reveal some details of the great novel which was then in the process of incubation.

"*She* insists on being married in a violet dress," said Joan, "with the organ playing the 'Funeral March of a Marionette.'"

"Oh, isn't that thrilling!" cried Miranda.

"But why does she insist upon these unusual arrangements?" asked Harold Jupp.

Joan brushed his question aside.

"It was symbolical of her."

"Yes. Linda would have done that," said Miranda. "I suppose her marriage turns out very unhappily?"

"It had to," said Joan, quite despondent over this unalterable necessity.

"Now, why?" asked Jupp in a perplexity.

"Her husband never understood her."

"What ho!" cried Dennis Brown, looking up from his scientific researches into "Form at a Glance."

"I expect that he talked racing all day," said Miranda.

Dennis Brown treated the rejoinder with contempt. His eyes were fixed sympathetically on the young writer-to-be.

"I hate crabbing any serious effort to elevate us, Joan, but, honestly, doesn't it all sound a little conventional?"

He could have used no epithet more deplorable. Joan shot at him one annihilating glance. Miranda bubbled with indignation.

"Don't notice them, Joan dear! They don't know the meaning of words. They are ribald, uneducated people. You call your heroine Linda? Linda—what?"

Mr. Jupp supplied a name.

"Linda Spavinsky," said he. "She comes of the ancient Scottish family of that name."

"Pig! O pig!" cried Joan, routed at last from her superior serenity; and a second afterwards her eyes danced and with a flash of sound white teeth she broke into honest laughter. She did her best to suppress her sense of fun, but it would get the better of her from time to time.

This onslaught upon Joan Whitworth took place on the Wednesday evening. Sir Chichester came into the room as it ended, with a telegram in his hand.

"Mario Escobar wires, Millie, that he is held up in London by press of work and will only be able to run down here on Friday for the night."

Hillyard looked up.

"Mario Escobar?"

"Do you know him?" asked Millie Splay.

"Slightly," answered Hillyard. "Press of work! What does he do?"

"Runs about with the girls," said Dennis Brown.

Sir Chichester Splay would not have the explanation.

"Nonsense, my dear Dennis, nonsense, nonsense! He has a great many social engagements of the most desirable kind. He is, I believe, interested in some shipping firms."

"I like him," said Millie Splay.

"And so do I," added Joan, "very much indeed." The statement was defiantly thrown at Harold Jupp.

"I think he is charming," said Miranda.

Harold Jupp looked from one to the other.

"That seems to settle it, doesn't it? But—"

"But what?" asked Sir Chichester.

"Need we listen to the ridiculous exhibitions of male jealousy?" Miranda asked plaintively.

"But," Harold Jupp repeated firmly, "I do like a man to have another address besides his club. Now, I will lay a nice five to one that no one in this room knows where Mario Escobar goes when he goes home."

A moment's silence followed upon Harold Jupp's challenge. To the men, the point had its importance. The women did not appreciate the importance, but they recognised that their own menfolk did, and they did not interrupt.

"It's true," said Sir Chichester, "I always hear from him with his club as his address. But it simply means that he lives at an hotel and is not sure that he will remain on."

Thus the little things of every day occupied the foreground of Rackham Park. Millicent Splay had her worries of which Joan Whitworth was the cause. She loved Joan; she was annoyed with Joan; she admired Joan; she was amused at Joan; and she herself could never have told you which of these four emotions had the upper hand. So inextricably were they intermingled.

She poured them out to Martin Hillyard, as they drove through the Park at Midhurst on the Thursday morning.

"What do you think of Joan?" she asked. "She is beautiful, isn't she, with that mass of golden hair and her eyes?"

"Yes, she is," answered Hillyard.

"And what a fright she is making of herself! She isn't *dressed* at all, is she? She is just—protected by her clothes."

Hillyard laughed and Millicent Splay sighed. "And I did hope she would have got over it all by Goodwood. But no! Really I could slap her. But I might have known! Joan never does things by halves."

"She seems thorough," said Hillyard, although he remembered, with some doubts as to the truth of his comment, moments now and again when more primitive impulses had bubbled up in Joan Whitworth.

"Thorough! Yes, that's the word. Oh, Mr. Hillyard, there was a time when she really dressed—*dressed*, you understand. My word, she was thorough then, too. I remember coming out of the Albert Hall on a Melba afternoon, when we could get nothing but a hansom cab, and a policeman actually had to lift her up into it like a big baby because her skirt was so tight. And look at her now!"

Millicent Splay thumped the side of the car in her vexation.

"But you mustn't think she's a fool." Lady Splay turned menacingly on the silent Hillyard.

"But I don't," he protested.

"That's the last thing to say about her."

"I never said it," declared Martin Hillyard.

"I should have lost my faith in you, if you had," rejoined Millicent Splay, even now hardly mollified.

But she could not avoid the subject. Here was a newcomer to Rackham Park. She could not bear that he should carry away a wrong impression of her darling.

"I'll tell you the truth about Joan. She has lived her sheltered life with us, and no real things have yet come near her. No real troubles, no deep joys. Her parents even died when she was too young to know them. But she is eighteen and alive to her fingertips. Therefore she's—expectant."

"Yes," Hillyard agreed.

"She is searching for the meaning, for the secrets of life, sure that there is a meaning, sure that there are secrets, if only she could get hold of them. But she hasn't got hold of them. She runs here. She runs there. She explores, she experiments. That's why she's dressed like a tramp and thinking out a book where the heroine gets married to the Funeral March of a Marionette. Oh, my dear person, it just means, as it always means with us poor creatures, that the right man hasn't come along."

Millie Splay leaned back in her seat.

"When he does!" she cried. "When he does! Did you see the magnolia this morning? It burst into flower during the night. Joan! I thought once that it might be Harold Jupp. But it isn't."

Lady Splay spoke with discouragement. She had the matchmaking fever in her blood. Martin Hillyard remembered her glance when he had casually spoken of Harry Luttrell. Then she startled him with words which he was never to forget, and in which he chose to find a real profundity.

"The right man has not come along. So Joan mistakes anything odd for something great, and thinks that to be unusual is to be strong. It's a mood of young people who have not yet waked up."

They drove to the private stand and walked through into the paddock. Millie Splay looked round at the gay and brilliant throng. She sighed.

"There she is, moping in the drawing-room over Prince Hohenstiel—whatever his name is. She *won't* come to Goodwood. No, she just won't."

Yet Joan Whitworth did come to Goodwood that year, though not upon this day.

No one in that household had read the newspapers so carefully each day as Martin Hillyard. As the prospect darkened each morning, he was in a distress lest a letter should not have been forwarded from his flat in London, or should have been lost in the post. Each evening when the party returned from the races his first question asked whether there was no telegram awaiting him. So regular and urgent were his inquiries that the house-party could not be ignorant of his preoccupation. And on the afternoon of the Thursday a telegram in its orange envelope was lying upon the hall-table.

"It's for you, Mr. Hillyard," said Lady Splay.

Hillyard held it in his hands. So the summons had come, the summons hoped for, despaired of, made so often into a whip wherewith he lashed his arrogance, the summons to serve.

"I shall have to go up to town this evening," he said.

Anxious faces gathered about him.

"Oh, don't do that!" said Harold Jupp. "We have just got to like you."

"Yes, wait until tomorrow, my dear boy," Sir Chichester suggested. Even Joan Whitworth descended to earth and requested that he should stay.

"It's awfully kind of you," stammered Martin. "But I am afraid that this is very important."

Lady Splay was practical.

"Hadn't you better see first?" she asked.

Hillyard, with his thoughts playing swiftly in the future like a rapier, was still standing stock-still with the unopened telegram in his hand.

"Of course," he said. "But I know already what it is."

The anxious little circle closed nearer as he tore open the envelope. He read:

> "*I have refused the Duke. Money is cash—I mean trash. Little one I am yours.*—Linda Spavinsky."

The telegram had been sent that afternoon from Chichester.

Hillyard gazed around at the serious faces which hemmed him in. It became a contest as to whose face should hold firm longest. Joan herself was the first to flee, and she was found rocking to and fro in silent laughter in a corner of the library. Then Hillyard himself burst into a roar.

"I bought that fairly," he admitted, and he went up several points in the estimation of them all.

The last day of the races came—all sunshine and hot summer; lights and shadows chasing across the downs, the black slopes of Charlton forest on the one side, parks and green fields and old brown houses, sloping to the silver Solent, upon the other; and in the centre of the plain, by Bosham water, the spire of Chichester Cathedral piercing the golden air. Paddock and lawn and the stands were filled until about two in the afternoon. Then the gaps began to show to those who were concerned to watch. Especially about the oval railings in the paddock, within which, dainty as cats and with sleek shining skins, the racehorses stepped, the crowd grew thin. And in a few moments, the word had run round like fire, "The officers had gone."

Hillyard stood reflecting upon the stupendous fact. Never had he so bitterly regretted that physical disqualification which banned him from their company. Never had he so envied Luttrell. He was in the uttermost depression when a small, brown-gloved hand touched his arm. He turned and saw Joan Whitworth at his side, her lovely face alive with excitement, her eyes most friendly. It was hardly at all the Joan he knew. Joan had courage, but to face Goodwood in the clothes she affected at Rackham Park was beyond it. From her grey silk stockings and suède shoes to the little smart blue hat which sat so prettily on her hair, she was, as Millicent Splay would have admitted, really dressed.

"There is a real telegram for you," she said. She held it out to him enclosed in an envelope which had been already opened.

"Please come to see me—Graham," he read, and the actual receipt of the message stirred within him such a whirl of emotion that, for a moment or two, Joan Whitworth spoke and he was not aware of it. Suddenly, however, he understood that she was speaking words of importance.

"I hope I did right to open it," she said. "Colonel Brockley rode over this morning to tell us that his son had been recalled to his battalion by a telegram. I knew you were expecting one. When this one came, I thought that it might be important and that you ought to have it at once. On the other hand it might be another telegram," and her face dimpled into smiles, "from Linda Spavinsky. I didn't know what to do about it. But Mario Escobar was quite certain that I ought to open it."

"Mario Escobar?" cried Hillyard.

"Yes. He had just arrived. He was quite certain that we ought to open it, so we did."

"We?" A note of regret in his voice made her ask anxiously:

"Was I wrong?"

Hillyard hastened to reassure her.

"Not a bit. Of course you were quite right, and I am very grateful."

Joan's face cleared again.

"You see, I thought that if it was important I could bring it over and drive you back again."

"Will you?" Hillyard asked eagerly. "But now you are here you ought to stay."

Joan would not hear of the proposal, and Hillyard himself was in a fever to be off. They found Sir Chichester and his wife in the paddock, and Hillyard wished his hosts good-bye. Mario Escobar, who had driven over with Joan Whitworth, was talking to them. Escobar turned to Martin Hillyard.

"We met at Sir Charles Hardiman's supper party. You have not forgotten? You are off? A new play, I hope, to go into rehearsal."

He smiled and bowed, and waved his hands. Hillyard went away with Joan Whitworth and mounted beside her into a little two-seated car which she had been accustomed to drive in her unregenerate days. She had not forgotten her skill, and she sent the little car spinning up and down the road into the hills. It was an afternoon of blue and gold, with the larks singing out of sight in the sky. The road wound up and down, dark hedges on one side, fields yellow with young wheat upon the other, and the scent of the briar-rose in the air. Joan said very little, and Hillyard was content to watch her as she drove, the curls blowing about her ears and her hands steady and sure upon the wheel as she swung the car round the corners and folds of the hills. Once she asked of him:

"Are you glad to go?"

He made no pretence of misunderstanding her.

"Very," he answered. "If the great trial is coming, I want to fall back into the rank and file. Pushing and splashing is for peace times."

"Oh, I understand that!" she cried.

These were the young days. The jealousies of Departments, the intrigues to pull this man down and put that man up, not because of his capacity or failure, but because he fitted or did not fit the inner politics of the Office, the capture of honours by the stay-at-homes—all the little miseries and horrors that from time immemorial have disfigured the management of wars—they lay in the future. With millions of people, as with this couple speeding among the uplands, the one thought was—the great test is at hand.

"You go up to London tonight, and it may be a long while before we see you," said Joan. She brought the car to a halt on the edge of Duncton Hill. "Look for luck and for memory at the Weald of Sussex," she cried with a little catch in her throat.

Fields and great trees, and here and there the white smoke of a passing train and beyond the Blackdown and the misty slopes of Leith Hill—Hillyard was never to forget it, neither that scene nor the eager face and shining eyes of Joan Whitworth against the blue and gold of the summer afternoon.

"You will remember that you have friends here, who will be glad to hear news of you," she said, and she threw in the clutch and started the car down the hill.

CHAPTER XI

Stella Runs To Earth

"You have been back in England long?" asked Stella Croyle.

"A little while," said Hillyard evasively.

It was the first week of September. But since his return from Rackham Park to London his days had been passed in the examination of files of documents; and what little time he had enjoyed free from that labour had been given to quiet preparations for his departure.

"You might have come to see me," Stella Croyle suggested. "You knew that I wished to see you."

"Yes, but I have been very busy," he answered. "I am going away."

Stella Croyle looked at him curiously.

"You too! You have joined up?"

Hillyard shook his head.

"No good," he answered. "I told you my lungs were my weak point. I am turned down—and I am going abroad. It's not very pleasant to find oneself staying on in London, going to a little dinner party here and there where all the men are oldish, when all of one's friends have gone."

Stella Croyle's face and voice softened.

"Yes. I can understand that," she said.

Hillyard watched her narrowly, but there was no doubt that she was sincere. She had received him with an air of grievance, and a hard accent in her voice. But she was entering now into a comprehension of the regrets which must be troubling him.

"I am sorry," she continued. "I never cared very much for women. I have very few friends amongst them. And so I am losing—every one." She held out her hand to him in sympathy. "But if I were a man and had been turned down by the doctors, I don't think that I could stay. I should go like you and hide."

She smiled and poured out two cups of tea.

"That is a habit of yours, even though you are not a man," Hillyard replied.

"What do you mean?"

"You run away and hide."

Stella looked at her visitor in surprise.

"Who told you that?"

"Sir Charles Hardiman."

Stella Croyle was silent for a few moments.

"Yes, that's true," and she laughed suddenly. "When things go wrong, I become rather impossible. I have often made up my mind to live entirely in the country, but I never carry the plan out."

She let Hillyard drink his tea and light a cigarette before she approached the question which was torturing her.

"You had a good time in the Sudan!" she began. "Lots of heads?"

"Yes. I had a perfect time."

"And your friend? Captain Luttrell. Did you meet him?"

Hillyard had pondered on the answer which he would give to her when she asked that question. If he answered, "Yes,"—why, then he must go on, he must tell her something of what passed between Luttrell and himself, how he delivered his message and what answer he received. Let him wrap that answer up in words, however delicate and vague, she would see straight to the answer. Her heart would lead her there. To plead forgetfulness would be merely to acknowledge that he slighted her; and she would not believe him. So he lied.

"No. I never met Luttrell. He was away down in Khordofan when I was on the White Nile."

Stella Croyle had turned a little away from Hillyard when she put the question; and she sat now with her face averted for a long while. Nothing broke the silence but the ticking of the clock.

"I am sorry," said Hillyard.

No doubt her disappointment was bitter. She had counted very much, no doubt, on this chance of the two men meeting; on her message reaching her lover, and a "little word" now and again from him coming to her hands. Some morning she would wake up and find an envelope in the familiar writing waiting upon the tray beside her tea—that, no doubt, had been the hope which she had lived on this many a day. Hillyard was not fool enough to hold that he understood either the conclusions at which women arrived, or the emotions by which they jumped to them. But he attributed these hopes and thoughts with some confidence to Stella Croyle—until she turned and showed him her face. The sympathy and gentleness had gone from it. She was white with passion and her eyes blazed.

"Why do you lie to me?" she cried. "I met Harry this morning."

Hillyard was more startled by the news of Luttrell's presence in London than confused by the detection of his lie.

"Harry Luttrell!" he exclaimed. "You are sure? He is in England?"

"Yes. I met him in Piccadilly outside Jerningham's"—she mentioned the great outfitters and provision merchants—"he told me that he had run across you in the Sudan. What made you say that you hadn't?"

Hillyard was taken at a loss.

"Well?" she insisted.

Hillyard could see no escape except by the way of absolute frankness.

"Because I gave him your message, Mrs. Croyle," he replied slowly, "and I judged that he was not going to answer it."

Stella Croyle was inclined to think that the world was banded against her, to deceive her and to do her harm. They had all been engaged, Hardiman and the rest of them, in keeping Harry Luttrell away from her: in defending him, whether he wished it or not, from the wiles of the enchantress. Stella Croyle was quick enough in the uptake where her wounded heart was not concerned, but she was never very clear in any judgment which affected Harry Luttrell. Passion and disappointment and hope drew veils between the truth and her, and she dived below the plain reason to this or that far-fetched notion for the springs of his conduct. Almost she had persuaded herself that Harry Luttrell, by the powerful influence of friends, was being kept against his will from her side. Her anger against Hillyard had sprung, not from the mere fact that he had lied to her, but from her fancy that he had joined the imaginary band of her enemies. She understood now that in this she had been wrong.

"I see," she said gently. "It was to spare me pain?"

"Yes."

Suddenly Stella Croyle laughed—and with triumph. She showed to Hillyard a face from which all the anger had gone.

"You need not have been so anxious to spare me. Harry is coming here this afternoon."

She saw the incredulity flicker in Hillyard's eyes, but she did not mind.

"Yes," she asserted. "He goes down this evening to a camp in the New Forest where his battalion is waiting to go to France. He starts at six from Waterloo. He promised to run in here first."

Hillyard looked at the clock. It was already half past four. He had not the faintest hope that Luttrell would come. Stella had no doubt pressed him to come. She had probably been a little importunate. Luttrell's promise was an excuse, just an excuse to be rid of her—nothing more.

"Luttrell has probably a great deal to do on this last afternoon," he suggested.

"Of course, he won't be able to stay long," Stella Croyle agreed. "Still, five minutes are worth a good deal, aren't they, if you have waited for them two years?"

She was impenetrable in her confidence. It clothed her about like armour. Not for a moment would she doubt—she dared not! Harry was coming back to the house that afternoon. Would he break something—some little china ornament upon the mantel-shelf? He generally knocked over something. What would it be today, the mandarin with the nodding head, or the funny little pot-bellied dwarf which she had picked up at Christie's the day before? Stella smiled delightedly as she selected this and that of her little treasures for destruction. Oh, today Harry Luttrell could sweep every glass or porcelain trinket she possessed into the grate—when once he had passed through the doorway—when once again he stood within her room. She sat with folded hands, hope like a rose in her heart, sure of him, so sure of him that she did not even watch the hands of her clock.

But the hands moved on.

"I will stay, if I may," said Hillyard uncomfortably. "I will go, of course, when——" and he could not bring himself to complete the sentence.

Stella, however, added the words, though in a quieter voice and with less triumph than she had used before.

"When he comes. Yes, do stay. I shall be glad."

Slowly the day drew in. The sunlight died away from the trees in the park. In the tiny garden great shadows fell. The dusk gathered and Hillyard and Stella Croyle sat without a word in the darkening room. But Stella had lost her pride of carriage. On the mantelpiece the clock struck the hour—six little tinkling silvery strokes. At that moment a guard was blowing his whistle on a platform of Waterloo and a train beginning slowly to move.

"He will have missed his train," said Stella in an unhappy whisper. "He will be here later."

"My dear," replied Hillyard, and leaning forward he took and gently shook her hand. "Soldiers don't miss their trains."

Stella did not answer. She sat on until the lamps were lit in the streets outside and in this room the dusk had changed to black night.

"No, he will not come," she said at last, in a low wail of anguish. She rose and turned to Hillyard. Her face glimmered against the darkness deathly white and her eyes shone with sorrow.

"It was kind and wise of you to wish to spare me," she said. "Oh, I can picture to myself how coldly he heard you. He never meant to come here this afternoon."

Stella Croyle was wrong, just as Hillyard had been. Harry Luttrell had meant to pay his farewell visit to Stella Croyle, knowing well that he was unlikely ever to come back, and understanding that he owed her it. But an incident drove the whole matter from his thoughts, and the incident was just one instance to show how wide a gulf now separated these two.

He had called at a nursing home close to Portland Place where a Colonel Oakley lay dying of a malignant disease. Oakley had been the chief spirit of reviving the moral and the confidence of the disgraced Clayfords. He had laboured unflinchingly to restore its discipline, to weld it into one mind, with dishonour to redeem, and a single arm to redeem it. He had lived for nothing else—until the internal trouble laid him aside. Luttrell called at half past three to tell him that all was well with his old battalion, and was met by a nurse who shook her head.

"The last two days he has been lying, except for a minute here and there, in a coma. You may see him if you like, but it is a question of hours."

Luttrell went into the bedroom where the sick man lay, so thin of face and hand, so bloodless. But it seemed that the Fates wished to deal the Colonel one last ironic stroke, before they let him die. For, while Luttrell yet stood in the room, Colonel Oakley's eyes opened. This last moment of consciousness was his, the very last; and while it still endured, suddenly, down Portland Place, with its drums beating, its soldiers singing, marched a battalion. The song and the music swelled, the tramp of young, active, vigorous soldiers echoed and reached down the quiet street. Colonel Oakley turned his face to his pillow and burst into tears; the bitterness of death was given him to drink in overflowing measure. It seemed as though a jibe was flung at him.

The tramp of the battalion had not yet died away when Oakley sank again into unconsciousness.

"It was pretty rough that he should just wake up to hear that and to know that he would never have part in it, eh?" said Luttrell, speaking in a low voice more to himself than to the nurse. "What he did for us! Pretty hard treatment, eh?"

Luttrell left the home with one thought filling his mind—the regiment. It had got to justify all Oakley's devotion; it had got somehow to make amends to him, even if he never was to know of it, for this last unfair stroke of destiny. Luttrell walked across London, dwelling upon the qualities of individual men in the company which was his command—how this man was quick, and that man stupid, and that other inclined to swank, and a fourth had a gift for reading maps, and a fifth would make a real marksman; and so he woke up to find himself before the bookstall in the station at Waterloo. Then he remembered the visit he had promised, but there was no longer any time. He took the train to the New Forest, and three days later went to France.

But of Luttrell's visit to Colonel Oakley, Stella Croyle never knew. And, again, very likely it would not have mattered if she had. They were parted too widely for insight and clear vision.

Hillyard carried away with him a picture of Stella's haunted and despairing face. It was over against him as he dined at his club, gleaming palely from out of darkness, the lips quivering, the eyes sad with all the sorrows of women. He could blame neither the one nor the other—neither Stella Croyle nor Harry Luttrell. One heart called to the other across too wide a gulf, and this heart on the hither side was listening to quite other voices and was deaf to her cry for help. But Hillyard was on the road along which Millicent Splay had already travelled. More and more he felt the case for compassion. He carried the picture of Stella's face home with him. It troubled his sleep; by constant gazing upon it he became afraid....

He waked with a start to hear a question whispered at his ear. "Where is she? How has she passed this night?" The morning light was glimmering between the curtains. The room was empty. Yet surely those words had been spoken, actually spoken by a human voice. . . . He took his telephone instrument in his hand and lifted the receiver. In a little while—but a while too long for his impatience—his call was acknowledged at the exchange. He gave Stella Croyle's number and waited. Whilst he waited he looked at his watch. The time was a quarter past seven.

An unfamiliar and sleepy voice answered him from her house.

"Will you put me on to Mrs. Croyle?" he requested, and the reply came back:

"Mrs. Croyle went away with her maid last night."

"Last night?" cried Hillyard incredulously. "But I did not leave the house myself until well after six, and she had then no plans for leaving."

Further details, however, were given to him. Mrs. Croyle had called up a garage whence cars can be hired. She had packed hurriedly. She had left at nine by motor.

"Where for?" asked Hillyard.

The name of an hotel in the pine country of Surrey was given.

"Thank you," said Hillyard, and he rang off.

She had run to earth in her usual way, when trouble and grief broke through her woman's armour and struck her down—that was all! Hillyard lighted a cigarette and rang for his tea. Yes, that was all! She was acting true to her type, as the jargon has it. But against his will, her face took shape before him, as he had seen it in the darkness of her room and ever since—ever since!

He rang again, and more insistently. He possessed a small, swift motorcar. Before the clocks of London had struck eight he was travelling westwards along the King's Road. Hillyard was afraid. He did not formulate his fears. He was not sure of what he feared. But he was afraid—terribly afraid; and for the first time anger rose up in his heart against his friend. Luttrell! Harry Luttrell! At this very moment he was changing direction in columns of fours upon the drill ground, happy in the smooth execution of the manœuvre by his men and untroubled by any thought of the distress of Stella Croyle. Well, little things must give way to great—women to the exigencies of drill!

Meanwhile, Hillyard grew more afraid, and yet more afraid. He swept down the hill to Cobham, passed between the Hut and the lake, and was through Ripley before the shutters in the shops were down. The dew was heavy in the air; all the fresh, clean smell of the earth was in that September morning. And as yet the morning itself was only half awake. At last the Hog's Back rose, and at a little inn, known for its comfort—and its *chef*—Hillyard's car was stopped.

"Mrs. Croyle?" Hillyard asked at the office.

"Her maid is here," said the girl clerk, and pointed.

Hillyard turned to a girl, pretty and, by a few years, younger than Stella Croyle.

"I have orders not to wake Mrs. Croyle until she rings," said the maid. Jenny Prask, she was called, and she spoke with just a touch of pleasant Sussex drawl. "Mrs. Croyle has not been sleeping well, and she looked for a good night's rest in country air."

The maid was so healthful in her appearance, so reasonable in her argument, that Hillyard's terrors, fostered by solitude, began to lose their vivid colours.

"I understand that," he stammered. "Yet, Jenny—"

Jenny Prask smiled.

"You are Mr. Hillyard, I think?"

"Yes."

"I have heard my mistress speak of you." Hillyard knew enough of maids to understand that "mistress" was an unusual word with them. Here, it seemed, was a paragon of maids, who was quite content to be publicly Stella Croyle's maid, whose gentility suffered no offence by the recognition of a mistress.

"If you wish, I will wake her."

Jenny Prask went up the stairs, Hillyard at her heels. She knocked upon the door. No answer was returned. She opened it and entered.

Stella Croyle was up and dressed. She was sitting at a table by the window with some sheets of notepaper and some envelopes in front of her, and her back was towards Hillyard and the open door. But she was dressed as she had been dressed the evening before when he had left her; the curtains in the room were drawn, and the electric lights on the writing-table and the walls were still burning. The bed had not been slept in.

Stella Croyle rose and turned towards her visitors. She tottered a little as she stood up, and her eyes were dazed.

"Why have you come here?" she asked faintly, and she fell rather than sat again in her chair.

Hillyard sprang forward and tore the curtains aside so that the sunlight poured into the room, and Stella opened and shut her eyes with a contraction of pain.

"I had so many letters to write," she explained, "I thought that I would sit up and get through with them."

Hillyard looked at the table. There were great black dashes on the notepaper and lines, and here and there a scribbled picture of a face, and perhaps now and again half a word. She had sat at that table all night and had not even begun a letter. Hillyard's heart was torn with pity as he looked from her white, tired face to the sheets of notepaper. What misery and unhappiness did those broad, black dashes and idle lines express?

"You must have some breakfast," he said. "I'll order it and have it ready for you downstairs by the time you are ready. Then I'll take you back to London."

The blood suddenly mounted into her face.

"You will?" she cried wildly. "In a reserved compartment, so that I may do nothing rash and foolish? Are you going to be kind too?"

She broke into a peal of shrill and bitter laughter. Then her head went down upon her hands, and she gave herself up to such a passion of sobbing and tears as was quite beyond all Hillyard's experience. Yet he would rather hear those sobs and see her bowed shoulders shaking under the violence of them than listen again to the dreadful laughter which had gone before. He had not the knowledge which could enable him to understand her sudden outburst, nor did he acquire that knowledge until long afterwards. But he understood that quite unwittingly he had touched some painful chord in that wayward nature.

"I am going to take you back in my motorcar," he said. "I'll be down-stairs with the breakfast ready."

She had probably eaten nothing, he reckoned, since teatime the day before. Food was the steadying thing she needed now. He went to the door which Jenny Prask held open for him.

"Don't leave her!" he breathed in a whisper.

Jenny Prask smiled.

"Not me, sir," she said fervently.

Hillyard remembered with comfort some words which she had spoken in appreciation of the loving devotion of her maid.

"In three-quarters of an hour," said Jenny; and later on that morning, with a great fear removed from his heart, Hillyard drove Stella Croyle back to London.

CHAPTER XII

In Barcelona

It was nine o'clock on a night of late August.

The restaurant of the Maison Dorée in the Plaza Cataluña at Barcelona looks across the brilliantly-lighted square from the south side. On the pavement in front of it and of its neighbour, the Café Continental, the vendors of lottery tickets were bawling the lucky numbers they had for sale. Even in this wide space the air was close and stale. Within, a few people left over in the town had strayed in to dine at tables placed against the walls under flamboyant decorations in the style of Fragonard. At a table Hillyard was sitting alone over his coffee. Across the room one of the panels represented a gleaming marble terrace overlooking a countryside bathed in orange light; and on the terrace stood a sedan chair with drawn curtains, and behind the chair stood a saddled white horse. Hillyard had dined more than once during the last few months at the Maison Dorée; and the problem of that picture had always baffled him. A lovers' tryst! But where were the lovers? In some inner room shaded from the outrage of that orange light which never was on sea or land? Or in the sedan chair? Or were their faces to be discovered, as in the puzzle pictures, in the dappling of the horse's flanks, or the convolutions of the pillars which supported the terrace roof, or the gilded ornamentations of the chair itself? Hillyard was speculating for the twentieth time on these important matters with a vague hope that one day the door of the sedan chair would open, when another door opened—the door of the restaurant. A sharp-visaged man with a bald forehead, a clerk, one would say, or a commercial traveller, looked round the room and went forward to Hillyard's table. He went quite openly.

The two men shook hands, and the newcomer seated himself in front of Hillyard.

"You will take coffee and a cigar?" Hillyard asked in Spanish, and gave the order to the waiter.

The two men talked of the heat, the cinematograph theatres at the side of the Plaza, the sea-bathing at Caldetas, and then the sharp-faced man leaned forward.

"Ramon says there is no truth in the story, señor."

Hillyard struck a match and held it to his companion's cigar.

"And you trust Ramon, Señor Baeza?"

Lopez Baeza leaned back with a gesture of unqualified assent.

"As often and often you can trust the peasant of my country," he said.

Hillyard agreed with a nod. He gazed about the room.

"There is no one interesting here tonight," he said idly.

"No," answered Lopez Baeza. "The theatres are closed, the gay people have gone to St. Sebastian, the families to the seaside. Ouf, but it is hot."

"Yes."

Hillyard dropped his voice to a whisper and returned to the subject of his thoughts.

"You see, my friend, it is of so much importance that we should make no mistake here."

"*Claro!*" returned Lopez Baeza. "But listen to me, señor. You know that our banks are behind the times and our post offices not greatly trusted. We have therefore a class of messengers."

Hillyard nodded.

"I know of them."

"Good. They are not educated. Most of them can neither read nor write. They are simply peasants. Yet they are trusted to carry the most important letters and great sums of money in gold and silver from place to place. And never do they betray their trust. It is unknown. Why, señor, I know myself of cases where rich men have entrusted their daughters to the care of the messengers, sure that in this way their daughters will arrive safely at their destination."

"Yes," said Hillyard. "I know of these men."

"Ramon Castillo is as honest as the best of them."

"Yes, but he is not one of them," said Hillyard. "He is a stevedore with thirty years of the quayside and at the port of Barcelona, where there are German ships with their officers and crews on board."

Hillyard was troubled. He drew from his pocket creased letters and read them for the twentieth time with a frowning countenance.

"There is so much at stake. Two hundred feluccas—two hundred motor-driven feluccas! And eighteen thousand men, on shore and sea? See what it means! On our side, the complete surveillance of the Western Mediterranean! On the other side—against us—two hundred travelling supply bases for submarines, two hundred signal stations. I want to be sure! I want neither to give the enemy the advantage by putting him upon his guard, nor to miss the great opportunity myself."

Lopez Baeza nodded.

"Why not talk with Ramon Castillo yourself?" he asked.

"That is what I want to do."

"I will arrange for it. When?"

"Tonight," said Hillyard.

Lopez Baeza lifted his hands in deprecation.

"Yes. I can take you to his house—now. But, señor, Ramon is a poor man. He lives in a little narrow street."

Hillyard looked quietly at Lopez Baeza. He had found men on the Mediterranean littoral whom he could trust with his life and everything that was his. But a good working principle was to have not overmuch faith in any one. A noisome little street in the lower quarters of Barcelona—who could tell what might happen after one had plunged into it?

"I will come with you," he said.

"Good," said Lopez. "I will go on ahead." And once more Hillyard's quiet eyes rested upon Baeza's face. "It is not wise that we should walk out together. There is no one here, it is true, but in the chairs outside the cafés—who shall say?"

"Yes. You go on ahead," Hillyard agreed. "That is wise."

Lopez rose.

"Give me five minutes, señor. Then down the Rambla. The second turning to the right, beyond the Opera House. You will see me at the corner. When you see me, follow!"

Hillyard rose and shook hands cordially with Lopez Baeza with the air of a man who might never see his friend again for years. Baeza commended him to God and went out of the restaurant on to the lighted footway.

Hillyard read through the two creased letters again, though he knew them by heart. They had reached him from William Lloyd, an English merchant at Barcelona, at two different dates. The first, written six weeks ago, related how Pontiana Tabor, a servant of the firm, had come into Lloyd's private office and informed him that on the night of the 27th June a German submarine had entered a deep cove at the lonely north-east point of the island of Mallorca, and had there been provisioned by José Medina's men, with José Medina's supplies, and that José Medina had driven out of Palma de Mallorca in his motorcar, and travelling by little-known tracks, had been present when the operation was in process. The name of a shoemaker in a street of Palma was given as corroboration.

The second letter, which had brought Hillyard post-haste off the sea into Barcelona, was only three days old. Once more Pontiana Tabor had been the bearer of bad news. José Medina had been seen entering the German Consulate in Barcelona, between eleven and twelve o'clock of the morning of August 22nd.

Hillyard was greatly troubled by these two letters.

"We can put José Medina out of business, of course," he reflected. For José Medina's tobacco factories were built at a free port in French territory. "But I want the man for my friend."

He put the letters back in his pocket and paid his bill. As he went out of the Maison Dorée, he felt in the right-hand pocket of his jacket to make sure that a little deadly life preserver lay ready to his hand.

He did not distrust Lopez Baeza. All the work which Baeza had done for him had, indeed, been faithfully and discreetly done. But—but there was always a certain amount of money for the man who would work the double cross—not so very much, but still, a certain amount. And Hillyard was always upon his guard against the intrusion of a contempt for the German effort. That contempt was easy enough for a man who, having read year after year of the wonders of the loud-vaunted German system of espionage, had come fresh from his reading into contact with the actual agents. Their habit of lining their pockets at the expense of their Government, their unfulfilled pretensions, their vanity and extravagance, and, above all, their unimaginative stupidity in their estimation of men—these things were apt in the early years of the war to bewilder the man who had been so often told to fall down before the great idol of German efficiency.

"The German agent works on the assumption that the mind of every foreigner reasons on German lines, but with inferior intelligence. But behind the agent is the cunning of Berlin, with its long-deliberated plans and its concocted ingenuity of method. And though on the whole they are countered, as with amazement they admit, by the amateurs from England, still every now and then—not very often—they do bring something off."

Thus Hillyard reasoned as he turned the corner of the Plaza Cataluña into the wide Rambla. It might be that the narratives of Pontiana Tabor and the denials of Ramon Castillo were all just part of one little subsidiary plan in the German scheme which was to reach its achievement by putting an inconvenient Englishman out of the way for good in one of the dark, narrow side streets of Barcelona.

After the hot day the Rambla, with its broad tree-shaded alley in the middle, its carriage-ways on each side of the alley, and its shops and footwalks beyond the carriage-ways, was crowded with loiterers. The Spaniard, to our ideas, is simple in his pleasure. To visit a cinematograph, to take a cooling temperance drink at the Municipal Kiosque at the top of the Rambla, and to pace up and down the broad walk with unending chatter—until daybreak—here were the joys of Barcelona folk in the days of summer. Further down at the lower end of the Rambla you would come upon the dancing halls and supper-cafés, with separate rooms for the national gambling game, "Siete y Media," but they had their own clientele amongst the bloods and the merchant captains from the harbour. The populace of Barcelona walked the Rambla under the great globes of electric light.

Hillyard could only move slowly through the press. Every one dawdled. Hillyard dawdled too. He passed the Opera House, and a little further down saw across the carriage-way, Lopez Baeza in front of a lighted tobacco shop at the corner of a narrow street. Hillyard crossed the carriage-way and Baeza turned into the street, a narrow thoroughfare between tall houses and dark as a cavern. Hillyard followed him. The lights of the Rambla were left behind, the houses became more slatternly and disreputable, the smells of the quarter were of rancid food and bad drains. Before a great door Baeza stopped and clapped his hands.

A jingle of keys answered him, and rising from the step of another house the watchman of the street crossed the road. He put a key into the door, opened it, and received the usual twopence. Baeza and Hillyard passed in.

"Ramon is on the top floor. We have to climb," said Baeza.

He lit a match, and the two men mounted a staircase with a carved balustrade, made for a king. Two stories up, the great staircase ended, and another of small, steep and narrow steps succeeded it. When Baeza's match went out there was no light anywhere; from a room somewhere above came a sound of quarrelling voices—a woman's voice high and shrill, a man's voice hoarse and drunken, and, as an accompaniment, the wailing of a child wakened from its sleep.

At the very top of the house Baeza rapped on a door. The door was opened, and a heavy, elderly man, wearing glasses on his nose, stood in the entrance with the light of an unshaded lamp behind him.

"Ramon, it is the chief," said Baeza.

Ramon Castello crossed the room and closed an inner door. Then he invited Hillyard to enter. The room was bare but for a few pieces of necessary furniture, but all was scrupulously clean. Ramon Castillo set forward a couple of chairs and asked his visitors to be seated. He was in his shirtsleeves, and he wore the rope-soled sandals of the Spanish peasant, but he was entirely at his ease. He made the customary little speech of welcome with so simple a dignity and so manifest a sincerity that Hillyard could hardly doubt him afterwards.

"It is my honour to welcome you not merely as my chief, but as an

Englishman. I am poor, and I take my pay, but Señor Baeza will assure you that for twenty-five years I have been the friend of England. And there are thousands and thousands of poor Spaniards like myself, who love England, because its law-courts are just, because there is a real freedom there, because political power is not the opportunity of oppression."

The little speech was spoken with great rapidity and with deep feeling; and, having delivered it, Ramon seated himself on the side of the table opposite to Hillyard and Baeza and waited.

"It is about Pontiana Tabor," said Hillyard. "He is making a mistake?"

"No, señor; he is lying," and he used the phrase which has no exact equivalent in the English. "He is a *sin verguenza*."

"Tell me, my friend," said Hillyard.

"Pontiana Tabor swears that José Medina was seen to enter the German Consulate before noon on August the 22nd. But on August the 21st Medina was in Palma, Mallorca; he was seen there by a captain of the Islana Company, and a friend of mine spoke to him on the quay. If, therefore, he was in the German Consulate here on the 22nd, he must have crossed that night by the steamer to Barcelona. But he did not. His name was not on the list of passengers, and although he might have avoided that, he was not seen on board or to come on board. I have spoken with officers and crew. José Medina did not cross on the 21st. Moreover, Señor Baeza has seen a letter which shows that he was certainly in Palma on the 23rd."

"That is true," said Baeza. "Medina was in Palma on the 21st, and in Palma on the 23rd, and he did not cross to Barcelona on the night of the 21st, nor back again to Palma on the night of the 22nd. Therefore he was not seen to visit the German Consulate on the morning of the 22nd, and, as Ramon says, Pontiana is lying."

"Why should Pontiana lie?" asked Hillyard.

Ramon took his pince-nez from the bridge of his nose, and, holding them between his finger and thumb, tapped with them upon his knee.

"Because, señor, there are other contrabandists besides José Medina; one little group at Tarragona and another near Garucha—and they would all be very glad to see José Medina get into trouble with the British and the French. His feluccas fly the British flag and his factories are on French soil. There would be an end of José Medina."

The letters were put in front of Hillyard. He read them over carefully, and at the end he said:

"If Pontiana Tabor lied in this case of the Consulate—and that seems clear—it is very likely that he lied also in the other. Yes."

As a matter of fact, Hillyard had reasons of his own to doubt the truth of the story which ascribed to Medina the actual provisioning of a submarine—reasons which had nothing whatever to do with José Medina himself.

The destruction of shipping by German submarines in this western section of the Mediterranean had an intermittent regularity. There would be ten successive days—hardly ever more than ten days—during which ships were sunk. Thereafter for three weeks, steamships and sailing ships would follow the course upon which they were ordered, without hurt or loss. After three weeks, the murderous business would begin again. There was but one explanation in Hillyard's opinion.

"The submarines come out of Pola. When they reach the line between the Balearics and the Spanish coast, they have oil for ten days' cruising, and then return to their base," he argued.

Now, if a submarine had been provisioned by José Medina in a creek of Mallorca, the ten days' cruise would be extended to three weeks. This had never happened. Moreover, the date fixed by Pontiana Tabor happened to fall precisely in the middle of one of those periods of three weeks during which the terror did not haunt those seas. Pontiana Tabor had not known enough. He had fixed his date at a venture.

"Yes," said Hillyard, rising from his chair. "I agree with you, Señor Ramon. Tabor is a liar. What troubled me was that I had no clue as to why he should lie. You have given me it, and with all my heart I thank you."

He shook the stevedore's hand and stood for a moment talking and joking with him upon other subjects. Hillyard knew the value of a smile and a jest and a friendly manner. Your very enemy in Spain will do you a good turn if you meet him thus. Then he turned to Baeza.

"I shall be back, perhaps, in a week, but perhaps not. I will let you know in the usual way."

The two men went down the stairs and into the street. It was empty now and black, but at the far end, as at the end of a tunnel, the Rambla blazed and roared and the crowds swung past like a procession.

"It is best that we should separate here," said Lopez Baeza, "if you have no further instructions."

"Touching the matter of those ships," Hillyard suggested.

"Señor Fairbairn has it in hand."

"Good. Then, my friend, I have no further instructions," said Hillyard. "I agree with you about Ramon. I will go first."

He shook hands with Baeza, crossed the road and disappeared into the mouthway of an alley which ran up the hill parallel to the Rambla. The alley led into another side street, and turning to the right, Hillyard slipped out into the throng beneath the trees. He sauntered, as idle and as curious as any in that broad walk. He took a drink at a café, neither hiding himself unnaturally nor ostentatiously occupying a chair at the edge of the awning. He sat there for half an hour. But when he rose again he made sure that no one was loitering to watch his movements. He sauntered up to the very end of the Rambla past the icecream kiosque. The great Plaza spread in front of him, and at the corner across the road stood a double line of motorcars, some for hire, others waiting for parties in the restaurants opposite. He walked across the roadway and disappeared in between the motorcars as if he intended to cross the Plaza by the footway to the Paseo de la Reforma. A second later a motorcar shot out from the line and took the road to Tarragona.

Hillyard was inside the car. The tall houses of the city gave place to villas draped in bougainvillea behind gardens of trees. Then the villas ceased and the car sped across the flats of Llobregat and climbed to the finest coast-road in the world. It was a night for lovers. A full moon, bright as silver, sailed in the sky; the broad, white road rose and dipped and wound past here and there a blue cottage, here and there a peasant mounted on his donkey and making his journey by night to escape the burning day. Far below the sea spread out most gently murmuring, and across a great wide path of glittering jewels, now a sailing-ship glided like a bird, now the black funnels of a steamer showed. So light was the wind that Hillyard could hear the kick of its screw, like the beating of some gigantic clock. He took his hat from his head and threw wide open his thin coat. After the heavy days of anxiety he felt a nimbleness of heart and spirit which set him in tune with the glory of that night. Suspicions, vague and elusive, had for so long clustered about José Medina, and then had come the two categorical statements, dates and hours, chapter and verse! He was still not sure, he declared to himself in warning. But he was sure enough to risk the great move—the move which he alone could make! He should no doubt have been dreaming of Joan Whitworth and fitting her into the frame of that August night. But he had not thought of her by one o'clock in the morning; and by one o'clock in the morning his motorcar had come to a stop on the deserted quay of Tarragona harbour under the stern of an English yacht.

CHAPTER XIII

Old Acquaintance

At six o'clock on the second morning after Hillyard's visit to Barcelona, the steam-yacht *Dragonfly* swept round the point of La Dragonera and changed her course to the south-east. She steamed with a following breeze over a sea of darkest sapphire which broke in sparkling cascades of white and gold against the rocky creeks and promontories on the ship's port side. Peasants working on the green terraces above the rocks stopped their work and stared as the blue ensign with the Union Jack in the corner broke out from the flagstaff at the stern.

"But it's impossible," cried one. "Only yesterday a French mail-steamer was chased in the passage between Mallorca and Minorca. It's impossible."

Another shaded his eyes with his hand and looked upon the neat yacht with its white deck and shining brass in contemptuous pity.

"Loco Inglés," said he.

The tradition of the mad Englishman has passed away from France, but it has only leaped the Pyrenees. Some crazy multi-millionaire was just running his head into the German noose. They gave up their work and settled down contentedly to watch the yacht, multi-millionaire, captain and crew and all go up into the sky. But the *Dragonfly* passed from their sight with the foam curling from her bows and broadening out into a pale fan behind her; and over the headlands for a long time they saw the streamer of her smoke as she drove in to Palma Bay.

Hillyard, standing by the captain's side upon the bridge, watched the great cathedral rise from out of the water at the end of the bay, towers and flying buttresses and the mass of brown stone, before even a house was visible. The *Dragonfly* passed a German cargo steamer which had sought refuge here at the outbreak of war. She was a large ship, full of oil, and she had been moved from the quay-side to an anchorage in the bay by the captain of the port, lest by design or inadvertence she should take fire and set the town aflame. There she lay, a source of endless misgiving to every allied ship which sailed these waters, kept clean and trim as a yacht, her full crew on board, her dangerous cargo below, in the very fairway of the submarine; and there the scruples of the Allies allowed her to remain while month followed month. Historians in later years will come across in this or that Government office in Paris, in London and in Rome, warnings, appeals, and accounts of the presence of this ship; and those anxious for a picturesque contrast may set against the violation of Belgium and all the "scrap of paper" philosophy, the fact that for years in the very centre of the German submarine effort in the Western Mediterranean, the German steamer *Fangturm*, with her priceless cargo of oil, was allowed by the scrupulous honour of the Allies to swing unmolested at her anchor in Palma Bay. Hillyard could never pass that great black ship in those neutral waters without a hope that his steering-gear would just at this moment play him false and swing his bows at full speed on to her side. The *Dragonfly* ran past her to the arm of the great mole and was moored with her stern to the quay. A small crowd of gesticulating idlers gathered about the ropes, and all were but repeating the phrases of the peasants upon the hillside, as Hillyard walked ashore down the gangway.

"But it's impossible that you should have come."

"Just outside there is one. The fisherman saw her yesterday."

"She rose and spoke to one of the fishing-boats."

"But it is impossible that you should have come here."

"Yet I am here," answered Hillyard, the very mad multi-millionaire. "What will you, my friends? Shall I tell you a secret? Yes, but tell no one else! The Germans would be most enraged if they found out that we knew it. There aren't any submarines."

A little jest spoken in a voice of good-humour, with a friendly smile, goes a long way anywhere, but further in Spain than anywhere else in the world. The small crowd laughed with Hillyard, and made way for him.

A man offered to him with a flourish and a bow a card advertising a garage at which motorcars could be hired for expeditions in the island. Hillyard accepted it and put it into his pocket. He paid a visit to his consul, and thereafter sat in a café for an hour. Then he strolled through the narrow streets, admired this and that massive archway, with its glimpse of a great stone staircase within, and mounted the hill. Almost at the top, he turned sharply into a doorway and ran up the stairs to the second floor. He knocked upon the door, and a maid-servant answered.

"Señor José Medina lives here?"

"Yes, señor."

"He is at home?"

"No, señor. He is in the country at his *finca*."

Hillyard thanked the girl, and went whistling down the stairs. Standing in the archway, he looked up and down the street with something of the air of a man engaged upon a secret end. One or two people were moving in the street; one or two were idling on the pavement. Hillyard smiled and walked down the hill again. He took the advertisement card from his pocket and, noting the address, walked into the garage.

"It will please me to see something of the island," he said. "I am not in Mallorca for long. I should like a car after lunch." He gave the name of a café between the cathedral and the quay. "At half past two? Thank you. And by which road shall I go for all that is most of Mallorca?"

This was Spain. A small group of men had already invaded the garage and gathered about Hillyard and the proprietor. They proceeded at once to take a hand in the conversation and offer their advice. They suggested the expedition to Miramar, to Alcudia, to Manacor, discussing the time each journey would take, the money to be saved by the shorter course, the dust, and even the gradients of the road. They had no interest in the business in the garage, and they were not at all concerned in the success of Hillyard's excursion. That a stranger should carry away with him pleasant recollections of the beauties of Mallorca, was a matter of supreme indifference to them all. But they were engaged in the favourite pursuit of the Spaniards of the towns. They were getting through a certain small portion of the day, without doing any work, and without spending any money. The majority favoured the road past Valdemosa, over the Pass of Soller to Miramar and its rocky coast on the north-east side of the island, as indeed Hillyard knew the majority must. For there is no road like it for beauty in the Balearics, and few in all Spain.

"I will go that way, then," said Hillyard, and he strolled off to his luncheon.

He drove afterwards over the plain, between groves of olive and almond trees with gnarled stems and branches white with dust, mounted by the twisting road, terraces upon his left and pine-clothed mountainside upon his right, past Valdemosa to the Pass. The great sweep of rock-bound coast and glittering sea burst upon his view, and the boom of water surging into innumerable caves was like thunder to his ears. At a little gate upon the road the car was stopped at a word from Hillyard.

"I am going in here," he said. "I may be a little while."

The chauffeur looked at Hillyard with surprise. Hillyard had never been to the house before, but he could not mistake it from the description which he had been given. He passed through an orchard to the door of an outrageous villa, built in the style of a Swiss chalet and glaring with yellow paint. A man in his shirt-sleeves came to the door.

"Señor José Medina?" Hillyard inquired.

He held out his card and was ushered into the room of ceremony which went very well with the exterior of the yellow chalet. A waxed floor, heavy white lace curtains at the windows, a table of walnut-wood, chairs without comfort, but with gold legs, all was new and never to be used and hideous. Hillyard looked around him with a nod of comprehension. This is what its proprietor would wish for. With a hundred old houses to select from for a model—no! This is the way his fancies would run. The one beauty of the place, its position, was Nature's. Hillyard went to the window, which was on the side of the house opposite to the door. He looked down a steep terraced garden of orange trees and bright flowers to the foam sparkling on the rocks a thousand feet below.

"You wished to see me, señor," and Hillyard turned with curiosity.

Twelve years had passed since he had seen José Medina, but he had changed less than Hillyard expected. Martin remembered him as small and slight, with a sharp mobile face and a remarkable activity which was the very badge of the man; and these characteristics he retained. He was still like quicksilver. But he was fast losing his hair, and he wore pince-nez. The dress of the peasant and the cautious manner of the peasant, both were gone. In his grey lounge suit he had the look of a quick-witted clerk.

"You wished to see me, señor," he repeated, and he laid the card upon the table.

"For a moment. I shall hope not to detain you long."

"My time and my house are yours."

José Medina had clearly become a *caballero* since those early days of adventure. Hillyard noted the point for his own guidance, thanking his stars meanwhile that the gift of the house was a meaningless politeness.

"I arrived at Palma this morning, in a yacht," said Hillyard.

José Medina was prepared for the information. He bowed. There had been neither smile nor, indeed, any expression whatever upon his face since he had entered the room.

"I have heard of the yacht," he said. "It is a fine ship."

"Yes."

José Medina looked at Hillyard.

"It flies the English flag."

Hillyard bowed.

"As do your feluccas, señor, I believe."

A mere twitch of the lips showed that Medina appreciated the point.

"But I," continued Hillyard, "am an Englishman, while you, señor—"

José Medina was not, if he could help it, to be forced to cry "a hit" again.

"Whereas I, señor, am a neutral," he answered. The twitch of the lips became a smile. He invited Hillyard to a chair, he drew up another himself, and the two men sat down over against one another in the middle of that bare and formal room.

That one word neutral, so delicately emphasised, warned Hillyard that José Medina was quite alive to the reason of his visit. He could, of course, have blurted it out at once. He could have said in so many words, "Your tobacco factories are on French soil, and your two hundred feluccas are nominally owned in Gibraltar. Between French and English we shall close you down unless you help." But he knew very well that he would have got no more than fair words if he had. It is not thus that delicate questions are approached in Spain. Even the blackmailer does not dream of bluntly demanding money, or exposing his knowledge that he will get it. He pleads decently the poverty of his family and the long illness of his mother-in-law; and with the same decency the blackmailed yields to compassion and opens his purse. There is a gentlemanly reticence to be observed in these matters and Hillyard was well aware of the rules. He struck quite a different note.

"I shall speak frankly to you, Señor Medina, as one *caballero* to another"; and José Medina bowed and smiled.

"I put my cards upon the table. I ask you whether in your heart you are for the Germans or for us."

José Medina hitched his chair a little closer and holding up one hand with fingers spread ticked off his points, as he spoke them, with the other.

"Let us see! First, you come to me, señor, saying you are English, and speaking Spanish with the accent of Valencia. Good! I might reply, señor, how do I know? I might ask you how I am to be sure that when that British flag is hauled down from your yacht outside the bay over there, it is not a German one which should take its place. Good! But I do not make these replies. I accept your word as a *caballero* that you are English and not an enemy of England laying a trap for me. Good!" He took off his eyeglasses and polished them.

"Now listen to me!" he continued. "I am a Spaniard. We of Spain have little grievances against England and France. But these are matters for the Government, not for a private person. And the Government bids us be neutral. Good! Now I speak as a private person. For me England means opportunity for poor men to become great and rich. You may say I have become rich without the opportunities of England. I answer I am one in many thousands. England means Liberty, and within the strict limits of my neutrality I will do what a man may for that great country."

Hillyard listened and nodded. The speech was flowing and spoken with great fervour. It might mean much. It might mean nothing at all. It might be the outcome of conviction. But it might again be nothing more than the lip-service of a man who knew very well that England and France could squeeze him dry if they chose.

"I wish," said Hillyard cordially, "that the captains of the ports of Spain spoke also with your voice."

José Medina neither assumed an ignorance of the German leanings of the port officials nor expressed any assent. But, as if he had realised the thought which must be passing in Hillyard's mind, he said:

"You know very well, señor, that I should be mad if I gave help to the Germans. I am in your hands. You and France have but to speak the word, and every felucca of mine is off the seas. But what then! There are eighteen thousand men at once without food or work thrown adrift upon the coast of Spain. Will not Germany find use for those eighteen thousand men?"

Hillyard agreed. The point was shrewd. It was an open, unanswerable reply to the unuttered threat which perhaps Hillyard might be prompted to use.

"I have spoken," continued José Medina. "Now it is for you, señor. Tell me what within the limits of my neutrality I can do to prove to you the sincerity of my respect for England?"

Hillyard took a sheet of paper and a pencil from his pocket. He drew a rough map.

"Here are the Balearic Islands; here, farther to the west, the Columbretes; here the African coast; here the mainland of Spain. Now watch, I beg you, señor, whilst I sketch in the routes of your feluccas. At Oran in Africa your factories stand. From them, then, we start. We draw a broad thick line from Oran to the north-east coast of Mallorca, that coast upon which we look down from these windows, a coast honeycombed with caves and indented with creeks like an edge of fine lace—a very store-house of a coast. Am I not right, Señor Don José?" He laughed, in a friendly good-humoured way, but the face of José Medina did not lose one shade of its impassiveness. He did not deny that the caves of this coast were the storehouse of his tobacco; nor did he agree.

"Let us see!" he said.

"So I draw a thick line, since all your feluccas make for this island and this part of the island first of all. From here they diverge—you will correct me, I hope, if I am wrong."

"I do not say that I shall correct you if you are wrong," said José Medina.

Hillyard was now drawing other and finer lines which radiated like the sticks of an outspread fan from the north-east coast of Mallorca to the Spanish mainland; and he went on drawing them, unperturbed by José's refusal to assist in his mapmaking. Some of the lines—a few—ended at the Islands of the Columbretes, sixty miles off Valencia.

"Your secret storehouse, I believe, señor," he remarked pleasantly.

"A cruiser of our Government examined these islands most carefully a fortnight ago upon representations from the Allies, and found nothing of any kind to excite interest," replied José Medina.

"The cruiser was looking for submarine bases, I understand, not tobacco," Martin Hillyard observed. "And since it was not the cruiser's commission to look for tobacco, why should it discover it?"

José Medina shrugged his shoulders. José Medina's purse was very long and reached very high. It would be quite impolitic for that cruiser to discover José Medina's tobacco stores, as Medina himself and Martin Hillyard, and the captain of the cruiser, all very well knew.

Martin Hillyard continued to draw fine straight lines westwards from the northern coast of Mallorca to the mainland of Spain, some touching the shore to the north of Barcelona, some striking it as far south as Almeria and Garrucha. When he had finished his mapmaking he handed the result to José Medina.

"See, señor! Your feluccas cut across all the trade-routes through the Mediterranean. Ships going east or going west must pass between the Balearics and Africa, or between the Balearics and Spain. We are here in the middle, and, whichever course those ships take, they must cross the lines on which your feluccas continually come and go."

José Medina looked at the map. He did not commit himself in any way. He contented himself with a question: "And what then?"

"So too with the German submarines. They also must cross and cross again in their cruises, those lines along which your feluccas continually come and go."

José Medina threw up his hands.

"The submarines! Señor, if you listen to the babblers on the quays, you would think that the seas are stiff with them! Schools of them like whales everywhere! Only yesterday Palma rang with the account of one. It pursued a French steamer between Minorca and Mallorca. It spoke to a fishing boat! What did it not do? Señor, there was no submarine yesterday in the channel between Minorca and Mallorca. If there had been I must have known."

And he sat back as though the subject were disposed of.

"But submarines do visit these waters, Señor Medina, and they do sink ships," replied Hillyard.

José Medina shrugged his shoulders and spread out his hands.

"*Claro!* And it is said that I supply them with their oil." He turned swiftly to Hillyard. "Perhaps you have heard that story, señor?"

Hillyard nodded.

"Yes. I did not believe it. It is because I did not believe it that I am here, asking your help."

"I thank you. It is the truth. I will tell you something now. Not one of my captains has ever seen one of those submarines, neither on this side nor on that," and Medina touched the lines which Hillyard had drawn on both sides of the Balearics on his chart. "Now, what can I do?"

"One simple thing, and well within your scruples as a neutral," replied Hillyard. "These submarines doubly break the laws of nations. They violate your territorial waters, and they sink merchant ships without regard for the crews."

"Yes," said José Medina.

"You have agents along the coast. I have friends too in every town, Englishmen who love both England and Spain, Spaniards who love both Spain and England. We will put, if you permit, your agents in touch with my friends."

"Yes," said José Medina innocently. "How shall we do that? We must have lists prepared."

Hillyard smiled gently.

"That is not necessary, señor. We know your agents already. If you will secretly inform them that those who speak in my name," and he took his card from the table, and gave it into Medina's hands, "are men to be trusted, it will be enough."

José Medina agreed.

"I will give them instructions."

"And yet another instruction if you will be so kind, to all your captains."

"Yes?"

"That they shall report at the earliest possible moment to your nearest agent ashore, the position of any submarine they have seen."

José Medina assented once more.

"But it will take a little time, señor, for me to pass that instruction round. It shall go from captain to captain, but it will not be prudent to give it out more widely. A week or two—no more—and every captain in my fleet shall be informed. That is all?"

Hillyard was already rising from his chair. He stood straight up.

"All except that they will be forbidden too," he added with a smile, "to supply either food or drink or oil to any enemy vessel."

José Medina raised his hands in protest.

"That order was given months ago. But it shall be repeated, and you can trust me, it shall be obeyed."

The two men went to the door of the villa, and stood outside in the garden. It seemed the interview was over, and the agreement made. But indeed the interview as Hillyard had planned it had hardly begun. He had a series of promises which might be kept or broken, and the keeping or breaking of them could not be checked. José Medina was very likely to be holding the common belief along that coast that Germany would surely win the war. He was in the perfect position to keep in with both sides were he so minded. It was not to content himself with general promises that Hillyard had brought the *Dragonfly* to Palma.

He turned suddenly towards José Medina with a broad laugh, and clapped him heartily upon the back.

"So you do not remember me, Señor José?"

Medina was puzzled. He took a step nearer to Hillyard. Then he shook his head, and apologised with a smile.

"I am to blame, señor. As a rule, my memory is not at fault. But on this occasion—yes."

Through the apology ran a wariness, some fear of a trick, some hint of an incredulity.

"Yet we have met."

"Señor, it must be so."

"Do you remember, Señor José, your first venture?" asked Hillyard. "Surely."

"A single sailing-felucca beached at one o'clock in the morning on the flat sand close to Benicassim."

José Medina did not answer. But the doubt which his politeness could not quite keep out of his face was changing into perplexity. This history of his first cargo so far was true.

"That was more than thirteen years ago," Hillyard continued. "Thirteen years last April."

José Medina nodded. Date, place, hour, all were correct. His eyes were fixed curiously upon his visitor, but there was no recognition in them.

"There were two carts waiting, to carry the tobacco up to the hills."

"Two?" José Medina interrupted sharply. "Let me think! That first cargo! It is so long ago."

Medina reflected carefully. Here was a detail of real importance which would put this Señor Hillyard to the test—if only he could himself remember. It was his first venture, yes! But there had been so many like to it since. Still—the very first. He ought to remember that! And as he concentrated his thoughts the veil of the years was rent, and he saw, he saw quite clearly the white moonlit beach, the felucca with its mast bent like a sapling in a high wind, and the great yard of the sail athwart the beam of the boat, the black shadow of it upon the sand, and the carts—yes, the carts!

"There were two carts," he agreed, and a change was just faintly audible in his voice—a change for which up till now Hillyard had listened with both his ears in vain. A ring of cordiality, a suggestion that the barriers of reserve were breaking down.

"Yes, señor, there were two carts."

Medina was listening intently now. Would his visitor go on with the history of that night!

And Hillyard did go on.

"The tobacco barrels were packed very quickly into the carts, and the carts were driven up the beach and across the Royal road, and into a track which led back to the hills."

José Medina suddenly laughed. He could hear the groaning and creaking of those thin-wheeled springless carts which had carried all his fortunes on that night thirteen years ago, the noise of them vibrating for miles in the air of that still spring night! What terror they had caused him! How his heart had leaped when—and lo! Hillyard was carrying on the tale.

"Two of the Guardia Civil stepped from behind a tree, arrested your carts, and told the drivers to turn back to the main road and the village."

"Yes."

"You ran in front of the leading cart, and stood there blocking the way. The Guardia told you to move or he would fire. You stood your ground."

"Yes."

"Why the Guardia did not fire," continued Hillyard, "who shall say? But he did not."

"No, he did not," José Medina repeated with a smile. "Why? It was Fate—Fortune—what you will."

"You sent every one aside, and remained alone with the guards—for a long time. Oh, for a long time! Then you called out, and your men came back, and found you alone with your horses and your carts. How you had persuaded the guards to leave you alone——"

"Quien sabe?" said Medina, with a smile.

"But you had persuaded them, even on that first venture. So," and now Hillyard smiled. "So we took your carts up in to the mountains."

"We?" exclaimed José. He took a step forward, and gazed keenly into Martin Hillyard's face. Hillyard nodded.

"I was one of your companions on that first night venture of yours thirteen years ago."

"*Claro!* You were certainly there," returned José Medina, and he was no longer speaking either with doubt or with the exaggerated politeness of a Spaniard towards a stranger. He was not even speaking as *caballero* to *caballero* the relationship to which, in the beginning, Hillyard had most wisely invited him. He was speaking as associate to associate, as friendly man to friendly man. "On that night you were certainly with me! No, let me think! There were five men, yes, five and a boy from Valencia—Martin."

He pronounced the word in the Spanish way as Marteen.

"Who led the horse in the first cart," said Hillyard, and he pointed to his visiting card which José Medina still held in his hand. José Medina read it again.

"Marteen Hillyard." He came close to Hillyard, and looked in his eyes, and at the shape of his features, and at the colour of his hair. "Yes, it is the little Marteen," he cried, "and now the little Marteen swings into Palma in his great steam yacht. Dios, what a change!"

"And José Medina owns two hundred motor-feluccas and employs eighteen thousand men," answered Hillyard.

José Medina held out his hand suddenly with a great burst of cordial, intimate laughter.

"Yes, we were companions in those days. You helped me to drive my carts up into the mountains. Good!" He patted Hillyard on the shoulder. "That makes a difference, eh? Come, we will go in again. Now I shall help you."

That reserve, that intense reserve of the Spaniard who so seldom admits another into real intimacy, and makes him acquainted with his private life, was down now. Hillyard had won. José Medina's house and his chattels were in earnest at Martin Hillyard's disposal. The two men went back through the house into a veranda above the steep fall of garden and cliff, where there were chairs in which a man could sit at his ease.

José Medina fetched out a box of cigars.

"You can trust these. They are good."

"Who should know if you do not?" answered Hillyard as he took one; and again José Medina patted him on the shoulder, but this time with a gurgle of delight.

"*El pequeño* Martin," he said, and he clapped his hands. From some recess of the house his wife appeared with a bottle of champagne and two glasses on a tray.

"Now we will talk," said José Medina, "or rather I will talk and you shall listen."

Hillyard nodded his head, as he raised the glass to his lips.

"I have learnt in the last years that it is better to listen than to talk," said he. "*Salut!*"

CHAPTER XIV

"Touching the Matter of Those Ships"

It has been said that Hillyard joined a service with its traditions to create. Indeed, it had everything to create, its rules, its methods, its whole philosophy. And it had to do this quickly during the war, and just for the war; since after the war it would cease to be. Certain conclusions had now been forced by experience quite definitely on Hillyard's mind. Firstly, that the service must be executive. Its servants must take their responsibility and act if they were going to cope with the intrigues and manœuvres of the Germans. There was no time for discussions with London, and London was overworked in any case. The Post Office, except on rare occasions, could not be used; telegrams, however ingenious the cipher, were dangerous; and even when London received them, it had not the knowledge of the sender on the spot, wherewith to fill them out. London, let it be admitted, or rather that one particular small section of London with which Hillyard dealt, was at one with Hillyard. Having chosen its men it trusted them, until such time as indiscretion or incapacity proved the trust misplaced; in which case the offender was brought politely home upon some excuse, cordially thanked, and with a friendly shake of the hand, shown the door.

Hillyard's second conclusion was that of one hundred trails, ten at the most would lead to any result: but you must follow each one of the hundred up until you reach proof that you are in a blind alley.

The third was the sound and simple doctrine that you can confidently look to Chance to bring you results, probably your very best results, if you are prepared and equipped to make all your profit out of chance the moment she leans your way. Chance is an elusive goddess, to be seized and held prisoner with a swift, firm hand. Then she'll serve you. But if the hand's not ready and the eye unexpectant, you'll see but the trail of her robe as she vanishes to offer her assistance to another more wakeful than yourself.

In pursuit of this conviction, Hillyard steamed out of Palma Bay on the morning of the day after his interview with José Medina, and crossing to the mainland cruised all the next night southwards. At six o'clock in the morning he was off a certain great high cape. The sea was smooth as glass. The day a riot of sunlight and summer, and the great headland with its high lighthouse thrust its huge brown knees into the water.

The *Dragonfly* slowed down and dawdled. Three men stood in the stern behind the white side-awning. Hillyard was on the bridge with his captain.

"I don't really expect much," he said, seeking already to discount a possible disappointment. "It's only a possibility, I don't count on it."

"Six o'clock off the cape," said the captain. "We are on time."

"Yes."

Both men searched the smooth sea for some long, sluggish, inexplicable wave which should break, or for a V-shaped ripple such as a fixed stake will make in a swiftly running stream.

"Not a sign," said the captain, disconsolately.

"No. Yet it is certainly true that the keeper of that lighthouse paid an amount equal to three years' salary into a bank three weeks ago. It is true that oil could be brought into that point, and stored there, and no one but the keeper be the wiser. And it is true that the *Acquitania* is at this moment in this part of the Mediterranean steaming east for Salonika with six thousand men on board. Let's trail our coat a bit!" said Hillyard, and the captain with a laugh gave an order to the signal boy by his side.

The boy ran aft and in a few seconds the red ensign fluttered up the flagstaff, and drooped in the still air. But even that provocation produced no result. For an hour and a half the *Dragonfly* steamed backwards and forwards in front of the cape.

"No good!" Hillyard at last admitted. "We'll get on to the *Acquitania*, and advise her. Meanwhile, captain, we had better make for Gibraltar and coal there."

Hillyard went to the wireless-room, and the yacht was put about for the great scarped eastern face of the Rock.

"One of the blind alleys," said Hillyard, as he ate his breakfast in the deck-saloon. "Next time perhaps we'll have better luck. Something'll turn up for sure."

Something was always turning up in those days, and the yacht had not indeed got its coal on board in Gibraltar harbour when a message came which sent Hillyard in a rush by train through Madrid to Barcelona. He reached Barcelona at half past nine in the morning, took his breakfast by the window of the smaller dining-room in the hotel at the corner of the Plaza Cataluña, and by eleven was seated in a flat in one of the neighbouring streets. The flat was occupied by Lopez Baeza who turned from the window to greet him.

"I was not followed," said Hillyard as he put down his hat and stick.

Habit had bred in him a vigilance, or rather an instinct which quickly made him aware of any who shadowed him.

"No, that is true," said Baeza, who had been watching Hillyard's approach from the window.

"But I should like to know who our young friend is on the kerb opposite, and why he is standing sentinel."

Lopez Baeza laughed.

"He is the sign and token of the commercial activity of Spain."

From behind the curtains, stretched across the window, both now looked down into the street. A youth in a grey suit and a pair of orange-coloured buttoned boots loitered backwards and forwards over about six yards of footwalk; now he smoked a cigarette, now he leaned against a tree and idly surveyed the passers by. He apparently had nothing whatever to do. But he did not move outside the narrow limits of his promenade. Consequently he had something to do.

"Yes," continued Baeza with a chuckle, "he is a proof of our initiative. I thought as you do three days ago. For it is just three days since he took his stand there. But he is not watching this flat. He is not concerned with us at all. He is an undertaker's tout. In the house opposite to us a woman is lying very ill. Our young friend is waiting for her to die, so that he may rush into the house, offer his condolences and present the undertaker's card."

Hillyard left the youth to his gruesome sentry-duty and turned back into the room. A man of fifty, with a tawny moustache, a long and rather narrow face and eyeglasses, was sitting at an office table with some papers in front of him.

"How do you do, Fairbairn?" Hillyard asked.

Fairbairn was a schoolmaster from the North of England, with a knowledge of the Spanish tongue, who had thrown up schoolmastering, prospects, everything, in October of 1914.

"Touching the matter of those ships," said Hillyard, sitting down opposite to Fairbairn.

Fairbairn grinned.

"It worked very well," said he, "so far."

Hillyard turned towards Lopez and invited him to a seat. "Let me hear everything," he said.

Spanish ships were running to England with the products of Cataluña and returning full of coal, and shipowners made their fortunes and wages ran high. But not all of them were content. Here and there the captains and the mates took with them in their cabin to England lists of questions thoughtfully compiled by German officers; and from what they saw in English harbours and on English seas and from what secret news was brought to them, they filled up answers to the questions and brought them back to the Germans in Spain. So much Hillyard already knew.

"A pilot, Juan de Maestre, went on board the ships, collected the answers, made a report and took it up to the German headquarters here. That Ramon Castillo found out," said Fairbairn. "Steps were taken with the crew. The ships would be placed on the black list. There would be no coal for them. They must be laid up and the crews dismissed. The crew of the *Saragossa* grasped the position, and the next time Juan de Maestre stepped on board he was invited to the forecastle, thumped, dropped overboard into the salubrious waters of the dock and left to swim ashore. Juan de Maestre has had enough. He won't go near the Germans any more. He is in a condition of extreme terror and neutrality. Oh, he's wonderfully neutral just now."

"We might catch him perhaps on the rebound!" Hillyard suggested.

"Lopez thinks so," said Fairbairn, with a nod towards Baeza.

"I can find him this evening," Baeza remarked.

The three men conferred for a little while, and as a consequence of that conference Lopez Baeza walked through the narrow streets of the old town to a café near the railway station. In a corner a small, wizened, square man was sitting over his beer, brooding unhappily. Baeza took a seat by his side and talked with Juan de Maestre. He went out after a few minutes and hired a motorcar from the stand in front of the station. In the car he drove to the park and went once round it. At a junction of two paths on the second round the car was stopped. A short, small man stepped out from the shadow of a great tree and swiftly stepped in.

"Drive towards Tibidabo," Baeza directed the driver, and inside the dark, closed car Baeza and Juan de Maestre debated, the one persuading, the other refusing. It was long before any agreement was reached, but when Baeza, with the perspiration standing in beads upon his face, returned to his flat in the quiet, respectable street, he found Martin Hillyard and Fairbairn waiting for him anxiously.

"*Hecho!*" he cried. "It is done! Juan de Maestre will continue to go on board the ships and collect the information and write it out for the Germans. But we shall receive an exact copy."

"How?" asked Hillyard.

"Ramon will meet a messenger from Juan. At eight in the morning of every second day Ramon is to be waiting at a spot which from time to time we will change. The first place will be the cinema opposite to the old Bull Ring."

"Good," said Hillyard. "In a fortnight I will return."

He departed once more for Gibraltar, cruised up the coast, left his yacht once more in the harbour of Tarragona and travelled by motorcar into Barcelona.

Fairbairn and Lopez Baeza received him. It was night, and hot with a staleness of the air which was stifling. The windows all stood open in the quiet, dark street, but the blinds and curtains were closely drawn before the lamps were lit.

"Now!" said Hillyard. "There are reports."

Fairbairn nodded grimly as he went to the safe and unlocked it.

"Pretty dangerous stuff," he answered.

"Reliable?" asked Hillyard.

Fairbairn returned with some sheets of blue-lined paper written over with purple ink, and some rough diagrams.

"I am sure," he replied. "Not because I trust Juan de Maestre, but because he couldn't have invented the information. He hasn't the knowledge."

Lopez Baeza agreed.

"Juan de Maestre is keeping faith with us," he said shortly, and, to the judgment of Lopez Baeza, Hillyard had learnt to incline a ready ear.

"This is the real thing, Hillyard," said Fairbairn, pulling at his moustache. "Look!"

He handed to Martin a chart. The points of the compass were marked in a corner. Certain courses and routes were given, and fixed lights indicated by which the vessel might be guided. There was a number of patches as if to warn the navigator of shallows, and again a number of small black cubes and squares which seemed to declare the position of rocks. There was no rough work in this chart. It was elaborately and skilfully drawn, the work of an artist.

"This is a copy made by me. Juan de Maestre left the original document with us for an hour," said Fairbairn, and he allowed Hillyard to speculate for a few seconds upon the whereabouts of that dangerous and reef-strewn sea. "It's not a chart of any bay or water at all. It's a plan of Cardiff by night for the guidance of German airships. Those patches are not shallows, but the loom in the sky of the furnaces. The black spots are the munition factories. Here are the docks," he pointed with the tip of his pencil. "The *Jesus-Maria* brought that back a week ago. Let it get from here to Germany, as it will do, eh? and a Zeppelin coming across England on a favourable night could make things hum in Cardiff."

Hillyard laid the sketch down and took another which Fairbairn held out to him.

"Do you see this?" Fairbairn continued. "This gives the exact line of the nets between the English and the Irish coasts, and the exact points of latitude and longitude where they are broken for the passage of ships, and the exact number and armament of the trawlers which guard those points."

Hillyard gazed closely at the chart. It gave the positions clearly enough, but it was a roughly-made affair, smudged with dingy fingers and uneven in its drawing. He laid it upon the table by the side of the map of Cardiff and compared one with the other.

"This," he said, touching the roughly-drawn map of a section of the Channel, "this is the work of the ship's captain?"

"Yes."

"But what of this?" and Hillyard lifted again the elaborate chart of Cardiff by night. "Some other hand drew this."

Fairbairn agreed.

"Yes. Here is the report which goes with the charts. The chart of Cardiff was handed to the captain in an inn on shore. It came from an unknown person, who is mentioned as B.45."

Hillyard seized upon the report and read it through, and then the others upon the top of that. Cloth, saddlery, equipment of various kinds were needed in England, and a great sea-borne trade had sprung up between the two countries, so that ships constantly went to and fro. In more than one of these reports the hieroglyph B.45 appeared. But never a hint which could lead to his detection—never anything personal, not a clue to his age, his business, his appearance, even his abode—nothing but this baffling symbol B.45.

"You have cabled all this home, of course," Hillyard observed to Fairbairn.

"Yes. They know nothing of the B.45. They are very anxious for any details."

"He seems to be a sort of letterbox," said Hillyard, "a centre-point for the gathering in of information."

Fairbairn shook his head.

"He is more active than that," he returned, and he pointed to a passage here and there, which bore him out. It was the first time that Martin Hillyard had come across this symbol, and he was utterly at a loss to conjecture the kind of man the symbol hid. He might be quite obscure, the tenant of some suburban shop, or, again, quite prominent in the public eye, the owner of a fine house, and generous in charities; he might be of any nationality. But there he was, somewhere under the oak-trees of England, doing his secret, mean work for the ruin of the country. Hillyard dreamed that night of B.45. He saw him in his dreams, an elusive figure without a face, moving swiftly wherever people were gathered together, travelling in crowded trains, sitting at the dinner-tables of the great, lurking at the corners of poor tenements. Hillyard hunted him, saw him deftly pocket a letter which a passing stranger as deftly handed him, or exchange some whispered words with another who walked for a few paces without recognition by his side, but though he hurried round corners to get in front of him and snatch a glance at his face, he could never come up with him. He waked with the sunlight pouring in between the lattices of his shutters from the Plaza Cataluña, tired and unrefreshed. B.45! B.45! He was like some figure from a child's storybook! Some figure made up of tins and sticks and endowed with malevolent life. B.45. London asked news of him, and he stalked through London. Where should Hillyard find his true image and counterpart?

It is not the purpose of this narrative to describe how one Christobal Quesada, first mate of the steamship *Mondragon*, utterly overreached himself by sending in a report of a British hospital ship, sure to leave the harbour of Alexandria with gun-carriages upon her deck; how the report was proved to be a lie; how it was used as the excuse for the barbarous sinking of the great ships laden with wounded, and ablaze from stern to stern with green lights, the red cross glowing amidships like a wondrous jewel; how Christobal Quesada was removed from his ship in a French port, and after being duly arraigned for his life, met his death against a prison wall. Fairbairn wrote to Martin Hillyard:

> *"The execution of Quesada has put an end to the whole wicked question. So long as the offender was only put in prison with the certainty of release at the end of the war, whilst his family lived comfortably on German money, the game went merrily on. But the return of the 'Mondragon,' minus her executed mate, has altered the whole position. Juan de Maestre has nothing whatever to do nowadays."*

Hillyard smiled with contentment. He could understand a German going to any lengths for Germany. He was prepared to do the same himself for his country. But when a neutral under the cloak of his neutrality meddles in this stupendous conflict for cash, for his thirty miserable pieces of silver, he could feel no inclination of mercy.

"Let the neutrals keep out!" he murmured. "This is not their affair. Let them hold their tongues and go about their own business!"

He received Fairbairn's letter in the beginning of the year 1916. He was still no nearer at that date to the discovery of B.45; nor were they any better informed in London. Hillyard could only wait upon Chance to slip a clue into his hand.

CHAPTER XV

In a Sleeping-Car

The night express from Paris to Narbonne and the Spanish frontier was due to leave the Quai d'Orsay station at ten. But three-quarters of an hour before that time the platform was already crowded, and many of the seats occupied. Hillyard walked down the steps a little before half past nine with the latest of the evening papers in his hand.

"You have engaged your seat, monsieur," the porter asked, who was carrying Hillyard's kit-bag.

"Yes," said Martin absently. He was thinking that on the boulevards the newsboys might now be crying a later edition of the papers than that which he held, an edition with still more details. He saw them surrounded in the darkened street by quiet, anxious groups.

"Will you give me your ticket, monsieur?" the porter continued, and as Hillyard looked at him vacantly, "the ticket for your seat."

Hillyard roused himself.

"I beg your pardon. I have a compartment in the sleeping-car, numbers eleven and twelve."

Amongst many old principles of which Martin Hillyard had first learned the wisdom during these last years, none had sunk deeper than this—that the head of an organisation cannot do the work of any of its members and hope that the machine will run smoothly. His was the task of supervision and ultimate direction. He held himself at the beck and call of those who worked under him. He responded to their summons. And it was in response to a very urgent summons from Fairbairn that he had hurried the completion of certain arrangements with the French authorities in Paris and was now returning to the south! But he was going very reluctantly.

It was July, 1916. The first battle of the Somme, launched some days past, was at its very climacteric. The casualties had been and were terrible. Even at this moment of night the fury of the attack was not relaxed. All through the day reports, exasperating in their brevity, had been streaming into Paris, and rumour, as of old, circled swift-winged above the city, making good or ill the deficiencies of the telegrams. One fact, however, had leaped to light, unassailably true. The Clayfords, stationed on the north of the line at Thiepval, had redeemed their name and added a new lustre to their erstwhile shining record. The devotion of the officers, the discipline of the men, had borne their fruits. At a most critical moment the Clayfords had been forced to change front against a flank attack, under a galling fire and in the very press of battle, and the long extended line had swung to its new position with the steadiness of veterans, and, having reached it, had stood fast. Hillyard rejoiced with a sincerity as deep as if he himself held his commission in that regiment. But the losses had been terrible; and Martin Hillyard was troubled to the roots of his heart by doubts whether Harry Luttrell were at this moment knowing the deep contentment that the fixed aim of his boyhood and youth had been fulfilled; or whether he was lying out on the dark ground beneath the stars unaware of it and indifferent. Hillyard nursed a hope that some blunder had been made, and that he would find his compartment occupied.

The controller, in his brown uniform with the brass buttons and his peaked cap, stood at the steps of the car with the attendant.

"Eleven and twelve," said Hillyard, handing to him his ticket.

The attendant, a middle-aged, stout man with a black moustache and a greasy face, shot one keen glance from under the peak of his cap at the occupant of numbers 11 and 12, and then led the way along the corridor.

The compartment was empty. Hillyard looked around it with a grudging eye.

"I am near the middle of the coach here, I think," he said.

"Yes, monsieur, quite in the middle."

"That is well," answered Hillyard. "I am an invalid, and cannot sleep when there is much motion."

He spoke irritably, with that tone of grievance peculiar to the man who thinks his health is much worse than it is.

"Can I get coffee in the morning?" he asked.

"At half past six, monsieur. But you must get out of the train for it."

Hillyard uttered an exclamation of disgust, and shrugged his shoulders. "What a country!" the gesture said as plainly as speech.

"But it is the war, monsieur!" the attendant expostulated with indignation.

"Oh, yes, I know! The war!" Hillyard retorted with ill humour. "Do I want a bath? I cannot have it. It is the war. If a waiter is rude to me, it is the war. If my steak is overcooked it is the war. The war! It is the excuse for everything."

He told the porter to place his bag upon the upper berth, and, still grumbling, gave him some money. He turned sharply on the attendant, who was smiling in the doorway.

"Ah, it seems to you funny that an invalid should be irritable, eh?" he cried. "I suppose it must be—damnably funny."

"Monsieur, there are very many men who would like tonight to be invalids with a sleeping compartment to themselves," returned the attendant severely.

"Well, I don't want to talk about it any more," said Hillyard roughly, and he shouldered his way out again on to the platform.

The attendant followed him. The smile upon his face was sleeker than ever. He was very amused and contented with his passenger in the compartment numbers 11 and 12. He took the cap off his head and wiped the perspiration from his forehead.

"Ouf! It is hot tonight." He looked after Hillyard with a chuckle, and remarked to the controller, "This is a customer who does not like his little comforts to be disarranged!"

The controller nodded contemptuously.

"They must travel—the English! The tourism—that is sacred, even if all Europe burns."

Hillyard strolled towards the stairs, and as he drew near to them his eyes brightened. A man about six years older than himself, tall, broad-shouldered, slim of waist, with a short, fair moustache, was descending towards him.

The war has killed many foolish legends, but none more foolish than the legend of the typical Frenchman, conceived as a short, rotund, explosive person, with a square, brown beard of curly baby-hair and a shiny silk hat with a flat brim. There have been too many young athletes of clean build on view whose nationality, language and the uniforms of powder-blue and khaki could alone decide. The more curious might, perhaps, if the youth were in mufti, cast a downward glance at the boots; but even boots were ceasing to be the sure telltale they once used to be. This man descending the stairs with a limp was the Commandant Marnier, of the 193rd Regiment, wounded in 1915, and now attached to the General Staff. He was in plain clothes; he was looking for Martin Hillyard, and no stranger but would have set him and the man for whom he was looking in the same category of races.

The Commandant Marnier saw Martin Hillyard clearly enough long before he reached the foot of the stairs. But nevertheless he greeted him with an appearance of surprise.

"But what luck!" he said aloud. "You leave by this train?"

"Yes. It may be that I shall find health."

"Yes, yes. So your friends will pray," returned the Commandant, falling into Hillyard's pace.

"The telegram we sent for you——" Marnier began.

"Yes!"

"There is an answer already. Your friend is unhurt. I have brought you a copy. I thought that perhaps I might catch you before your train started."

He gave the slip of typewritten message into Hillyard's hand.

"That was most kind of you," said Hillyard. "You have removed a great anxiety. It would have been many days before I should have received this good news if you had not gone out of your way to hurry with it here."

Hillyard was moved, partly by the message, partly by the consideration of Marnier, who now waved his thanks aside.

"Bah! We may not say 'comrade' as often as the Boche, but perhaps we are it all the more. I will not come further with you towards your carriage, for I have still a few things to do."

He shook Hillyard by the hand and departed. Hillyard turned from him towards his sleeping-car, but though his chief anxiety was dispelled, his reluctance to go was not. And he looked at the long, brightly-lit train which was to carry him from this busy and high-hearted city with a desire that it would start before its time, and leave him a derelict upon the platform. He could not bend his thoughts to the work which was at his hand. The sapphire waters of the South had quite lost their sparkle and enchantment. Here, here, was the place of life! The exhilaration of his task, its importance, the glow of thankfulness when some real advantage was won, a plot foiled, a scheme carried to success—these matters were all banished from his mind. Even the war-risk of it was forgotten. He thought with envy of the men in trenches. Yet the purpose of his yacht was long since known to the Germans; the danger of the torpedo was ever present on her voyages, and the certainty that if she were sunk, and he captured, any means would be taken to force him to speak before he was shot, was altogether beyond dispute. Even at this moment he carried hidden in a matchbox a little phial, which never left him, to put the sure impediment between himself and a forced confession of his aims and knowledge. But he was not aware of it. How many times had he seen the red light at Europa Point on Gibraltar's edge change to white, sometimes against the scarlet bars of dawn, sometimes in the winter against a wall of black! But on the platform of the Quai d'Orsay station, in a bustle of soldiers going on short leave to their homes, and rattling with pannikins and iron-helmets, he could remember none of these consolations.

He reached his carriage.

"Messieurs les voyageurs, en route!" cried the controller.

"What a crowd!" Hillyard grumbled. "Really, it almost disposes one to say that one will never travel again until this war is over."

He walked along the corridor to his compartment and sat down as the train started with a jerk. The door stood open, and in a few minutes the attendant came to it.

"Who is in the next compartment on the other side of the lavatory?" Hillyard asked.

"A manufacturer of Perpignan and his wife."

"Does he snore?" Hillyard asked. "If he snores I shall not sleep. It should be an offence against your bylaws for a traveller to snore."

He crossed one leg across his knee and unlaced his shoe.

The attendant came into the room.

"It is possible, monsieur, that I might hurry and fetch you your coffee in the morning," he said.

"It is worth five francs to you if you do," replied Hillyard.

"Then monsieur will not move from his compartment until luncheon. I will see to it. Monsieur will bolt his door, and in the morning I will knock when I bring the coffee."

"Good," returned Hillyard ungraciously.

The attendant retired, and Hillyard closed the door. But the ventilating lattice in the lower part of the door was open, and Hillyard could see the legs of the attendant. He was waiting outside—waiting for what? Hillyard smiled to himself and took down his bag from the upper berth. He had hardly opened it when the attendant knocked and entered.

"You will not forget, monsieur, to bolt your door. In these days it is not wise to leave it on the latch."

"I won't forget," Hillyard replied surlily, and once more the attendant retired; and again he stood outside the door. He did not move until the bolt was shot. The attendant seemed very pleased that this fool of a tourist who thought of nothing but his infirmities should safely bolt the door of the compartments numbers 11 and 12; and very pleased, too, to bring to this churlish, discontented traveller his coffee in the morning, so that he need not leave compartments numbers 11 and 12 unguarded. Hillyard chuckled as the attendant moved away.

"I am to be your watchdog, am I? Your sentinel? Very well! Come, let me deserve your confidence, my friend."

The train thundered out of the tunnel and through the suburbs of Paris. Hillyard drew a letter from Fairbairn out of his pocket and read it through.

"Compartments numbers 11 and 12 on the night train from the Quai d'Orsay station to Cerbère. Good!" murmured Hillyard. "Here I am in compartments numbers 11 and 12. Now we wait until the married couple from Perpignan and the attendant are comfortably asleep."

He undressed and went to bed, but he did not sleep. He lay in the berth in the darkness, listening intently as the train rushed out of Paris across the plains of France. Once or twice, as the hours passed, he heard a stealthy footstep in the corridor outside, and once the faintest possible little click told that the latch of his door had been lifted to make sure that the bolt was still shot home in its socket. Hillyard smiled.

"You are safe, my friend," he breathed the words towards the anxious one in the corridor. "No one can get in. The door is locked. The door of the dressing-room too. Sleep in your corner in peace."

The train sped over a moonlit country, spacious, unhurt by war. It moved with a steady, rhythmical throb, like an accompaniment to a tune or a phrase, ever repeated and repeated Hillyard found himself fitting words to the pulsation of the wheels. "Berlin . . . Berne . . . Paris . . . Cerbère . . . Barcelona . . . Madrid . . . Aranjuez and the world"; and back again, reversing the order: "Madrid . . . Barcelona . . . Cerbère . . . Paris . . . Berne . . . Berlin."

But the throb of the train set the interrogation at the end of the string of names. So that the sequence of them was like a question demanding confirmation. . . .

Towards three in the morning, when there was no movement in the corridor and the lights were blue and dim, Hillyard silently folded back his bedclothes and rose. In the darkness he groped gently for the door of the lavatory between his compartment and the compartment of the manufacturer of Perpignan. He found the handle, and pressed it down slowly; without a creak or a whine of the hinges the door swung open towards him. Through the clatter he could hear that the manufacturer of Perpignan was snoring. But Hillyard did not put his trust in snores. He crept with bare feet across the washing-room, and, easing over the handle of the further door, locked the manufacturer out. Again there had been no sound. He shut the door of his own compartment lest the swing of the train should set it banging and arouse the sleepers. Towards the corridor there was a window of painted glass, and through this window a pale, dim light filtered in. Hillyard noticed, for the first time, that a small diamond-shaped piece of the coloured glass was missing, at about the level of a man's head. It was advisable that Martin Hillyard should be quick—or he might find the tables turned. With his ears more than ever alert, he set up the steps for the upper berth, in the lavatory, and whilst he worked his eyes watched that little aperture at the level of a man's head, which once a diamond-shaped piece of coloured glass had closed. . . .

The door of the manufacturer was unlocked, the steps folded in their place, and Hillyard back again in his bed before two minutes had passed. And once more the throb of the train beat into a chain of towns which went backwards and forwards like a shuttle in his brain. But there was no note of interrogation now.

"Berlin . . . Berne . . . Paris . . . Cerbère . . . Barcelona . . . Madrid . . . Aranjuez and the world"; and with a thump the train set a firm full stop to the sequence. Across the broad plain, meadowland and plough, flower-garden and fruit the train thundered down to the Pyrenees. Paris was far away now, and the sense of desolation at quitting it quite gone from Hillyard's breast.

"Berlin . . . Berne . . . Paris . . . Cerbère . . . Barcelona . . . Madrid."

Here was one of the post-roads by which Germany reached the outer world. Others there were beyond doubt. Sweden and Rotterdam, Mexico and South America—but here was one, and tomorrow, nay, today, the communication would be cut, and Germany so much the poorer.

The train steamed into Cerbère at one o'clock of the afternoon.

"Every one must descend here, monsieur, for the examination of luggage and passports," said the attendant.

"But I am leaving France!" cried Hillyard. "I go on into Spain. Why should France, then, examine my luggage?"

"It is the war, monsieur."

Hillyard lifted up his hands in indignation too deep for words. He gathered together his bag and his coat and stick, handed them to a porter and descended. He passed into the waiting-room, and was directed by a soldier with a fixed bayonet to take his place in the queue of passengers. But he said quietly to the soldier:

"I would like to see M. de Cassaud, the Commissaire of Police."

Hillyard was led apart; his card was taken from him; he was ushered instantly into an office where an elderly French officer sat in mufti before a table. He shook Hillyard cordially by the hand.

"You pass through? I myself hope to visit Barcelona again very soon. Jean, wait outside with monsieur's baggage," this to the porter who had pushed in behind Hillyard. M. de Cassaud rose and closed the door. He had looked at Hillyard's face and acted quickly.

"It is something more than compliments you want from me, monsieur. Well, what can I do?"

"The second sleeping-car, compartments numbers 11 and 12," said Hillyard urgently. "In the water-tank of the lavatory there is a little metal case with letters from Berlin for Barcelona and Madrid. But wait, monsieur!"

M. de Cassaud was already at the door.

"It is the attendant of the sleeping-car who hides them there. If he can be called into an office quietly on some matter of routine and held there whilst your search is made, then those in Madrid and Barcelona to whom these letters are addressed may never know they have been sent at all!"

M. de Cassaud nodded and went out. Hillyard waited nervously in the little whitewashed room. It was impossible that the attendant should have taken fright and bolted. Even if he bolted, it would be impossible that he should escape across the frontier. It was impossible that he should recover the metal case from the water-tank, while the carriage stood openly at the platform of Cerbère station. He would be certain to wait until it was shunted into the cleaning shed. But so many certainties had been disproved, so many possibilities had come to pass during the last two years, that Hillyard was sceptical to his fingertips. M. de Cassaud was a long time away. Yes, certainly M. de Cassaud was a very long—and the door opened, and M. de Cassaud appeared.

"He is giving an account of his blankets and his towels. There are two soldiers at the door. He is safe. Come!" said the Commissaire.

They crossed the platform to the carriage, whilst Hillyard described the attendant's anxiety that he should bolt his door. "No doubt he gave the same advice to the manufacturer of Perpignan," Hillyard added.

It was M. de Cassaud who arranged and mounted the steps in the tiny washing-room.

"Look, monsieur," said Hillyard, and he pointed to the little aperture in the coloured glass of the window. "One can see from the corridor what is going on in this room. That is useful. If a traveller complains—bah, it is the war!" and Hillyard laughed.

M. de Cassaud looked at the window.

"Yes, that is ingenious," he said.

He drained off the water, folded back his sleeve, and plunged his arm into the tank. Then he uttered a little cry. He drew up into the light an oblong metal can, like a sandwich-case, with the edges soldered together to make it water-tight. He slipped it into his pocket and turned again to the window. He looked at it again curiously.

"Yes, that is ingenious," he said softly, like a man speaking to himself. Then he led the way back to his office, looking in at the guard-room on the platform to give an order on the way.

The soldered edges of the case were quickly split asunder and a small package of letters written on very thin paper revealed.

"You will let me take these on with me," pleaded Martin. "You shall have them again. But some of them may want a special treatment of which we have the secret."

M. de Cassaud was doubtful about the propriety of such a procedure.

"After all I found them," Martin urged.

"It would be unusual," said M. de Cassaud. "The regulations, you know——"

Martin Hillyard smiled.

"The regulations, for you and me, my friend, are those we make ourselves."

M. de Cassaud would admit nothing so outrageous to his trained and rather formal mind. But he made a list of these letters and of their addresses as though he was undecided. He had not finished when a sergeant entered and saluted. The attendant of the sleeping-car had been taken to the depot. He had been searched and a pistol had been found upon him. The sergeant laid a very small automatic Colt upon the table and retired. M. de Cassaud took up the little weapon and examined it.

"Do you know these toys, Monsieur Hillyard?" he asked.

"Yes. They are chiefly used against the mosquitoes."

"Oh, they will kill at twenty-five paces," continued the Commissaire; and he looked quickly at Hillyard. "I will tell you something. You ran some risk last night when you explored that water-tank. Yes, indeed! It would have been so easy. The attendant had but to thrust the muzzle of this through the opening of the window, shoot you dead, raise an alarm that he had caught you hiding something, and there was he a hero and you a traitor. Yes, that is why I said to you the little opening in the window was ingenious! Ah, if he had caught you! Yes, if he had caught you!"

Martin was quick to take advantage.

"Then let me have those letters! I will keep my French colleagues informed of everything."

"Very well," said M. de Cassaud, and he suddenly swept the letters across to Hillyard, who gathered them up hastily and buttoned them away in his pocket before de Cassaud could change his mind.

"It is all very incorrect," said the Commissaire reproachfully.

"Yes, but it is the war," replied Hillyard. "I have the authority of the attendant of the sleeping-car for saying so."

CHAPTER XVI

Tricks of the Trade

"Now!" said Hillyard.

Fairbairn fetched a couple of white porcelain developing dishes to the table. Hillyard unlocked a drawer in his bureau. They were in the deck-saloon of the *Dragonfly*, steaming southwards from Valencia. Outside the open windows the brown hillsides, the uplands of olive trees and the sun-flecked waves slipped by in a magical clear light; and the hiss of the beaded water against the ship's planks filled the cabin with a rustle as of silk. Hillyard drew a deep breath of excitement as he took out from the drawer the letters he had carried off from M. de Cassaud. He had travelled straight through Barcelona to Valencia with the letters in his pocket, picking up Fairbairn at the Estación de Francia on the way, and now, in the sunlight and in the secrecy of the open sea, they were to appraise the value of their catch.

They sat at the table and examined them, opening the envelopes with the skill and the care which experience had taught them. For, even though this post-road was henceforth closed it might possibly be worth while to send forward these letters. One or two were apparently family letters for German soldiers, interned at Pampluna; one or two were business communications from firms in Berlin to their agents in Spain; and these seemed genuine enough.

"They may be of value to the War Trade Board," said Fairbairn; and he put them aside for dispatch to London. As he turned back Hillyard cried suddenly:

"Here we are!"

He had come to the last letter of the little heap. He was holding the envelope in front of him and he read out the address:

"Mr. Jack Williams,
"Alfredo Menandez, 6,
"Madrid."

Fairbairn started up, and tugging at his moustache, stared at the envelope over Hillyard's shoulder.

"By Jove!" he said. "We may have got something."

"Let us see!" returned Hillyard, and he opened the envelope.

As he spread out the letter both men laughed. The date of the month had been corrected by the writer—thus:

8
"*July* 2~~7~~th, 1916."

There was no doubt any longer in either of these two men's minds that hidden away under the commonplaces of a letter of affection was a message of grave importance.

"They are full of clever tricks in Berlin," said Hillyard cheerfully. He could afford to contemplate that cleverness with complacency, for it was now to serve his ends.

There was a German official of high importance living in the Calle Alfredo Menandez, although not at number 6 in that street. The street was a short one with very few numbers in it; and it had occurred to the German official to point out to the postman in that street that if letters came to English names in that street of which the owners could not be discovered, they were probably for the governess of his children, who had a number of English relations moving about Spain, and was accustomed to receive their letters for them, and in any case, five pesetas would be paid for each of them. Shortly after, letters had begun to arrive addressed to English nonexistent people in the quiet little Calle Alfredo Menandez, sometimes from Allied countries, sometimes from Holland, or from Port-Bou over against Cerbère in Spain; and every one of these found its natural way to the house of the German official. The choice of English names had a certain small ingenuity in that, when passing through the censorship of Allied countries, they were a little more likely to be taken at their face value than letters addressed to foreigners.

So far so good. But the German high official was a very busy person; and letters might find their way into his hands which were really intended for English persons and not for him at all. Accordingly, to make all clear, to warn him that here indeed was a letter deserving his kind attention, that little trifling alteration in the date was adopted; as though a man writing on the 28th had mislaid the calendar or newspaper and assigned the 27th to the day of writing, and afterwards had discovered his mistake. It was no wonder accordingly that hope ran high in both Fairbairn and Hillyard as they read through this letter; although, upon the face of it, it was nothing but a sentimental effusion from a sister to a brother.

"We have got to clear all this nonsense away first," said Hillyard.

Fairbairn took the letter, and placing it on one of the developing dishes, poured over it a liquid from a bottle.

"That won't take very long," he said.

Meanwhile Hillyard busied himself with the second of the two white porcelain dishes. He brought out a cruet stand from a cupboard at the side of the stove and filled the dish half full of vinegar. He added water until the liquid rose within half an inch of the rim, and rocked the dish that the dilution might be complete. Next he took a new copying-pencil from the pen-tray on his bureau and stripping the wood away with his knife, dropped the blue lead into the vinegar and water. This lead he carefully dissolved with the help of a glass pestle.

"There! It's ready," he said.

"I, too," added Fairbairn.

He lifted out of the developing dish a wet sheet of writing paper which was absolutely blank. Not one drop of the black ink which had recorded those sentimental effusions remained. It was just a sheet of note-paper which had accidentally fallen into a basin of water.

"That's all right," said Hillyard; and Fairbairn gently slid the sheet into the dish in front of Hillyard. And for a while nothing happened.

"It's a clever trick, isn't it?" Hillyard used the words again, but now with a note of nervousness. "No unlikely paraphernalia needed. Just a copying pencil and some vinegar, which you can get anywhere. Yes, it's a clever trick!"

"If it works," Fairbairn added bluntly.

Both men watched the dish anxiously. The paper remained blank. The solution did not seem to work. It was the first time they had ever made use of it. The coast slid by unnoticed.

"Lopez was certain," said Fairbairn, "quite certain that this was the developing formula."

Hillyard nodded gloomily, but he did not remove his eyes from that irresponsive sheet.

"There may be some other ingredient, something kept quite secret—something known only to one man or two."

He sat down, hooking his chair with his foot nearer to the table.

"We must wait."

"That's all there is to be done," said Fairbairn, and they waited; and they waited. They had no idea, even if the formula should work, whether the writing would flash up suddenly like an over-exposed photographic plate, or emerge shyly and reluctantly letter by letter, word by word. Then, without a word spoken, Fairbairn's finger pointed. A brown stain showed on the whiteness of the paper—just a stroke. It was followed by a curve and another stroke. Hillyard swiftly turned the oblong developing dish so that the side of it, and not the end, was towards him now.

"The writing is across the sheet," he said, and then with a cry, "Look!"

A word was coming out clear, writing itself unmistakably in the middle of the line, at the bottom of the sheet—a signature. Zimmermann!

"From the General Staff!" said Hillyard, in a whisper of excitement. "My word!" He looked at Fairbairn with an eager smile of gratitude. "It's your doing that we have got this—yours and Lopez Baeza's!"

Miraculously the brown strokes and curves and dots and flourishes trooped out of nothing, and fell in like sections and platoons and companies with their due space between them, some quick and trim, some rather slovenly in their aspect, some loitering; but in the end the battalion of words stood to attention, dressed for inspection. The brown had turned black before Hillyard lifted the letter from the solution and spread it upon a sheet of blotting paper.

"Now let us see!" and they read the letter through.

One thousand pounds in English money were offered for reliable information as to the number of howitzers and tanks upon the British front.

A second sum of a thousand pounds for reliable information as to the manufacture of howitzers and tanks in England.

"So far, it's not very exciting," Hillyard remarked with disappointment, as he turned the leaf. But the letter progressed in interest.

A third sum of a thousand pounds was offered for a list of the postal sections on the British front, with the name, initials and rank of a really good and reliable British soldier in each section who was prepared to receive and answer correspondence.

Fairbairn chuckled and observed:

"I think Herr Zimmermann might be provided with a number of such good and reliable soldiers selected by our General Staff," and he added with a truculent snort, "We could do with that sum of a thousand pounds here. You must put in a claim for it, Hillyard. Otherwise they'll snaffle it in London."

Fairbairn, once a mild north-country schoolmaster, of correct phraseology and respectable demeanour, had, under the pressure of his service, developed like that white sheet of notepaper. He had suffered

> *"A sea-change
> Into something rich and strange"*

and from a schoolmaster had become a buccaneer with a truculent manner and a mind of violence. London, under which name he classed all Government officials, offices, departments, and administrations, particularly roused his ire. London was ignorant, London was stupid, London was always doing him and the other buccaneers down, was always snaffling something which he ought to have. Fairbairn, uttering one snort of satisfaction, would have shot it with his Browning.

"Get it off your chest, old man," said Hillyard soothingly, "and we'll go on with this letter. It looks to me as if——" He was glancing onwards and checked himself with an exclamation. His face became grave and set.

"Listen to this," and he read aloud, translating as he went along.

> *"Since the tubes have been successful in France, the device should be extended to England. B45 is obviously suitable for the work. A submarine will sink letters for the Embassy in Madrid and a parcel of the tubes between the twenty-seventh and the thirtieth of July, within Spanish territorial waters off the Cabo de Cabron. A green light will be shown in three short flashes from the sea and it should be answered from the shore by a red and a white and two reds."*

Hillyard leaned back in his chair.

"B45," he cried in exasperation. "We get no nearer to him."

"Wait a bit!" Fairbairn interposed. "We are a deal nearer to him through Zimmermann's very letter here. What are these tubes which have been so successful in France? Once we get hold of them and understand them and know what end they are to serve, we may get an idea of the kind of man obviously suitable for handling them."

"Like B45," said Hillyard.

"Yes! The search will be narrowed to one kind of man. Oh, we shall be much nearer, if only we get the tubes—if only the Germans in Madrid don't guess this letter's gone astray to us."

Hillyard had reflected already upon that contingency.

"But why should they? The sleeping-car man is held *incomunicado*. There is no reason why they should know anything about this letter at all, if we lay our plans carefully."

He folded up the letter and locked it away in the drawer. He looked for a while out of the window of the saloon. The yacht had rounded the Cabo San Antonio. It was still the forenoon.

"This is where José Medina has got to come in," he declared. "You must go to Madrid, Fairbairn, and keep an eye on Mr. Jack Williams.

Meanwhile, here José Medina has got to come in."

Fairbairn reluctantly agreed. He would much rather have stayed upon the coast and shared in the adventure, but it was obviously necessary that a keen watch should be kept in Madrid.

"Very well," he said, "unless, of course, you would like to go to Madrid yourself."

Hillyard laughed.

"I think not, old man."

He mounted the ladder to the bridge and gave the instructions to the Captain, and early that evening the *Dragonfly* was piloted into the harbour of Alicante. Hillyard and Fairbairn went ashore. They had some hours to get through before they could take the journey they intended. They sauntered accordingly along the esplanade beneath the palm trees until they came to the Casino. Both were temporary members of that club, and they sat down upon the cane chairs on the broad sidewalk. A military band was playing on the esplanade a little to their right, and in front of them a throng of visitors and townspeople strolled and sat in the evening air. Hillyard smiled as he watched the kaleidoscopic grouping and regrouping of men and children and women. The revolutions of his life, a subject which in the press of other and urgent matters had fallen of late into the background of his thoughts, struck him again as wondrous and admirable. He began to laugh with enjoyment. He looked at Fairbairn. How dull in comparison the regular sequences of his career!

"I wandered about here barefoot and penniless," he said, "not so very long ago. On this very pavement!" He struck it with his foot, commending to Fairbairn the amazing fact. "I have cleaned boots," and he called to a boy who was lying in wait with a bootblack's apparatus on his back for any dusty foot. "Chico, come and clean my shoes." He jested with the boy with the kindliness of a Spaniard, and gave him a shining peseta. Hillyard was revelling in the romance of his life under the spur of the excitement which the affair of the letter had fired in him. "Yes, I wandered here, passing up and down in front of this very Casino."

And Fairbairn saw his face change and his eyes widen as though he recognised some one in the throng beneath the trees.

"What is it?" Fairbairn asked, and for a little while Hillyard did not answer. His eyes were not following any movements under the trees. They saw no one present in Alicante that day. Slowly he turned to Fairbairn, and answered in voice of suspense:

"Nothing! I was just remembering—and wondering!"

He remained sunk in abstraction for a long time. "It can't be!" at grips with "If it could be!" and a rising inspiration that "It was!" A man had once tried him out with questions about Alicante, a man who was afraid lest he should have seen too much. But Hillyard had learnt to hold his tongue when he had only inspirations to go upon, and he disclosed nothing of this to Fairbairn.

Later on, when darkness had fallen, the two men drove in a motorcar southwards round the bay and through a shallow valley to the fishing village of Torrevieja. When you came upon its broad beach of shingle and sand, with its black-tarred boats hauled up, and its market booths, you might dream that you had been transported to Broadstairs—except for one fact. The houses are built in a single story, since the village is afflicted with earthquakes. Two houses rise higher than the rest, the hotel and the Casino. In the Casino Hillyard found José Medina's agent for those parts sitting over his great mug of beer; and they talked together quietly for a long while.

Thus Martin Hillyard fared in those days. He played with life and death, enjoying vividly the one and ever on the brink of the other, but the deep, innermost realities of either had as yet touched him not at all.

CHAPTER XVII

On a Cape of Spain

The great cape thrusts its knees far out into the Mediterranean, and close down by the sea on the very point a lighthouse stands out from the green mass like a white pencil. South-westwards the land runs sharply back in heights of tangled undergrowths and trees, overhangs a wide bay and drops at the end of the bay to the mouth of a spacious, empty harbour. Eastwards the cape slopes inland at a gentler angle with an undercliff, a narrow plateau, and behind the plateau mountain walls. Two tiny fishing villages cluster a mile or two apart at the water's edge, and high up on the cape's flanks here and there a small rude settlement clings to the hillside. There are no roads to the cape. From the east you may ride a horse towards it, and lose your way. From the west you must approach by boat. So remote and unvisited is this region that the women in these high villages, their homes cut out of the actual brown rock, still cover their faces with the Moorish veil.

There are no roads, but José Medina was never deterred by the lack of roads. His business, indeed, was a shy one, and led him to prefer wild country. A high police official in one great town said of him:

"For endurance and activity there is no one like José Medina between the sea and the Pyrenees. You think him safe in Mallorca and look! He lands one morning from the steamer, jumps into a motorcar, and in five minutes—whish!—he is gone like the smoke of my cigarette. He will drive his car through our mountains by tracks, of which the guardia civil does not even know the existence."

By devious tracks, then, now through narrow gullies in brown and barren mountains, now striking some village path amidst peach trees and marguerites, José Medina drove Martin Hillyard down to the edge of the sea. Here amongst cactus bushes in flower, with turf for a carpet, a camp had been prepared near to one of the two tiny villages. José Medina was king in this region. The party arrived in the afternoon of the twenty-sixth day of the month, all of the colour of saffron from the dust-clouds the car had raised, and Hillyard so stiff and bruised with the intolerable jolting over ruts baked to iron, that he could hardly climb down on to the ground. He slept that night amidst such a music of birds as he had never believed possible one country could produce. Through the night of the twenty-sixth he and José Medina watched; their lanterns ready to their hands. Lights there were in plenty on the sea, but they were the lights of acetylene lamps used by the fishermen of those parts to attract the fish; and the morning broke with the lighthouse flashing wanly over a smooth sea, pale as fine jade.

"There are three more nights," said Hillyard. He was a little dispirited after the fatigue of the day before and the long, empty vigil on the top of the day.

The next watch brought no better fortune. There was no moon; the night was of a darkness so clear that the stars threw pale and tremulous paths over the surface of the water, and from far away the still air vibrated from time to time with the throbbing of propellers as the ships without lights passed along the coast.

Hillyard rose from the blanket on which he and José Medina had been lying during the night. It had been spread on a patch of turf in a break of the hill some hundreds of feet above the sea. He was cold. The blanket was drenched and the dew hung like a frost on bush and grass.

"It looks as if they had found out," he said.

"This is only the second night," said José Medina.

"It all means so much to me," replied Hillyard, shivering in the briskness of the morning.

"Courage, the little Marteen!" cried José Medina. "After breakfast and a few hours' sleep, we shall take a rosier view."

Hillyard, however, could not compose himself to those few hours. The dread lest the Germans should have discovered the interception of their letters weighed too heavily upon him. Even in the daylight he needs must look out over that placid sunlit sea and imagine here and there upon its surface the low tower and grey turtle-back of a submarine. Success here might be so great a thing, so great a saving of lives, so dire a blow to the enemy. Somehow that day slowly dragged its burning hours to sunset, the coolness of the evening came, and the swift darkness upon its heels, and once more, high up on the hillside, the vigil was renewed. And at half past one in the morning, far away at sea, a green light, bright as an emerald, flashed thrice and was gone.

"Did I not say to you, 'Have courage'?" said José Medina.

"Quick! the Lanterns!" replied Hillyard. "The red first! Good! Now the white. So! And the red again. Now we must wait!" and he sank down again upon the blanket. All the impatience and languor were gone from him. The moment had come. He was at once steel to meet it.

"Yes," said José Medina, "we shall see nothing more now for a long while."

They heard no sound in that still night; they saw no gleam of lights. It seemed to Hillyard that æons passed before José touched him on the elbow and pointed downwards.

"Look!" he whispered excitedly.

Right at their very feet the long, grim vessel lay, so near that Hillyard had the illusion he could pitch a stone on to the conning tower. He now held his breath, lest his breathing should be heard. Then the water splashed, and a moment afterwards the submarine turned and moved to sea. They gave it five minutes, and then climbed down to a tiny creek. A rowing-boat lay in readiness there, with one man at the tiller and two at the oars.

"You saw it, Manuel?" said Medina as he and Hillyard stepped in.

"Yes, Señor José. It was very close. Oh, they know these waters!"

The oars churned the phosphorescent water into green fire, and the foam from the stem of the boat sparkled as though jewels were scattered into it by the oarsmen as they rowed. They stopped alongside a little white buoy which floated on the water. The buoy was attached to a rope; that again to a chain. A mat was folded over the side of the boat and the chain drawn cautiously in and coiled without noise. Hillyard saw the two men who were hauling it in bend suddenly at their work and heave with a greater effort.

"It is coming," said one of them, and the man at the tiller went forward to help them. Hillyard leaned over the side of the heavy boat and stared down into the water. But the night was too dark for him to see anything but the swirl of green fire made by the movement of the chain and the fire-drops falling from the links. At last something heavy knocked against the boat's flanks.

"Once more," whispered the man from the tiller. "Now!"

And the load was perched upon the gunwale and lowered into the boat. It consisted of three square and bulky metal cases, bound together by the chain.

"We have it, my friend Marteen," whispered José Medina, with a laugh of sheer excitement. He was indeed hardly less stirred than Hillyard himself. "Not for nothing did the little Marteen lead the horse across the beach of Benicassim. Now we will row back quickly. We must be far away from here by the time the world is stirring."

The boatmen bent to their oars with a will, and the boat leaped upon the water. They had rowed for fifty yards when suddenly far away a cannon boomed. The crew stopped, and every one in the boat strained his eyes seawards. Some one whispered, and Hillyard held up his hand for silence.

Thus they sat immobile as figures of wax for the space of ten minutes. Then Hillyard relaxed from his attention.

"They must have got her plump with the first shot," he said; and, indeed, there was no other explanation for that boom of a solitary cannon across the midnight sea.

José Medina laughed.

"So the little Marteen had made his arrangements?"

"What else am I here for?" retorted the little Marteen, and though he too laughed, a thrill of triumph ran through the laugh. "It just needed that shot to round all off. I was so afraid that we should not hear it, that it might never be fired. Now it will never be known, if your men keep silent, whether they sunk their cargo or were sunk with it on board."

The crew once more drove the blades of their oars through the water, and did not slacken till the shore was reached. They clambered up the rocks to their camp bearing their treasure, and up from the camp again to the spot where José's motorcar was hidden. José talked to the boatmen while the cans were stowed away in the bottom of the car, and then turned to Hillyard.

"There will be no sign of our camp at daybreak. The tent will be gone—everything. If our luck holds—and why should it not?—no one need ever know that the Señor Marteen and his friend José Medina picnicked for three days upon that cape."

"But the lighthouse-keepers! What of them?" objected Hillyard. In him, too, hope and excitement were leaping high. But this objection he offered up on the altars of the gods who chastise men for the insolence of triumph.

"What of them?" José Medina repeated gaily. "They, too, are my friends this many a year." He seated himself at the wheel of the car. "Come, for we cannot drive fast amongst these hills in the dark."

Hillyard will never forget to the day of his death that wild passage through the mountains. Now it was some sudden twist to avoid a precipice, now a jerk and a halt whilst José stared into the darkness ahead of him; here the car jolted suddenly over great stones, then it sank to the axle in soft dust; at another place the bushes whipped their faces; and again they must descend and build a little bridge of boughs and undergrowth over a rivulet. But so high an elation possessed him that he was unconscious both of the peril and the bruises. He could have sung aloud. They stopped an hour after daybreak and breakfasted by the side of the car in a high country of wild flowers. The sun was hidden from them by a barrier of hills.

"We shall strike an old mine-road in half an hour," said José Medina, "and make good going."

They came into a district of grey, weathered rock, and, making a wide circuit all that day, crept towards nightfall down to the road between Aguilas and Cartagena; and once more the sea lay before them.

"We are a little early," said Medina. "We will wait here until it is dark. The carabineros are not at all well disposed to me, and there are a number of them patrolling the road."

They were above the road and hidden from it by a hedge of thick bushes. Between the leaves Hillyard could see a large felucca moving westwards some miles from the shore and a long way off on the road below two tiny specks. The specks grew larger and became two men on horses. They became larger still, and in the failing light Hillyard was just able to distinguish that they wore the grey uniform of the Guardia Civil.

"Let us pray," said Medina with a note of anxiety in his voice, "that they do not become curious about our fishing-boat out there!"

As he spoke the two horsemen halted, and did look out to sea. They conversed each with the other.

"If I were near enough to hear them!" said José Medina, and he suddenly turned in alarm upon Hillyard. "What are you doing?" he said.

Hillyard had taken a large .38 Colt automatic pistol from his pocket. His face was drawn and white and very set.

"I am doing nothing—for the moment," he answered. "But those two men must ride on before it is dark and too late for me to see them."

"But they are of the Guardia Civil," José Medina expostulated in awed tones.

To the Spaniard, the mere name of the Guardia Civil, so great is its prestige, and so competent its personnel, inspires respect.

"I don't care," answered Hillyard savagely. "In this war why should two men on a road count at all? Let them go on, and nothing will happen."

José Medina, who had been assuming the part of protector and adviser to his young English friend, had now the surprise of his life. He found himself suddenly relegated to the second place and by nothing but sheer force of character. Hillyard rested the point of his elbow on the earth and supported the barrel of his Colt upon his left forearm. He aimed carefully along the sights.

"Let them go on!" he said between his teeth. "I will give them until the last moment—until the darkness begins to hide them. But not a moment longer. I am not here, my friend, for my health. I am here because there is a war."

"The little Marteen" was singularly unapparent at this moment Here was just the ordinary appalling Englishman who had not the imagination to understand what a desperately heinous crime it would be to kill two of the Guardia Civil, who was simply going to do it the moment it became necessary, and would not lose one minute of his sleep until his dying day because he had done it. José Medina was completely at a loss as he looked into the grim indifferent face of his companion. The two horsemen were covered. The Colt would kill at more than five hundred yards, and it had no more to do than carry sixty. And still those two fools sat on their horses, and babbled to one another, and looked out to sea.

"What am I to do with this loco Inglés?" José Medina speculated, wringing his hands in an agony of apprehension. He had no share in those memories which at this moment invaded Martin Hillyard, and touched every fibre of his soul. Martin Hillyard, though his eye never left the sights of his Colt nor his mind wavered from his purpose, was with a subordinate consciousness stealing in the dark night up the footpath between the big, leafy trees over the rustic railway bridge to the summit of the hill. He was tramping once more through lanes, between fields, and stood again upon a hillock of Peckham Rye, and saw the morning break in beauty and in wonder over London. The vision gained from the foolish and romantic days of his boyhood, steadied his finger upon the trigger after all these years.

Then to José's infinite relief the two horsemen rode on. The long, black, shining barrel of the Colt followed them as they dwindled on the road. They turned a corner, and as Hillyard replaced his pistol in his pocket, José Medina rolled over on his back, and clapped his hands to his face.

"You might have missed," he gasped. "One of them at all events."

Hillyard turned to him with a grin. The savage was not yet exorcised.

"Why?" he asked. "Why should I have missed one of them? It was my business not to."

José Medina flung up his hands.

"I will not argue with you. We are not made of the same earth."

Hillyard's face changed to gentleness.

"Pretty nearly, my friend," he said, and he laid a hand on José Medina's shoulder. "For we are good friends—such good friends that I do not scruple to drag you into the same perils as myself."

Hillyard had not wasted his time during those three years when he loafed and worked about the quays of Southern Spain. He touched the right chord now with an unerring skill. Hillyard might be the mad Englishman, the loco Inglés! But to be reckoned by one of them as one of them—here was an insidious flattery which no one of José Medina's upbringing could possibly resist.

At nightfall they drove down across the road on to the beach. A rowing-boat was waiting, and Medina's manager from Alicante beside the boat on the sand. The cases were quickly transferred from the car to the boat.

"We will take charge of the car," said José to his manager, and he stepped into the boat, and sat down beside Hillyard. "This is my adventure. I see it through to the end," he explained.

A mile away the felucca picked them up. Hillyard rolled himself up in a rug in the bows of the boat. He looked up to the stars tramping the sky above his head.

"And gentlemen in England now a-bed."

Drowsily he muttered the immemorial line, and turning on his side slept as only the tired men who know they have done their work can sleep. He was roused in broad daylight. The felucca was lying motionless upon the water; no land was anywhere in sight; but above the felucca towered the tall side of the steam yacht *Dragonfly*.

Fairbairn was waiting at the head of the ladder. The cases were carried into the saloon and opened. The top cases were full of documents and letters, some private, most of them political.

"These are for the pundits," said Hillyard. He put them back again, and turned to the last case. In them were a number of small glass tubes, neatly packed in cardboard boxes with compartments lined with cotton wool.

"This is our affair, Fairbairn," he said. He took one out, and a look of perplexity crept over his face. The tube was empty. He tried another and another, and then another; every one of the tubes was empty.

"Now what in the world do you make of that?" he asked.

The tubes had yet to be filled and there was no hint of what they were to be filled with.

"What I am wondering about is why they troubled to send the tubes at all?" said Fairbairn slowly. "There's some reason, of course, something perhaps in the make of the glass."

He held one of the tubes up to the light. There was nothing to distinguish it from any one of the tubes in which small tabloids are sold by chemists.

Hillyard got out of his bureau the letter in which these tubes were mentioned.

"'They have been successful in France,'" he said, quoting from the letter. "The scientists may be able to make something of them in Paris. This letter and the tubes together may give a clue. I think that I had better take one of the boxes to Paris."

"Yes," said Fairbairn gloomily. "But——" and he shrugged his shoulders.

"But it's one of the ninety per cent, which go wrong, eh?" Hillyard finished the sentence with bitterness. Disappointment was heavy upon both men. Hillyard, too, was tired by the tension of these last sleepless days. He had not understood how much he had counted upon success.

"Yes, it's damnably disheartening," he cried. "I thought these tubes might lead us pretty straight to B45."

"B45!"

The exclamation came from José Medina, who was leaning against the doorpost of the saloon, half in the room, half out on the sunlit deck. He had placed himself tactfully aloof. The examination of the cases was none of his business. Now, however, his face lit up.

"B45." He shut the door and took a seat at the table. "I can tell you about B45."

CHAPTER XVIII

The Uses of Science

It was Hillyard's creed that chance will serve a man very capably, if he is equipped to take advantage of its help; and here was an instance. The preparation had begun on the morning when Hillyard took the *Dragonfly* into the harbour of Palma. Chance had offered her assistance some months later in an hotel at Madrid; as Medina was now to explain.

"The day after you left Mallorca," said José Medina, "it was known all over Palma that you had come to visit me."

"Of course," answered Martin.

"I was in consequence approached almost immediately, by the other side."

"I expected that. It was only natural."

"There is a young lady in Madrid," continued José Medina.

"Carolina Muller?"

"No."

"Rosa Hahn, then."

"Yes," said José Medina.

José rose and unlocking a drawer in his bureau took out from it a sheaf of photographs. He selected one and handed it with a smile to Hillyard. It was the portrait of a good-looking girl, tall, dark, and intelligent, but heavy about the feet, dressed in Moorish robes, and extended on a divan in Oriental indolence against a scene cloth which outdid the luxuries of Llalla Rookh.

"That's the lady, I think."

Medina gazed at the picture with delight. He touched his lips with his fingers, and threw a kiss to it. His sharp, sallow face suddenly flowered into smiles.

"Yes. What a woman! She has real intelligence," he exclaimed fervently.

José Medina was in the habit of losing his heart and keeping his head a good many times in an ordinary year.

"It's an extraordinary thing," Martin Hillyard remarked, "that however intelligent they are, not one of these young ladies can resist the temptation to have her portrait taken in Moorish dress at the photographer's in the Alhambra."

José Medina saw nothing at all grotesque or ridiculous in this particular foible.

"They make such charming pictures," he cried.

"And it is very useful for us, too," remarked Hillyard. "The photographer is a friend of mine."

José was still gazing at the photograph.

"Such a brain, my friend! She never told a story the second time differently, however emotional the moment. She never gave away a secret."

"She probably didn't know any," said Hillyard.

But José would not hear of such a reason.

"Oh, yes! She has great influence. She knows people in Berlin—great people. She is their friend, and I cannot wonder. What an intelligence!"

Martin Hillyard laughed.

"She seems to have fairly put it over you at any rate," he said. He was not alarmed at José Medina's fervour. For he knew that remarkable man's capacity for holding his tongue even in the wildest moments of his temporary passions. But he took the photograph away from Medina and locked it up again. The rapturous reminiscences of Rosa Hahn's intelligence checked the flow of that story which was to lead him to B45.

"So you know about her?" José said with an envious eye upon the locked drawer.

"A little," said Martin Hillyard.

Rosa Hahn was a clerk in the office of the Hamburg-Amerika Line before the war, and in the Spanish Department. She was sent to Spain in the last days of July, 1914, upon Government work, and at a considerable salary, which she enjoyed. She seemed indeed to have done little else, and Berlin, after a year, began to complain. Berlin had a lower opinion of both her social position and her brains than José Medina had formed. Berlin needed results, and failing to obtain them, proceeded to hint more and more definitely that Rosa had better return to her clerk's stool in Hamburg. Rosa, however, had been intelligent enough to make friends with one or two powerful Germans in Spain; and they pleaded for her with this much success. She was given another three months within which period she must really do something to justify her salary. So much Martin Hillyard already knew; he learnt now that José Medina had provided the great opportunity. To snatch him with his two hundred motor feluccas and his eighteen thousand men from the English—here was something really worth doing.

"What beats me," said Hillyard, "is why they didn't try to get at you before."

"They didn't," said Medina.

Rosa, it seemed, used the argument which is generally sound; that the old and simple tricks are the tricks which win. She discovered the hotel at which José Medina stayed in Madrid, and having discovered it she went to stay there herself. She took pains to become friendly with the manager and his staff, and by professing curiosity and interest in the famous personage, she made sure not only that she would have fore-warning of his arrival, but that José Medina himself would hear of a charming young lady to whom he appealed as a hero of romance. She knew José to be of a coming-on disposition—and the rest seemed easy. Only, she had not guarded against the workings of Chance.

The hotel was the Hotel de Napoli, not one of the modern palaces of cement and steel girders, built close to the Prado, but an old house near the Puerto del Sol, a place of lath and plaster walls and thin doors; so that you must not raise your voice unless you wish your affairs to become public property. To this house José Medina came as he had many times come before, and Chance willed that he should occupy the next room to that occupied by Rosa Hahn. It was the merest accident. It was the merest accident, too, that José Medina whilst he was unpacking his bag heard his name pronounced in the next room. José Medina, with all his qualities, was of the peasant class with much of the peasant mind. He was inquisitive, and he was suspicious. Let it be said in his defence that he had enemies enough ready to pull him down, not only, as we have seen, amongst his rivals on the coast, but here, amongst the Government officials of Madrid. It cost him a pretty penny annually to keep his balance on the tightrope, as it was. He stepped noiselessly over to the door and listened. The voices were speaking in Spanish, one a woman's voice with a guttural accent.

"Rosa Hahn," said Hillyard as the story was told to him in the cabin of the yacht.

"The other a man's voice. But again it was a foreign voice, not a Spaniard's. But I could not distinguish the accent."

"Greek, do you think?" asked Hillyard. "There is a Levantine Greek high up in the councils of the Germans."

José Medina, however, did not know.

"Here were two foreigners talking about me, and fortunately in Spanish. I was to arrive immediately; Rosa was to make my acquaintance. What my relations were with this man, Hillyard—yes, you came into the conversation, my friend, too—I was quickly to be persuaded to tell. Oh—you have a saying—everything in your melon patch was lovely."

"Not for nothing has the American tourist come to Spain," Hillyard murmured.

"Then their voices dropped a little, and your B45 was mentioned—once or twice. And a name in connection with B45 once or twice. I did not understand what it was all about."

"But you remember the name!" Fairbairn exclaimed eagerly.

"Yes, I do."

"Well, what was it?"

It was again Fairbairn who spoke. Hillyard had not moved, nor did he even look up.

"It was Mario Escobar," said José Medina; and as he spoke he knew that the utterance of the name awakened no surprise in Martin Hillyard. Hillyard filled his pipe from the tobacco tin, and lighted it before he spoke.

"Do you know anything of this Mario Escobar?" he asked, "you who know every one?"

José Medina shrugged his shoulders, and threw up his hands.

"There was some years ago a Mario Escobar at Alicante," and José Medina saw Hillyard's eyes open and fix themselves upon him with an unblinking steadiness. Just so José Medina imagined might some savage animal in a jungle survey the man who had stumbled upon his lair.

"That Mario Escobar, a penniless, shameless person, was in business with a German, the German Vice-Consul. He went from Alicante to London."

"Thank you," said Hillyard. He rose from his chair and went to the window. But he saw nothing of the deck outside, or the sea beyond. He saw a man at a supper party in London a year before the war began, betraying himself by foolish insistent questions uttered in fear lest his close intimacy with Germans in Alicante should be known.

"I have no doubt that Mario Escobar came definitely to England, long before the war, to spy," said Hillyard gravely. He returned to the table, and took up again one of the empty glass tubes.

"I wonder what he was to do with these."

José Medina had opened the door of the saloon once more. A beam of sunlight shot through the doorway, and enveloped Hillyard's arm and hand. The tiny slim phial glittered like silver; and to all of them in the cabin it became a sinister engine of destruction.

"That, as you say, is your affair. I must go," said José, and he shook hands with Hillyard and Fairbairn, and went out on to the deck. "*Hasta luego!*"

"*Hasta ahora!*" returned Hillyard; and José Medina walked down the steps of the ladder to his felucca. The blue sea widened between the two vessels; and in a week, Hillyard descended from a train on to the platform of the Quai D'Orsay station in Paris. He had the tubes in his luggage, and one box of them he took that morning to Commandant Marnier at his office on the left bank of the river with the letter which gave warning of their arrival.

"You see what the letter says," Hillyard explained. "These tubes have been very successful in France."

Marnier nodded his head:

"If you will leave them with me, I will show them to our chemists, and perhaps, in a few days, I will have news for you."

For a week Hillyard took his ease in Paris and was glad of the rest in the midst of those strenuous days. He received one morning at his hotel, a batch of letters, many of which had been written months before. But two were of recent date. Henry Luttrell wrote to him:

> "*My battalion did splendidly and our debt to old Oakley is great. There is only a handful of us left and we are withdrawn, of course, from the lines. By some miracle I escaped without a hurt. Everybody has been very generous, making it up to us for our bad times. The Corps Commander came and threw bouquets in person, and we hear that D.H. himself is going out of his way to come and inspect us. I go home on leave in a fortnight and hope to come back in command of the battalion. Perhaps we may meet in London. Let me hear if that is possible.*"

The second letter had been sent from Rackham Park, and in it Millie Splay wrote:

> "*We have not heard from you for years. Will you be in England this August? We are trying to gather again our old Goodwood party. Both Dennis Brown and Harold Jupp will be home on leave. There will be no Goodwood of course, but there is a meeting at Gatwick which is easily reached from here. Do come if you can and bring your friend with you, if he is in London and has nothing better to do. We have all been reading about him in the papers, and Chichester is very proud of belonging to the same mess, and says what a wonderful thing it must be to be able to get into the papers like that, without trying to.*"

Hillyard could see the smile upon Lady Splay's face as she wrote that sentence. Hillyard laughed as he read it but it was less in amusement as from pleasure at the particular information which this sentence contained. Harry Luttrell had clearly won a special distinction in the hard fighting at Thiepval. There was not a word in Harry's letter to suggest it.

There would not be. All his pride and joy would be engrossed by the great fact that his battalion had increased its good name.

There was a closing sentence in Millie Splay's letter which brought another smile to his lips.

"Linda Spavinsky is, alas, going as strong as ever. She was married last meek, in violet, as you will remember, to the Funeral March of a Marionette and already she is in the throes of domestic unhappiness. Her husband, fleshy, of course, red in the face, and accustomed to sleep after dinner, simply won't *understand her."*

Here again Hillyard was able to see the smile on Millicent Splay's face, but it was a smile rather rueful and it ended, no doubt, in a sigh of annoyance. Hillyard himself was caught away to quite another scene. He was once more in the small motorcar on the top of Duncton Hill, and looked out over the Weald of Sussex to the Blackdown and Hindhead, and the slopes of Leith Hill, imagined rather than seen, in the summer haze. He saw Joan Whitworth's rapt face, and heard her eager cry.

"Look out over the Weald of Sussex, so that you can carry it away with you in your breast. Isn't it worth everything—banishment, suffering—everything? Not the people so much, but the earth itself and the jolly homes upon it!"

A passage followed which disturbed him:

"There are other things too. My magnolia is still in bud. I dread a blight before the flower opens."

It was a cry of distress—nothing less than that—uttered in some moment of intense depression. Else it would never have been allowed to escape at all.

Hillyard folded up the letter. He would be going home in any case. There were those tubes. There was B45. He had enjoyed no leave since he had left England. Yes, he would go down to Rackham Park, and take Harry Luttrell with him if he could.

Two days later the Commandant Marnier came to see him at the Ritz Hotel. They dined together in a corner of the restaurant.

"We have solved the problem of those tubes," said Marnier. "They are nothing more nor less than time-fuses."

"Time-fuses!" Hillyard repeated. "I don't understand."

"Listen!"

Marnier looked around. There was no one near enough to overhear him, if he did not raise his voice; and he was careful to speak in a whisper.

"Two things." He ticked them off upon his fingers. "First, hydrofluoric acid when brought into contact with certain forms of explosive will create a fire. Second, hydrofluoric acid will bite its way through glass. The thicker the glass, the longer the time required to set the acid free. Do you follow?"

"Yes," said Hillyard.

"Good! Make a glass tube of such thickness that it will take hydrofluoric acid four hours and a half to eat its way through. Then fill it with acid and seal it up. You have a time-fuse which will act precisely in four hours and a half."

"If it comes into contact with the necessary explosive," Hillyard added.

"Exactly. Now attend to this! Our workmen in our munition factories work three hours and a half. Then they go to their luncheon."

"Munition factories!" said Hillyard with a start.

"Yes, my friend. Munition factories. We are short of labour as you know. Our men are in the firing line. We must get labour from some other source. And there is only one source."

"The neutrals," Hillyard exclaimed.

"Yes, the neutrals, and especially the neutrals who are near to us, who can come without difficulty and without much expense. We have a good many Spanish workmen in our munition factories and three of these factories have recently been burnt down. We have the proof now, thanks to you, that those little glass tubes so carefully manufactured in Berlin to last four hours and a half and no more, set the fires going."

"Proof, you say?" Hillyard asked earnestly. "It is not probability or moral certainty? It is actual bedrock proof?"

"Yes. For once our chemists had grasped how these tubes could be used, we knew what to look for when the workmen were searched on entering the factory. Two days ago we caught a man. He had one of these little tubes in his mouth and in the lining of his waistcoat, just a little high explosive, so little was necessary that it must escape notice unless you knew what to search for. Yes, we caught him and he, the good fellow, the good honest neutral"—it would be difficult to describe the bitterness and scorn which rang through Marnier's words, "has been kind enough to tell me how he earned his German pay as well as his French wages."

Hillyard leaned forward.

"Yes, tell me that!"

"On his way to the factory in the morning, he makes a call."

"Yes."

"The one on whom he calls fills the tube or has it just filled and gives it to the workman. The time fuse is set for four hours and a half. The workman has so arranged it that he will reach the factory half an hour after the tube is filled. He passes the searcher. At his place he takes off his waistcoat and hangs it up and in the pocket, just separated from the explosive by the lining of the waistcoat, he places, secretly, the tube. The tube has now four hours of life and the workman three and a half hours of work. When the whistle goes to knock off for luncheon, the workman leaves his waist coat still hanging up on the peg and goes out in the stream. But half an hour afterwards, halfway through the hour of luncheon, the acid reaches the explosive. There is a tiny explosion in that empty hall, not enough to make a great noise, but quite enough to start a big fire; and when the workmen return, the building is ablaze. No lives are lost, but the factory is burnt down."

Hillyard sat for a little while in thought.

"Perhaps you can tell me," he said at length. "I hear nothing from England or very little; and naturally. Are we obtaining Spanish workmen, too, for our munition factories?"

"Yes."

It was clear now why B45 was especially suitable for this work. B45 was Mario Escobar, a Spaniard himself.

"And filling the tubes! That is simple?"

"A child could do it," answered Marnier.

"Thank you," said Martin Hillyard.

The next evening he left Paris and travelling all night to Boulogne, reached London in the early afternoon of the following day. Twenty months had passed since he had set foot there.

CHAPTER XIX

Under Grey Skies Again

Hillyard landed in England athirst for grey skies. Could he have chosen the season of the year which should greet him, he would have named October. For the ceaseless bright blue of sea and heaven had set him dreaming through many a month past, of still grey mornings sweet with the smell of earth and thick hedgerows and the cluck of pheasants. But there were at all events the fields wondrously green after the brown hillsides and rusty grass, the little rich fields in the frames of their hedges, and the brown-roofed houses and the woods splashing their emerald branches in the sunlight. Hillyard travelled up through Kent rejoicing. He reached London in the afternoon, and leaving his luggage in his flat walked down to the house in the quiet street behind the Strand whence Commodore Graham overlooked the Thames.

But even in this backwater the changes of the war were evident. The brass plates had all gone from the door post and girls ran up and down the staircases in stockings which some Allied fairies had woven on Midsummer morning out of cobwebs of dew. They were, however, as unaware as of old of any Commodore Graham. Was he quite certain that he wanted to see Commodore Graham. And why? And, after all, was there a Commodore Graham? Gracious damsels looked blandly at one another, with every apparent desire to assist this sunburnt stranger. It seemed to Hillyard that they would get for him immediately any one else in the world whom he chose to name. It was just bitterly disappointing and contrarious that the one person he wished to see was a Commodore Graham. Oh, couldn't he be reasonable and ask for somebody else?

"Very well," said Hillyard with a smile. "There was a pretty girl with grey eyes, and I'll see her."

"The description is vague," said the young lady demurely.

"She is Miss Cheyne."

"Oh!" said one.

"Oh!" said another; and

"Will you follow me, please?" said a third, who at once became businesslike and brisk, and led him up the stairs. The door was still unvarnished. Miss Cheyne opened it, wearing the composed expression of attention with which she had greeted Hillyard when he had sought admission first. But her face broke up into friendliness and smiles, when she recognised him, and she drew him into the room.

"The Commodore's away for a week," she said. "He had come to the end: no sleep, nerves all jangled. He is up in Scotland shooting grouse."

Hillyard nodded. His news could wait a week very well, since it had waited already two years.

"And you?" he asked.

"Oh, I had a fortnight," replied Miss Cheyne, her eyes dancing at the recollection. It was her pleasure to sail a boat in Bosham Creek and out towards the Island. "Not a day of rain during the whole time."

"I think that I might have a month then, don't you?" said Hillyard, and Miss Cheyne opined that there would be no objection.

"But you will come back in a week," she stipulated, "won't you? The Commodore will be here on Thursday, and there are things accumulating which he must see to. So will you come on Friday?"

"Friday morning," Hillyard suggested.

Thursday was the day on which he should have travelled down to Rackham Park, but if he could finish his business on Friday morning, he would only lose one day.

"Friday morning then," said Miss Cheyne, and made a note of it.

Hillyard had thus a week in which to resume his friendships, arrange to write, at some distant time, a play, revisit his club and his tailor, and revel, as at a pageant, in the fresh beauty, the summer clothes, the white skin and clean-limbed boyishness of English girls. He went through, in a word, the first experiences of most men returned from a long sojourn in other climes; and they were ordinary enough. But the week was made notable for him by one small incident.

It was on the Monday and about five o'clock in the afternoon. He was walking from the Charing Cross Road towards Leicester Square, when, from a doorway ahead of him, a couple emerged. They did not turn his way but preceded him, so that he only saw their backs. But he had no doubt who one of the couple was. The fair hair, the tall, slim, long-limbed figure, the perverse sloppiness of dress which could not quite obscure her grace of youth, betrayed the disdainful prodigy of Rackham Park. The creator of Linda Spavinsky swam ahead of him. Had he doubted her identity, a glance at the door from which she had emerged would have dispelled the doubt. It was the entrance to a picture gallery, where, cubes and curves having served their turn and gone, the rotundists were having an innings. Everybody and everything was in rounds, palaces and gardens and ships and Westminster Bridge, and men and women were all in circles. The circle was the principle of life and art. Joan Whitworth would be drawn to the exhibition as a filing to a magnet. Undoubtedly Joan Whitworth was ahead of Hillyard and he began to hurry after her. But he checked himself after a few paces. Or rather the aspect of her companion checked him. His appearance was vaguely familiar, but that was all. It was not certainly Sir Chichester Splay, for the all-sufficient reason that the Private View had long gone by; since the very last week of the exhibition was announced in the window. Moreover, the man in front of him was younger than Sir Chichester.

The couple, however, crossed the road to the Square Garden, and Hillyard saw the man in profile. He stopped so suddenly that a man walking behind him banged heavily against his back. The man walked on and turned round after he had passed to stare at Hillyard. For Hillyard stood stock still, he was unaware that any one had run into him, in all his body his lips alone moved.

"Mario," he whispered. "Mario Escobar!"

The man who had been so far the foremost in his thoughts during the last weeks that he never thought that he could have failed to recognise him. Mario Escobar! And with Joan Whitworth. Millicent Splay's letter flashed back into his memory. The distress which he had seemed to hear loud behind the written words—was this its meaning and explanation? Joan Whitworth and Mario Escobar! Certainly Joan knew him! He was sitting next to her on the night when "The Dark Tower" was produced, sitting next to her, and talking to her. Sir Charles Hardiman had used some phrase to describe that conversation. Hillyard was strangely anxious to recapture the phrase. Escobar was talking to her with an air of intimacy a little excessive in a public place. Yes, that was the sentence.

Hillyard walked on quickly to his club.

"Is Sir Charles Hardiman here?" he asked of the hall porter.

"He is in the card-room, sir."

Martin Hillyard went up the stairs with a sense of relief. His position was becoming a little complicated. Mario Escobar was B45, and a friend of Joan Whitworth, and a friend of the Splays. There was one point upon which Martin Hillyard greatly needed information.

Hardiman, a little heavier and broader and more obese than when Hillyard had last seen him, was sitting by a bridge table overlooking the players. He never played himself, nor did he ever bet upon the game, but he took a curious pleasure in looking on, and would sit in the card-room by the hour engrossed in the fall of the cards. The sight of Hillyard, however, plucked him out of his occupation.

"So you're back!" he cried, heaving himself heavily out of his chair and shaking hands with Martin.

"For a month."

"I hear you have done very well," Sir Charles continued. "Have a whisky-and-soda."

"Thanks."

Hardiman touched the bell and led the way over to a sofa.

"Lucky man! The doctor's read the Riot Act to me! I met Luttrell in the Mall this morning, on his way back from Buckingham Palace. He had just been given his D.S.O."

Hardiman began to sit down, but the couch was low, and though he began the movement lazily, it went suddenly with a run, so that the springs of the couch jumped and twanged and his feet flew from beneath him.

"Yes, he has done splendidly," said Martin. "His battalion too. That's what he cares about."

Sir Charles needed a moment or two after he had set down to recover his equipoise. He wiped his forehead with his handkerchief.

"Luttrell told me you were both off to Rackham Park this week for Gatwick."

"That's right! But I shan't get down until Friday afternoon," said Hillyard.

The waiter put the glass of whisky-and-soda at his side, and he took a drink from it.

"Perhaps you are going too," he suggested.

Hardiman shook his head.

Hillyard was silent for a minute. Then he asked another question.

"Do you know who is going to be there beside Luttrell and myself?"

Sir Charles smiled.

"I don't know, but I fancy that you won't find him amongst the guests."

Hillyard was a little startled by the answer, but he did not betray the least sign of surprise. He pursued his questions.

"You know whom I have in my mind?"

"I drew a bow at a venture," answered Sir Charles.

"Shall I name him?" asked Hillyard.

"I will," returned Sir Charles. "Mario Escobar."

Hillyard nodded. He took another pull at his whisky-and-soda. Then he lit a cigarette and leaned forward, with his elbows upon his knees; and all the while Sir Charles Hardiman, his body in a majestic repose, contemplated him placidly. Hardiman had this great advantage in any little matter of debate; he never wished to move. Place him in a chair, and he remained, singularly immobile.

"Since you were so quick to guess at once the reason of my question," continued Hillyard, "I can draw an inference. Mario Escobar has been at Rackham Park a good deal?"

Sir Charles Hardiman's smile broadened.

"Even now you don't express your inference," he retorted. "You mean that Mario Escobar has been at Rackham Park too much." He paused whilst he drew out his cigarette-case and selected a cigarette from it. "And I agree," he added. "Mario Escobar is too picturesque a person for these primitive days."

Hillyard was not sure what Sir Charles Hardiman precisely meant. But on the other hand he was anxious to ask no direct questions concerning Escobar. He sought to enter in by another gate.

"Primitive?" he said.

"Yes. We have become rather primitive, especially the women. They have lost a deal of self-consciousness. They exact less. They give more—oh, superbly more! It's the effect of war, of course. They have jumped down off their little pinnacles. Let me put it coarsely. They are saved from rape by the fighting man, and they know it. Consequently all men benefit and not least," Sir Charles lit his cigarette, "that beast of abomination, the professional manipulator of women, the man who lives by them and on them, who cajoles them first and blackmails them afterwards, who has the little attentions, the appealing voice, in fact all the tricks of his trade ready at his fingers' ends. However, Millie Splay's awake to the danger now."

"Danger!" Hillyard sharply exclaimed.

"Quite right. It's too strong a word. I take it back," Hardiman agreed at once. But he was not in the habit of using words wildly. He had said exactly what he meant to say, and having aroused the attention which he meant to arouse, he calmly withdrew the word. "I rubbed it into Chichester's thick head that Escobar was overmuch at Rackham Park, and in the end—it percolated."

Much the same account of Escobar, with this instance of Rackham Park omitted, was given to Hillyard by Commodore Graham on the Friday morning.

"He is the kind of man whom men loathe and women like. He runs about London, gets a foot in here and there. You know what London is, even now in the midst of this war, with its inability to be surprised, and its indifference to strange things. You might walk down Regent Street dressed up as a Cherokee Indian, feathers and tomahawk and all, and how many

Cockneys would take the trouble to turn round and look at you twice? It was pretty easy for Escobar to slip about unnoticed."

Commodore Graham bent his head over the case of tubes which Hillyard had brought with him.

"We'll have a lookout kept for these things. There have been none of them in England up till now."

Martin Hillyard returned to the personality of Mario Escobar.

"Did you suspect him before?" he asked.

Commodore Graham pushed the cigarettes towards Hillyard.

"Scotland Yard has kept an eye on him. That sort of adventurer is always dangerous."

He rang the bell, and on Miss Cheyne's appearance called for what information the office had concerning Mario Escobar. Miss Cheyne returned with a book in which Escobar's dossier was included.

"Here he is," said Graham, and Hillyard, moving across to the bureau, followed Graham's forefinger across the written page. He was agent for the Compania de Navigacion del Sur d'España—a German firm on the black list, headquarters at Alicante. Escobar severed his connection with the company on the outbreak of war.

Graham raised his head to comment on the action.

"That, of course, was camouflage. But it checked suspicion for a time. Suspicion was first aroused," and he resumed reading again, "by his change of lodging. He lived in a small back bedroom in a boarding-house in Clarence Street, off Westbourne Grove, and concealed his address, having his letters addressed to his club, until February, 1915, upon which date he moved into a furnished flat in Maddox Street. Nothing further, however, happened to strengthen that suspicion until, in the autumn of that year, a letter signed Mario was intercepted by the censor. It was sent to a Diego Perez, the Director of a fruit company at Murcia, for Emma Grutsner."

"You sent me a telegram about her," exclaimed Hillyard, "in November."

Commodore Graham's forefinger travelled along the written lines and stopped at the number and distinguishing sign of the telegram, sent and received.

"Yes," continued Graham. "Here's your answer. 'Emma Grutzner is the governess in a Spanish family at Torrevieja, and she goes occasionally, once a month or so, to the house of Diego Perez in Murcia.'"

"Yes, yes! I routed that out," said Hillyard. "But I hadn't an idea that Mario Escobar was concerned in it."

"That wasn't mentioned?" asked the Commodore.

"No. I already knew, you see, of B45. If just a word had been added that it was Mario who was writing to Emma Grutzner we might have identified him months ago."

"Yes," answered Graham soothingly and with a proper compunction. He was not unused to other fiery suggestions from his subordinates that if only the reasons for his telegrams and the information on which his questions were based, were sent out with the questions themselves, better results in quicker time could be obtained. Telegrams, however, were going out and coming in all day; a whole array of cipherers and decipherers lived in different rookeries in London. Commodore Graham's activities embraced the high and the narrow seas, great Capitals and little tucked-away towns and desolate stretches of coast where the trade-winds blew. No doubt full explanations would have led in many cases to more satisfactory conclusions. But fuller explanations were out of all possibility. Even with questions fined down to the last succinct syllable the cables groaned. None of the objections were raised, however, by Commodore Graham. It was his business to keep men like Hillyard who were serving him well to their own considerable cost, in a good humour. Remorse was the line, not argument.

"What a pity! I *am* sorry," protested the Commodore. "It's my fault! There's nothing else to be said. I am to blame about it."

Martin Hillyard began to feel some compunction that he had ever suggested a fault in the composition of the telegram. But then, it was his business not to betray any such tenderness.

"If we could have in the future a little more information from London, it would save us a good deal of time," he said stonily. "Sometimes a surname is hurled at us, and will we find him, please, and cable home all details?"

"Yes, that is very wrong," the Commodore agreed. "We will have that changed." Then a bright idea appeared to occur to him. His face lighted up. "After all, in this instance the mistake hasn't done any real harm. For we have got our friend Mario Escobar now, and without these tubes and this letter from Berlin about the use of them and José Medina's account of the conversation in the next room we shouldn't have got him. The German governess wasn't enough. He's, after all, a neutral. Besides, there was nothing definite in his letter. But now——"

"Now you can deal with him?" asked Hillyard eagerly.

"To be sure," replied the Commodore. "We have no proof here to put him on his trial. But we have reasonable ground for believing him to be in communication with our enemies for the purpose of damaging us, and that's quite enough to lock him up until the end of the war."

He reached out his hand for the telephone and asked for a number.

"I am ringing up Scotland Yard," he said to Hillyard over the top of the instrument; and immediately Hillyard heard a tiny voice speaking as if summoned from another planet.

"Hallo!" cried Graham. "Is that you, A.C.? You remember Mario Escobar? Good. I have Hillyard here from the Mediterranean with a clear case. I'll come over and see you."

Mr. "A.C.", whose real name was Adrian Carruthers, thereupon took up the conversation at the other end of the line. The lines deepened upon the Commodore's forehead as he listened. Then he turned to Hillyard, and swore softly and whole-heartedly.

"Mario Escobar has vanished."

"But I saw him myself," Hillyard exclaimed. "I saw him in London."

"When?"

"On Monday afternoon."

Graham lifted the mouthpiece to his lips again.

"Wait a bit, A.C. Hillyard saw the man in London on Monday afternoon."

Again A.C. spoke at the other end from an office in Scotland Yard. Graham put down the instrument with a bang and hung up the receiver.

"He vanished yesterday. Could he have seen you?"

Hillyard shook his head.

"I think not."

"Oh, we'll get him, of course. He can't escape from the country. And we will get him pretty soon," Graham declared. He looked out of the window on to the river. "I wonder what in the world alarmed him, since it wasn't you?" he speculated slowly.

But both Scotland Yard and Commodore Graham were out of their reckoning for once. Mario Escobar was not alarmed at all. He had packed his bag, taken the tube to his terminus, bought his ticket and gone off in a train. Only no one had noticed him go; and that was all there was to it.

CHAPTER XX

Lady Splay's Preoccupations

"It's a good race to leave alone, Miranda," said Dennis Brown. "But if you want to back something, I should put a trifle on Kinky Jane."

"Thank you, Dennis," Miranda answered absently. She was standing upon the lawn at Gatwick with her face towards the line of bookmakers upon the far side of the railings. These men were shouting at the full frenzy of their voices, in spite of the heat and the dust. The ring was crowded, and even the enclosure more than usually full.

"But you won't get any price," Harold Jupp continued, and he waved an indignant arm towards the bookmakers. "I never saw such a crowd of pinchers in my life."

"Thank you, Harold," Miranda replied politely. She was aware that he was advising her, but the nature of the advice did not reach her mind. She was staring steadily in front of her.

Dennis Brown and Harold Jupp looked at one another in alarm. They knew well that sibylline look on the face of Miranda Brown. She was awaiting the moment of inspiration. She was all wrapped up in expectation of it. At times she glanced at her race-card, whilst a thoughtful frown puckered her pretty forehead, as though the name of the winning filly might leap out in letters of gold.

Dennis shook his head dolefully. For the one thing sure and certain was that the fatal moment of inspiration would come to Miranda in time to allow her to reach the railings before the start. Suddenly a name uttered by an apoplectic gentleman in a voice breaking with fine passion reached her ears, with the odds attached to it of nine to one.

Miranda's face cleared of all its troubles.

"Oh, why didn't I think of that before?" she said in an extremity of self-reproach. She walked straight to the apoplectic gentleman, followed by the unhappy pair of scientific punters.

"Callow Girl is nine to one, isn't it?"

The apoplectic gentleman smiled winningly.

"To you, missie."

Miranda laughed.

"I'll have ten pounds on it," she said, and did not hear the gasp of her husband behind her. She made a note of the bet in her little pocketbook.

"That's ninety pounds, anyway," she said, turning to her companions.

"They will just buy that simple little Callot frock with the embroidery."

Yes, racing was as easy as that to Miranda Brown. She wanted a simple little Callot frock which would cost ninety pounds, and Callow Girl was obviously marked out to win it for her.

"Then I shall be a Callot girl," she said gaily, and as neither of her companions enjoyed her witticism she stamped her small foot in vexation.

"Oh, how dull you both are!" she cried.

"Well, you see," Dennis rejoined, "we've had rather a bad day."

"So have I," returned Miranda indignantly. "Yet I keep up my spirits."

A look of blank amazement overspread the face of Dennis Brown. He gazed around as one who should say, "Did you ever see anything so amazing outside the Ark?"

Miranda corrected her remark with a laugh.

"Well, I mean I haven't won as much as I should have if I had backed winners." For she had really mastered the science of the race-course. She knew how to go racing. Her husband paid her losses and she kept her winnings.

Harold Jupp took her seriously by the arm.

"You ought to go into a home, Miranda," he advised. "You really ought. That little head was never meant for all this weighty thought."

Miranda walked across to the little stone terrace which looks down the course.

"Don't be foolish, Harold, but go and collect Colonel Luttrell if you can find him, whilst I see my filly win," she said. "Dennis has already gone to find the car and we propose to start immediately this race is over."

Miranda ascended the grass slope and saw the fillies canter down towards the starting post. From the chatter about her she gathered that the odds on Callow Girl had shortened. It was understood that a sum of money had been laid on her at the last moment. She was favourite before the flag was dropped and won by half a length. Miranda ran joyously down the slope.

"What did I tell you, Harold? Aren't I wonderful? And have you found Colonel Luttrell? You know Millie told us to look out for him?" she cried all in a breath.

Luttrell had written to Lady Splay to say that he would try to motor to Gatwick in time for the last races; and that he would look out for Jupp and Dennis Brown, whom he had already met earlier in the week at a dinner party given by Martin Hillyard.

"There's no sign of him," Harold Jupp answered.

There were two more races, but the party from Rackham Park did not wait for them. They drove over the flat country through Crawley and Horsham and came to the wooded roads between high banks where the foliage met overhead, and to the old stone bridges over quiet streams. Harold Jupp was home from Egypt, Dennis Brown from Salonika, and as the great downs, with their velvet forests, seen now over a thick hedge, now in an opening of branches like the frame of a locket, the marvel of the English countryside in summer paid them in full for their peril and endurance.

"I have a fortnight, Miranda," said Dennis, dropping a hand upon his wife's. "Think of it!"

"My dear, I have been thinking of nothing else for months," she said softly. Terrors there had been, nights and days of them, terrors there would be, but she had a fortnight now, perfect in its season, and in the meeting of old friends upon familiar ground—a miniature complete in beauty, like the glimpses of the downs seen through the openings amongst the boughs.

"Yes, a whole fortnight," she cried and laughed, and just for a second turned her head away, since just for a second the tears glistened in her eyes.

The car turned and twisted through the puzzle of the Petworth streets and mounted on to the Midhurst road. The three indefatigable race-goers found Lady Splay sitting with Martin Hillyard in the hall of Rackham Park.

"You had a good day, I hope," she said.

"It was wonderful," exclaimed Dennis Brown. "We didn't make any money except Miranda. But that didn't matter."

"All our horses were down the course," Harold Jupp explained. "They weren't running in their form at all"; and he added cheerfully: "But the war may be over before the winter, and then we'll go chasing and get it all back."

Millicent Splay rang for tea, just as Joan Whitworth came into the hall.

"You didn't see Colonel Luttrell then?" asked Lady Splay.

"No."

"He'll come down later then." She had an eye for Joan Whitworth as she spoke, but Joan was so utterly indifferent as to whether Colonel Luttrell would arrive or not that she could not stifle a sigh. She had gathered Luttrell into the party with some effort and now it seemed her effort was to be fruitless. Joan persisted in her mood of austere contempt for the foibles of the world. She was dressed in a gown of an indeterminate shade between drab and sage-green, which did its best to annul her. She had even come to sandals. There they were now sticking out beneath the abominable gown.

"She can't ruin her complexion," thought Millicent Splay. "That's one thing. But if she could, she would. Oh, I would love to smack her!"

Joan, quite unaware of Millie Splay's tingling fingers and indignant eyes, sat reading "Ferishtah's Fancies." Other girls might set their caps at the soldiers. Joan had got to be different. She had even dallied with the pacifists. Martin Hillyard had carried away so close a recollection of her on that afternoon when she had driven him through the golden sunset over Duncton Hill and of the brave words she had then spoken that he had to force himself to realise that this was indeed she.

Millicent Splay had three preoccupations that afternoon but none pressed upon her with so heavy a load of anxiety as her preoccupation concerning Joan Whitworth.

Martin crossed the room to Joan and sat upon the couch beside her.

"Didn't I see you in London, Miss Whitworth, on Monday afternoon?" he asked.

Joan met his gaze steadily.

"Did you? It was possible. I was in London on Monday. Where did you think you saw me?"

"Coming out of a picture gallery in Green Street."

Joan did not flinch, nor drop her eyes from his.

"Yes, you saw me," she replied. Then with a challenge in her voice she added distinctly, so that the words reached, as they were meant to reach, every one in that room. "I was with Mario Escobar."

The room suddenly grew still. Two years ago, Martin Hillyard reflected, Harold Jupp or Dennis would have chaffed her roundly about her conquest, and she would have retorted with good humour. Now, no one spoke, but a little sigh, a little movement of uneasiness came from Millie Splay. Joan did not take her eyes from Hillyard's face. But the blood mounted slowly over her throat and cheeks.

"Well?" she asked, and the note of challenge was a trifle more audible in her quiet voice. And since he was challenged, Hillyard answered:

"He is a German spy."

The words smote upon all in the room like a blow. Joan herself grew pale. Then she replied:

"People say that nowadays of every foreigner."

The moment of embarrassment was prolonged to a full minute—during which no one spoke. Then to the relief of every one, Sir Chichester Splay entered the hall. He had been sitting all day upon the

Bench. He had to attend the Flower Show in Chichester during the next week. Really the life of a country notable was a dog's life.

"You are going to make a speech at Chichester, Sir Christopher?" Jupp inquired.

"Oh no, my boy," replied Sir Chichester. "Make a speech indeed! And in this weather! Nothing would induce me. Me for the back benches, as our cousins across the Atlantic would say."

He spoke pompously, yet with a certain gratification as though Harold Jupp had asked him to dignify the occasion with a speech.

"Have the evening papers not arrived yet?" he asked, looking with suspicious eyes on Dennis Brown.

"No, I am not sitting on them this time," said Dennis.

"And Colonel Luttrell?"

After the evening papers, Sir Chichester thought politely of his guests. Millie Splay replied with hesitation. While the others of the company were shaking off their embarrassment, she was sinking deeper into hers.

"Colonel Luttrell has not come yet. Nor—nor—the other guest who completes our party."

Her voice trailed off lamentably into a plea for kind treatment and gentleness. Here was Millie Splay's second preoccupation. As it was Sir Chichester's passion to see his name printed in the papers, so it was Millie's to gather in the personages of the moment under her roof. She had promised that this party should be just a small one of old friends with Luttrell as the only newcomer. But personages were difficult to come by at this date, since they were either deep in work or out of the country altogether. They had to be brought down by a snap shot, and very often the bird brought down turned out to be a remarkably inferior specimen of his class. Millie Splay had been tempted and had fallen; and she was not altogether easy about the quality of her bird, now on its descent to her feet.

"I didn't know any one else was coming," said Sir Chichester, who really didn't care how much Lady Splay gratified her passion, so long as he got full satisfaction for his.

"No, nor any one else," said Dennis Brown severely. "He is a stranger."

"To you," replied Millie Splay, showing fight.

Harold Jupp advanced and planted himself firmly before her.

"Do you know him yourself, Lady Splay?" he asked.

"But of course I do," the poor lady exclaimed. "How absurd of you, Harold, to ask such a question! I met him at a party when Joan and I were in London at the beginning of this week." She caught again at her fleeting courage. "So I invited him, and he's coming this afternoon. I shall send the motor to meet him in an hour from now. So there's an end of the matter."

Harold Jupp shook his head sagely.

"We must see that the plate is all locked up safely tonight."

"There! I knew it would be like this," cried Millie Splay, wringing her hands. She remembered, from a war correspondent's article, that to attack is the only successful defence. She turned on Jupp.

"I won't be bullied by you, Harold! He's a most charming person, with really nice manners," she emphasised her praise of the absent guest, "and if only you will study him whilst he is here—all of you, you will be greatly improved at the end of your visit."

Harold Jupp was quite unimpressed by Millie Splay's outburst. He remained severely in front of her, judge, prosecutor and jury all in one, and all relentlessly against her.

"And what is his name?"

Lady Splay looked down and looked up.

"Mr. Albany Todd," she said.

"I don't like it," said Harold Jupp.

"No," added Dennis Brown sadly from a corner. "We can't like it, Lady Splay."

Lady Splay turned with her most insinuating smile towards Brown.

"Oh, Dennis, do be nice and remember this isn't your house," she cried. "You can be so unpleasant if you find any one here you don't like. Mr. Albany Todd's quite a famous person."

Harold Jupp, of the inquiring mind, still stood looking down on Lady Splay without any softening of his face.

"What for?" he asked.

Lady Splay groaned in despair.

"Oh, I was sure you were going to ask that. You are so unpleasant." She put her hand to her forehead. "But I know quite well. Yes, I do." Her face suddenly cleared. "He is a conversationalist—that's it—a great conversationalist. He is the sort of man," she spoke as one repeating a lesson, "who would have been welcome at the breakfast table of Mr. Rogers."

"Rogers?" Harold Jupp asked sternly. "I don't know him."

"And probably never will, Harold, I am sorry to say," said Lady Splay triumphantly. "Mr. Rogers was in heaven many years ago." She suddenly changed her note and began to implore. "Oh, do be pleasant, you and Dennis!"

Harold Jupp's mouth began to twitch, but he composed it again, with an effort, to the stern lines befitting the occasion.

"I'll tell you what I think, Lady Splay," said he, pronouncing judgment. "Your new guest's a Plater."

The dreadful expected word was spoken. Lady Splay broke into appeals, denials, threats. "Oh, he isn't, he isn't!" She turned to her husband. "Chichester, exert your authority! He's not a Plater really. He's not right down the course. And even if he were, they've got to be polite to him."

Sir Chichester, however, was the last man who could be lured into the expression of a definite opinion.

"My dear, I never interfere in the arrangements of the house. You have your realm. I have mine. I am sure those papers are being kept in the servants' hall," and he left the room hurriedly.

"Oh, how mean men are!" cried Millie; and they all began to laugh.

Lady Splay saw a glimpse of hope in their laughter and became much more cheerful.

"As you are not racing, dear," she said to Joan, "he will be quite a pleasant companion for you."

Sir Chichester returned with the evening papers. Dennis and Miranda and Harold Jupp rose to go upstairs and change into flannels; and suddenly, a good hour before his time, Harper, the butler, announced:

"Mr. Albany Todd."

Mr. Albany Todd was a stout, consequential personage, and ovoid in appearance. Thin legs broadened out to very wide hips, and from the hips he curved in again to a bald and shiny head, which in its turn curved inwards to a high, narrow crown. Lady Splay casting a look of appeal towards her refractory young guests hurried forward to meet him.

"This is my husband." She presented him to the others. "I was going to send the motorcar to meet the seven o'clock train."

"Oh, thank you, Lady Splay," Mr. Albany Todd returned in a booming voice. "I have been staying not more than twenty miles from here, with a dear old friend, a rare and inestimable being, Lord Bilberry, and he was kind enough to send me in."

"What, old man Bilberry," cried Harold Jupp. "Isn't he balmy?"

"Balmy, sir?" Mr. Todd asked in surprise. "He takes the air every morning, if that is what you mean." He turned again to Lady Splay. "He keeps the most admirable table. You must know him, Lady Splay. I will see to it."

"Thank you," said Millie Splay humbly.

"Ah, muffins!" said Mr. Albany Todd with glistening eyes. He ate one and took another. "These are really as good as the muffins I ate at a wonderful weekend party a fortnight ago."

The chatter of the others ceased. The great conversationalist, it seemed, was off. Miranda, Dennis, Harold Jupp, Sir Chichester, even Joan looked up with expectation.

"Yes," said Lady Splay, encouraging him. She looked around at her guests. "Now you shall see," she seemed to say.

"How we laughed! What sprightly talk! The fine flavour of that party is quite incommunicable. Just dear old friends, you see, intimate, congenial friends."

Mr. Albany Todd stopped. It appeared that he needed a question to be put to him. Lady Splay dutifully put it.

"And where did this party take place, Mr. Albany Todd?"

Mr. Albany Todd smiled and dusted the crumbs from his knees.

"At the Earl of Wimborough's little place in the north. Do you know the Earl of Wimborough? No? You must, dear lady! I will see to it."

"Thank you," said Millie Splay.

Harold Jupp looked eagerly at the personage, and said, "I hope Wimborough won't go jumping this winter."

"Jumping!" cried Mr. Albany Todd turning indignantly. "I should think not indeed! Jumping! Why, he is seventy-three!"

He was utterly scandalised that any one should attribute the possibility of such wayward behaviour to the venerable Earl. In his agitation he ate another muffin. After all, if the nobleman did go jumping in the winter why should this young and horsey man presume to criticise him.

"Harold Jupp was drawing a distinction between flat racing and steeple-chasing, Mr. Albany Todd," Sir Chichester suavely explained.

"Oh, I see." Mr. Albany Todd was appeased. He turned a condescending face upon Joan Whitworth.

"And what are you reading, Miss Whitworth?"

"What ho!" interposed Harold Jupp.

Joan shot at him a withering glance.

"It wouldn't interest you." She smiled on Mr. Albany Todd. "It's Browning."

"Well, that's just where you are wrong," returned Jupp. "Browning's the only poet I can stick. There's a ripping thing of his I learnt at school."

> "'I sprang to the saddle and Joris and he,
> I galloped, Dirck galloped, we galloped all three.'"

"Oh," exclaimed Miranda eagerly, "a horse race!"

"Nothing of the sort, Miranda. I am thoroughly ashamed of you," said Harold in reproof. "It's 'How they Brought the Good News from Ghent to Aix.'"

Here Joan intervened disdainfully.

"But that's not Browning!"

Lady Splay looked perplexed.

"Are you sure, Joan?"

Joan tossed her head.

"Of course, it's Browning all right," she explained, "but it's not Browning if you understand me."

The explanation left that company mystified. Harold Jupp shook his head mournfully at Joan, and tapped his forehead.

"Excessive study, Joan, has turned that little head. The moment I saw you in sandals I said to myself, 'Joan couldn't take the hill.'"

Joan wrinkled her nose, and made a grimace at him. What rejoinder she would have made no one was to know. For Mr. Albany Todd finding himself unduly neglected burst into the conversation with a complete irrelevance.

"I am so happy. I shot a stag last autumn."

Both Dennis Brown and Harold Jupp turned to the great conversationalist with real interest.

"How many stone?" asked Dennis.

"I used a rifle," replied Mr. Albany Todd coldly. He did not like to be made fun of; and suddenly a ripple of clear laughter broke deliciously from Joan.

Lady Splay looked agitatedly around for succour. Oh, what a mistake she had made in bringing Mr. Albany Todd into the midst of these ribald young people. And after all—she had to admit it ruefully, he was a bit of a Plater. Dennis Brown, however, hurried to the rescue. He came across the room to Joan, and sat down at her side.

"I haven't had a word with you, Joan."

"No," she answered.

"And how's the little book going on? Do tell me! I won't laugh, upon my word."

Joan herself tried not to. "Oh, pig, pig!" she exclaimed, but she got no further in her anathema for Miranda drew up a stool, and sat in admiration before her.

"Yes, do tell us," she pleaded. "It's all so wonderful."

Miranda, however, was never to hear. Mr. Albany Todd leaned forward with an upraised forefinger, and a smile of keen discernment.

"You are writing a book, Miss Whitworth," he said, as if he had discovered the truth by his own intuition, and expected her to deny the impeachment. "Ah, but you are! And I see that you *can* write one."

"Now, how?" asked Harold Jupp.

Mr. Albany Todd waved the question aside. "The moment I entered the hall, and saw Miss Whitworth, I said to myself, 'There's a book there!' Yes, I said that. I knew it! I know women."

Mr. Albany Todd closed his eyelids, and peeped out through the narrowest possible slits in the cunningest fashion. "Some experience you know. I am the last man to boast of it. A certain almost feminine sensibility—and there you have my secret. I read the character of women in their eyebrows. A woman's eyebrows. Oh, how loud they speak! I looked at Miss Whitworth's eyebrows, and I exclaimed, 'There is a book there—and I will read it!'"

Joan flamed into life. She clasped her hands together.

"Oh, will you?" The question was half wonder, half prayer.

No man could have shown a more charming condescension than did Mr. Albany Todd at this moment.

"Indeed, I will. I read one book a year—never more. A few sentences in bed in the morning, and a few sentences in bed at night. Yours shall be my book for 1923." He took a little notebook and a pencil from his pocket. "Now what title will it have?"

"'A Woman's Heart, and Who Broke It,'" replied Joan, blushing from her temples to her throat.

Miranda repeated the title in an ecstasy of admiration, and asked the world at large: "Isn't it all wonderful?"

"'And Who Broke It,'" quoted Mr. Albany Todd as he wrote the title down. He put his pocketbook away.

"The volume I am reading now——"

"Yes?" said Joan eagerly. With what master was she to find herself in company? She was not to know.

"——was given to me exquisitely bound by a very dear friend of mine, now alas! in precarious health!—the Marquis of Bridlington," said Mr. Albany Todd—an audible groan from Harold Jupp; an imploring glance from Millie Splay, and to her immense relief the butler ushered in Harry Luttrell. He was welcomed by Millie Splay, presented to Sir Chichester, and surrounded by his friends. He was a trifle leaner than of old, and there were lines now where before there had been none. His eyes, too, had the queer, worn and sunken look which was becoming familiar in the eyes of the young men on leave. Joan Whitworth watched him as he entered, carelessly—for perhaps a second. Then her book dropped from her hand upon the carpet—that book which she had so jealously read a few minutes back. Now it lay where it had fallen. She leaned forward, as though above all she wished to hear the sound of his voice. And when she heard it, she drew in a little breath. He was speaking and laughing with Sir Chichester, and the theme was nothing more important than Sir Chichester's Honorary Membership of the Senga Mess.

"Lucky fellow!" cried Sir Chichester. "No trouble for you to get into the papers, eh! Publicity waits on you like a valet."

"But that's just the kind of valet I can't afford in my profession," said Harry.

The conversation was all trivial and customary. But Joan Whitworth leaned forward with a light upon her face that had never yet burnt there. Colonel Luttrell was presented to Mr. Albany Todd, who was most kind and condescending. Joan looked suddenly down at her bilious frock, and the horror of her sandals was something she could hardly bear. They would turn to her next. Yes, they would turn to her! She looked desperately towards the great staircase with its broad, shallow steps which ran up round two sides of the hall. Millie Splay was actually beginning to turn to her, when Dennis Brown came unconsciously to her rescue.

"We looked out for you at Gatwick," he said.

"I only just reached the race course in time for the last race," said Harry Luttrell. "Luckily for me."

"Why luckily?" asked Harold Jupp in surprise.

"Because I backed the winner," replied Luttrell.

The indefatigable race-goers gathered about him a little closer; and Joan Whitworth rose noiselessly from her chair.

"Which horse won?" asked Harold Jupp.

"Loman!" Harold Jupp stared at Dennis Brown. Incredulity held them as in bonds.

"But he couldn't win!" they both cried in a breath.

"He did, you know, and at a long price."

"What on earth made you back him?" asked Dennis Brown.

"Well," Luttrell answered, "he was the only white horse in the race."

Miranda uttered a cry of pleasure. She recognised a brother. "That's an awfully good reason," she cried. But science fell with a crash. Dennis Brown took his "Form at a Glance" from his pocket, and sadly began to tear the pages across. Harold Jupp looked on at that act of sacrilege.

"It doesn't matter," he said, and offered his invariable consolation. "Flat racing's no use. We'll go jumping in the winter."

But Harold Jupp was never again to go jumping in the winter. Long before steeple chasing began that year, he was lying out on the flat land beyond the Somme, with a bullet through his heart.

Dennis Brown returned "Form at a Glance" to his pocket; and Millie Splay drew Harry Luttrell away from the group.

"I want to introduce you to Joan Whitworth," she said, and she turned to the chair in which Joan had been sitting a few moments ago.

It was empty.

"Why, where in the world has Joan gone to?" she exclaimed.

"She has fled," explained Jupp. "Joan saw his 'Form at a Glance,' without any book. She saw that he was incapable of the higher Life, and she has gone."

"Nonsense, Harold," cried Millicent Splay in vexation. She turned towards the stairs, and she gave a little gasp. A woman was standing on the second step from the floor. But it was not Joan, it was Stella Croyle.

"I thought you had such a bad headache," said Lady Splay, after a perceptible pause.

"It's better now, thank you," said Stella, and coming down the remaining steps, she advanced towards Harry.

"How do you do, Colonel Luttrell?" she asked.

For a moment he was taken aback. Then with the blood mounting in his face, he took a step forwards and shook hands with her easily.

"So you know one another!" said Lady Splay.

"We have known each other for a long while," returned Stella Croyle.

So that was why Stella Croyle had proposed herself for the week! Lady Splay had been a little surprised; so persistently had Stella avoided anything in the shape of a party. But this time Stella had definitely wished to come, and Millie Splay in her loyalty had not hesitated to welcome her. But she had been a little curious. Stella's visit, indeed, was the third, though the least, of her preoccupations. The Ball on the Thursday of next week at the Willoughby's! Well, Stella was never lacking in tact. That would arrange itself. But as Millie Splay looked at her, recognised her beauty, her eager advance to Harry Luttrell, and Harry Luttrell's embarrassment, she said to herself, for quite other reasons:

"If I had guessed why she wanted to come, nothing would have persuaded me to have her."

Millie Splay had more reason to repeat the words before the week was out.

CHAPTER XXI

The Magnolia Flowers

"I hadn't an idea that we should find her here," said Hillyard. "Lady Splay told me so very clearly that Mrs. Croyle always timed her visits to avoid a party."

Hillyard was a little troubled lest he should be thought by his friend to have concurred in a plot to bring about this meeting.

"I suppose that Hardiman told her you were coming to Rackham Park. I haven't seen her until this moment, since I returned."

"That's all right, Martin," Luttrell answered.

The two men were alone in the hall. The tennis players had changed, and were out upon the court. Millie Splay had dragged Stella Croyle away with her to play croquet. Luttrell moved to a writing-table.

"You are going to join the tennis players," he said. Hillyard was already dressed for the game, and carried a racket in his hand. "I must write a letter, then I will come out and watch you."

"Right," said Martin, and he left his friend to his letter.

The hall was very still. A bee came buzzing in at the open window, made a tour of the flower-vases, and flew out again into the sunshine. From the lawn the cries of the tennis players, the calls of thrush and blackbird and dishwasher, were wafted in on waves of perfume from the roses. It was very pleasant and restful to Harry Luttrell after the sweat and labour of France. He sighed as he folded his letter and addressed it to a friend in the War Office.

A letterbox stood upon a table close to the staircase. He was carrying his letter over to it, when a girl came running lightly down the stairs and halted suddenly a step or two from the bottom. She stood very still where Stella Croyle had stood a few minutes ago, and like Stella, she looked over the balustrade at Harry Luttrell. Harry Luttrell had reached the letterbox when he caught sight of her, but he quite forgot to drop his letter through the slit. He stood transfixed with wonder and perplexity; wonder at her beauty; perplexity as to who she was.

Martin Hillyard had spoken to him of Joan Whitworth. By the delicious oval of her face, the deep blue of her eyes, the wealth of rippling bright hair, the soft bloom of colour on her cheeks, and her slim, boyish figure—the girl should rightly be she. But it couldn't be! No, it couldn't! This girl's lips were parted in a whimsical friendly smile; her eyes danced;

she was buoyant with joy singing at her heart. Besides—besides——! Luttrell looked at her clothes. She wore a little white frock of chiffon and lace, as simple as could be, but even to a man's eyes it was that simplicity which is the last word of a good dressmaker. A huge rose of blue and silver at her waist was its only touch of colour. With it she wore a white, broad-brimmed hat of straw with a great blue bow and a few narrow streamers of blue ribbon floating jauntily, white stockings and shoes, cross-gartered round her slender ankles with shining ribbons. Was it she? Was it not? Was Martin Hillyard crazy or the whole world upside down?

"You must be Colonel Luttrell," his gracious vision exclaimed, with every appearance of surprise.

"I am," replied Luttrell. He was playing with his letter, half slipping it in, and then drawing it back from the box, and quite unaware of what he was doing.

"We had better introduce ourselves, I think. I am Joan Whitworth."

She held out her hand to him over the balustrade. He had but to reach up and take it. It was a cool hand, and a cordial one.

"Martin Hillyard has talked to me about you," he said.

"I like him," she replied. "He's a dear."

"He told me enough to make me frightened at the prospect of meeting you."

Joan leaned over the banister.

"But now that we have met, you aren't really frightened, are you?" she asked in so wistful a voice, and with a look so deeply pleading in her big blue eyes that no young man could have withstood her.

Harry Luttrell laughed.

"I am not. I am not a bit frightened. In fact I am almost bold enough to ask you a question."

"Yes, Colonel Luttrell?"

The invitation was clear enough. But the Colonel was suddenly aware of his audacity and faltered.

"Oh, do ask me, Colonel Luttrell!" she pleaded. The old-fashioned would have condemned Joan Whitworth as a minx at this moment, but would have softened the condemnation with a smile forced from them by her winning grace.

"Well, I will," replied Luttrell, and with great solemnity he asked, "How is Linda Spavinsky?"

Joan ran down the remaining steps, and dropped into a chair. A peal of laughter, silvery and clear, and joyous rang out from her mouth.

"Oh, she's not at all well today. I believe she's going. Her health was never very stable."

Then her mood changed altogether. The laughter died away, the very look of it faded from her face. She stood up and faced Harry Luttrell. In the depths of her eyes there appeared a sudden gravity, a certain wistfulness, almost a regret.

She spoke simply:

> *"Iram indeed is gone with all his rose,*
> *And Jamshyd's seven-ringed cup—where, no one knows!*
> *But still a ruby kindles in the vine,*
> *And many a garden by the water blows."*

She had the air of one saying good-bye to many pleasant follies which for long had borne her company—and saying good-bye with a sort of doubt whether that which was in store for her would bring a greater happiness.

Harry Luttrell had no answer, and no very distinct comprehension of her mood. But he was stirred by it. For a little while they looked at one another without any words. The air about them in that still hall vibrated with the emotions of violins. Joan Whitworth was the first to break the dangerous silence.

"I am afraid that up till now, what I have liked, I have liked tremendously, but I have not always liked it for very long. You will remember that in pity, won't you?" she said lightly.

Harry Luttrell was quick to catch her tone.

"I shall remember it with considerable apprehension if I am fortunate enough ever to get into your good books." His little speech ended with a gasp. The letter which he was holding carelessly in his fingers had almost slipped from them into the locked letter box.

Joan crossed to where he stood.

"That's all right," she said. "You can post your letter there. The box is cleared regularly."

"No doubt," Harry Luttrell returned. "But I am no longer sure that I am going to post it."

The letter to his friend at the War Office contained an earnest prayer that a peremptory telegram should be sent to him at Rackham Park, at an early hour on the next morning, commanding his return to London.

He looked up at Joan.

"You despise racing, don't you?"

"I am going to Gatwick tomorrow."

"You are!" he cried eagerly.

"Of course."

He stood poising the letter in the palm of his open hand. The thought of Stella Croyle bade him post it. The presence of Joan Whitworth, and he was so conscious of her, paralysed his arm. Some vague sense of the tumult within him passed out from him to her. An intuition seized upon her that that letter was in some way vital to her, in some way a menace to her. Any moment he might post it! Once posted he might let it go. She drew a little sharp breath. He was standing there, so still, so quiet and slow in his decision. It became necessary to her that words should be spoken. She spoke the first which rose to her lips.

"You are going to stay for the Willoughbys' ball, aren't you?"

Harry Luttrell smiled.

"But you despise dancing."

"I? I adore it!"

She smiled as she spoke, but she spoke with a queer shyness which took him off his feet. He slowly tore the letter across and again across and then into little pieces and carried them to the waste-paper basket.

The action brought home to her with a shock that there was a letter which she, in her turn, must write, must write and post in that glass letterbox, oh, without any hesitation or error, this very evening. She thought upon it with repugnance, but it had to be written and done with. It was the consequence of her own folly, her own vanity. Harry Luttrell returned to her but he did not remark the trouble in her face.

"When I left England," he said slowly, "people were dancing the tango. That is—one couple which knew the dance, was dancing it in the ballroom, and all the others were practising in the passage. That's done with, I suppose?"

"Quite," said Joan.

Harry Luttrell heaved a sigh.

"I should have liked to have practised with you in the passage," he said ruefully.

"Still, there are other dances," Joan Whitworth suggested. "The one-step?"

"That's going for a walk," said Harry Luttrell.

"In an unusual attitude," Joan added demurely. "Do you know the fox-trot?"

"A little."

"The twinkle step?"

"Not at all."

"I might teach you that," Joan suggested.

"Oh, do! Teach it me now! Then we'll dance it in the passage."

"But every one will be dancing it in the ballroom," Joan objected.

"That's why," said Harry Luttrell, and they both laughed.

Joan looked towards the gramophone in the corner of the room. She was tempted, but she must have that letter written first. She would dance with Harry Luttrell with an uneasy mind unless that letter were written and posted first.

"Will you put a record ready on the gramophone, whilst I write a note," she suggested. "Then I'll teach you. It's quite a short note."

Joan sat in her turn at the writing table. She wrote the first lines easily and quickly enough. But she came to explanations, and of explanations she had none to offer. She sat and framed a sentence and it would not do. Meanwhile the gramophone was open and ready, the record fitted on to the disc of green baize and her cavalier in impatient attendance. She must be quick. But the quicker she wanted to be, the more slowly her thoughts moved amongst awkward sentences which she must write. She dashed off in the end the standard phrase for such emergencies. "I will write to you tomorrow," addressed and stamped her letter and dropped it into the letter box. The letter fell in the glass box with the address uppermost. But Joan did not trouble about that, did not even notice it; a weight was off her mind.

"I am ready," she said, and a few seconds later the music of "The Long Trail" was wafted to the astonished ears of the tennis players in the garden. They paused in their game and then Dennis Brown crept to the window of the hall and looked cautiously in. He stood transfixed; then turned and beckoned furiously. The lawn-tennis players forsook their rackets, Lady Splay and Stella Croyle their croquet mallets. Dennis Brown led them by a back way up to the head of the broad stairs. Here a gallery ran along one side of the hall. Voices rose up to them from the floor above the music of the gramophone.

Joan's: "That's the twinkle."

Luttrell's: "It's pretty difficult."

"Try it again," said Joan. "Oh, that's ever so much better."

"I shall never dare to dance it with any one else," said Luttrell.

"I really don't mind very much about that," Joan responded dryly.

Millie Splay could hardly believe her ears. Cautiously she and her party advanced on tiptoe to the balustrade and looked down. Yes, there the pair of them were, now laughing, now in desperate earnest, practising the fox-trot to the music of the gramophone.

"Do I hold you right?" asked Harry.

"Well—I shan't break, you know," Joan answered demurely, and then with a little sigh, "That's better."

Under her breath Stella Croyle murmured passionately, "Oh, you minx!"

As the record ran out a storm of applause burst from the gallery.

"Oh, Joan, Joan," cried Harold Jupp, shaking his head reproachfully. "There's the poet kicked right across the room."

"Where?" asked Harry Luttrell, looking round for the book.

"Oh, it doesn't matter," said Joan impatiently. "It's only an old volume of Browning."

Cries of "Shame" broke indignantly from the race-goers, and Joan received them with imperturbable indifference. Harry Luttrell, however, went on his knees and discovering the book beneath a distant sofa, carefully dusted it.

"Did you ever read 'How they Brought the Good News from Ghent to Aix'?" he asked.

The audience in the gallery waited in dead silence for Joan Whitworth's answer. It came unhesitatingly clear and in a voice of high enthusiasm.

"Isn't it the most wonderful poem he ever wrote?"

The gallery broke into screams, catcalls, hisses and protests against Joan's shameless recantation.

"It's Browning, of course, but it's not Browning at all, if you understand me," Dennis Brown exclaimed with every show of indignation; and the whole party trooped away again to their tennis and their croquet.

Harry Luttrell placed the book upon a table and turned to Joan.

"Now what would you like to do?" he asked.

Joan shrugged her shoulders.

"We might cut into the next tennis set," she said doubtfully.

"You could hardly play in those shoes," said Harry Luttrell.

Joan contemplated a heel of formidable height. Oh, where were the sandals of the higher Life?

"No, I suppose not. Of course, there's a—but it wouldn't probably interest you."

"Wouldn't it?" cried Harry Luttrell.

"Well, it's a maze. Millie Splay is rather proud of it. The hedges are centuries old." She turned innocent eyes on Harry Luttrell. "I don't know whether you are interested in old hedges."

It is to be feared that "minx" was the only right word for Joan Whitworth on this afternoon. Harry Luttrell expressed an intense enthusiasm for great box hedges.

"But they aren't box, they are yew," said Joan, stopping at once.

Harry Luttrell's enthusiasm for yew hedges, however, was even greater and more engrossing than his enthusiasm for box ones. A pagoda perched upon a bank overlooked the maze and a narrow steep path led down into it between the hedges. Joan left it to her soldier to find the way. There was a stone pedestal with a small lead figure perched upon the top of it in the small clear space in the middle. But Harry Luttrell took a deal of time in reaching it. If, however, their progress was slow, with many false turnings and sudden stops against solid walls of hedge, it was not so with their acquaintanceship; each turn in the path brought them on by a new stage. They wandered in the dawn of the world.

"Suppose that I had never come to Rackham Park!" said Harry Luttrell, suddenly turning at the end of a blind alley. "I almost didn't come. I might have altogether missed knowing you."

The terrible thought smote them both. What risks people ran to be sure. They might never have met. They might have never known what it was to meet. They might have lived benighted, not knowing what lovely spirit had passed them by. They looked at one another with despairing eyes. Then a happy thought occurred to Joan.

"But, after all, you did come," she exclaimed.

Harry Luttrell drew a breath. He was relieved of a great oppression.

"Why, yes," he answered in wonderment. "So I did!"

They retraced their steps. As the sun drew towards its late setting, by an innocent suggestion from Joan here, a little question there, Harry Luttrell was manœuvred towards the centre of the maze. Suddenly he stopped with a finger on the lips. A voice reached to them from the innermost recess—a voice which intoned, a voice which was oracular.

"What's that?" he asked in a whisper.

Joan shook her head.

"I haven't an idea."

As yet they could hear no words. Words were flung from wall to wall of the centre space and kept imprisoned there. It seemed that the presiding genius of the maze was uttering his invocation as the sun went down. Joan and Harry Luttrell crept stealthily nearer, Harry now openly guided by a light touch upon his arm as the paths twisted. Words—amazing words—became distinctly audible; and a familiar voice. They came to the last screen of hedge and peered through at a spot where the twigs were thin.

In the very middle of the clear space stood Sir Chichester Splay, one hand leaning upon the pedestal, the other hidden in his bosom, in the very attitude of the orator; and to the silent spaces of the maze thus he made his address:

"Ladies and gentlemen! When I entered the tent this afternoon and took my seat upon the platform, nothing was further from my thoughts than that I should hear myself proposing a vote of thanks to our indefatigable chairman!"

Sir Chichester was getting ready for the Chichester Flower Show, at which, certainly, he was not going to make a speech. Oh dear, no! He knew better than that.

"In this marvellous collection of flowers, ladies and gentlemen, we can read, if so we will, a singular instance of co-ordination and organisation—the Empire's great needs today——"

Harry Luttrell and Joan stifled their laughter and stole away out of hearing.

"We won't breathe a word of it," said Joan.

"No," said Harry.

They had a little secret now between them—that wonderful link—a little secret; and to be sure they made the most of it. They could look across the dinner-table at one another with a smile in which no one else could have a share. If Sir Chichester spoke, it would be just to kindle that swift glance in lovers' eyes from which the heart takes fire. Love-making went at a gallop in nineteen hundred and sixteen; it jumped the barriers; it danced to a lively and violent tune. Maidens, as Sir Charles Hardiman had pronounced, had become more primeval. Insecurity had dropped them down upon the bedrock elemental truths. Men were for women, women for men, especially for those men who went out with a cheery song in their mouths to save them from the hideous destiny of women in ravaged lands. The soldier was here today on leave, and God alone knew where he would be tomorrow, and whether alive, or perhaps a crippled thing like a child!

Joan Whitworth and Harry Luttrell had been touched by the swift magic of those days; he, when he had first seen her in the shining armour of her youth upon the steps of the stairs; she, when Harry had first entered the hall and spoken his few commonplace words of greeting. This was the hour for them, the hour at the well with the desert behind them and the desert in front, the hour within the measure of which was to be forced the essence of many days. When they returned to the hall they found most of the small party gathered there before going up to dress for dinner; and there was that in the faces of the pair which betrayed them. Hillyard looked quickly round the hall, as a qualm of pity for Stella Croyle seized him. But he could not see her. "Thank Heaven she has already gone up to dress," he said to himself. A marriage between Joan Whitworth and the Harry Luttrell of today, the man freed now from the great obsession of his life and trained now to the traditional paths, was a fitting thing, a thing to be welcomed. Hillyard readily acknowledged it. But he had more insight into the troubled soul of Stella Croyle than any one else in that company.

"No one's bothering about her," he reflected. "She came here to set up her last fight to win back Harry. She is now putting on her armour for it. And she hasn't a chance—no, not one!"

For Harry's sake he was glad. But he was a creator of plays; and his training led him to seek to understand, and to understand with the sympathy of his emotions, the points of view of others who might stand in a contrast or a relation. He walked up the stairs with a heart full of pity when Millicent Splay caught him up.

"What did I tell you?" she said, brimful with delight. "Just look at Joan! Is there a girl anywhere who can match her?"

Martin looked down over the balustrade at Joan in the hall below.

"No," he said slowly. "Not one whom I have ever seen."

The little note of melancholy in his voice moved Millie Splay. She was all kindness in that moment of her triumph. She turned to Martin Hillyard in commiseration. "Oh, don't tell me that you are in love with her too! I should be so sorry."

"No, I am not," Martin Hillyard hastened to reassure her, "not one bit."

The commiseration died on the instant in Millicent Splay.

"Well, really I don't see why you shouldn't be," she said coldly. "You will go a long way before you find any one to equal her."

Her whole attitude demanded of him an explanation of how he dared not to be in love with her darling.

"A very long way," Martin Hillyard agreed humbly. "All the way probably."

Lady Splay was mollified, and went on to her room. Down in the hall, Harry Luttrell turned to Joan.

"This is going to be a wonderful week for me."

"I am very glad," answered Joan, and they went up the stairs side by side.

CHAPTER XXII

Jenny Prask

"I have put out the blue dress with the silver underskirt, madam," said Jenny Prask, knowing well that nothing in Stella Croyle's wardrobe set off so well her dark and fragile beauty.

"Very well, Jenny."

Stella Croyle answered listlessly. She was discouraged by her experience of that afternoon. She had come to Rackham Park, certain of one factor upon her side, but very certain of that. She would find no competitor, and lo! the invincible competitor, youth, had put on armour against her! Stella looked in the mirror. She was thirty, and in the circle within which she moved, thirty meant climbing reluctantly on to the shelf.

"Don't you think, Jenny, the blue frock makes me look old?"

Jenny Prask laughed scornfully.

"Old, madam! You! Just fancy!"

Stella Croyle, living much alone, had made a companion of her maid. There was nothing of Mrs. Croyle's history which Jenny Prask did not know, and very few of her hopes and sorrows were hidden from her.

"My gracious me, madam! There will be nobody to hold a candle to you here!" she said, with a sniff, as she helped Stella to undress.

Stella looked in the glass. Certainly there was not a line upon the smoothness of her cheeks; her dark hair had lost none of its gloss. She took her features one by one, and found no trace of change. Nor, indeed, scrutinised in that way did Stella show any change. It was when you saw her across a room that you recognised that girlhood had gone, and that there was a woman in the full ripeness of her beauty.

"Yes," she said, and her listlessness began to disappear. She turned away from the mirror. "Come, Jenny!" she cried, with a hopeful smile. She was saying to herself, "I have still a chance."

Jenny rattled on while she assisted her mistress. Stella's face changed with her mood, more than most faces. Disappointment and fatigue aged her beyond due measure. Jenny Prask was determined that she could go down to dinner tonight looking her youngest and best.

"I went for a walk this evening with Mr. Marvin. He's Colonel Luttrell's soldier-servant, and quite enthusiastic, he was, madam."

"Was he, Jenny?"

"Quite! The men in his company loved him—a captain he was then.

He always looked after their dinner. A bit strict, too, but they don't mind that."

Jenny was busy with Stella Croyle's hair; and the result satisfied her.

"There won't be anybody else tonight, madam," she said.

"Won't there, Jenny?" said Mrs. Croyle, incredulously. "There'll be Miss Whitworth."

Jenny Prask sniffed disdainfully.

"Miss Whitworth! A fair sight I call her, madam, if I may say so. I never did see such clothes! And how she keeps a maid for more than a week beats me altogether. What I say, madam, is those who button in front when they should hook behind are a fair washout."

Stella laughed.

"I'm afraid that you'll find, Jenny, that Miss Whitworth will hook behind tonight."

Jenny went on unaffected by the rejoinder. She had her little item of news to contribute to the contentment of her mistress.

"Besides, Miss Whitworth is in love with the foreign gentleman. Oh, madam, if you turn as sharp as that, I can't but pull your hair."

"Which foreigner?"

"That Mario Escobar." Jenny looked over Stella's head and into the reflection of her eyes upon the mirror. "I don't hold with foreigners myself, madam. A little ridiculous they always seem to me, with their chatter and what not."

"And you believe Miss Whitworth's in love with him."

"Outrageous, Mr. Harper says. Quite the talk of the servants' hall, it is. Why, even this afternoon she wrote him a letter. Mr. Harper showed it me after he took it out of the letterbox to post it. 'That's her 'and,' says he—and there it was, Mario Escobar, Esquire, the Golden Sun Hotel, Midhurst—"

"Midhurst?" cried Stella with a start. She looked eagerly at the reflection of Jenny Prask. "Mr. Escobar is staying in an hotel at Midhurst?"

"Yes, madam."

"And Miss Whitworth wrote to him there this afternoon?"

"It's gospel truth, madam. May it be my last dying word, if it isn't!" said Jenny Prask.

The blood mounted into Stella Croyle's face. Since that was true—and she did not doubt Jenny Prask for a moment—Jenny would have given anything she had to save her mistress trouble, and Stella knew it. Since it was true, then, that Mario Escobar was staying hidden away in a country hotel five miles off, and that Joan was writing to him, why, after all, she had no rival.

Her spirits rose with a bound. She had a week, a whole week, in the company of Harry Luttrell; and what might she not do in a week if she used her wits and used her beauty! Stella Croyle ran down the stairs like a girl.

Jenny Prask shut the door, and, opening a wardrobe, took from a high shelf Mrs. Croyle's dressing-bag. She opened it, and from one of the fittings she lifted out a bottle. The bottle was quite full of a white, colourless liquid. Jenny Prask nodded to herself and carefully put the bottle back. There was very little she did not know about the proceedings of her mistress. Then she went out of the room into the gallery, and peeped down to watch the other guests assemble. She saw Miranda Brown, Stella, Sir Chichester Splay, Dennis and Harry Luttrell come from their different rooms and gather in the hall below. From a passage behind her, a girl, butterfly-bright, flashed out and danced joyously down the stairs. A newcomer, thought Jenny, with a pang of alarm for her mistress! But she heard the newcomer speak, and heard her spoken to. It was Joan Whitworth.

"Oh!" Jenny Prask gasped.

Undoubtedly Joan "hooked behind" tonight. What had come over her? Jenny asked. Her quick mind realised that Mario Escobar was not answerable for the change since Mario Escobar was miles away at Midhurst. Besides, according to Mr. Harper, this flirtation with Escobar had been going on a year and more.

Jenny Prask looked from Joan to Harry Luttrell. She saw them drawn to one another across the hall and move into the dining-room side by side. She turned back with a little moan of disappointment into Stella Croyle's bedroom; and whilst she tidied it, more than once she stopped to wring her hands.

Stella Croyle, however, kept her good spirits through the evening. For after dinner Harry Luttrell, of his own will, came straight to her in the drawing-room.

"Oh, Wub," she said in a whisper as she drew her skirt aside to make room for him upon the couch. "Oh, Wub, what years it is since I have seen you."

When the old nickname fell upon Harry's ears, he looked quickly about him to see where Joan Whitworth sat. But she was at the other end of the room.

"Yes, it is a long time."

"Stockholm!" said Stella, dwelling upon the name. She lowered her voice. "Wub, I suffered terribly after you went away. Oh, it wasn't a good time. No, it wasn't!"

"Stella, I am very sorry," he said gently. He knew himself this day the glories and the pangs of love. He was sunk ocean-deep one moment in the sense of his unworthiness, the next he knocked his head against the stars on the soaring billow of his pride. He could not but feel for Stella, who had passed through the same furnace. He could not but grieve that the wondrous book of which he was racing through the first pages had been closed for her by him. Might she not open it again, some time, with another at her side?

"Wub, tell me what you have been doing all these years," she said.

He began the tale of them in the short, reluctant, colloquial phrases which the English use to strip their achievements of any romantic semblance until Millicent Splay sailed across the room and claimed him for a table of bridge.

"He will be safer there," she said to herself.

"Yes, but she had to take him away," Stella's thoughts responded. She was dangerous then in Millie Splay's judgment. The sweet flattery set Stella smiling. She went up to her room rejoicing that she had chosen that week to visit Rackham Park. She was playing a losing game, but she did not know it.

Thus the very spirit of summer seemed to inform the gathering. Saturday brought up no clouds to darken the clear sky. Harold Jupp and Dennis Brown actually scored four nice wins at Gatwick on horses which, to celebrate the week, miraculously ran to form. Miranda under these conditions would have inevitably lost, but by another stroke of fortune no horse running had any special blemish, name, colour or trick calculated to inspire her. Sir Chichester was happy too, for he saw a lady reporter write down his name in her notebook. So was Mr. Albany Todd. For he met the Earl of Eltringham, with whom he had a passing acquaintance; and his lordship, being complimented upon his gardens, of which *Country Life* had published an account, was moved to say in the friendliest manner: "You must propose yourself for a weekend, Mr. Todd, and see them."

As for Joan and Harry Luttrell, it mattered little where they were, so that they were together. They walked in their own magical garden.

It fell to Martin Hillyard to look after Stella Croyle, and the task was not difficult. She kept her eyes blindfold to what she did not wish to see. She had a chance, she said to herself, recollecting her talk with Harry last night, and the news of Joan which Jenny Prask had given to her. She had a chance, if she walked delicately.

"Old associations—give them opportunity, and they renew their strength," she thought. "Harry is afraid of them—that's all."

On the Monday evening Jenny Prask brought a fresh piece of gossip which strengthened her hopes.

"Miss Whitworth had a letter from him this morning," said Jenny. "She wouldn't open it at the breakfast-table, Mr. Harper says. Quite upset she was, he says. She took it upstairs to her room just as it was."

"It might have been from some one else," answered Stella.

"Oh, no, madam," replied Jenny. "It had the Midhurst postmark, and Mr. Harper knows his handwriting besides. Mr. Harper's very observant."

"He seems to be," said Stella.

"Miss Whitworth answered the letter at once, and took it out to the village and posted it with her own hands," Jenny continued.

"Are you sure?" cried Mrs. Croyle.

"I saw her go with my own eyes, I did. She went in her own little run-about, and was back in a jiffy, with a sort of 'There-I've-done-it!' look about her. Oh, there's something going on there, madam—take my word for it! She's a deep one, Miss Whitworth is, and no mistake. Will you wear the smoke-grey tonight, madam? I am keeping the pink for the ball on Thursday."

Stella allowed a moment or two to pass before she answered.

"I shan't go to the Willoughbys' ball, Jenny."

Jenny Prask stared in dismay.

"You won't, madam!"

"No, Jenny. But I want you to be careful not to mention it to any one. I shall dress as if I was going, but at the last moment I shall plead a head-ache and stay behind."

"Very well, madam," said Jenny. But it seemed to her that Stella was throwing down her arms. Stella, however, had understood, upon hearing of the invitation for Lady Splay's party, that she could do nothing else. The Willoughbys were strict folk. Mrs. Croyle could hardly hope to go without some rumour of her history coming afterwards to the ears of that family; and the family would hold her presence as a reproach against Millie Splay. Stella had herself proposed her plan to Millie, and she noted the relief with which it was received.

"You will be careful not to mention it to a soul, Jenny," Stella insisted.

"My goodness me, madam, I never talk," replied Jenny. "I keep my ears open and let the others do that."

"I know, Jenny," said Stella, with a smile. "I can't imagine what I should do without you."

"And you never will, madam, unless it's your own wish and doin',"
said Jenny heartily. "I have talked it over with Brown"—Brown was Mrs.
Croyle's chauffeur—"and he's quite willin' that I should go on with you
after we are married."

"Then, that's all right," said Stella.

Many a one looking backwards upon some terrible and unexpected
tragedy will have noticed with what care the great dramaturgist so wove his
play that every little unheeded event in the days before helped directly to
create the final catastrophe. It happened on this evening that Stella went
downstairs earlier than the other guests, and in going into the library in
search of an evening paper, found Sir Chichester standing by the telephone instrument.

"Am I in your way?" she asked.

"Not a bit, Stella," he answered. "In fact, you might help me by
looking up the number I want." He raised the instrument, and playing
with the receiver as he stood erect, remarked, "Although I am happy to
think that I shall not be called upon to deliver any observations on the
occasion of the Chichester flower show next Thursday, I may as well ask
one of the newspapers if their local correspondent would give the ceremony some little attention."

Stella Croyle took up the telephone book.

"Which newspaper is it to be, Sir Chichester?"

"The *Harpoon*, I think. Yes, I am sure. The *Harpoon*."

Stella Croyle looked up the number and read out:

"Gerrard, one, six, two, double three."

Sir Chichester accordingly called upon the trunk line and gave the
number.

"You will ring me up? Thank you," he said, and replacing the receiver,
stood in anxious expectancy.

"I thought that your favourite paper was the *Daily Flashlight*?" Stella
observed.

"That's quite true, Stella. It was," Sir Chichester explained naïvely.
"But I have noticed lately a regrettable tendency to indifference on the
part of the *Flashlight*. The management is usually too occupied to converse
with me when I ring it up. On the other hand, I am new to the *Harpoon*.
Hallo! Hallo! This is Sir Christopher Splay speaking," and he delivered his
message. "Thank you very much," said Sir Chichester as he hung up the
receiver. "Really most courteous people. Yes, most courteous. What is their
number, Stella? I must remember it."

Stella read it out again.

"Gerrard, one, six, two, double three," and thus she, too, committed the number to memory.

CHAPTER XXIII

Plans for the Evening

The library at Rackham Park was a small, oblong room, with a big window upon the garden. It opened into the hall on the one side and into the dining-room on the other, and in one corner the telephone was installed. At half past eight on the night of the dance at Harrel, this room was empty and in darkness. But a second afterwards the door from the hall was opened, and Joan stood in the doorway, the light shimmering upon her satin cloak and the silver embroidery of her frock. She cast an anxious look behind her and up the staircase. It seemed as if some movement at the angle made by the stairs and the gallery caught her eye, for she stepped back for a clearer view, and listened with a peculiar intentness. She saw nothing, however, and heard nothing. She entered the library swiftly and closed the door behind her, so that the room fell once more upon darkness save for a thread of gold at the bottom of the other door behind which the men of the party were still sitting over their wine. She crossed the room towards the window, stepping cautiously to avoid the furniture. She was quite invisible. But for a tiny rustle of the lace flounces on her dress one would have sworn the room was empty. But when she was halfway across a sudden burst of laughter from the dining-room brought her to a stop with her hand upon her heart and a little sob not altogether stifled in her throat. It meant so much to her that the desperate adventure of this night should be carried through! If all went well, as it must—oh, as it surely must!—by midnight she would be free of her terrors and distress.

The laughter in the dining room died down. Joan stole forward again. She drew away the heavy curtains from the long window, and the moonlight, clear and bright like silver, poured into the room and clothed her in its soft radiance. She drew back the bolts at the top and bottom of the glass door and turned the key in the lock. She touched the glass and the door swung open upon the garden, easily, noiselessly. She drew it close again and leaving it so, raised her hands to the curtains at the side. As she began carefully to draw them together, so that the rings should not rattle on the pole, the door from the hall was softly and quickly opened, and the switch of the electric lights by the side of the door pressed down. The room leapt into light.

Joan swung round, her face grown white, her eyes burning with fire. She saw only Jenny Prask.

"I hope I don't intrude, miss," said Jenny respectfully. "I came to find a book."

The blood flowed back into Joan's cheeks.

"Certainly, Jenny, take what you like," said Joan, and she draped the curtains across the window.

"Thank you, miss."

Jenny chose a book from the case upon the table and without a glance at Joan or at the window, went out of the room again. Joan watched her go. After all, what had Jenny seen? A girl whose home was there, drawing the curtains close. That was all. Joan shook her anxiety off. Jenny had left the door of the library open and some one came running down the stairs whistling as she ran. Miranda Brown dashed into the room struggling with a pair of gloves.

"Oh, how I hate gloves in this weather!" she cried. "Well, here I am, Joan. You wanted to speak to me before the others had finished powdering their noses. What is it?"

"I want you to help me."

"Of course I will," Miranda answered cheerily. "How?"

Joan closed the door and returned to Miranda, who, having drawn the gloves over her arm, was now struggling with the buttons.

"I want you, when we reach Harrel——"

"Yes."

"To lend me your motorcar for an hour."

Miranda turned in amazement towards her friend. But one glance at her face showed that the prayer was made in desperate earnest. Miranda Brown caught her friend by the arm.

"Joan!"

"Yes," Joan Whitworth answered, nodding her head miserably. "That's the help I want and I want it dreadfully. Just for an hour—no more."

"Joan, my dear—what's the matter?" asked Miranda gazing into Joan Whitworth's troubled face.

"I don't want you to ask me," the girl answered. "I want you to help me straight off without any questions. Otherwise——" and Joan's voice shook and broke, "otherwise—oh, I don't know what will happen to me!"

Miranda put her arm round Joan Whitworth's waist. "Joan! You are in real trouble!"

"For the first time!" said Joan.

"Can't I——?"

"No," Joan interrupted. "There's only the one way, Miranda."

She sat down upon a couch at Miranda's side and feverishly caught her hand. "Do help me! You can't tell what it means to me! . . . And I should hate telling you! Oh, I have been such a fool!"

Joan's face was quivering, and so deep a compunction was audible in her voice, so earnest a prayer was to be read in her troubled eyes, that Miranda's doubt and anxiety were doubled.

"I don't know what I shall do, if you don't help me," Joan said miserably as she let go of Miranda. Her hands fluttered helplessly in the air. "No, I don't know!"

Miranda was thoroughly disturbed. The contrast between the Joan she had known until this week, good-humoured, a little aloof, contented with herself and her ambitions, placid, self-contained, and this lovely girl, troubled to the heart's core, with her beseeching eyes and trembling lips touched her poignantly, meltingly.

"Oh, Joan, I don't like it!" she whispered. "What mad thing have you done?"

"Nothing that can't be put right! Nothing! Nothing!" Joan caught eagerly at the argument. "Oh, I was a fool! But if you'll only help me tonight, I am sure everything will be arranged."

The words were bold enough, but the girl's voice trailed off into a low, unsteady whisper, as terror at the rash plan which she had made and must now carry through caught at her heart. "Oh, Miranda, do be kind!"

"When do you want the car?" asked Miranda.

"Immediately after we get to Harrel."

"Joan!"

Miranda herself was growing frightened. She stood torn with indecision. Joan's distress pleaded on the one side, dread of some tragic mystery upon the other. For the first time in her life Joan was in some desperate crisis of destiny. Her feet and hands twitched as though she were bound fast in the coils of a net she could not break. What wisdom of experience could she bring to help her to escape? On what wild and hopeless venture might she not be set?

"Yes, yes," Joan urged eagerly. "I have thought it all out. I want you to tell your chauffeur privately to return along the avenue after he has set you down. There's a road on the right a few yards down. If he will turn into that and wait behind the big clump of rhododendrons I will join him immediately."

"But it will be noticed that you have gone. People will ask for you," Miranda objected.

"No, I shall be back again within the hour. There will be a crowd of people. And lots won't imagine that I should ever come to the dance at all." Even at that moment a little smile played about the lips. "And if the ball had been a week ago, I shouldn't have gone, should I? I should still be wearing sandals," she explained, as she looked down at the buckles of her trim satin slippers, "and haughtily wishing you all good night in the hall here. No, it will be easy enough. I shall just shake hands with Mrs. Willoughby, pass on with the rest of our party into the ballroom and then slip out by the corridor at the side of the park."

"It's dangerous, Joan!" said Miranda.

"Oh, I know, but——" Joan rose suddenly with her eyes upon the door. "The others are coming. Miranda, will you help me? I would have driven over to Harrel in my own little car. But it's open and I should have got blown about until everybody would have begun asking why in the world I used it. Oh, Miranda, quick!"

Her ears had heard the voices already in the hall. Miranda heard them too. In a moment the door would be thrown open. She must make up her mind now.

"Very well. The first turning to the right down the avenue and behind the rhododendrons. I'll tell the chauffeur."

"And no one else! Not even Dennis!"

"Joan!"

"No, not even Dennis! Promise me."

Millie Splay was heard to be inquiring for them both.

"Very well. I promise!"

"Oh, thank you! Thank you."

The door from the hall was opened upon that cry of gratitude and Millie Splay looked in.

"Oh, there you are." A movement of chairs became audible in the dining-room. "And those men are still sitting over their miserable cigars."

"They are coming," said Joan, and the next moment the dining-room door was thrown open and Sir Chichester with his guests trooped out from it.

"Now then, you girls, we ought to be off," he cried as if he had been waiting with his coat on for half an hour. "This is none of your London dances. We are in the country. You won't any of you get any partners if you don't hurry."

"Well, I like that!" returned Millie Splay. "Here we all are, absolutely waiting for you!"

Mr. Albany Todd approached Joan.

"You will keep a dance for me?"

"Of course. The third before supper," answered Joan.

Already Sir Chichester was putting on his coat in the hall.

"Come on! Come on!" he cried impatiently, and then in quite another tone, "Oh!"

The evening papers had arrived late that evening. They now lay neatly folded on the hall table. Sir Chichester pounced upon them. The throbbing motorcars at the door, the gay figures of his guests were all forgotten. He plumped down upon a couch.

"There!" cried Millie Splay in despair. "Now we can all sit down for half an hour."

"Nonsense, my dear, nonsense! I just want to see whether there is any report of my little speech at the Flower Show yesterday." He turned over the leaves. "Not a word apparently, here! And yet it was an occasion of some importance. I can't understand these fellows."

He tossed the paper aside and took up another. "Just a second, dear!"

Millie Splay looked around at her guests with much the same expression of helpless wonderment which was so often to be seen on the face of Dennis Brown, when Miranda went racing.

"It's the limit!" she declared.

There were two, however, of the party, who were not at all distressed by Sir Chichester's procrastination. When the others streamed into the hall, Joan lingered behind, sedulously buttoning her gloves which were buttoned before; and Harry Luttrell returned to assist her. The door was three-quarters closed. From the hall no one could see them.

"You are going to dance with me in the passage," he said.

Joan smiled at him and nodded. Now that Miranda had given way, Joan's spirits had revived. The colour was bright in her cheeks, her eyes were tender.

"Yes, but not at once."

"Why?"

"I'll finish my duty dances first," said Joan in a low voice. She did not take her eyes from his face. She let him read, she meant him to read, in her eyes what lay so close at her heart. Harry Luttrell read without an error, the print was so large, the type so clear. He took a step nearer to her.

"Joan!" he whispered; and at this, his first use of her Christian name, her face flowered like a rose.

"Thank you!" she said softly. "Oh, thank you!"

Harry Luttrell looked over his shoulder. They had the room to themselves, so long as they did not raise their voices.

"Joan," he began with a little falter in his voice. Could he have pleaded better in a thousand fine speeches, he who had seen his men wither about him on the Somme, than by that little timorous quaver in his voice? "Joan, I have something to ask of you tonight. I meant to ask it during a dance, when you couldn't run away. But I am going to ask it now."

Joan drew back sharply.

"No! Please wait!" and as she saw his face cloud, she hurried on. "Oh, don't be hurt! You misunderstand. How you misunderstand! Take me in to supper tonight, will you? And then you shall talk to me, and I'll listen." Her voice rose like clear sweet music in a lilt of joy. "I'll listen with all my heart, my hands openly in yours if you will, so that all may see and know my pride!"

"Joan!" he whispered.

"But not now! Not till then!"

Harry Luttrell did not consider what scruple in the girl's conscience held him off. The delay did not trouble him at all. She stood before him, radiant in her beauty, her happiness like an aura about her.

"Joan," he whispered again, and—how it happened who shall say?—in a second she was within his arms, her heart throbbing against his; her hands stole about his shoulders; their lips were pressed together.

"Harry! Oh, Harry!" she murmured. Then very gently she pushed him from her. She shook her head with a wistful little smile.

"I didn't mean you to do that," she said in self-reproach, "until after supper."

In the hall Sir Chichester threw down the last of the newspapers in a rage. "Not a word! Not one single miserable little word! I don't ask much, goodness knows, but——" and his voice went up in an angry incredulity. "Not one word! And I thought the *Harpoon* was such a good paper too!"

Sir Chichester sprang to his feet. He glanced at his guests. He turned upon his wife.

"God bless my soul, Millie, what *are* we waiting for? I'll tell you girls what it is. Unless we get off at once, we had better not go at all. Where's Joan? Where's Luttrell?"

"Here we are!" cried Luttrell from the library, and in a lower tone to Joan, he observed, "What a bore people are to be sure, aren't they?"

The guilty couple emerged into the hall. Sir Chichester surveyed them with severity.

"I don't know whether you have heard about it, Luttrell, but there's a ball tonight at Harrel, and we all rather thought of going to it," he remarked with crushing sarcasm.

"I am quite ready, sir," replied Harry humbly. Sir Chichester was mollified.

"Very well then. We'll go."

"But Mrs. Croyle isn't down yet," said Miranda.

"Stella isn't going, dear," answered Millie Splay; and a cry of dismay burst from Joan.

"Not going!"

The consternation in the girl's voice was so pronounced that every eye in that hall turned to her in astonishment. There was consternation, too, most legible in her widely-opened eyes. Her cheeks had lost their colour. She stood for a fleeting moment before them all, an image of terror. Then she caught at an excuse.

"Stella's ill then—since she's not going."

"It's not as bad as all that, dear," Lady Splay hastened to reassure her. "She complained of a racking headache at dinner. She has gone to bed."

The blood flowed back into Joan's cheeks.

"Oh, I see!" she observed slowly. "That is why her maid came to the library for a book!"

But she was very silent throughout the quarter of an hour, which it took them to drive to Harrel. There was somebody left behind at Rackham Park that night. Joan had overlooked one possibility in contriving her plan, and that possibility, now developed into fact, threatened to ruin all. One guest remained behind in the house, and that one Joan's rival.

CHAPTER XXIV

Jenny Prask is Interested

Rackham was a red Georgian mansion with great windows in flat rows, and lofty rooms made beautiful by the delicate tracery of the ceilings. It has neither wings nor embellishments but stood squarely in its gardens, looking southwards to the Downs. The dining-room was upon the east side, between that room and the hall was the library, of which the window faced the north. Mrs. Croyle's bedroom, however, was in the south-west corner and from its windows one could see the smoke of the train as it climbed from Midhurst to the Cocking tunnel, and the gap where the road runs through to Singleton.

"You won't be going to bed yet, madam, I suppose," said Jenny.

She had not troubled to bring upstairs into the room the book which she had picked out at random from the stand that was lying on the hall table.

"No, Jenny. I will ring for you when I want you," said Stella.

Stella was dispirited. Her week was nearly at an end. Tomorrow would be the last day and she had gained nothing, it seemed, by all her care. Harry was kind—oh, ever so much kinder than in the old days when they had been together—more considerate, more thoughtful. But the skies of passion are stormily red, and so effulgent that one walks in gold. Consideration, thoughtfulness—what were these pale things worth against one spurt of fire? Besides, there was the ball tonight. He would dance with *her*, would seek the dim open spaces of the lawns, the dark shadows of the great elms, with her—with Joan.

"I'll ring for you, Jenny," she repeated, as her maid stood doubtfully by the door. "I am quite right."

"Very well, madam."

Stella Croyle's eyes were drawn when she was left alone to that cupboard in which her dressing-bag was stowed away. But she arrested them and covered them with her hands.

"This is my last chance," she said to herself aloud in the anguish of her spirit. If it failed, there was nothing in front of her but a loneliness which each year must augment. Youth and high spirits or the assumption of high spirits—these she must have if she were to keep her place in her poor little circle—and both were slipping from her fast. "This is my last chance." She stood in front of her mirror in her dancing frock, her dark hair exquisitely dressed, her face hauntingly wistful. After all, she was beautiful. Why shouldn't she win? Jenny thought that she could.

At that moment Jenny was slipping noiselessly along a corridor to the northern side of the house. The lights were all off; a pencil of moonlight here and there from an interstice in the curtains alone touched her as she passed. At one window she stopped, and softly lifted the blind. She looked out and was satisfied.

"Thought so!" she murmured, with a little vindictive smile. Just beneath her was that long window of the library which Joan had been at such pains to arrange.

Jenny stationed herself by the window. The night was very still. She could hear the voices of the servants in the dining-room round the angle of the house, and see the light from its windows lying in frames upon the grass. Then the light went out, and silence fell.

From time to time the hum of a motorcar swelled and diminished to its last faint vibrations on the distant road; and as each car passed Jenny stiffened at her post. She looked at her watch, turning the dial to the moonlight. It was ten minutes past nine now. The cars had left Rackham Park well before nine. She would not have long to wait now! As she slipped her watch again into her waistband she drew back with an instinctive movement, although the window at which she stood had been this last half hour in shadow. For under a great copper beech on the grass in front of her a man was standing. The sight of him was a shock to her.

She wondered how he had come, how long he had been there—and why? Some explanation flashed upon her.

"My goodness me!" she whispered. "You could knock me down with a hairpin. So you could!"

Whilst she watched that solitary figure beneath the tree, another motor whizzed along the road. The noise of its engine grew louder—surely louder than any which, standing at this window, she had heard before. Had it turned into the park? off the main road. Was it coming to the house? Before Jenny could answer these questions in her mind, the noise ceased altogether. Jenny held her breath; and round the angle of the house a girl came running swiftly, her skirt sparkling like silver in the moonlight, and a white cloak drawn about her shoulders. She drew open the window of the library and passed in. A few seconds passed. Jenny imagined her stealthily opening the door into the hall, and listening to make sure that the servants were in their own quarters and this part of the house deserted. Then the girl reappeared at the window and made a sign. From beneath the tree the man ran across the grass. His face was turned towards

Jenny, and the moonlight revealed it. The man was Mario Escobar.

Jenny drew a little sharp breath. She heard the window ever so gently latched. Suddenly the light blazed out from the room and then, strip by strip, vanished, as if the curtains had been cautiously drawn. The garden, the house resumed its aspect of quiet; all was as it had been when Jenny Prask first lifted the window of the corridor. Jenny Prask crept cautiously away.

"Fancy that!" she said to herself, with a little chuckle of triumph.

In the room below Mario Escobar and Joan Whitworth were talking.

CHAPTER XXV

In a Library

"You insisted that I should see you. You have something to say to me," said Joan. She was breathing more quickly than usual and the blood fluttered in her cheeks, but she faced Mario Escobar with level eyes, and spoke without a tremor in her voice. So far everything had happened just as she had planned. There were these few difficult minutes now to be grappled with, and afterwards the ordeal would be ended, that foolish chapter in her life altogether closed. "Will you please be quick?" she pleaded.

But Mario Escobar was in no hurry to answer. He had never imagined that Joan Whitworth could look so beautiful. He had never dreamed that she would take so much trouble. Mario Escobar understood women's clothes, and his eyes ran with a sensation of pleasure over her delicate frock with its shining bands, its embroidery of silver and flounces of fine lace, down to her slim brocaded shoes. He had not, indeed, thought very much of her in the days when Linda Spavinsky was queen. She had been a sort of challenge to him, because of her aloofness, her indifference. Women were his profession, and here was a queer outlandish one whom it would be amusing to parade as his. So he had set to work; he had a sense of art, he could talk with ingenuity on artistic matters, and he had flattered Joan by doing so; but always with a certain definite laughter and contempt for her. Now her beauty rather swept him off his feet. He looked at her in amazement. Why this change? And—the second question for ever in his mind—how could he profit by it?

"I don't understand," he said slowly, feeling his way. "We were good friends—very good friends." Joan neither denied nor agreed. "We had certain things in common, a love of art, of the finer things of life. I made enemies, of course, in consequence. Your racing friends——" He paused. "Milly Splay, who would have matched you with some dull, tiresome squire accustomed to sleep over his port after dinner, the sort of man you are drawing so brilliantly in your wonderful book." A movement of impatience on Joan's part perplexed him. Authors! You can generally lay your praise on with a trowel. What in the world was the matter with Joan? He hurried on. "I understood that I was making enemies. I understood, too, why I was no longer invited to Rackham Park. I was a foreigner. I would as soon visit a picture gallery as shoot a pheasant. I would as soon appreciate your old gates and houses in the country as gallop after a poor little fox on the downs. Oh, yes, I wasn't popular. That I understand. But you!" and his voice softened to a gentle reproach. "You were different! And you had the courage of your difference! Since I was not invited to Rackham Park, I was to come down to the inn at Midhurst. I was to drive over—publicly, most publicly—and ask for you. We would show them that there were finer things in the world than horse-racing and lawn tennis. Oh, yes. We arranged it all at that wonderful exhibition of the New School in Green Street."

Joan writhed a little at her recollection of the pictures of the rotundists and of the fatuous aphorisms to which she had given utterance.

"I come to Midhurst accordingly, and what happens? You scribble me out a curt little letter. I am not to come to Rackham Park. I am not to try to see you. And you are writing tomorrow. But tomorrow comes, and you don't write—no, not one line!"

"It was so difficult," Joan answered. She spoke diffidently. Some of her courage had gone from her; she was confronted with so direct, so unanswerable an accusation. "I thought that you would understand that I did not wish to see you again. I thought that you would accept my wish."

Mario Escobar laughed unpleasantly.

"Why should I?"

"Because most men have that chivalry," said Joan.

Mario Escobar only smiled this time. He smiled with narrowed eyes and a gleam of white teeth behind his black moustache. He was amused, like a man who receives ridiculous answers from a child.

"It is easy to see that you have read the poets—Joan," he replied deliberately.

Joan's face flamed. Never had she been addressed with so much insolence. Chaff she was accustomed to, but it was always chaff mitigated by a tenderness of real affection. Insolence and disdain were quite new to her, and they hurt intolerably. Joan, however, was learning her lessons fairly quickly. She had to get this meeting over as swiftly and quietly as she could, and high words would not help.

"It's true," she admitted meekly. "I know very little."

Joan looked very lovely as she stood nervously drumming with her gloved fingers on a little table which stood between them, all her assurance gone.

Mario Escobar lived always on the whirling edge of passion. The least extra leap of the water caught him and drew him in. He gazed at Joan, and the computing look which cast up her charms made her suddenly hot from head to foot. The good-looking, pretentious fool whom it had been amusing to exhibit amidst the black frowns of her circle had suddenly become exquisitely desirable for herself as a prize, with her beauty, her dainty care to tend it, and her delicious clothes. She would now be a real credit! Escobar took a step towards her.

"After all," he said, "we were such good friends. We had little private interests which we did not share with other people. Surely it was natural that I should wish to see you again."

Mario was speaking smoothly enough now. His voice, his eyes actually caressed her. She was at pains to repress a shiver of physical repulsion. But she remembered his letter very clearly. It had expressed no mere wish to see her. It had claimed a right with a vague threat of making trouble if the right were not conceded. She had recognised the right, not out of the fear of the threat so much—although that weighed with her, as out of a longing to have done with him for good and all. Instinct had told her that this was the last type of man to find favour in Harry Luttrell's eyes, that she herself would be lowered from her high pedestal in his heart, if he knew of the false friendship.

"Well, I agreed to see you," she replied. "But I have to go back to the ball. Will you please to be quick?"

"The time and the place were of your own choice."

"My choice!" Joan answered. "I had no choice. A girl amongst visitors in a country house—when is she free? When is she alone? She can keep to her room—yes! But that's all her liberty. Let her go out, there will be some one at her side."

"If she is like you—no doubt," said Escobar, and again he smiled at her covetously. Joan shook the compliment off her with a hitch of her shoulders.

"We could have met in a hundred places," Mario continued.

"I could have come to call on you as we arranged."

"No!" cried Joan with more vigour than wisdom in her voice. She had a picture of him, of the embarrassment of the Splays and her friends, of the disapproval of Harry Luttrell.

Escobar was quick when he dealt with women, quick and sensitive. The passionate denial did not escape him. He began to divine the true cause of this swift upheaval and revolution in her.

"You could have sent me a card for the Willoughbys' dance. It would have been easy enough for us to meet there."

Again she replied, "No!" A note of obstinacy was audible.

"Why?"

Joan did not answer at all.

"I'll tell you," Escobar flashed out at her angrily. "You wouldn't be seen with me any more! Suddenly, you would not be seen with me—no, not for the world! That's the truth, isn't it? That's why you come secretly back and bid me meet you in an empty house."

"Hush!" pleaded Joan.

Mario Escobar's voice had risen as his own words flogged him to a keener indignation.

"Why should I care if all the world hears me?" he replied roughly. "Why should I consider you, who turn me down the moment it suits you, without a reason? It's fairly galling to me, I assure you."

Joan nodded her head. Mario Escobar had some right upon his side, she was ready to acknowledge.

"I beg your pardon," she said simply. "Won't you please be content with that and leave things as they are?"

"When you are a little older you will know that you can never leave things as they are," answered Mario. "I was looking forward to a week of happiness. I have had a week of torment. For lesser insults than yours, men kill in my country."

There were other differences, too, between her country and his. Joan did not cry out, or burst into tears or flinch in any way. She was alone in this room; there was no one, as far as she knew, within the reach of her voice. She had chosen this meeting-place, not altogether because the house would be empty, but because in this first serious difficulty of her life she would be amongst familiar things and draw from them confidence and strength, and a sense of security. With Mario Escobar in front of her, his face ablaze with passion, the security vanished altogether. Yet all the more she was raised to the top of her courage.

"Then I shall tell you the truth," she answered gently. "You speak to me of our friendship. It was never anything serious to me. It was a taunt—a foolish taunt to other people."

Mario Escobar flinched, as if she had struck him in the face.

"Yes, I hurt you," she went on in the same gentle voice, which was not the least element in Escobar's humiliation. "I am very sorry. I tried not to hurt you. I am very ignorant, as you have told me, but I wouldn't believe it till a week ago. I made it my pride to be different from anybody else. I believed that I was different. I was a fool. I wouldn't listen. Even during the war. I have shut myself up away from it, trying not to share in the effort, not to feel the pride and the sorrow, pretending that it was just a horrible, sordid business altogether beneath lofty minds! That's one of the reasons why I chose you for my friend! I was flinging my glove in the face of the little world I knew. I had *got* to be different. It's all very shameful to tell, and I am sorry. Oh, how I am sorry!"

Her sorrow was most evident. She had sunk down upon a couch, her fair head drooping and the tears now running down her cheeks in the bitterness of her shame. But Mario Escobar was untouched by any pity. If any thought occurred to him outside his burning humiliation, it was prompted by the economy of the Spaniard.

"She'll spoil that frock if she goes on crying," he said to himself, "and it was very expensive."

"I have nothing but remorse to offer in atonement," she went on. "But that remorse is very sincere——"

Mario Escobar swept her plea aside with a furious gesture.

"So that's it!" he cried. "You were just making a fool of me!" That she, this pretty pink and white girl, should have been making a show of him, parading him before her friends, exhibiting him, using him as a challenge—just as in fact he had been using her, and with more success! Only to think of it hurt him like a knife. "Your remorse!" he cried scornfully. "There's some one else, of course!"

Joan sat up straight and stiff. Escobar might have laid a lash across her delicate shoulders.

"Yes," she said defiantly.

"Some one who was not here a week ago?"

"Yes."

To Escobar's humiliation was now added a sudden fire of jealousy. For the first time tonight, as woman, as flesh and blood, she was adorable, and she owed this transformation, not to him, no, not in the tiniest fraction of a degree to him, but to some one else, some dull boor without niceties or deftness, who had stormed into her life within the week. Who was it? He had got to know. But Joan was hardly thinking of Escobar. Her eyes were turned from him.

"He has set me free from many vanities and follies. If I am grieved and ashamed now, I owe it thankfully to him. If my remorse is bitter, it is because through him I have a gleam of light which helps me to understand."

"And you have told him what you have told me?"

"No, but I shall tonight when all this is over, when I go back to Harrel."

Mario Escobar moved closer to her.

"Are you so sure that you are going back to Harrel tonight?" he asked in a low voice.

"Yes," she replied, and only after she had spoken did the menace of his voice force itself into her mind as something which she must take into account. She looked up at him startled, and as she looked her wonderment turned into stark fear. The cry that in his country men killed had left her unmoved. But she was afraid now, desperately afraid, all the more afraid because she thought of the man searching for her through the reception-rooms at Harrel.

"We are alone here in an empty quarter of the house. So you arranged it," he continued. "Good! Women do not amuse themselves at my expense without being paid for it."

Joan started up in a panic, but Escobar seized her shoulders and forced her down again.

"Sit still," he cried savagely. Then his face changed. For the first time for many minutes his lips parted in a smile of pleasure.

"You are very lovely, Joan. I love to see you like that—afraid—trembling. It is the beginning of recompense."

Joan had tumbled into a deeper pit than any she had dreamed of. In desperation she cast about for means to climb out of it. The secrecy of this meeting—that must go. But, even so, was there escape? The bell? Before she could be halfway across the room, he would be holding her in his arms. A cry? Before it was half uttered, he would have stifled her mouth. No, she must sit very still and provoke no movement by him.

Mario Escobar was a creature of unhealthy refinements. He wanted to know, first, who was the man who had touched this indifferent maiden into warm life. The knowledge would be an extra spice to his pleasure.

"Who are staying in the house?" he asked. It would be amusing to make his selection, and discover if he were right.

"Dennis Brown, Harold Jupp"—Joan began, puzzled by his question, yet welcoming it as so much delay.

"I don't want to hear about them," Mario Escobar replied. "Tell me of the newcomers!"

"Martin Hillyard—" Joan began again, and was aware that Mario Escobar made a quick startled movement and gasped. Martin Hillyard's name was a pail of cold water for Escobar.

"Does Hillyard know that I am at Midhurst?" he asked sharply.

"No," Joan answered.

There was something which Hillyard had told her about Mario Escobar, something which she had rejected and dismissed altogether from her thoughts. Then she remembered. Escobar was an enemy working in

England against England. She had given the statement no weight whatever. It was the sort of thing people said of unconventional people they disliked in order to send them to Coventry. But Escobar's start and Escobar's question put a different value upon it. Joan caught at it. Of what use could it be to her? Of some use, surely, if only she had the wit to divine it. But she was in such a disorder of fear and doubt that every idea went whirling about and about in her mind. She raised her hand to her forehead, keeping her eyes upon Escobar. She felt as helpless as a child. Almost she regretted the love which had so violently mastered her. It had made clear to her her ignorance and so stripped her of all assurance and left her defenceless.

But even in the tumult of her thoughts, she began to recognise a change. The air was less charged with terror. There was less of passion and anger in Mario Escobar, and more of speculation. He watched her in a gloomy silence, and each moment she took fresh heart. With a swift movement he seated himself on the couch beside her.

Joan sprang up with a little cry, and her heart thumping in her breast.

"Hush!" said Escobar. Yes, it was now he who pleaded for secrecy and a quiet voice.

There was a stronger passion in Mario than the love of women, and that was the love of money. Women were to him mainly the means to money. They were easier to get, too, if you were not over particular. Money was a rare, shy thing, except to an amazing few who accumulated it by some obscure, magnetic attraction; and opportunities of acquisition were not to be missed.

"Hush!" he said. "You treated me badly, Joan. It was right that I should teach you a lesson—frighten you a little, eh?"

He smiled at her with eyes half closed and eyelids cunningly blinking. Now that her fears were weakening Joan found his impertinence almost insufferable. But she held her tongue and waited.

"But you owe me a return, don't you?"

Joan did not move.

"A little return—which will cost you nothing at all. You know that I represent a line of ships. You can help me. We have rivals, with active agents. You shall find out for me exactly what Martin Hillyard is doing in the Mediterranean, and why he visits in a yacht the ports of Spain. You will find this out for me, so that I may know whether he is acting for my rivals. Yes."

"He is not," answered Joan.

"You will find this out for me, so that I may know," Escobar repeated smoothly. "Exactly what he is doing in the Mediterranean, what special plans, and why he visits in a yacht the ports of Spain. You promise me that knowledge, and you can go straight back to your dancing."

"I have no knowledge," said Joan quietly.

"But you can obtain it," Escobar insisted. "He is a friend of yours. Exactly what he is doing—is it not so?"

So Martin's accusation was true. Joan nodded her head, and Escobar, with a smile of relief, took the gesture as a consent to his proposal.

"Good!" he said, rising from the couch. "Then all is forgiven! You will make some notes——"

"I will do nothing of the kind," said Joan quietly, but she was white to the edge of her lips, and she trembled from head to foot. But there was no room any more for fear in her. She was in a heat of anger which she had never known. "Oh, that you should dare!" and her words choked her.

Mario Escobar stared at her.

"You refuse?"

"With all my soul."

Escobar took a step towards her, but she did not move.

"You are alone with me, when you should be dancing at the ball. You made the appointment, chose the hour, the place . . . even if you scream, there will be a scandal, a disgrace."

"I don't care."

"And the man you are in love with, eh? That makes a difference," he said, as he saw the girl falter. "Do we think of him?"

"No," said Joan. "We incur the disgrace."

She saw his eyes open wide with terror. He drew a step away from her. "Oh!" he exclaimed, in a long-drawn whisper; and he looked at Joan with incredulity and hatred. "You——" he used some Spanish word which Joan did not catch. It would have told her little if she had caught it. It was "Cabron," a harmless, inoffensive word which has become in Spain the ultimate low word of abuse. "You have laid a trap for me."

Joan answered him in a bewilderment. "I have laid no trap for you," and there was so much scorn and contempt in her voice that Escobar could hardly disbelieve her.

But he was shaken. He was in a panic. He was in a haste to go. Money—yes. But you must live in order to enjoy it.

"I will give you a day to think over my proposal," he said, stammering the words in his haste. And then, "Don't write to me! I will find a means," and, almost before she was aware of his movements, he had snatched up his cap, and the room was empty. The curtain was torn aside; the glass door stood open; beyond it the garden lay white in the light of the moon.

"A trap?" Joan repeated his accusation in a perplexity. She turned and she saw the door, the door behind her, which Escobar had faced, the door into the hall, slowly open. There had been no turning of the handle, it was unlatched before. Yet Joan had seen to it that it was shut before ever she beckoned Mario Escobar into the room. Some one, then, had been listening. Mario Escobar had seen the handle move, the door drawn ajar. Joan saw it open now to its full width, and in the entrance Stella Croyle.

CHAPTER XXVI

A Fatal Kindness

Joan picked up her cloak and arranged it upon her shoulders. She did not give one thought to Stella, or even hear the words which Stella began nervously to speak. Her secret appointment would come to light now in any case. It would very likely cost her—oh, all the gold and glamour of the world. It would be bandied about in gossip over the tea-tables, in the street, at the Clubs, in the Press. Sir Chichester ought to be happy, at all events. The thought struck her with a wry humour, and brought a smile to her lips. He would accomplish his dream. Without effort, without a letter or a telephone call, or a rebuff, he would have such publicity as he could hardly have hoped for. "Who is that?" Joan made up a little scene. "That? Oh, don't you know? That's Sir Chichester Splay. You must have heard of Sir Chichester! Why, it was in his house that the Whitworth girl, rather pretty but an awful fool, carried on with the spy-man."

Joan was a little overstrung. All the while she was powdering her nose in front of a mirror and removing as best she could the traces of tears, and all the while Mrs. Croyle was stammering words and words and words behind her. Joan regretted that Stella was not going to the Willoughbys' ball. If she had been, she would probably be carrying some rouge in her little handbag, and Joan might have borrowed some.

"Well, since you haven't got any with you, I must go," said Joan, bursting suddenly into Stella's monologue. But she had caught a name spoken just before Stella stopped in her perplexity at Joan's outbreak.

"Harry Luttrell!" Joan repeated. What in the world had Stella Croyle got to say to her about Harry Luttrell? But Stella resumed her faltering discourse and the sense of her words penetrated at last to Joan's brain and amazed her.

Joan was to leave Harry Luttrell alone.

"You are quite young," said Stella, "only twenty. What does he matter to you? You have everything in front of you. With your looks and your twenty years you can choose where you will. You have lovers already—"

"I?" Joan interrupted.

"Mario Escobar."

Joan repeated the name with such a violence of scorn that for a moment Stella Croyle was silenced.

"Mario Escobar!"

"He was here with you a moment ago."

Joan answered quietly and quite distinctly:

"I wish he were dead!"

Stella Croyle fell back upon her first declaration.

"You must leave my Wub alone."

Joan laughed aloud, harshly and without any merriment. She checked herself with an effort lest she should go on laughing, and her laughter turn uncontrollably into hysteria and tears. Here was Mrs. Croyle, a grown woman, standing in front of her like a mutinous obstinate child, looking like one too, talking like one and bidding Joan leave her Wub alone. Whence did she get that ridiculous name? It was all degrading and grotesque.

"Your Wub! Your Wub!" she cried in a heat. "Yes, I am only twenty, and probably I am quite wrong and stupid. But it seems to me horrible that we two women should be wrangling over a man neither of us had met a week ago. I'll have no more of it."

She flung towards the window, but Stella Croyle cried out, "A week ago!" and the cry brought her to a stop. Joan turned and looked doubtfully at Mrs. Croyle. After all, that ridiculous label had not been pasted on to Harry Luttrell as a result of a week's acquaintance. Harry Luttrell had certainly talked to Stella through the greater part of an evening, his first evening in the house, but they had hardly been together at all since then. Joan came back slowly into the room.

"So you knew Colonel Luttrell before this week?"

"We were great friends a few years ago."

It was disturbing to Joan that Harry Luttrell had never spoken to her of this friendship. Was it possible that Stella had a claim upon him of which she herself knew nothing? She sat down at a table in front of Mrs. Croyle.

"Tell me," she said.

Once, long ago, upon the deck of the *Dragonfly* at Stockholm, Stella had cried out to Harry Luttrell, "Oh, what a cruel mistake you made when you went out of your way to be kind!" Joan was now to hear how that cry had come to be uttered by a woman in the nethermost distress. She knew, of course, that Stella was married at the age of seventeen and had been divorced, but little more than that.

"There was a little girl," said Stella, "my baby. I lost her."

She spoke very simply. She had come to the end of efforts and schemes, and was very tired. Joan's anger died away altogether in her heart.

"Oh, I am very sorry," she replied. "I didn't know that you had a little girl."

"Yes. Look, here is her portrait." Stella Croyle drew out from her bosom a locket which hung night and day against her heart, and showed it to Joan across the table. "But I don't know whether she is little any more. She is thirteen now."

Joan gazed at the painted miniature of a lovely child with the eyes and the hair of Stella Croyle.

"And you lost her altogether?" she asked with a rising pity.

"Not at first," answered Stella. "I was allowed by the Court to have her with me for one month in every year. And I lived the other eleven months for the one, the wonderful one."

Stella's face softened indescribably. The memory of her child did for her what all her passion for Harry Luttrell could not do. It restored her youth. Her eyes grew tender, her mouth quivered, the look of conflict vanished altogether.

"We had good times together, my baby and I. I took her to the sea. It sounds foolish, but we were more like a couple of children together than mother and daughter"; and Joan, looking at the delicate, porcelainlike figure in front of her, smiled in response.

"Yes, I can understand that."

"She was with me every minute," Stella Croyle resumed. "I watched her so, I gave her so much of me that when I had seen her off at the station with her nurse at the end of the month, I was left behind, as weak and limp as an invalid. I lived for her, Joan, believe that at all events in my favour! There was no one else."

"I do believe it."

"Then one year in the winter she did not come to me."

"They kept her back!" cried Joan. "But you had the right to her."

"Yes. And I went down to Exeter to her father's house, to fetch her away."

It was curious that Stella Croyle, who was speaking of her own distressful life, told her story with a quiet simplicity of tone, as if she had bent her neck in submission to the hammer strokes of her destiny; whereas Joan, who was but listening to griefs of another, was stirred to a compassion which kindled her face and made her voice shake.

"Oh, they hadn't sent her away! She was waiting for you," she cried eagerly.

"She was waiting for me. Yes! But it was no longer my baby who was waiting. They had worked on her, Robert, my husband—and his sisters.

They had told her—oh, more than they need! That I was bad."

"Oh!" breathed Joan.

"Yes, they were a little cruel. They had changed baby altogether. She was just eight at that time." Stella stopped for a moment or two. Her voice did not falter but her eyes suddenly swam with tears. "She used to adore me—she really and truly did. Now her little face and her eyes were like flint. And what do you think she said to me? Just this! 'Mummy, I don't want to go with you. If you take me with you, you'll spoil my holidays!'"

Joan shot back in her chair.

"But they had taught her to say that?"

Stella Croyle shook her head.

"They had taught her to dislike me. My little girl has character. She wouldn't have repeated the words, because she had been taught them. No, she meant them."

"But a day or two with you and she would have forgotten them. Oh, she *did* forget them!"

In her great longing to comfort the woman, whose deep anguish she divined beneath the quiet desolation of her voice, Joan overleapt her own knowledge. She was still young enough to will that past events had not occurred, and that things true were false.

"I didn't take her," replied Stella Croyle. "I wouldn't take her. I knew baby—besides she had struck me too hard."

"You came away alone!" whispered Joan.

"In the cab which I had kept waiting at the door to take us both away."

"That's terrible!" said Joan. The child with her lovely face set like flint in the room, the mother creeping out of the house and stumbling alone into the fly at the door—the picture was vivid before her eyes. Joan wrung her hands with a little helpless gesture, and a moan upon her lips. Almost it seemed that these sad things were actually happening to *her*, so poignantly she felt them.

"Oh, and you had all that long journey back to London, the journey you had dreamt of for eleven months with your baby at your side—you had now to take it alone."

Stella Croyle shook her head.

"No! There was just one and only one of my friends—and not at all a great friend—who had the imagination to understand, as you understand too, Joan, just what that journey would have meant to me, if anything had gone wrong, and the kindness to put himself out to make its endurance a little easier."

Joan drew back quickly.

"Harry Luttrell," she whispered.

"Yes. He had once been stationed at Exeter. He knew Robert Croyle and the sisters. He guessed what might happen to me. Perhaps he knew that it was going to happen."

So, when Stella, having pulled down her veil that none might see her face, was stumbling along the platform in search of an empty carriage, a hand was very gently laid upon her and Harry Luttrell was at her side. He had come all the way from London to befriend her, should she need it. If he had seen her with her little girl, he would have kept out of sight and himself have returned to London by a later train.

"That was fine," cried Joan.

"Fine, yes!" answered Stella. "You realise that, Joan, and you have never been in real trouble, or known what men are when kindness interferes with their comfort. I am not blaming people, but women do get the worst of it, if they are fools enough—wicked enough if you like, to do as I did. I knew men—lots of them. I was bound to. I was fair game, you see."

Joan's forehead wrinkled. The doors of knowledge had been opening very rapidly for her during the last few minutes. But she was still often at a loss.

"Fair game. Why? I don't understand."

"I had been divorced. Therefore I wasn't dangerous. Complications couldn't follow from a little affair with me." Stella explained bitterly. "I had men on my doorstep always. But not one of these men who protested and made love to me, would have put themselves out to do what Harry Luttrell did. It was fine—yes. But for three years I have been wondering whether Harry Luttrell would not really have been kinder if he had thought of his own comfort too, and had never travelled to Exeter to befriend me."

"Why?" asked Joan.

"I should have thrown myself out of the carriage and saved myself—oh, so much sorrow afterwards," Stella Croyle answered in so simple and natural a voice that Joan could not disbelieve her.

Joan clasped her hands before her eyes and then gazed again at Stella sitting in front of her, with pity and wonder. It was so hard for her to understand that this pretty woman, who made it her business to be gay, whom she had met from time to time in this house and had chatted with and forgotten, had passed through so dreadful an ordeal of suffering and humiliation. She was to look closer still into the mysteries which were being revealed to her.

Harry Luttrell had held Stella in his arms just as if she had been a child herself whilst the train rushed through the bleak winter country. Stella had behaved like a child, now sobbing in a passion of grief, now mutinous in a passion of rage, now silent and despairing under the weights that nothing, neither sympathy, nor grief, nor revolt, can lift.

"He took me home. He stayed with me. Oh, it wasn't love," cried Stella. "He was afraid."

"Afraid!" asked Joan. She wished to know every least detail of the story now.

"Afraid lest I should take—something . . . as I wished to do . . . as during the trouble of the divorce I learned to do."

She related little ridiculous incidents which Joan listened to with a breaking heart. Stella could not sleep at all after her return. She lived in a little house with a big garden on the northern edge of London, and all night she lay awake, listening to the patter of rain on melancholy trees, and thinking and thinking. Harry Luttrell kept her from the drugs in her dressing-case. She had no anodyne for her sorrows—but one.

"You will laugh," said Stella with a little wry smile of her own, "when I tell you what it was. It was a gramophone. I got Harry to set it going, whilst I lay in bed—to set it playing ragtime. While it was playing, I stopped thinking. For I had to keep time in my brain with the beat of the tune. And so, at last, since I couldn't think, or remember, I fell asleep. The gramophone saved me"; and again Joan was smitten by the incongruity of Stella with her life. She had eaten of all that nature allots to women—love, marriage, the birth of children, the loss of them—and there she was, to this day half-child, and quite incompatible with what she had suffered and endured.

"After a fortnight I got quieter of course," said Stella. "And suddenly a change sadder than anything I have told you took place in me. I suppose that I had gone through too much on baby's account for me. I lost something more than my baby, I lost my want to have her with me."

She remained silent for a little while reviewing the story which she had told.

"There, that's all," she said, rising suddenly. "It's no claim at all, of course. I know that very well. Harry left me at Stockholm four years ago;" and suddenly Joan's face flushed scarlet. She had been absorbed in Stella's sorrows, she had admired that kind action of Harry Luttrell's which had brought so much trouble in its train. It needed that reminder that Harry had only left Stella Croyle at Stockholm to bring home the whole part which Harry had taken in the affair. Now she understood; a flame of sudden jealousy confused her; and with it came a young girl's distaste as though some ugly reptile had raised its head amongst flowers.

"I never saw Harry again until this week, except for a minute outside a shop one morning in Piccadilly. But he hasn't married during those four years, so I always kept a hope that we should be somewhere together again for a few days, and that afterwards he would come back to me."

"That's why you chose this week to come to Rackham Park?"

"Yes," answered Stella Croyle; and she laughed harshly. "But I hadn't considered you."

Joan looked helplessly at her companion. Stella had not one small chance of the fulfilment of her hope—no, not one—even if she herself stood a million miles away. Of that Joan was sure. But how was she to say so to one who was blind and deaf to all but her hope, who would not listen, who would not see? Mario Escobar had left his gloves behind him on a couch. Joan saw them, and remembered to whom they belonged, and her thoughts took another complexion. Harry Luttrell! What share had she now in his life? She rose abruptly and pushed back her chair.

"Oh, I'll stand aside," she said, "never fear! We are to talk things over tonight. I shall say 'No.'"

She had turned again to the window, but a startled question from Stella Croyle stayed her feet.

"Harry has asked you to marry him?"

"He was going to," Joan faltered. The sense of her own loss returned upon her, she felt utterly alone, all the more alone because of the wondrous week which had come to so desolate an end tonight. "Here in this little room, not two hours ago. But I asked him to wait until supper time tonight. Here—it was here we stood!"

Joan looked down. Yes, she had been standing in this very spot, the table here upon her left, that chair upon her right, that trifolium in the pattern of the carpet under her feet, when Harry Luttrell had taken her in his arms. What foolish thing was Stella Croyle saying now?

"I take back all that I have said to you. If Harry has spoken to you already I have lost—that's all. I didn't know," she said. Her cheeks were white, her eyes suddenly grown large with a horror in them which Joan could not understand.

"Yes, it's all over. I have lost," she kept repeating in a dreadful whisper, moistening her dry lips with her tongue between her sentences.

"Oh, don't think that I am standing aside out of pity," Joan answered her. "Tomorrow I shall be impossible as a wife for Harry Luttrell." The words fell upon ears which did not hear. It would not have mattered if Stella had heard. Since Harry Luttrell was that night asking Joan to marry him, the hopes upon which she had so long been building, which Jenny Prask had done so much to nurse and encourage, withered and crumbled in an instant.

"I must go back and dance," said Joan with a shiver.

She left Stella Croyle standing in the room like one possessed with visions of terrible things. Her tragic face and moving lips were to haunt Joan for many a month afterwards. She went out by the window and ran down the drive to the spot where she had left Miranda's car halfway between the lodge and the house. The gates had been set open that night against the return of the party from Harrel. Joan drove back again under the great over-arching trees of the road. It was just ten o'clock when she slipped into the ballroom and was claimed by a neighbour for a dance.

CHAPTER XXVII

The Rank and File

Martin Hillyard crammed a year's enjoyment into the early hours of that night. He danced a great deal and had supper a good many times; and even the girl who had passed the season of 1914 in London and said languidly, "Tell me more," before he had opened his mouth, failed to ruffle his enjoyment.

"If I did, you would scream for your mother," he replied, "and I should be turned out of the house and Sir Chichester would lose his position in the county. No, I'll tell you less. That means we'll go and have some supper."

He led a subdued maiden into the supper-room and from that moment his enjoyment began to wane. For, at a little table near to hand, sat Joan Whitworth and Harry Luttrell, and it was clear to him from the distress upon their faces that their smooth courtship had encountered its obstacles. A spot of anger, indeed, seemed to burn in Joan's cheeks. They hardly spoke at all.

Half an hour later, he came face to face with Joan in a corridor.

"I have been looking for you for a long while," she cried in a quick, agitated voice. "Are you free for this dance?"

"Yes."

Martin Hillyard lied without compunction.

"Then will you take me into the garden?"

He found a couple of chairs in a corner of the terrace out of the hearing of the rest.

"We shall be quiet here," he said. He hoped that she would disclose the difficulty which had risen between herself and Harry, and seek his counsel as Harry's friend. It might be one of the little trifling discords which love magnifies until they blot out the skies and drape the earth in temporary mourning. But Joan began at once nervously upon a different topic.

"You made a charge against Mario Escobar the other day. I did not believe it. But you spoke the truth. I know that now."

She stopped and gazed woefully in front of her. Then she hurried on.

"I can prove it. He demands news of your movements in the Mediterranean. If it is necessary I must come forward publicly and prove it. It will be horrible, but of course I will."

Martin looked at her quickly. She kept her eyes averted from him. Her fingers plucked nervously at her dress. There was an aspect of shame in her attitude.

"It will not be necessary, Joan," he answered. "I have quite enough evidence already to put him away until the end of the war."

Joan turned to him with quivering lips.

"You are sure. It means so much to me to escape—what I have no right to escape, I can hardly believe it."

"I am quite sure," replied Martin Hillyard.

Joan breathed a long, fluttering sigh of relief. She sat up as though a weight had been loosed from her shoulders. The trouble lifted from her face.

"You need not call upon me at all?"

"No."

"I don't want to shirk—any more," she insisted. "I should not hesitate."

"I know that, Joan," he said with a smile. She looked out over the gardens to the great line of hills, dim and pleasant as fairyland in the silver haze of the moonlight. Her eyes travelled eastwards along the ridge and stopped at the clump of Bishop's Ring which marks the crest of Duncton Hill, and the dark fold below where the trees flow down to Graffham.

"You ask me no questions," she said in a low, warm voice. "I am very grateful."

"I ask you one. Where is Mario Escobar tonight?"

"At Midhurst," and she gave him the name of the hotel.

Martin Hillyard laughed. Whilst the police were inquiring here and searching there and watching the ports for him, he was lying almost within reach of his hand, snugly and peacefully at Midhurst.

"But I expect that he will go from Midhurst now," Joan added, remembering his snarl of fear when the door had opened behind her, and the haste with which he had fled.

Hillyard looked at his watch. It was one o'clock in the morning.

"You are in a hurry?" she asked.

"I ought to send a message." He turned to Joan. "You know this house, of course. Is there a telephone in a quiet room, where I shall not be interrupted or be drowned out, voice and ears by the music?"

"Yes, Mrs. Willoughby's sitting-room upstairs. Shall I ask her if you may use it?"

"If you please."

Joan left Martin standing in one of the corridors and rejoined him after a few minutes. "Come," she said, and led the way upstairs to the room. Martin called up the trunk line and gave a number.

"I shall have to wait a few minutes," he said.

"You want me to go," answered Joan, and she moved towards the door reluctantly.

"No. But you will be missing your dances."

Joan shook her head. She did not turn back to him, but stood facing the door as she replied; so that he could not see her face.

"I had kept all the dances after supper free. If I am not in the way I would rather wait with you."

"Of course."

He was careful to use the most commonplace tone with the thought that it would steady her. The trouble which this telephone message would finally dispel was clearly not all which distressed her. She needed companionship; her voice broke, as though her heart were breaking too. He saw her raise a wisp of handkerchief to her eyes; and then the telephone bell rang at his side. He was calling at a venture upon the number which Commodore Graham had rung up in the office above the old waterway of the Thames.

"Is that Scotland Yard?" he asked, and he gave the address at which Mario Escobar was to be found. "But he may be gone tomorrow," he added, and hearing a short "That's all right," he rang off.

"Now, if you will get your cloak, we might go back into the garden."

They found their corner of the terrace unoccupied and sat for a while in silence. Hillyard recognised that neither questions nor any conversation at all were required from him, but simply the sympathy of his companionship. He smoked a cigarette while Joan sat by his side.

She stretched out her hand towards the Bishop's Ring, small as a button upon the great shoulder of the Down.

"Do you remember the afternoon when I drove you back from Goodwood?"

"Yes."

"You said to me, 'If the great trial is coming, I want to fall back into the rank and file.' And I cried out, 'Oh, I understand that!'"

"I remember."

"What a fool I was!" said Joan. "I didn't understand at all. I thought that it sounded fine, and that was why I applauded. I am only beginning to understand now. Even after I had agreed with you, my one ambition was to be different."

Her voice died remorsefully away. From the window further down the terrace the yellow light poured from the windows and fought with the moonlight. The music of a waltz floated out upon the yearning of many violins. There was a ripple of distant voices.

"All this week," Joan began again, "I have found myself standing unexpectedly in a strong light before a mirror and utterly scared by the revelation of what I was . . . by the memory of the foolish things which I had done. From one of the worst of them, you have saved me tonight. You are very kind to me, Martin."

It was the first time he had ever heard her use his Christian name.

"I should like to be kinder, if you'll let me," he said. "I am not blind. I was in the supper-room when you and Harry were there. It was for him that you had kept all the last dances free. And you are here, breaking your heart. Why?"

Joan shook her head. A little sob broke from her against her will. But this matter was between her and Harry Luttrell. She sought no counsel from any other.

"Then I am very grieved for both of you," said Hillyard. Joan made a movement as if she were about to rise. "Will you wait just a moment?" Martin asked.

He guessed that some hint of Stella Croyle's story had reached the girl's ears. He understood that she would be hurt, and affronted; that she would feel herself suddenly steeped in vulgarities; and that she would visit her resentment sharply upon her lover, and upon herself at the same time. And all this was true. But Martin was not sure of it. He meant to tread warily, lest if he stumbled, the harm should be the more complete.

"I have known Harry Luttrell a long while," he said. "No woman ever reached his heart until he came home from France this summer. No woman I believe, could have reached it—not even you, Joan, I believe, if you had met him a year ago. He was possessed by one great shame and one great longing—shame that the regiment with which he and his father were bound up, had once disgraced itself—longing for the day to come when it would recover its prestige. Those two emotions burnt in him like white flames. I believe no other could have lived beside them."

Joan would not speak, but she concentrated all her senses to listen. A phrase which Stella Croyle had used—Harry had feared to become "the slovenly soldier"—began to take on its meaning.

"On the Somme the shame was wiped out. Led by such men as Harry—well, you know what happened. Harry Luttrell came home freed at last from an overwhelming obsession. He looked about him with different eyes, and there you were! It seems to me a thing perfectly ordained, as so few things are. I brought him down here just for a pleasant week in the country—without another thought beyond that. All this week I have been coming to think of myself as an unconscious agent, who just at the right time is made to do the right thing. Here was the first possible moment for Harry Luttrell—and there you were in the path—just as if you without knowing it, had been set there to wait until he came over the fields to you."

He turned to her and took her hand in his. He had his sympathies for Stella Croyle, but her hopes held no positive promise of happiness for either her or Harry Luttrell—a mere flash and splutter of passion at the best, with all sorts of sordid disadvantages to follow, quarrels, the scorn of his equals, the loss of position, the check to advancement in his profession. Here, on the other hand, was the fitting match.

"It would be a great pity," he said gently, "if anything were now to interfere."

He stood up and after a moment Joan rose to her feet. There was a tender smile upon her lips and her eyes were shining. She laid a hand upon his arm.

"I shall have to get you a wife, Martin," she said, midway between laughter and tears. "It wouldn't be fair on us if you were to escape."

This was her way of thanking him.

CHAPTER XXVIII

The Long Sleep

The amazing incident which cut so sharply into these tangled lives occurred the next morning at Rackham Park. Some of the house party straggled down to a late breakfast, others did not descend at all. Harry Luttrell joined Millie Splay upon the stairs and stopped her before she entered the breakfast-room.

"I should like to slip away this morning, Lady Splay," he said. "My servant is packing now."

Millie Splay looked at him in dismay.

"Oh, I am so sorry," she said. "I was hoping that this morning you and Joan would have something to say to me."

"I did too," replied Harry with a wry smile. "But Joan turned me down with a bang last night."

Lady Splay plumped herself down on a chair in the hall.

"Oh, she is the most exasperating girl!" she cried. "Are you sure that you didn't misunderstand her?"

"Quite."

Lady Splay sat for a little while with her cheek propped upon her hand and her brows drawn together in a perplexity.

"It's very strange," she said at length. "For Joan meant you to ask her to marry you. She has been deliberately showing you that you weren't indifferent to her. Joan would never have done that if she hadn't meant you to ask her; or if she hadn't meant to accept you." She rose with a gesture of despair.

"I give it up. But oh, how I'd love to smack her!" and with that unrealisable desire burning furiously in her breast, Lady Splay marched into the breakfast-room. Dennis Brown and Jupp were already in their white flannels at the table. Miranda ran down into the room a moment afterwards.

"Joan's the lazy one," she said, looking round the table. She had got to bed at half past four and looked as fresh as if she had slept the clock round. "What are you going to eat, Colonel Luttrell?"

Luttrell was standing by her at the side table, and as they inspected the dishes they were joined by Mr. Albany Todd.

"You were going it last night," Jupp called to him, with a note of respect in his voice. "For a top-weight you're the hottest thing I have seen in years. Stay another week in our academic company, and we shall discover so many excellent qualities in you that we shall be calling you Toddles."

"And then in the winter, I suppose, we'll go jumping together," said Mr. Albany Todd.

Like many another round and heavy man, Mr. Albany Todd was an exceptionally smooth dancer. His first dance on the night before he had owed to the consideration of his hostess. Sheer merit had filled the rest of his programme; and he sat down to breakfast now in a high good humour. Sir Chichester stumped into the room when the serious part of the meal was over, and all the newspapers already taken. He sat down in front of his kidney and bacon and grunted.

"Any news in *The Times*, Mr. Albany Todd?"

"No! No!" replied Mr. Albany Todd in an abstracted voice, with his head buried between the pages. "Would you like it, Sir Chichester?"

He showed no intention of handing it over; and Sir Chichester replied with as much indifference as he could assume,

"Oh, there's no hurry."

"No, we have all the morning, haven't we?" said Mr. Albany Todd pleasantly.

Sir Chichester ate some breakfast and drank some tea. "No news in your paper is there, Dennis, my boy?" he asked carelessly.

"Oh, isn't there just?" cried Dennis Brown. "Oppifex and Hampstead Darling are both running in the two-thirty at Windsor."

Sir Chichester grunted again.

"Racing! It's wonderful, Mr. Albany Todd, that you haven't got the disease during the week. There's a racing microbe at Rackham."

"But I am not so sure that I have escaped," returned Mr. Albany Todd. "I am tempted to go jumping in the winter."

"You must keep your old Lords out if you do," Harold Jupp urged earnestly. "Bring in your Dukes and your Marquises, and we poor men are all up the spout."

Thus they rattled on about the breakfast table; cigarettes were lighted, Miranda pushed back her chair; in a minute the room would be deserted. But Millie Splay uttered a little cry of horror, so sharp and startling that it froze each person into a sudden immobility. She dropped the newspaper upon her knees. Her hands flew to her face and covered it.

"What's the matter, Millie?" cried Sir Chichester, starting up in alarm. He hurried round the table. Some stab of physical pain had caused Millie's cry—he shared that conviction with every one else in the room. But Millie lifted her head quickly.

"Oh, it's intolerable!" she exclaimed. "Chichester, look at this!" She thrust the paper feverishly into his hands. Sir Chichester smoothed its crumpled leaves as he stood beside her.

"Ah, the *Harpoon*," he said, his fear quite allayed. He knew his wife to have a somewhat thinner skin than himself. "You are exaggerating no doubt, my dear. The *Harpoon* is a good paper and quite friendly."

But Millie Splay broke in upon his protestations in a voice as shrill as a scream.

"Oh, stop, Chichester, and look! There, in the third column! Just under your eyes!"

And Sir Chichester Splay read. As he read his face changed.

"Yes, that won't do," he said, very quietly. He carried the newspaper back with him to his chair and sat down again. He had the air of a man struck clean out of his wits. "That won't do," he repeated, and again, with a rush of angry blood into his face, "No, that won't do." It seemed that Sir Chichester's harmless little foible had suddenly received more than its due punishment.

The newspaper slipped from his fingers on to the floor, whilst he sat staring at the white tablecloth in front of him. But no sooner did Harold Jupp at his side make a movement to pick the paper up than Sir Chichester swooped down upon it in a flash.

"No!" he said. "No!" and he began to fold it up very carefully. "It's as Millie says, a rather intolerable invention which has crept into the social news. I must consider what steps we should take."

There was another at that table who was as disturbed as Sir Chichester and Lady Splay. Martin Hillyard knew nothing of the paragraph which had caused this consternation in his hosts; and he had asked no questions last night. But he remembered every word that Joan had said. She had seen Mario Escobar somewhere since leaving Rackham Park—that was certain; and Mario Escobar had demanded information. "Demanded" was the word which Joan had used. Mario Escobar was of the blackmailing type. Martin's heart was in his mouth.

"An invention about us here?" he asked.

"About one of us," answered Sir Chichester; and Martin dared ask no more.

Harry Luttrell, however, had none of Martin's knowledge to restrain him.

"In that case, sir, wouldn't it be wiser to read it now, aloud?" he suggested. "It can't be suppressed now. Sooner or later every one will hear of it."

Every one agreed except Hillyard. To him Harry Luttrell seemed wilfully to be rushing towards catastrophe.

"Yes . . . yes," said Sir Chichester slowly. He unfolded his newspaper again and read; and of all those who listened no one was more amazed than Hillyard himself. Mario Escobar had no hand in this abominable work. For this is what Sir Chichester read:

> "'A mysterious and tragic event has occurred at Rackham Park, where Sir Chichester Splay, the well-known Baronet——'" He broke off to observe, "Really, it's put quite civilly, Millie. It's a dreadful mistake, but so far as the wording of the Editor is concerned it's put really more considerately than I noticed at first."

"Oh, please go on," cried Millie.
"Very well, my dear," and he resumed.

> "Sir Chichester Splay, the well-known Baronet, is entertaining a small party. At an early hour this morning Mrs. Croyle, one of Sir Chichester's guests, died under strange circumstances."

Miranda uttered a little scream.
"Died!" she exclaimed.
"Yes, listen to this," said Sir Chichester. "Mrs. Croyle was discovered lying upon her side with her face bent above a glass of chloroform. The glass was supported between her pillows and Mrs. Croyle's fingers were still grasping it when she was discovered."

A gasp of indignation and horror ran round that breakfast table when Sir Chichester had finished.

"It's so atrociously circumstantial," said Mr. Albany Todd.

"Yes." Sir Chichester seized upon the point. "That's the really damnable point about it. That's real malice. This report will linger and live long after the denial and apology are published."

Lady Splay raised her head.

"I can't imagine who can have sent in such a cowardly lie. Enemies of us? Or enemies of Stella?"

"We can think that out afterwards, Lady Splay," said Harold Jupp. He was of a practical matter-of-fact mind and every one turned to listen to his suggestion. "The first thing to do is to get the report contradicted in the evening papers."

"Of course."

There was something to be done. All grasped at the doing of it in sheer relief—except one. For as the men rose, saying; one "I'll look after it"; and another "No, you'd better leave it to me," Luttrell's voice broke in upon them all, with a sort of dreadful fatality in the quiet sound of it.

"Where is Mrs. Croyle now?" he asked, and he was as white as the tablecloth in front of him.

There was no further movement towards the door. Slowly the men resumed their seats. A silence followed in which person after person looked at Stella's empty place as though an intensity of gaze would materialise her there. Miranda was the first bravely to break through it.

"She hasn't come down yet," she said, and Millie Splay seized upon the words.

"No, she never comes down for breakfast—never has all this week."

"Yes, that's true," returned Dennis Brown with an attempt at cheerfulness.

"Besides—what makes—the idea—impossible," said Sir Chichester, "is the publication this morning. There wouldn't have been time. . . . It's clearly an atrocious piece of malice." He was speaking with an obvious effort to convince himself that the monstrous thing was false. But he collapsed suddenly and once more discomfort and silence reigned in the room.

"Stella's not well," Millie Splay took up the tale. "That's why she is seldom seen before twelve. Those headaches of hers——" and suddenly she in her turn broke off. She leaned forward and pressed the electric bell upon the tablecloth beside her. That small trivial action brought its relief, lightened the vague cloud of misgiving which since Luttrell had spoken, had settled upon all.

"You rang, my lady," said Harper in the doorway.

"Yes, Harper. We were making some plans for a picnic today and we should like to know if Mrs. Croyle will join us. Can you find out from her maid whether she is awake?"

It was superbly done. There was not a quaver in Lady Splay's voice, not a sign of agitation in her manner.

"I'll inquire, my lady," replied Harper, and he left the room upon his errand.

"One thing is certain," Mr. Albany Todd broke in. "I was watching Harper over your shoulder, Lady Splay. He hasn't seen the paragraph. There's nothing known of it in the servants' hall."

Sir Chichester nodded, and Millie Splay observed:

"Harper's so imperturbable that he always inspires me with confidence. I feel that nothing out of the way could really happen whilst he was in the house." And her attitude of tension did greatly relax as she thought, illogically enough, of that stolid butler. A suggestion made by Martin Hillyard set them to work whilst they waited.

"Let us see if the report is in any of the other papers," and all immediately were busy with that examination—except one again. And that one again, Harry Luttrell. He sat in his place motionless, his eyes transfixed upon some vision of horror—as if he *knew*, Martin said to himself, yes, as if all these questions were futile, as if he *knew*.

But no other newspaper had printed the paragraph. They had hardly assured themselves of this fact, when Harper once more stood in the doorway.

"Mrs. Croyle gave orders last night to her maid that she was not to be disturbed until she rang, my lady," he said.

"And she has not rung?" Millie asked.

"No, my lady."

Miranda suddenly laughed in an odd fashion and swayed in her chair.

"Miranda!" Millie Splay brought her back to her self-control with a sharp cry of rebuke. Then she resumed to Harper.

"I will take the responsibility of waking Mrs. Croyle. Will you please, ask her maid to rouse Mrs. Croyle, and inquire whether she will join us this morning. We shall start at twelve."

"Very well, my lady."

There was no longer any pretence of ease amongst the people seated round the table. A queer panic passed from one to the other. They were awed by the imminence of dreadful uncomprehended things. They waited in silence, like people under a spell, and from somewhere in the house above their heads, there sounded a loud rapping upon a door. They held their breath, straining to hear the grate of a key in a lock, and the opening of that door. They heard only the knocking repeated and repeated again. It was followed by a sound of hurrying feet.

Jenny Prask ran down the great main staircase, and burst into the breakfast room, her face mottled with terror, her hand spread above her heart to still its wild beating.

"My lady! My lady! The door's locked. I can get no answer. I am afraid."

Sir Chichester rose abruptly from his chair. But Jenny Prask had more to say.

"The key had been removed. My lady, I looked through the keyhole. The lights are still burning in the room."

"Oh!"

Martin Hillyard had started to his feet. He remembered another time when the lights had been burning in Stella Croyle's room in the full blaze of a summer morning. She was sitting at the writing-table then. She had been sitting there all through the night making meaningless signs and figures upon the paper and the blotting-pad in front of her. The full significance of that flight of the unhappy Stella to the little hotel below the Hog's Back was now revealed to him. But between that morning and this, there was an enormous difference. She had opened her door then in answer to the knocking.

"We must get through that door, Lady Splay," he said. Sir Chichester was already up and about in a busy agitation.

"Yes, to be sure. It's just an ordinary lock. We shall easily find a key to fit it. I'll take Harper with me, and perhaps, Millie, you will come."

"Yes, I'll come," said Millie quietly. After her first shock of horror and surprise when she had first chanced upon the paragraph in the *Harpoon*, she had been completely, wonderfully, mistress of herself.

"The rest of you will please stay downstairs," said Sir Chichester, as he removed the key from the door of the room. Jenny Prask was not thus to be disposed of.

"Oh, my lady, I must go up too!" she cried, twisting her hands together. "Mrs. Croyle was always very kind to me, poor lady. I must come!"

"She won't keep her head," Sir Chichester objected, who was fast losing his. But Milly Splay laid her hand upon the girl's arm.

"Yes, you shall come with us, Jenny," she said gently, and the four of them moved out of the room.

The others followed them as far as the hall, and stood grouped at the foot of the staircase.

"Miranda, would you like to go out into the air?" Dennis Brown asked with solicitude of his wife.

"No, dear, I am all right. I—oh, poor woman!" and with a sob she dropped her face in her hands.

"Hush!" Luttrell called sharply for silence, and a moment afterwards, a loud shrill scream rent the air like lightning.

Miranda cowered from it.

"Jenny Prask!" said Hillyard.

"Then—then—the news is true," faltered Miranda, and she would have fallen but for the arm of her husband about her waist.

They waited until Sir Chichester came down the stairs to them. He was shaken and trembling. He, the spectator of dramas, was now a character in one most tragically enacted under his own roof.

"The report is true to the letter," he said in a low voice. "Dennis, will you go for McKerrel, the doctor. You know his house in Midhurst. Will you take your car, and bring him back. There is nothing more that we can do until he comes." He stood for a little while by the table in the hall, staring down at it, and taking particular note of its grain.

"A curious thing," he said. "The key of her room is missing altogether."

To no one did it come at this moment that the disappearance of the key was to prove a point of vast importance. No one made any comment, and Sir Chichester fell to silence again. "She looked like a child sleeping," he said at length, "a child without a care."

Then he sat down and took the newspaper from his pocket. Mr. Albany Todd suddenly advanced to Harry Luttrell. He had been no less observant than Martin Hillyard.

"You alone, Colonel Luttrell," he said, "were not surprised."

"I was not," answered Harry frankly. "I was shocked, but not surprised. For I knew Mrs. Croyle at a time when she was so tormented that she could not sleep at all. During that time she learnt to take drugs, and especially that drug in precisely that way that the newspaper described."

The men drifted out of the hall on to the lawn, leaving Sir Chichester brooding above the outspread sheets of the *Harpoon*. Here was the insoluble sinister question to which somehow he had to find an answer. Stella Croyle died late last night, in the country, at Rackham Park; and yet in this very morning's issue of the newspaper, her death with every circumstance and detail was truthfully recorded, hours before it was even known by anybody in the house itself.

"How can that be?" Sir Chichester exclaimed in despair. "How can it be?"

CHAPTER XXIX

Jenny Puts Up Her Fight

Stella, the undisciplined! She had flung out of the rank and file, as long ago Sir Charles Hardiman had put it, and to this end she had come, waywardness exacting its inexorable price. Harry Luttrell, however, was not able to lull his conscience with any such easy reflections. He walked with Martin Hillyard apart in the garden.

"I am to blame," he cried. "I took on a responsibility for Stella when I went out of my way to do one kind, foolish thing. . . . Yet, she would have killed herself if I hadn't—as she has done five years afterwards! . . . I couldn't leave her when I had brought her home . . . she was in such misery! . . . and it couldn't have gone on. . . . Old Hardiman was right about that. . . . It would have ended in a quarrel when unforgivable words would have been used. . . . Yet, perhaps, if that had happened she wouldn't have killed herself. . . . Oh, I don't know!"

Martin Hillyard had never seen Harry Luttrell so moved or sunk in such remorse. He did not argue, lest he should but add fuel to this high flame of self-reproach. Life had become so much easier as a problem with him, so much inner probing and speculation and worry about small vanities had been smoothed away since he had been engaged day after day in a definite service which was building up by a law deduced here, an inspired formula there, a tradition for its servants. The service, the tradition, would dissolve and blow to nothing, when peace came again. Meanwhile there was the worth of traditional service made clear to him, in an indifference to the little enmities which before would have hurt and rankled, in a freedom from doubt when decision was needed, above all in a sort of underlying calm which strengthened as his life became more turbulently active.

"It's a clear principle of life which make the difference," he said, hesitating, because to say even so much made him feel a prig. "Stella just drifted from unhappiness to unhappiness——"

But Harry Luttrell had no attention to give to him.

"I simply couldn't have gone on," he cried. "It wasn't a question of my ruin or not. . . . It was simply beyond me to go on. . . . There were other things more powerful. . . . You know! I once told you on the river above Kennington Island. . . . Oh, my God, I am in such a tangle of argument—and there she is up there—only thirty, and beautiful—such a queer, wayward kid—'like a child sleeping.'"

He quoted Sir Chichester's phrase, and hurried away from his friend.

"I shall be back in a little while," he muttered. His bad hour was upon him, and he must wrestle with it alone.

Martin Hillyard returned to the hall, and found Sir Chichester with the doctor, a short, rugged Scotsman. Dr. McKerrel was saying:

"There's nothing whatever for me to do, Sir Chichester," he said. "The poor creature must have died somewhere about one o'clock of the morning." He saw Sir Chichester with a start fall once more to reading the paragraph in the *Harpoon*, and continued with a warmth of admiration, "Eh, but those newspaper fellows are quick! I saw the *Harpoon* this morning, and it was lucky I did. For I'd ha' been on my rounds otherwise when that young fellow called for me."

"It was good of you to come so quickly," said Sir Chichester.

"I shall charge for it," replied Dr. McKerrel. "I'll just step round to the Peace Officer at once, and I'll be obliged if you'll not have that glass with the chloroform touched again. I have put it aside."

Martin Hillyard was disturbed.

"There will have to be an inquest then?" he asked.

"Aye, but there wull."

"In a case of this kind," Sir Chichester suggested, "it would be better if it could be avoided."

"But it can't," answered Dr. McKerrel bluntly. "And for my part, I tell you frankly, Sir Chichester, I have no great pity for poor neurotic bodies like the young lady upstairs. If she had had a little of my work to do, she would have been too tired in the evening to think about her worries." He looked at the disconsolate Baronet with a sudden twinkle in his eye. "Eh, man, but you'll get all the publicity you want over this case."

Sir Chichester had no rejoinder to the quip; and his unwonted meekness caused McKerrel to relent. He stopped at the door, and said:

"I'll give you a hint. The coroner can cut the inquest down to the barest necessary limits, if he has got all the facts clear beforehand. If he has got to explore in the dark, he'll ask questions here and questions there, and you never know, nor does he, what he's going to drag out to light in the end. But let him have it all clear and straight first! There's only one character I know of, more free from regulations and limitations and red-tape than a coroner, and that's the police-sergeant who runs the coroner. Goodday to you."

A telegram was brought to Martin Hillyard whilst McKerrel was yet speaking; and Hillyard read it with relief. Mario Escobar had been taken that morning as he was leaving the hotel for the morning train to London. He was now on his way to an internment camp. So that complication was smoothed out at all events. He agreed with Sir Chichester Splay that it would be prudent to carry out McKerrel's suggestion at once.

"I will make the document out," said Sir Chichester importantly. Give him a little work which set him in the limelight as the leader of the Chorus, and nothing could keep down his spirits. He took a sheet of foolscap, a blotting pad, a heavy inkstand, and a quill pen—Sir Chichester never used anything but a quill pen—to the big table in the middle of the hall, and wrote in a fair, round hand:

"The case of Mrs. Croyle."

and looked at his work and thought it good.

"It looks quite like a *cause célèbre*, doesn't it?" he said buoyantly. But he caught Martin Hillyard's eye, and recovered his more becoming despondency. Harry Luttrell came in as the baronet settled once more to his task. He laid a shining key upon the table and said:

"I found this upon the lawn. It looked as if it might be the key of Mrs. Croyle's room."

It was undoubtedly the key of a door. "We'll find out," said the baronet. Harper was sent for and commissioned to inquire. He returned in a few minutes.

"Yes, sir, it is the key of Mrs. Croyle's room." He laid it upon the table and went out of the room.

"I suppose it is then," said Harry Luttrell. "But I am a little puzzled."
"Oh?"

"It wasn't lying beneath Mrs. Croyle's window as one might have expected. But at the east side of the house, below the corridor, and almost in front of the glass door of the library."

Both of his hearers were disturbed. Sir Chichester took up the key, and twisted it this way and that, till it flashed like a point of fire in the sunlight; as though under such giddy work it would yield up its secret for the sake of peace. He flung it on the table again, where it rattled and lay still.

"I can't make head or tail of it," Sir Chichester cried. Martin Hillyard opened his mouth to speak and thought better of it. He could not falter in his belief that Stella had destroyed herself. The picture of her that morning in Surrey, with the lamps burning in her room and the bed untouched, was too vivid in his memory. What she had tried to do two years ago, she had found the courage to do today.

That was sure. But it was not all. There was some one in the shadows who meant harm, more harm than was already accomplished. There was malevolence at work. The discovery of the key in that position far from Stella's window assured him of it. The aspect of the key itself as it lay upon the table made the assurance still more sure. But whom was this malevolence to hurt? And how? At what moment would the hand behind the curtain strike? And whose hand would it be? These were questions which locked his lips tight. It was for him to watch and discover, for he alone overlooked the battlefield, and if he failed, God help his friends at Rackham Park. Mario Escobar? Mario Escobar could at all events do no harm now.

Sir Chichester explained to Harry Luttrell Dr. McKerrel's suggestion.

"Just a clear, succinct statement of the facts. The witnesses, and what each one knows and is ready to depose. I shall put the statement before the coroner, who is a very good fellow, and we shall escape with as little scandal as possible. Now, let me see——" Sir Chichester put on his glasses. "The most important witness, of course, will be Stella's maid."

Sir Chichester rang the bell, and in answer to his summons Jenny came down the stairs. Her eyes were red with weeping and she was very pale. But she bore herself steadily.

"You wanted me, sir?" she asked. Her eyes travelled from one to the other of the three men in the hall. They rested for a little moment longer upon Harry Luttrell than upon the rest; and it seemed to Hillyard that as they rested there they glittered strangely, and that the ghost of a smile flickered about her mouth.

"Yes," said Sir Chichester, pompously. "You understand that there will have to be an inquiry into the cause of Mrs. Croyle's death; and one wants for the sake of everybody, your dead mistress more than any one, that there should be as little talk as possible."

Jenny's voice cut in like ice.

"Mrs. Croyle had no reason that I know of to fear the fullest inquiry."

"Quite so! Quite so!" returned Sir Chichester, shifting his ground. "But it will save time if we get the facts concisely together."

Jenny stepped forward, and stood at the end of the table opposite to the baronet.

"I am quite willing, sir," she said respectfully, "to answer any question now or at any time"; and throughout the little interrogatory which followed she never once changed from her attitude of respect.

"Your name first."

"Jenny Prask," and Sir Chichester wrote it down.

"You have been Mrs. Croyle's maid for some time."

"For three and a half years, sir."

"Good!" said Sir Chichester, with the air of one who by an artful question has elicited a most important piece of evidence.

"Now!" But now he fumbled. He had come to the real examination, and was at a loss how to begin. "Yes, now then, Jenny!" and again he came to a halt.

Whilst Jenny waited, her eyes once glittered strangely under their half dropped lids; and Martin Hillyard followed the direction of their gaze to the door-key lying upon the table beside Sir Chichester's hand.

"Jenny," said Sir Chichester, who had at last formulated a question. "You informed us that Mrs. Croyle instructed you last night not to call her until she rang. That, no doubt, was an unusual order for her to give."

"No, sir."

Sir Chichester leaned back in his chair.

"Oh, it wasn't?"

"No, sir."

Sir Chichester looked a little blank. He cast about for another line of examination.

"You are aware, of course, Jenny, that your mistress was in the habit of taking drugs—chloroform especially."

"Never, sir," answered Jenny.

"You weren't aware of it?" exclaimed Sir Chichester.

"She never took them."

Harry Luttrell made a little movement. He stared in perplexity at Jenny Prask, who did not once remove her calm and respectful eyes from Sir Chichester Splay. She waited in absolute composure for the next question. But the question took a long time to formulate. Sir Chichester had framed no interrogatory in a sequence; whereas Jenny's answers were pat, as though, sitting by the bed whereon her dead mistress lay, she had thought out the questions which might be asked of her and got her answers ready. Sir Chichester began to get flurried. At every conjecture which he expressed, Jenny Prask slammed a door in his face.

"But you told me——" he cried, turning to Harry Luttrell and so broke off. "Are you speaking the truth, Jenny?"

Suddenly Jenny's composure broke up. The blood rushed into her face. She shouted violently:

"I swear it! If it was my last dying word, I do! Chloroform indeed!"

She became sarcastic. "What an idea! Just fancy!"

Sir Chichester threw down his pen. He was aghast before the conclusion to which his examination was leading him.

"But, if Stella didn't put that glass of chloroform between her pillows—herself—of her own accord—why then, whilst she was asleep——" He would not utter the inevitable induction. But it was clear enough, hideous enough to all of them. Why then, whilst she was asleep, some one entered the room, placed the chloroform where its deadly fumes would do their work, locked her door upon her and tossed the key out on to the lawn. A charge of murder—nothing less.

"Don't you see what you are suggesting, Jenny," Sir Chichester spluttered helplessly.

"I am suggesting nothing, sir," the maid answered stolidly. "I am answering questions."

She was lying, of course! Hillyard had not a doubt of it. Jenny Prask was the malevolent force of which he was in search. So much had, at all events, sprung clear from Sir Chichester's blunderings. And some hint, too, of the plan which malevolence had formed—not more than a hint! That Jenny Prask intended to sustain a charge of murder Martin did not believe. She was of too strong a brain for that folly. But she had some clear purpose to harm somebody; and Martin's heart sank as he conjectured who that some one might, nay must, be. Meanwhile, he thought, let Sir Chichester pursue his questioning. He got glimpses through that clouded medium into Jenny Prask's mind.

"You must realise, Jenny, the unfortunate position into which your answers are leading you," said Sir Chichester with a trace of bluster.

Hillyard could have laughed. As if she didn't realise exactly the drift and meaning of every word which she uttered. Jenny was not at all perturbed by Sir Chichester's manner. Her face took on a puzzled look.

"I don't understand, sir."

"No? Let me make it clear! If your mistress never took drugs, if she did not place the glass of chloroform in the particular position which would ensure her death, then, since you, her maid, were alone in this part of the house with her and were the last person to see her alive——"

"No, sir," Jenny Prask interrupted.

Sir Chichester stared. He was more and more out of his depth, and these were waters in which expert swimming was required.

"I don't understand. Do you say that somebody saw Mrs. Croyle after she had dismissed you for the night?"

"Yes, sir."

"Will you please explain?"

The explanation was as simple as possible. Jenny had first fetched a book for her mistress from the library, before the house-party left for the ball. She then had supper and went to Mrs. Croyle's room. It was then about half past nine, so far as she could conjecture. Her mistress, however, was not ready for bed, and dismissed Jenny, saying that she would look after herself. Jenny thereupon retired to her own bedroom and wrote a letter. After writing it, she remembered that she had not put out the distilled water which Mrs. Croyle was in the habit of using for her toilet. She accordingly returned to Mrs. Croyle's bedroom, and to her surprise found it empty. She waited for a quarter of an hour, and then becoming uneasy, went downstairs into the hall. She heard her mistress and some one else talking in the library. Their voices were raised a little as though they were quarrelling.

"Quarrelling!" Sir Chichester Splay cried out the word in dismay. His hand flapped feebly on the table. "I am afraid to go on. . . . What do you think, Hillyard? I am afraid to go on. . . ."

"We must go on," said Luttrell quietly. He was very white. Did he guess what was coming, Hillyard wondered? At all events he did not falter. He took the business of putting questions altogether out of his host's hands.

"Was the somebody a man or a woman?"

"A woman, sir."

"Did you recognise her voice?"

"Yes, sir."

"Who was it?"

"Miss Whitworth."

Harry Luttrell nodded his head as if he had, during these last minutes, come to expect that answer and no other. But Sir Chichester rose up in wrath and, leaning forward over the table, shook his finger threateningly at the girl.

"Now you know you are not speaking the truth. Miss Whitworth was at Harrel last night with the rest of us."

"Yes, sir, but she came back to Rackham Park almost at once," said Jenny; and Harry Luttrell's face showed a sign of anxiety. After all, he hadn't seen Joan himself in the ballroom until well after ten o'clock. "I should have known that it was Miss Whitworth even if I had not heard her voice," and Jenny described how, on fetching Mrs. Croyle's book, she had seen Joan unlatch the glass door of the library.

Sir Chichester was shaken, but he pushed his blotting-paper here and his pen there, and pished and tushed like a refractory child.

"And how did she get back? I suppose she ran all the way in her satin shoes and back again, eh?"

"No, sir, she came back in Mrs. Brown's motorcar. I saw it from my bedroom window waiting in the drive."

"Ah! Now that we can put to the test, Jenny," cried Sir Chichester triumphantly. "And we will——" He caught Hillyard's eye as he moved towards the door in order to summon Miranda from the garden. Hillyard warned him with an almost imperceptible shake of the head. "Yes, we will, in our own time," he concluded lamely. His anger burst out again. "Joan, indeed! We won't have her mixed up in this sordid business, it's bad enough as it is. But Joan, no! To suggest that Joan came straight back from the Willoughbys' dance in order to quarrel with a woman whom she was seeing every day here, and, having quarrelled with her, afterwards—— No, I won't speak the word. It's preposterous!"

"But I don't suggest, sir, that Miss Whitworth came back in order to quarrel with my mistress," Jenny Prask returned, as soon as Sir Chichester's spate of words ran down. "I only give you the facts I know. I am quite sure that Miss Whitworth can quite easily explain why she came back to Rackham Park last night. There can't be any difficulty about that!"

Jenny Prask had kept every intonation of her voice under her control. There was no hint of irony or triumph. She was a respectful lady's maid, frankly answering questions about her dead mistress. But she did not so successfully keep sentinel over her looks. She could not but glance from time to time at Harry Luttrell savouring his trouble and anxiety; and when she expressed her conviction that Joan could so easily clear up these mysteries, such a flame of hatred burnt suddenly in her eyes that it lit Martin Hillyard straight to the heart of her purpose.

"So that's it," he thought, and was terrified as he grasped its reach. An accusation of murder! Oh, nothing so crude. But just enough suggestion of the possibility of murder to make it absolutely necessary that Joan Whitworth should go into the witness box at the coroner's inquest and acknowledge before the world that she had hurried secretly back from Harrel to meet Mario Escobar in an empty house. Mario Escobar too! Of all people, Mario Escobar! Jenny Prask had builded better than she knew. That telegram which Martin had welcomed with so much relief but an hour ago taunted him now. The scandal would have been bad enough if Mario Escobar were nothing more than the shady hunter of women he was supposed to be. It would be ten times louder now that Mario Escobar had been interned as a traitor within twelve hours of the secret meeting!

Some escape must be discovered from the peril. Else the mud of it would cling to Joan all her life. She would be spoilt. Harry Luttrell, too! If he married her, if he did not. But Martin could not think of a way out. The whole plan was an artful, devilish piece of hard-headed cunning. Martin fell to wondering where was Jenny Prask's weak joint. She certainly looked, with her quiet strength, as if she had not one at all.

To make matters worse, Miranda Brown chose this moment to re-enter the hall. Sir Chichester, warned already by Martin, threw the warning to the winds.

"Miranda, you are the very person to help us," he cried. "Now listen to me, my dear, and don't get flurried. Think carefully, for your answer may have illimitable consequences! After your arrival at Harrel last night, did Joan return here immediately in your car?"

Sir Chichester had never been so impressive. Miranda was frightened and changed colour. But she had given her promise and she kept it pluckily.

"No," she answered.

Jenny Prask permitted herself to smile her disbelief. Sir Chichester was triumphant.

"Well, there's an end of your pretty story, my girl," he said. "You wanted to do a little mischief, did you? Well, you haven't! And here, by a stroke of luck, is Joan herself to settle the matter."

He sat down and once more he drew his sheet of foolscap in front of him. He could write his clear succinct statement now, write it in "nervous prose." He was not quite sure what nervous prose actually was, but he knew it to be the correct medium to use on these occasions.

Meanwhile Joan ran down the stairs.

"I am afraid I have been very lazy this morning," she cried. She saw Harry Luttrell, she coloured to the eyes, she smiled doubtfully and said in a little whimsical voice, "We didn't after all, practise in the passage."

Then, and only then, did she realise that something was amiss. Millie Splay in her desire to spare her darling the sudden shock of learning what calamity had befallen the house that night had bidden Joan's maid keep silence. She herself would break the news. But Millie Splay was busy with telegrams to Robert Croyle and Stella's own friends, and all the sad little duties which wait on death; and Joan ran down into the midst of the debate without a warning.

Martin Hillyard would have given it to her, but Sir Chichester was hot upon his report.

"Joan, my dear," he said confidently. "There's a little point—not in dispute really—but—well there's a little point. It has been said that you came straight back here last night from Harrel?"

Joan's face turned slowly white. She stood with her great eyes fixed upon Sir Chichester, still as an image, and she did not answer a word. Harry Luttrell drew in a quick breath like a man in pain. Sir Chichester was selecting a new pen and noticed nothing.

"It's ridiculous, of course, my dear, but I must put to you the formal question. Did you?"

"Yes," answered Joan, and the pen fell from Sir Chichester's hand.

"But—but—how did you come back?"

"I borrowed Miranda's car."

Miranda's legs gave under her and she sank down with a moan in a chair.

"But Miranda denies that she lent it," said Sir Chichester in exasperation.

"I asked her to deny it."

"Why?"

Joan's eyes for one swift instant swept round to Harry Luttrell. She swayed. Then she answered:

"I can't tell you."

Sir Chichester rose to his feet and tore his sheet of foolscap across.

"God bless my soul!" he said to himself rather than to any of that company. "God bless my soul!" He moved away from the table. "I think I'll go and see Millie. Yes! I'll consult with Millie," and he ascended the stairs heavily, a very downcast and bewildered man. It seemed as though old age had suddenly found him out, and bowed his shoulders and taken the spring from his limbs. Something of this he felt himself, for he was heard to mutter as he passed along the landing to his wife's sitting-room:

"I am not the man I was. I feel difficulties more"; and so he passed from sight.

Harry Luttrell turned then to Joan.

"Miss Whitworth," he began and got no further. For the blood rushed up into the girl's face and she exclaimed in a trembling voice:

"Colonel Luttrell, I trust that you are not going to ask me any questions."

"Why?" he asked, taken aback by the little touch of violence in her manner.

"Because, at twelve o'clock last night, I refused you the right to ask them."

The words were not very generous. They were meant to hurt and they did. They were meant to put a sharp, quick end to any questioning; and in that, too, they succeeded. Harry Luttrell bowed his head in assent and went out into the garden. For a moment afterwards Martin Hillyard, Joan and Jenny Prask stood in silence; and in that silence once more Martin's eyes fell upon the key of Stella's room. The earth had moved since the interrogatory had begun and the sunlight now played upon the key and transmuted it into a bright jewel. Martin Hillyard stepped forward and lifted it up. A faint, a very faint light, as from the far end of a long tunnel began to glimmer in his mind.

"I must think it out," he whispered to himself; and at once the key filled all his thoughts. He turned to Joan:

"Will you watch, please?" He opened the drawer in the table and laid the key inside it. Then he closed the drawer and locked it and took the key of the drawer out of the lock.

"You see, Joan, what I have done? That key is locked in this drawer, and I hold the key of the drawer. It may be important."

Joan nodded.

"I see what you have done. And now, will you please leave me with Jenny Prask?"

The smile was very easy to read now in Jenny's face. She could ask nothing better than to be left alone with Joan.

Martin hesitated.

"I think, Joan, that you ought to see Lady Splay before you talk to any one," he counselled gently.

"Is everybody going to give me orders in this house?" Joan retorted with a quiet, dangerous calm.

Martin Hillyard turned and ran swiftly up the stairs. There was but one thing to do. Lady Splay must be fetched down. But hurry as he might, he was not in time. For a few seconds Joan and Jenny Prask were alone in the hall, and all Jenny's composure left her on the instant. She stepped quickly over to Joan, and in a voice vibrating with hatred and passion, she hissed:

"But you'll have to say why you came back. You'll have to say who you came back to see. You'll have to say it publicly too—right there in court. It'll be in all the papers. Won't you like it, Miss Whitworth? Just fancy!"

Joan was staggered by the attack. The sheer hatred of Jenny bewildered her.

"In court?" she faltered. "What do you mean?"

"That Mrs. Croyle died of poison last night in her room," answered Jenny.

Joan stared at her. "Last night, after we had talked—she killed herself—oh!" The truth reached her brain and laid a chill hand upon her heart. She rocked backwards and forwards as she stood, and with a gasping moan fell headlong to the ground. She had fainted. For a little while Jenny surveyed her handiwork with triumph. She bent down with a laugh.

"Yes, it's your turn, you pretty doll. You've got to go through it! You won't look so young and pretty when they have done with you in the witness-box. Bah!"

Jenny Prask was a strenuous hater. She drew back her foot to kick the unconscious girl as she lay at her feet upon the floor. But that insult Millie Splay was in time to prevent.

"Jenny," she cried sharply from the balustrade of the landing.

Jenny was once more the quiet, respectful maid.

"Yes, my lady. You want me? I am afraid that Miss Whitworth has fainted."

CHAPTER XXX

A Revolution in Sir Chichester

Upon that house which had yesterday rung with joyous life now fell gloom and sorrow and grave disquiet. Millie Splay drew Miranda, Dennis Brown and Harold Jupp aside.

"You three had better go," she said. "You have such a little time for holidays now; and I can always telegraph for you if you should be wanted."

Miranda bubbled into little sympathetic explosions.

"Oh, Millie, I'll stay, of course. These boys can go. But Joan will want some one."

Millie, however, would not hear of it.

"You're a brick, Miranda. But I have ordered the car for you all immediately after luncheon. Joan's in bed, and wants to see no one. She seems heartbroken. She will say nothing. I can't understand her."

There was only one at Rackham Park who did, and to him Millie Splay turned instinctively.

"I should like you to stay, if you will put up with us. I think Chichester feels at a loss, and he likes you very much."

"Of course I'll stay," replied Hillyard.

Mr. Albany Todd drifted away to the more congenial atmosphere of a dowager duchess's dower-house in the Highlands, where it is to be hoped that his conversational qualities were more brilliantly displayed than in the irreverent gaiety of Rackham. Millie Splay meant to keep Harry Luttrell too. She hoped against hope. This was the man for her Joan, and whether he was wasting his leave miserably in that melancholy house troubled her not one jot.

"It would be so welcome to me if you would put off your departure," she said. "I am sure there is some dreadful misunderstanding."

Luttrell consented willingly to stay, and they went into the library, where Sir Chichester was brooding over the catastrophe with his head in his hands and the copy of the *Harpoon* on the floor beside him.

"No, I can't make head or tail of it," he said, and Harper the butler came softly into the room, closing the door from the hall.

"There's a reporter from the *West Sussex Advertiser*, sir, asking to see you," he said, and Sir Chichester raised his head, like an old hunter which hears a pack of hounds giving tongue in the distance.

"Where is he?"

"In the hall, sir."

The baronet's head sank again between his shoulders.

"Tell him that I can't see him," he said in a dull voice.

The butler was the only man in the room who could hear that pronouncement with an unmoved face, and he owed his imperturbability merely to professional pride. Indeed, it was almost unthinkable that a couple of hours could produce so vast a revolution in a man. Here was a reporter who had come, without being asked, to interview Sir Chichester Splay, and the baronet would not see him! The incongruity struck Sir Chichester himself.

"Perhaps it will seem rather impolite, eh, Luttrell? Rather hard treatment on a man who has come so far? What do you think, Hillyard? I suppose I ought to see him for a moment—yes." Sir Chichester raised his voice in a sharp cry which contrasted vividly with the deliberative sentences preceding it. "Harper! Harper!" and Harper reappeared. "I have been thinking about it, Harper. The unfortunate man may lose his whole morning if I don't see him. We all agree that to send him away would be unkind."

"He has gone, sir."

"Gone?" exclaimed Sir Chichester testily. "God bless my soul! Did he seem disappointed, Harper?"

"Not so much disappointed, sir, as, if I may utilise a vulgarism, struck of all a heap, sir."

"That will do, Harper," said Millie Splay, and Harper again retired.

"Struck all of a heap!" said Sir Chichester sadly. "Well he might be!" He looked up and caught Harry's eye. "They say, Luttrell, that breaking a habit is only distressing during the first few days. With each refusal of the mind to yield, the temptation diminishes in strength. I believe that to be so, Luttrell."

"It is very likely, sir," Harry replied.

Harper seemed to be perpetually in and out of the library that morning. For he appeared with a little oblong parcel in his hand. Sir Chichester did not notice the parcel. He sprang up, and with a distinct note of eager pleasure in his voice, he cried:

"He has come back! Then I really think——"

"No, sir," Harper interrupted. "These are cigarettes."

"Oh, yes," Hillyard stepped forward and took the parcel from the table. "I had run out, so I sent to Midhurst for a box."

"Oh, cigarettes!" Sir Chichester's voice sagged again. He contemplated the little parcel swinging by a loop of string from Martin's finger. His face became a little stern. "That's a bad habit, Hillyard," he observed, shaking his head. "It will grow on you—nicotine poisoning may supervene at any moment. You had better begin to break yourself of it at once. I think so."

"Chichester!" cried Millie Splay. "What in the world are you doing?"

Sir Chichester was gently but firmly removing the parcel from Martin's hands, whilst Martin himself looked on, paralysed by the aggression.

"A little strength of character, Hillyard. . . . You saw me a minute ago. . . . The first few days, I believe, are trying."

Martin sought to retrieve his cigarettes, but Sir Chichester laid them aside upon a high mantelpiece, as if Hillyard were a child and could not reach them.

"No, don't disappoint me, Hillyard! I am sure that you, too, can rise above a temptation. Why should I be the only one?"

But Hillyard did not answer. Sir Chichester's desire that he should have a companion in sacrifice set a train of thought working in his mind. In the hurry and horror of that morning something had been forgotten—something of importance, something which perhaps, together with the key locked away in the hall table, might set free Joan's feet from the net in which they were entangled. He looked at his watch.

"Will you lend me your car, Harry, for a few hours?" he asked suddenly.

"Yes."

"Then I'll go," said Martin. "I will be back this afternoon or evening, Lady Splay." He went to the door, but was delayed by a box of Corona cigars upon a small table. "I'll take one of your cigars, Sir Chichester," he said drily.

"Anything in the house, of course, my boy," began the baronet hospitably, and pulled himself up. "A very bad habit, Hillyard. You disappoint me."

A trick of secrecy grows quickly upon men doing the work to which Martin Hillyard had been assigned during the last two years. Nothing is easier than to reach a frame of mind which drives you about with your finger to your lips, whispering "Hush! hush!" over the veriest trifles. Hillyard had not reached that point, but, like many other persons of his service, he was on the way to it. He gave no information now to any one of his purpose or destination, not even to Millie Splay, who came out with him alone into the hall, yearning for some crumb of hope. All that he said to her was:

"It is possible that I may be later than I think; but I shall certainly be back tonight." And he drove off in Luttrell's powerful small car.

It was, in fact, ten o'clock when Hillyard returned to Rackham Park. There was that in his manner which encouraged the inmates to hope some way out had been discovered. Questions were poured upon him, and some information given. The date of the inquest had been fixed for the next Monday, and meanwhile no statement of any kind had been put before the coroner. Jenny had not yielded by an inch. She would certainly tell her story with all the convincing force behind it of her respectful quiet manner and her love for her mistress.

"I have something to tell you," said Martin. "But I have had no dinner, and am starving. I will tell you whilst I eat."

"Shall I fetch Joan down?" Millie Splay asked eagerly.

"Better to wait," said Martin. He imagined in what a fever of anxiety Joan would be. It would be time enough to lift her to hope when it was certain that the hope would not crumble away to dust.

Joan was at that moment lying on her bed in the darkness of her room, her face towards the moonlit garden, and such a terror of the ordeal to be faced the next Monday in her thoughts as turned her cold and sent her heart fluttering into her throat. Mario Escobar had been taken away that morning. The news had reached Rackham, as it had reached every other house in the countryside. Joan knew of it, and she felt soiled and humiliated beyond endurance as she thought upon her association with the spy.

The picture of the room crowded with witnesses, and people whom she knew, and strangers, whilst she gave the evidence which would turn their liking for her into contempt and suspicion would fade away from before her eyes, and the summer afternoon on Duncton Hill glow in its place. She had bidden Hillyard look at the Weald of Sussex, that he might carry the smell of its soil, the aspect of its blooms and dark woodlands and brown cottages away with him as a treasure to which he could secretly turn like a miser to his gold; and she herself, with them ever before her eyes, had forgotten them altogether. To sink back into the rank and file—how fine she had thought it, and how little she had heeded it! Now she had got to pay for her heedlessness, and she buried her face in her pillows and lay shivering.

Meanwhile, in the dining-room downstairs, Millie Splay, Sir Chichester and Harry Luttrell gathered about Martin at the table whilst he ate cold beef and drank a pint of champagne.

"I went up to London to see some one on the editorial staff of the *Harpoon*," Martin explained. "There were two questions I wanted answers for, if I could get them. You see, according to McKerrel—and you, Sir Chichester, say that he is a capable man—Stella Croyle died at one in the morning."

"Yes," Sir Chichester agreed.

"*About* one," Harry Luttrell corrected, with the exactness of the soldierly mind.

"'About' will do," Martin rejoined. "For newspapers go to press early nowadays. The *Harpoon* would have been made up, and most of the editorial staff would have gone home an hour—yes, actually an hour—before Mrs. Croyle died here at Rackham in Sussex. Yet the news is in that very issue. How did that happen? How did the news reach the office of the *Harpoon* an hour before the event occurred?"

"Yes, that is what has been bothering me," added Sir Chichester.

"Well, that was one question," Martin resumed. "Here's the other. How, when the news had reached the *Harpoon* office, did it get printed in the paper?"

Millie Splay found no difficulty in providing an explanation of that.

"It's sensational," she said disdainfully.

Martin shook his head.

"I don't think that's enough. The *Harpoon*, like lots of other newspapers, has its social column, and in that column, no doubt, a paragraph like this one about Stella would have a certain sensational value. But supposing it wasn't true! A libel action follows, follows inevitably. A great deal would be said about the unscrupulous recklessness involved; the judge would come down like a cartload of bricks and the paper would get badly stung. No editor of any reliable paper would run such a risk. No sub-editor, left behind with power to alter and insert, would have taken the responsibility. Before he printed that item of news he would want corroboration of its truth. That's certain. How did he get it? It was true news, and it was corroborated. But, again, it was corroborated before the event happened. How?"

"I haven't an idea," cried Sir Chichester. "I thought I knew something about getting things into the papers, but I see that I am a baby at it."

"It's much the more difficult question of the two," Hillyard agreed. "But we will go back to the first one. How did the news reach the *Harpoon* office yesterday night? Perhaps you can guess?" and he looked towards Harry Luttrell.

Luttrell, however, was at a loss.

"It's beyond me," he replied, and Martin Hillyard understood how that one morning at the little hotel under the Hog's Back had given to him and him alone the key by which the door upon these dark things might be unlocked.

"The news arrived in the form of a letter marked urgent, which was handed in by the chauffeur of a private motorcar just after midnight. Of the time there is no doubt. I saw the editor myself. The issue would already have gone to press, but late news was expected that night from France, and the paper was waiting for it. Instead this letter came."

A look of bewilderment crept into the faces of the group about the table.

"But who in the world could have written it?" cried Sir Chichester in exasperation.

"It was written over your name."

"Mine?"

The bewilderment in Millie Splay's face deepened into anxiety. She looked at her husband with a sudden sinking of her heart. Had his foible developed into a madness? Such things had been. A little gasp broke from her lips.

"But not in your handwriting," Hillyard hastened to add.

"Whose then?" asked Harry Luttrell suddenly.

"Stella's," answered Hillyard.

A shiver ran from one to the other of that small company, and discomfort kept them silent. A vague dread stole in upon their minds. It was as though some uncanny presence were in the room. They had eaten with Stella Croyle in this room, played with her out there in the sunlit garden, and only one of them had suspected the overwhelming despair which had driven her so hard. They began to blame themselves. "Poor woman! Poor woman!" Millie Splay whispered in a moan.

Sir Chichester broke the silence.

"But we left Stella here when we went to Harrel," he began, and Hillyard interrupted him.

"There's no doubt that Stella sent the message," he said. "Your car, Mrs. Brown's and Luttrell's, were all used to take us to Harrel. One car remained in your garage—Stella's."

"But there wouldn't be time for that car to reach London." Sir Chichester fought against Hillyard's statement. He did not want to believe it. He did not want to think of it. It brought him within too near a view of that horrid brink where overtried nature grows dizzy and whirls down into blackness.

"Just time," Hillyard answered relentlessly, "if you will follow me. Joan certainly returned here last night—that I know, as you know. But she was back again in the ballroom at Harrel within a few minutes of ten o'clock. She must have left Mrs. Croyle a quarter before ten—that, at the latest."

"Yes," Millie Splay agreed.

"Well, I have myself crossed Putney Bridge after leaving here, within ten minutes under the two hours. And that in the daytime. Stella had time enough for her purpose. It was night and little traffic on the road. She writes her letter, sends Jenny with it to the garage, and the car reaches the *Harpoon* office by twelve."

"But its return?" asked Sir Chichester.

"Simpler still. Your gates were left open last night, and we returned from Harrel at four in the morning. Stella's chauffeur hands in his letter, comes back by the way he went and is home here at Rackham an hour and a half before we thought of saying good-bye to Mrs. Willoughby. That is the way it happened. That is the way it must have happened," Hillyard concluded energetically. "For it's the only way it could have happened."

Luttrell, though he had been a listener and nothing else throughout Martin's statement, had cherished a hope that somehow it might be discovered that Stella had died by an accident. That she should die by her own hand, in this house, under the same roof as Joan, and because of one year which had ended at Stockholm—oh, to him a generation back!—was an idea of irrepressible horror. He could not shake off some sense of guiltiness. He had argued with it all that day, discovering the most excellent contentions, but at the end, not one of them had succeeded in weakening in the least degree his inward conviction that he had his share in Stella's death. Unless her death was an accident, unless, using her drug, she fell asleep and so drifted unintentionally out of life! He still caught at that hope.

"Are you sure that the handwriting was Stella's?" he asked.

"Quite. I saw the letter."

"Did the editor give it to you?"

"No, he had to keep it for his own protection."

"That's a pity," said Harry. A pity—or a relief, since, without that evidence before his eyes, he could still insist upon his pretence.

"Not such a great pity," answered Martin, and taking a letter from his pocket he threw it down upon the table, with the ghost of a smile upon his face. "What do you think I have been doing during the last two years?" he asked drily.

Harry pounced upon the letter and his first glance dispelled his illusion—nay, proved to him that he had never had faith in it. For he saw, without surprise, the broad strokes and the straight up-and-down letters familiar to him of old. Stella had always written rather like a man, a man without character. He had made a joke of it to her in the time before the little jokes aimed by the one at the other had begun to rasp.

"Yes, she wrote the letter and signed it with Sir Chichester's name."

Millie Splay reached out for the letter.

"Stella took a big risk," she said. "I don't understand it. She must have foreseen that Chichester's hand was likely to be familiar in the office."

"No, Millie," said Sir Chichester suddenly, and he spurred his memory. "Of course! Of course! Stella helped me with the telephone one day this week in the library there. I told her that I was new to the *Harpoon*." He suddenly beat upon the table with his fist. "But why should she write the letter at all? Why should she want her death here, under these strange conditions, announced to the world? A little cruel I call it—yes, Millie, a little cruel."

"Stella wasn't cruel," said Lady Splay.

"She wasn't," Hillyard agreed. "I know why she wrote that. She wrote it to strengthen her hand and will at the last moment. The message was sent, the announcement of her death would be published in the morning, was already in print. Just that knowledge would serve as the final compulsion to do what she wished to do. She wrote lest her courage and nerve should at the last moment fail her, as to my knowledge they had failed her before."

"Before!" cried Millie. "She had tried before! Oh, poor woman!"

"Yes," said Hillyard, and he told them all of the vague but very real fear which had once driven him into Surrey in chase of her; of her bedroom with the bed unslept in and the lights still burning in the blaze of a summer morning; of herself sitting all night at her writing-table, making dashes and figures upon the notepaper and unable to steel herself to the last dreadful act.

Martin Hillyard gave no reason for her misery upon that occasion, nor did any one think to inquire. He just told the story from his heart, and therefore with a great simplicity of words. There was not one of those who heard him, but was moved.

"Yet there were perhaps a couple of hours in her life more grim and horrible than any in that long night," he went on, "the hours between ten o'clock and midnight yesterday."

"Ah, but we don't know how they were spent," began Sir Chichester.

"We know something," returned Martin gravely. "I told you that that letter was corroborated before the paragraph it contained was inserted in the paper."

"Yes," said Lady Splay.

"Whilst they were waiting for the news from France, which did not come, they rang you up from the *Harpoon* office. Yes: they rang up Rackham Park."

Harry Luttrell snatched up the letter once more from the table. Yes, there across the left-hand corner was printed Sir Chichester's telephone number and the district exchange.

"They were answered by a woman. Of that there's no doubt. And the woman assured them that Stella Croyle was dead. This was at a quarter-past twelve."

There was a movement of horror about the table, and then, with dry lips, Millie Splay whispered:

"Stella!"

"Yes. It must have been," answered Hillyard. "Oh, she had thought out her plan to its last detail. She knew the letter might not be enough. So, whilst we were all dancing at Harrel, she sat alone from ten to midnight in that library, waiting for the telephone to ring, hoping perhaps—for all we know—at the bottom of her heart that it would not ring. But it did, and she answered."

The picture rose vividly before them all. Harrel, with its lighted ballroom and joyous dancers on the one side; the silent library on the other, with Stella herself in all her finery, sitting with her haggard eyes fixed upon the telephone, whilst the slow minutes passed.

"That's terrible," said Millie Splay in a low voice; and such a wave of pity swept over the four people that for a long while no further word was said. Joan upstairs in her room was forgotten. Any thought of resentment in that Stella had used Sir Chichester's name was overlooked by the revelation of the long travail of her soul.

"I remember that she once said to me, 'Women do get the worst of it when they kick over the traces,'" Hillyard resumed. "And undoubtedly they do. On the other hand you have McKerrel's hard-headed verdict, 'If these poor neurotic bodies had any work to do they wouldn't have so much time to worry about their troubles.' Who shall choose between them? And what does it matter now? Stella's gone. She will strain her poor little unhappy heart no more against the bars."

CHAPTER XXXI

Jenny and Millie Splay

After a time their thoughts reverted to the living.

"There's Joan," said Millie Splay. "Jenny Prask hates her. She means to drag her into some scandal."

"If she can," said Martin. He went out into the hall and returned with the key of Stella Croyle's room. He held it up before them all.

"This key was found on the lawn outside the library window this morning by Luttrell. Jenny has never referred to it since she ran downstairs this morning crying out that the key was not in the lock. It was lying on the hall table all through the time when Sir Chichester was questioning her, and she said never a word about it. She was much too clever. But she saw it. I was watching her when she did see it. There was no concealing the swift look of satisfaction which flashed across her face. I haven't a doubt that she herself dropped the key where it was found."

"Nor I," Luttrell agreed with a despairing vehemence, "but we can't prove it. Jenny Prask is going to know nothing of that key. 'No, no, no, no!' she is going to say, 'Ask Miss Whitworth! Miss Whitworth came back from Harrel. Miss Whitworth was the last person to see Mrs. Croyle alive. Ask her!' It is Jenny Prask or Miss Whitworth. We are up against that alternative all the time. And Jenny holds all the cards. For she knows, damn her, what happened here last night."

"She did hold all the cards this morning," Hillyard corrected. "She doesn't now. Look at this key! There was a heavy dew last night. It was wet underfoot in the garden at Harrel."

"Yes," said Millie.

"How is it then that there's no rust upon the key?" and as he asked the question he twirled the key so that the light flashed upon stem and wards until they shone like silver. "No, this key was placed where you found it, Luttrell, not last night, but this morning after the sun had dried the grass."

"But we came home by daylight," Sir Chichester interposed. "They might argue that Joan might have slipped downstairs before she went to bed, with the key in her hand."

"But she wouldn't have chosen that spot in front of the library window. She might have flung it from her window, she might conceivably have slipped round the house and laid it under Mrs. Croyle's window. But to place it in front of the library to which room she returned from

Harrel—no."

"Yes," said Sir Chichester doubtfully. "I see. Joan can make good that point. Yes, she can explain that." And Millie Splay broke in with impatience:

"Explain it! Of course. But what we want is to avoid that she should have to explain anything, that she should be called as a witness at all!"

There lay the point of trouble. To it, they came ceaselessly back, revolving in the circle of their vain argument. Joan had something to conceal, and Jenny Prask was determined that she should disclose it, and Jenny Prask held the means by which to force her.

"But that's just what I am driving at," continued Martin. "We can't afford to be gentle here. There's no lie Jenny Prask wouldn't tell to force Joan into the witness box. We have got to deal relentlessly with Jenny Prask. A woman's voice spoke from this house over the telephone to London at a quarter-past twelve last night, and said that Stella was dead. Whose voice? Not Joan's. Joan was having supper with Luttrell at twelve o'clock. I saw her, others, too, saw her of course. Whose voice then? Stella's, as we say—as we know. But if not Stella's, as Jenny Prask says—why then there is only one other woman's voice which could have given the news."

"Jenny's," cried Millie with a sudden upspring of hope.

"Yes, Jenny Prask's."

Millie Splay rose from her chair swiftly and rang the bell; and when Harper answered it, she said:

"Will you ask Jenny to come here?"

"Now, my lady?"

"Now."

Harper went out of the room and Millie turned again to her friends.

"Will you leave this to me?" she asked.

Sir Chichester was inclined to demur. A few deft and pointed questions, very clear, such as might naturally occur to Hillyard or Luttrell, or Sir Chichester himself might come in usefully to put the polish, as it were, on Millie's spade work. Harry Luttrell smiled grimly.

"We didn't exactly cover ourselves with glory this morning," he said. "I think that we had better leave it to Lady Splay."

Sir Chichester reluctantly consented, and they all waited anxiously for Jenny's appearance. That she would fight to the last no one doubted. Would she fight even to her own danger?

Jenny came into the room, quietly respectful, and without a trace of apprehension.

"You sent for me, my lady."

"Yes, Jenny."

Jenny closed the door and came forward to the table.

"Do you still persist in your story of this morning?" Lady Splay asked.

"Yes, my lady."

"You did not see your mistress at all after Miss Whitworth had talked with her in the library?"

"No, my lady."

"Jenny, I advise you to be quite sure before you speak."

"I am not to be frightened, my lady," said Jenny Prask, with a spot of bright colour showing suddenly in her cheeks.

"I am not trying to frighten you," Millie Splay returned. "But some unexpected news has reached us which, if you persist, will place you in an awkward position."

Jenny Prask smiled. She turned again to the door.

"Is that all, my lady?"

"You had better hear what the news is."

"As you please, my lady."

Jenny stopped and resumed her position.

"The announcement of Mrs. Croyle's death appeared in the *Harpoon* this morning. The news was left at the *Harpoon* office by a chauffeur with a private car at midnight—Mrs. Croyle's car."

"It never left the garage last night," said Jenny fiercely.

"You know that for certain?"

"I am engaged to the chauffeur," she replied with a smile; and Millie Splay looked sharply up.

"Oh," she murmured slowly, after a pause. "Thank you, Jenny. Yes, thank you."

The quiet satisfaction of Millie Splay's voice puzzled Jenny and troubled her security. She watched Lady Splay warily. From that moment her assurance faltered, and with the loss of her ease, she lost something, too, of her respectful manner. A note of impertinence became audible.

"Very happy, I'm sure," she said.

"The motorcar delivered the message at midnight," Lady Splay resumed, "and—this is what I ask your attention to, Jenny—the editor, in order to obtain corroboration of the message before he inserted it in his paper, rang up Rackham Park."

Lady Splay paused for Jenny's comment, but none was uttered then. Jenny was listening with a concentration of all her thoughts. Here was a new fact of which she was ignorant, creeping into the affair. Whither did it lead? Did it strike her weapon from her hand? Upset her fine plan of avenging her dear mistress's most unhappy life? She would not believe it.

"He rang up Rackham Park—mark the time, Jenny—at a few minutes after twelve," said Lady Splay impressively, and Jenny's uneasiness was markedly increased.

"Fancy that!" she returned flippantly. "But I don't see, my lady, what that has to do with me."

"You will see, Jenny," Lady Splay continued with gentleness. "He got an answer."

Jenny turned that announcement over in her mind.

"An answer, did he?"

"Yes, Jenny, and an answer in a woman's voice."

A startled cry broke from the lips of Jenny Prask. Her cheeks blanched and horror stared suddenly from her eyes. She understood whose voice it must have been which answered the question from London. Before her, too, the pitiful vision of the lonely woman waiting for the shrill summons of the telephone bell to close the door of life upon her, rose clear; and such a flood of grief and compassion welled up in her as choked her utterance.

"Oh!" she whispered, moaning.

"Whose voice was it, Jenny?"

At the question Jenny rallied. All the more dearly because of that vision, should Joan Whitworth pay, the shining armour of her young beauty be pierced, her pride be humbled, her indifference turned to shame.

"I can't think, my lady—unless it was Miss Whitworth's."

"I asked you to mark the time, Jenny. A few minutes after midnight. Miss Whitworth was at that moment in the supper-room at Harrel. She was seen there. The woman's voice which answered was either Mrs. Croyle's or yours."

Nothing could have been quieter or gentler than Millie Splay's utterance. But it was like a searing iron to the shoulders of Jenny Prask.

"Mine!" The word was launched in a cry of incredulous anger. "It wasn't mine. Oh, as if I would do such a thing! The idea! Well, I never did!"

"I don't believe it was yours, Jenny," said Millie Splay.

"Granted, I'm sure," returned Jenny Prask, tossing her head.

"But how many people will agree with me?" Millie Splay went on.

"I don't care, my lady."

"Don't you? You will, Jenny," said Millie in a hard and biting tone which contrasted violently with the smoothness of her earlier questions. "You are trying, very maliciously, to do a great injury to a young girl who had never a thought of hurting your mistress, and you have only succeeded in placing yourself in real danger."

Jenny tried to laugh contemptuously.

"Me in danger! Goodness me, what next, I wonder?"

"Just listen how your story works out, Jenny," and Millie Splay set it out succinctly step by step.

"Mrs. Croyle never took chloroform as a drug. Mrs. Croyle had no troubles. Mrs. Croyle was quite gay this week. Yet she was found dead with a glass of chloroform arranged between her pillows, so that the fumes must kill her—and Jenny Prask was her maid. A motorcar took the news of Mrs. Croyle's death to London before it had occurred and took the news from Rackham Park. There was only one motorcar in the garage—Mrs. Croyle's—and Mrs. Croyle's chauffeur was engaged to Jenny Prask, Mrs. Croyle's maid. London then telephones to Rackham Park for corroboration of the news, and a woman's voice confirms it—an hour before it was true. There are only two women to choose from, Mrs. Croyle and Jenny Prask, her maid. But since Mrs. Croyle never took drugs, and had no troubles or thoughts of suicide and was quite gay, it follows that Jenny Prask—"

At this point Jenny interrupted in a voice in which fear was now very distinctly audible. "Why, you can't mean—Oh, my lady, you are telling me that—oh!"

"Yes, it begins to look black, Jenny, but I am not at the end," Millie Splay continued implacably. Jenny was not the only woman in that house who could fight if her darling was attacked. "You proceed to direct suspicion at a young girl with the statement that you never saw your mistress after half past nine that night or helped her to undress; and to complete your treachery, you take the key of Mrs. Croyle's door which you found inside her room this morning, and threw it where it may avert inquiry from you and point it against another."

Jenny Prask flinched. The conviction with which Lady Splay announced as a fact the opinion of the small conclave about the table quite deceived her.

"So you know about the key?" she said sullenly. And about the table ran a little quiver of relief. With that question, Jenny Prask had delivered herself into their hands.

"Yes."

Jenny stood with a mutinous face and silent lips. Lady Splay had marshalled in their order the items of the case which would be made against her, if she persisted in her lie. How would she receive them? Persist, reckless of her own overthrow, so long as she overthrew Joan Whitworth too? Or surrender angrily? The four people watched for her answer with anxiety; and it was given in a way which they least expected. For Jenny covered her face with her hands, her shoulders began to heave and great tears burst out between her fingers and trickled down the backs of her hands.

"It's unbearable," she sobbed. "I would have given my life for her—that's the truth. Oh, I know that most maids serve their mistresses for what they can get out of them. But she was so kind to me—wherever she went she was thoughtful of my comfort. Oh, if I had guessed what she meant to do! And I might have!"

The truth came out now. Stella Croyle had given the letter to Jenny, and Jenny herself had taken it to the garage and sent the chauffeur off upon his journey. She had no idea of what the letter contained. Stella was in the habit of inhaling chloroform; she carried a bottle of it in her dressing-case—a bottle which Jenny had taken secretly from the room and smashed into atoms after Doctor McKerrel's departure. She had already conceived her plan to involve Joan in so much suspicion that she must needs openly confess that she had returned from Harrel to meet Mario Escobar in the empty house.

"Mario Escobar!" Millie Splay exclaimed. "It was he." She turned pale. Sir Charles Hardiman had spoken frankly to her of Escobar. A creature of the shadows—it was rumored that he lived on the blackmailing of women. Joan was not out of the wood then! Martin Hillyard was quick to appease her fears.

"He will not trouble you," and when Jenny had gone from the room he added, "Mario Escobar was arrested this morning. He will be interned till the end of the war and deported afterwards."

Lady Splay rose, her face bright with relief.

"Thank you," she said warmly to Hillyard. "I am going up to Joan." At the door she stopped to add, "Now that it's over, I don't mind telling you that I admire Jenny Prask. Out-and-out loyalty like hers is not so common that we can think lightly of it."

Martin Hillyard turned to Sir Chichester.

"And now, if you will allow me, I will open my box of cigarettes."

Harry Luttrell went back to his depot the next morning, without seeing Joan again. Millicent Splay wrote to him during the next week. The inquest had been confined within its proper limits. Jenny Prask had spoken the truth in the witness box, and from beginning to end there had been no mention of Joan or Mario Escobar. A verdict of temporary insanity had been returned, and Stella now lay in the village churchyard. Harry Luttrell drew a breath of relief and turned to his work. For six weeks his days and nights were full; and then came twenty-four hours' leave and a swift journey into Sussex. He arrived at Rackham Park in the dusk of the evening. By a good chance he found Joan with Millie Splay and Sir Chichester alone.

Sir Chichester welcomed him with cordiality.

"My dear fellow, I am delighted to see you. You will stay the night, of course."

"No," Harry answered. "I must get back to London this evening."

He took a cup of tea, and Sir Chichester, obtuse to the warning glances of his wife, plunged into an account of the events which had followed his departure.

"I drew out a statement. Nothing could have been more concise, the coroner said. What's the matter, Millie? Why don't you leave me alone? Oh—ah—yes," and he hummed a little and spluttered a little, and then with an air of the subtlest craft he remarked, "There are those plans for the new pig-sties, Millie, which I am anxious to show you."

He was manœuvred at last from the room. Harry Luttrell and Joan Whitworth were left standing opposite to one another in the room.

"Joan," Harry Luttrell said, "in ten days I go back to France."

With a queer little stumble and her hands fluttering out she went towards him blinded by a rush of tears.

CHAPTER XXXII

"But Still a Ruby Kindles in the Vine"

Between the North and South Downs in the east of Sussex lies a wide tract of pleasant homely country which, during certain months of those years, was subject to a strange phenomenon. Listen on a still day when the clouds were low, or at night when the birds were all asleep, and you heard a faint, soft thud, so very faint that it was rather a convulsion of the air than an actual sound. Fancy might paint it as the tap of an enormous muffled drum beaten at a giant's funeral leagues and leagues away. It was not the roll of thunder. There was no crash, however distant, along the sky. It was just the one soft impact with a suggestion of earth-wide portentous force; and an interval followed; and the blurred sound again. The dwellers in those parts, who had sons and husbands at the war, made up no fancies to explain it. They listened with a sinking of the heart; for what they heard was the roar of the British guns at Ypres.

Into this country Martin Hillyard drove a small motorcar on a day of October two years afterwards. Until this week he had not set foot in his country of the soft grey skies since he had left Rackham Park. He had hurried down to Rackham as soon as he had reported to his Chief, but not with the high anticipation of old days. In what spirit would he find his friends? How would Joan meet him? For sorrow had marked her cross upon the door of that house as upon so many others in the land.

Martin had arrived before luncheon.

"Joan is hunting today," said Millie, "on the other side of the county. She will catch a train back."

"I can fetch her," Hillyard returned. "She is well?"

"Yes. She was overworked and ordered a rest. She has been with us a fortnight and is better. She was very grateful for your letters. She sent you a telegram because she could not bear to write."

Martin had understood that. He had had little news of her during the two years—a few lines about Harry in the crowded obituaries of the newspapers after the attack in 1917 on the Messines Ridge, where he met his death, and six months afterwards the announcement that a son was born.

"Joan's distress was terrible," said Millie. "At first she refused to believe that Harry was killed. He was reported as 'missing' for weeks; and during those weeks Joan, with a confident face—whatever failings of the heart beset her during the night vigils none ever knew—daily sought for news of him at the Red Cross office at Devonshire House. There had been the usual rumours. One officer in one prison camp had heard of Harry Luttrell in another. A sergeant had seen him wounded, not mortally. A bullet had struck him in the foot. Joan lived upon these rumours. Finally proof came—proof irrefutable.

"Joan collapsed then," said Millie Splay. "We brought her down here and put her to bed. She cried—oh, day and night!—she who never cried! We were afraid for her—afraid for the child that was coming."

Millie Splay smiled wistfully. "She had just two weeks with Harry. They were married before he left for France in 'sixteen, and then had another week together in the January of 'seventeen at his house in the Clayford country. That was all." Millie Splay was silent for a few minutes. Then she resumed cheerfully:

"But she is better now. She will talk of him, indeed, likes at times to talk of him; she is comforted by it, and the boy"—Millie's face became radiant—"the boy is splendid. You shall see him."

Martin was shown the boy. He seemed to him much like any other boy of his age, but such remarkable things in the way of avoirdupois poundage and teething, serenity of temper and quickness of apprehension were explained to him that he felt that he must be in the presence of a prodigy.

"Chichester will want to see you. He is in the library. He is Chairman of our Food Committee. You may have seen it in the papers," said Millie with a smile. "He is back in the papers again, you know."

"Good. Then he won't object to me smoking a cigarette," said Martin.

He motored over in the afternoon to the house on the other side of Sussex where he was to find Joan. He drove her away with him, and as they came to the top of a little crest in the flat country, Martin stopped the car and looked about him.

"I never cease to be surprised by the beauty of this country when I come home to it."

"Yes, but I wish *that* would stop."

That was the dull and muffled boom of the great guns across the sea. They sat and listened to it in silence.

"There it comes again!" said Joan in a quiet voice. "Oh, I do wish it would stop! What has happened to me, has happened to enough of us."

As Millie had said, she was glad to talk of Harry Luttrell to his friends; and she talked simply and naturally, with a little note of wistfulness heard in all the words.

"We were going to have a small house in London and spend our time between it and the old Manor at Clayford. . . . Harry had seen the house. . . . He was always writing that I must watch for it to come into the market. . . . It had a brass front door. There we should be. We could go out when we wished, and when we wished we could be snug behind our own brass door." Joan laughed simply and lovingly as she spoke. Hillyard had never seen her more beautiful than she was at this moment. If grief had taken from her just the high brilliancy of her beauty, it had added to it a most appealing tenderness.

"After all," she said again, "Harry fulfilled himself. I love to think of that. The ambition of his life—young as he was he saw it realised and helped—more than all others, except perhaps one old Colonel—to realise it. And he left me a son . . . to carry on. . . . There will be no stigma on the Clayfords when my boy gets his commission. Won't I tell him why? Won't I just tell him!"

And the soft October evening closed in upon them as they drove.

THE END